BETWEEN RIVER
AND MOUNTAIN

ALSO BY SALLY WALKER BRINKMANN

Wicked Women and Other Stories
Rebel Traveler: A Romance of Time Travel

BETWEEN RIVER AND MOUNTAIN

SALLY WALKER BRINKMANN

WILDSIDE PRESS

ACKNOWLEDGEMENTS

I gratefully acknowledge the invaluable advice and guidance of Victor J. Banis, the late Joe McCabe, and John Betancourt, Publisher, Wildside Press, LLC. Many others commented on various drafts of the manuscript. I would like to thank Abbie Brown, Sandy Campbell, Kate Shunney, Constance Dowrick, and Lindsay Unger. I am also grateful to the Martinsburg Writer's Group and the Morgan County Writer's Group.

This story is a work of fiction; however, it is based on historical facts and events. Many of the characters are based on actual individuals living at the time, while some characters and events are purely fictitious.

Published by Wildside Press LLC.
www.wildsidebooks.com

CHAPTER 1

MORGAN COUNTY, VIRGINIA

SUMMER, 1861

The old man turned the team south onto the Hancock Road and the farm wagon lumbered toward Bath. Rob sat on the wagon seat next to Pa and looked back at dark clouds rolling off the mountains to the north. The sound of approaching horses got his attention and he searched the dusty road ahead. Before Pa could move the team out of the way, a troop of Confederate cavalry was upon them.

The captain rode up to the wagon and raised a gloved hand. "Hold on, farmer, this is your chance to become a hero in the Army of Virginia."

"Outta my way."

The cavalry captain nodded and his men started to drag Tom Johnson out of the wagon. Rob managed to grab his father's coat and tried to pull the big man back onto the wagon seat. Heavily muscled from years of hard work, Tom put up a good fight. Cursing and kicking at the soldiers, he fended them off for a short time.

"Damn conscript gang," he shouted. "You ain't got no right."

Rob looked around at the empty road and his fear grew. "Leave my pa alone," he yelled. But he lost his grip on Tom's coat as the soldiers yanked him off the wagon. Rob grabbed the horsewhip and lashed out at the nearest man.

The captain maneuvered his horse closer. "Leave this ornery old man. Take the boy."

Tom lifted his head and stopped struggling. "You don't want the boy. He won't be no good to you." Twisting out of his attackers' grip, Tom drew himself up and appraised the captain. "Can you use any horses? Mounts would be more use to you than me or the boy."

"What horses? How many?"

"I'll show you what I have, Captain. Meet me on River Road where the road to Horse Ridge turns off. Be there at eight tonight."

"If you're not there, old man, I'll find you." The captain turned his horse and headed toward Bath. His troops raised a cloud of dust as they rode after him.

Tom Johnson cursed the Confederate cavalry all the way into the town of Bath. "Jump in the back and look over them egg crates," he ordered. "That bitch at the Pavilion Hotel ain't gonna give us nothing for cracked eggs."

"None got broke," Rob reported as he swung his lanky frame back onto the wagon seat. "What deal did you make with that Rebel captain?" Rob brushed his long hair out of his eyes and watched his father.

"It ain't none of your concern, but I'd rather be a horse thief than a dead hero in any army." He looked at his son. "Things are changing fast, boy, and we gotta find new ways to get by."

As they entered town, the wagon rumbled by dusty shop fronts and taverns. The park, site of the springs and bathhouses for the wealthy, was a serene green space in the middle of the small country town. A few well-dressed visitors strolled near the spa or sat in groups on the Pavilion Hotel's long columned porch. Since the onset of the war, the hotel had seen a steady decline in reservations.

At the Pavilion kitchen door, Tom reined in the horses and grabbed Rob's arm. "Don't ever get no notion of joining up, boy. Have you ever seen either side lift a finger to look after us here in these mountains? Hell, no. They'll march you off to some flatland battleground and when you're dead it won't make no difference to them bastards." Tom glared at his son. "Listen to me. I tried to tell Billy, but he was crazy to go to war. Now he's been gone for two months and we ain't heard a word. Well, both sides can burn in hell. We need to look after ourselves here."

* * * *

After they traded at the Pavilion, Pa went off to find his drinking buddies and Rob drove the wagon to O'Ferrall's. Located on Fairfax Street above the town park, O'Ferrall's Coffee House catered to travelers and local folks. In the dark low-ceilinged kitchen, Mrs. O'Ferrall gave Rob a bowl of slippery potpie. As he ate, he watched Mary, the proprietor's pretty black-haired daughter, but she didn't seem to notice him. He knew he looked scruffy and unkempt. His dark hair curled to the collar of his rough work shirt. Since Ma had died, there was no one who chided him about his appearance.

Rob was so engrossed in his thoughts that Mary took him by surprise when she sat down beside him. She was close enough that he caught the scent of cinnamon on her clothes.

"Hello, Rob." She smiled at him. "We just got a letter from my brother, Trip. He's joined a cavalry company. Have you heard from Billy?"

"No, we ain't heard," Rob answered. "Pa's starting to worry."

"I'm glad you're still at home." Mary watched him closely. "I was hoping you'd do me a great favor." She handed him a small envelope. "Could you take this to Fannie Swann down at Alpine Station?"

Rob left O'Ferrall's with the envelope safe in his pocket. Settling down in the wagon seat to wait for Pa, he wove daydreams about pretty Mary O'Ferrall. When a light rain began to fall, he headed back to the farm alone. The evening chores had to be done. He only hoped Pa would have a little of the market money left when he came home.

* * * *

The next morning Rob found Pa sprawled in a chair, his head resting on the kitchen table. Reeking of whiskey, he cursed when Rob tried to rouse him. That was when Rob spotted the ten dollar Yankee note clutched in the old man's hand. So he must have traded horses with the Rebel cavalry last night. He never came home with this much money won at cards.

Rob put Mary O'Ferrall's letter in his pocket, grabbed some stale cornbread and ran out the door. At Alpine Station he found Fannie Swann on the riverbank staring over at the northern shore of the Potomac. Her red hair and blue dress made her stand out like a beacon. Yankee pickets shuffling up and down in their assigned areas often stopped to wave at her. Fannie did not wave back.

"Fannie." She turned toward him. "Mary O'Ferrall asked me to bring you this letter." He knew the way he must look: a skinny farm boy, and ragged at that.

Fannie took the letter and slipped it in her pocket. "Thanks, Rob." She gestured across the river. "I don't hate those Yankee soldiers over in Hancock. They're just boys, most of them. But I hate having the Union Army sitting on our doorstep." She turned away from the river and started walking back toward Alpine Station.

Cornrows flanked the path through fertile bottomland. Rob saw that this corn was much higher than the Johnson's crop, growing in shallow hill soil. But now he couldn't keep his eyes off Fannie Swann's rounded hips as they glided from side-to-side not two feet ahead of him on the path. They walked in silence. Passing the entrance to Charles Swann's small general store, Rob saw that the old man was busy with a customer. There were three other buildings at Alpine, but the store and the railroad platform were the center of activity. A freight train was pulling away from the station, and the smoke from its boiler drifted up over the purple hills.

Fannie glanced back at Rob. "Pa doesn't let me help out much in the store. He says I'm too outspoken to the Yankee folks." She smiled at him. "Your brother used to come into the store with your father. Do you hear from him now that he's in the army?"

"Ain't heard nothing from Billy yet," Rob mumbled. "We're missing him on the farm."

As he was leaving, Fannie grabbed his hand. "Rob, it's important for Mary O'Ferrall and me to keep in touch. It's too dangerous for us to travel the roads these days, so we need your help. Come by in a few days."

As he continued up the ridge road toward the farm, Rob thought about Fannie and Mary O'Ferrall. They were several years older than he was and they usually ignored him, so their sudden friendship was puzzling. He might only be an errand boy, but he wasn't just 'Billy Johnson's little brother' anymore.

* * * *

The afternoon sun beat down on his back as Rob walked along the ridge toward home. Low clouds hung over the blue ridges to the west and a lone hawk circled the valley. The Johnson farm was made up of one hundred rocky acres set in rolling hills a mile above the river. The house and barn, built by his great-grandfather, were of rugged but solid construction, meant to withstand mountain winds and snows.

As Rob pushed open the farmhouse door, the reek of alcohol hit him. His father lay sprawled on the floor, his breath coming in gasps. Although he was a big man, his clothes hung on him and his skin had taken on an unhealthy gray tinge.

When Billy left home, Rob hadn't known what to do with his father. But now he knelt down and went through Pa's pockets; one dollar and fifteen cents in coins fell out. Rob added most of the coins to the stash he kept hidden in the back of the cupboard. When Pa sobered up, he would never remember how much money he'd carried home. Rob shoved a pillow under the old man's head before opening all the windows. Finally, he measured coffee into the pot, stirred up the fire in the cook stove and made the evening meal.

Glancing back at his father lying in the middle of the small sparsely furnished kitchen, Rob thought it was good Ma hadn't lived to see this. She was gone and few reminders of her were left. Pa had sold her prized pieces of good furniture and odds and ends of fine china. All that remained was her favorite blue teapot, which sat alone on the top shelf of the cupboard.

With a little time on his hands, Rob sat on the porch and watched the clouds hanging over the ridge tops. He dreamed of Fannie, of her red-gold hair and the soft curve of her breast in the blue dress. The warm evening air carried the smell of simmering beans and side meat through the open door.

Movement to his left caught his attention. "Damn it, Nate, you sure know how to sneak up on a person."

Nate Fields held up a stringer of bass. "Never come visiting empty-handed. You want to fry these up?" He grinned as he stood sniffing by the open door. "Got something cooking?"

Following Rob into the house, Nate surveyed Tom Johnson sprawled on the floor. "So the old man ain't good these days. He's gonna up and die on you soon. Happened to my pa." He looked shrewdly at Rob. "Then what the hell you gonna do? You oughta join up with me. Soon as I get together enough money to smooth my way into the army, I'm signing on with the 21st Virginia."

Nate eased his lean frame onto the bench by the table. Sandy hair fell over his narrow, hazel eyes as he watched Rob. "Got a little cornbread left over? Ain't had nothing to eat since yesterday."

Rob threw the bass into a pan sizzling with hot bacon grease. "I thought about joining up like Billy did, but Pa ain't keen on the idea." Rob shoved some stale cornbread toward his guest.

"Come to think of it, don't know if the Confederate Army would take you. You're on the young side." Nate gave him an appraising look.

"You're only a year older. Besides, I'm needed at home."

"What, looking after the old man here?"

"Yeah, trying to keep the farm going and helping out a few local ladies."

"What ladies?" Nate asked with his mouth full of cornbread.

"Down at Alpine Station and over to O'Ferrall's in town."

"Them two! God help you, boy. They're up to spying on the Yankees. Don't get caught at it on the Maryland side of the river. They hang spies." Nate clutched his neck and swayed back and forth.

Rob shrugged and served up the food. He and Nate carried their plates to the porch and ate hungrily.

Later, Nate offered to help with the evening chores. Mostly, he stood around and watched as Rob pitched hay into the manger for the two milk cows and three heifers. Nate scratched old Bessie behind the ears and she nuzzled his shoulder before starting to feed.

"Always had a way with animals," he said. "Matter of fact, I just called them fish outta the water today."

Rob grinned, but he had the uncanny feeling it might be true. Nate had always had a way with animals.

"You best be finding a hiding place for these here cows," Nate advised. "Raiding parties already riding through these hills."

"Nobody but the damn Yankee Army bothers us around here."

"These men ain't from around here. I've seen them driving horses and cattle down the Valley Road. You don't wanta mess with them."

Rob hauled two buckets of water from the cistern. "What about the cave up on the mountain? Let's go have a look."

* * * *

The boys reached the shallow cave just as darkness closed in on the pine woods. Dragging brush from the opening, they entered the cave, which was little more than a ledge overhang. Rob lit a match, illuminating the rough moss-covered walls. A dank musty smell filled the small space.

"Remember when we used to hide up here from your pa?" Nate's lop-sided grin made Rob relax.

"Yeah, when you stole his chewing tobacco and we got sick." Rob said, but he realized that he'd heard too many lies and too many broken promises from Nate in the past. Trust was hard to hold onto with him. He'd grown up rootless and rough, but he'd survived. Most of his family had not.

"Matter of fact," Nate drawled. "I need to find a hiding place for a crate I picked up today. Whadaya say?"

* * * *

Back in the barn, Rob lit the oil lantern while Nate carefully pulled a large crate from the hay. Prying open the lid with his knife, he lifted out a Colt revolver and savored the look of wonder on Rob's face. "Pretty nice, eh? Got ten of them. Take one. Never know when you may have need of it, times being what they are."

"Where'd you get these guns?" Rob took the proffered revolver. "Says 'U.S. Army' on the crate."

"Them Bluebellies ain't particular how they unload supplies off canal boats. It was easy to drag this here crate off. I went across the river to see my Uncle Joe," Nate continued. "He's a lockkeeper on the canal now. Wanted to tell him about Ma. She didn't suffer Daddy's death too hard. Ran off with a neighbor man. Joe said it's about what he would have expected."

Nate pounded the crate lid down with his knife handle. "So after I got done visiting, I come across these fool Yankees supposed to be unloading a canal boat. Sergeant wasn't around, so half of them was sleeping and the other half was playing cards."

Rob sighted down the barrel of the new Colt. "How'd you get the crate back here? Couldn't float it across the river."

"Well, as luck would have it, I found an old flatboat by the shore. Poled across and left the boat hidden in brush near your landing place. That boat's yours now."

Rob turned the gun in his hands, scraping off the protective tallow. The metal shone dully in the lantern light. "You're crazy, Nate. If the Yankees had caught you, they'd have thrown you in jail."

"Don't worry, I ain't never gonna sit in no jail. Okay if I store this crate up in the cave?"

Rob nodded. "Sure, it's fine by me. Best to go now before Pa wakes up."

* * * *

When the boys got back to the farmhouse, they found Pa still sprawled on the kitchen floor. Nate helped Rob half-carry, half-drag the old man to his bedroom. Rousing as they heaved him into bed, Pa muttered curses and then shouted at them to get out.

"He's one mean old cuss," Nate said when he and Rob were back in the kitchen. "Got any coffee left?"

Rob put the pot back on the cook stove and stirred up the fire, then sat down across the table from his guest. Nate eyed Rob intently. "I been doing some thinking on how easy it would be to rob a canal boat. Take two men. Never know what you might pick up. Later on, you and me, Rob, we'll do it. Whadaya say?"

"I ain't interested. I got enough problems," Rob said, yawning. "I'm going to bed. You're welcome to sleep in the barn if you want."

That night Rob wasn't thinking of Nate or his crazy schemes. The old springs groaned as he sat on the side of the bed. Reaching down, he picked up the broken shard of glass he'd stashed under the bed. It had been part of his mother's hand mirror, left in the dump down in the hollow. Pa must have thrown it there after he'd sold the fancy silver frame. Though it had been cracked years ago, Rob remembered Ma gazing at her image as she brushed her hair.

The broken mirror reflected his face in the dim light of the oil lamp. His high cheekbones and light blue eyes were like his mother's, but he'd inherited his large full lips from Pa. He knew this feature kept him from any claim of being handsome. Yet, Ma had married Tom Johnson, hadn't she?

Rob wondered if he'd find a woman. He thought of Fannie and the slow rolling movement of her hips as she'd walked through the cornfield. He longed for the touch of a woman, for Fannie's touch. Falling back on the bed, he kicked off his boots, replaced the shard carefully and turned out the lamp. He spent the time between waking and sleeping envisioning what it would be like to make love to Fannie and could almost feel her small firm body in his arms. Then he found himself committing the act his mother had warned him was on the pathway to hell. Finally, he was able to fall asleep.

* * * *

A few days later Rob walked down River Road to the Swann's place. He had paid his neighbor, old Miss McKenny, one dozen eggs to trim his unruly hair and thought he looked presentable. Charles Swann offered work and set him to splitting firewood, but he saw no sign of Fannie.

About an hour later he heard her call his name. Setting down the axe, he watched her walk toward him. The sun glinted off her red-gold hair and even the shapeless gingham dress couldn't hide the curves of her young body.

Fannie smiled at him and beckoned. "I'm hoping you'll walk with me down to my Uncle Johnson Orrick's farm."

"I'd like to go with you." Rob tried not to sound too eager. "But I can't just up and leave your daddy's woodpile. I'll be done in about an hour."

For an instant, he saw the flash of anger in her blue eyes. Then she smiled and nodded. "Yes, that will be fine."

* * * *

Johnson Orrick had been a delegate to the Virginia State Convention and had voted for secession in April. Rob knew the Orricks were several cuts above him and Pa on the local social ladder, but was always surprised at the grandeur of their home. Wicker rocking chairs sat on the long columned porch and potted plants stood near the front door. Though only a mile of dusty road separated the Swann and Orrick homes, the gap between the families was clear to Rob.

Worried about his appearance, he'd doused himself with cold water at the Swann's well, but he knew his hosts would be dismayed by the clumsy country boy Fannie had brought with her. Sitting in the parlor, Rob was awed by the velvet drapes and the Turkey rugs covering the polished floors.

Johnson Orrick was a powerfully built heavy-set man who seemed very sure of himself. "We're just beginning this fight," he told his young visitors. "There's much we can do on the border to gather information. Remember, any army depends on accurate intelligence."

Mrs. Orrick, a tall stern-faced woman, nodded her approval as her husband continued. "I've heard that General Jackson is not happy with Union troops patrolling just forty miles from his headquarters. They say he may arrive here in force before the new year."

Millie, the Negro house servant, entered quietly with a tray of tea and cakes. The Orricks were one of the few local families to keep slaves. As Millie served the refreshments, she stopped abruptly in front of Rob and stared at him. A tiny, light-skinned woman with searching dark eyes, Millie served him, nodded slightly and moved on. No one else noticed.

Johnson Orrick and his wife were going over the lists Fannie and the O'Ferralls had compiled. Names of local families who would hide Confederate patrols were listed by area. Rob tried to follow the conversation, but the incident with Millie had spooked him. Their hosts had related several tales of her power, calling it second sight.

When he and Fannie left, Millie appeared out of nowhere and approached Rob. "There's a yellow-haired boy, a soldier, who will die in a terrible battle before this moon is out." Then she turned and abruptly walked toward the river.

"That crazy old woman is talking about my brother." Rob watched Millie's stooped figure disappear into the shadows.

"Don't believe her. She's just trying to scare us. The Negroes are on the Union side in this war." Fannie took his hand and steered him toward her home. "Remember, Pa owes you wages. Forget crazy old Millie."

Charles Swann paid him generously, throwing in a little tobacco. Rob thanked the old man and had started toward River Road when Fannie caught up with him.

She handed him a warm peach pie covered with a checkered cloth. "Rob, Ma sent this for your supper." She smiled at him. "Now that you've met my Uncle Orrick, you see how important our work is. We need you, Rob."

* * * *

On the first market day in July, Pa cursed under his breath as he tried to maneuver the wagon through the streets of Bath. Crowds of farmers and townsfolk loitered near the courthouse and gray-coated soldiers were everywhere. The Confederate Army occupied the town.

Rob took care unloading the milk cans and carrying them into the Pavilion Hotel kitchen. The cook, Mabel McCabe, screamed like a banshee if a drop spilled. Today, the proprietor, Colonel John Strother himself, held the door open for Rob.

"All this excitement over the damn Rebel Army," the colonel said in greeting. Rob knew the Strothers were Yankees and made no bones about it. The old man's son, David, was an officer in the Union Army. David had also drawn most of the artwork hanging on the hotel walls. He signed his name "Porte Crayon," not Strother.

Rob turned at the sound of raised voices by the kitchen door. "You shorted me on the last bill, Tom. You better make it right," Mabel yelled.

"Calm down, woman." Pa strode out the door and Rob raced after him.

At O'Ferrall's, the kitchen was filled with Rebel soldiers and Rob could see their officer sitting with Mrs. Jane O'Ferrall out in the dining room. The men were wolfing down stacks of hotcakes, grits, and gravy.

"Isn't it grand." Mary handed Rob payment for the order in Confederate scrip. "At last our boys are here in town. I know you can't wait to join up."

The truth was Rob had no desire at all to go to war, but he knew this thought was best kept quiet. This wasn't their war, even if Billy had volunteered. Billy, like most of these men in the kitchen, had wanted to get away from home, but Rob had no notion of leaving. As Pa said, the war couldn't last forever and those who left might have nothing to come home to.

Back outside, he found his father dozing on the wagon seat so Rob took the reins and clucked the old horses into a plodding walk. He knew he'd better get out of town while they still had the market money. On the Hancock Road they were stopped by pickets guarding the road.

"What's your business, mister?" The first man looked at Pa, now wide awake.

"It ain't none of your concern, but I'm on my way home. Outta my way."

The soldiers stepped back sullenly and turned toward the next travelers. Rob had heard grumbling in town about the pickets. He wondered how long the Rebel troops would stay.

* * * *

When they reached the farm, Nate Fields was waiting on the porch. "Got a message from your red-haired lady love," he drawled as he followed Rob to the barn. "She wants you to go to church with her family on the fourth of July. The Rebel colonel's gonna speak." Nate lent a hand with the horses. "Told her you wasn't much on church going."

"I'll go if Fannie wants me to," Rob said.

"Fannie don't always say what she means." Nate leaned against the door. "I know you got a lot more schooling than me and I ain't been around women like Fannie much, but I know people. I watch them." He smiled lazily at Rob. "Take them Bluebellies camped near my uncle. I can tell you which ones will stand and fight, which ones will run, and which ones will pick valuables off the corpses. As for Fannie." Nate hesitated. "She's using you, Rob. You ain't nothing to her."

"You got it wrong. I ain't no fool." But the look in Rob's eyes proved him a liar.

* * * *

The Methodist church was filled to overflowing on the evening of July fourth. The Swann family was near the front, with Fannie seated between her father and Rob. He knew her beauty had not gone unnoticed, whereas he had been completely overlooked. He tried to hide his worn boots under the pew in front of him.

The O'Ferralls and the Orricks sat nearby. Colonel Edmundson's command, all splendidly turned out, filled the back of the church. Rob wondered how he'd look in a gray uniform and pictured the admiration in Fannie's eyes.

The congregation hushed as the Colonel's voice filled the church. "We are Virginians; this is our land. We will not tolerate vipers in our midst who pledge loyalty to the Union," he thundered. Rob was jolted to attention as he heard the audience stir.

"These men should be exiled from Virginia. Their property should be confiscated." Edmundson paused and looked sternly at the audience. "They are enemies of the Confederate States of America. Hang the traitors!"

A commotion took place in the church as John Strother and other Northern sympathizers hurriedly left. The Confederate colonel droned on for almost two more hours. No one else left, but not everyone looked happy. Rob ignored the colonel's words. Sitting this close to Fannie was all he wanted.

* * * *

A few days later, Rob was finishing up chores when the sound of military drums echoed off the hills to the north. He had heard from the Swanns that Colonel Lew Wallace's Indiana Regiment was moving down the National Road from Cumberland and now the Indiana Yankees had finally reached Hancock. As he left the barn, he saw Fannie running up the lane toward him.

She caught sight of him and stopped. "Rob, we've got to get word to town about the Yankees." Fannie collapsed on the grass and Rob threw himself down beside her.

"The Indiana boys gonna stay?"

"Our friends in Hancock say probably not for long. Truth is, we don't know." Fannie's face was flushed. She was winded from the climb up to the farm.

To Rob she was more beautiful than ever. "I'll go into town for you, but don't worry. Even if they had a mind to, it would take them troops a good while to cross the river."

When Rob steered the wagon team into town, he saw that the Confederate soldiers were hurriedly packing up and preparing to move out. Word had already reached here, he realized, and Colonel Edmundson, who'd had so much to say on the fourth of July, was on the run.

As it turned out, Colonel Wallace's Regiment marched through Hancock and continued to Hagerstown. But even their fleeting presence had been enough to rid Bath of Rebel control.

* * * *

As the month of July wore on, Rob took on all of the farm work, though some fields went untended. Pa had started spending most of his time away. When he was home, he was either sleeping off a drunk, or, like today, he was bad-tempered and accusing.

"This all the money left from last week's market orders?" Pa rasped. "Should've sent you to the army and kept Billy here. He would've known how to handle them thieving hotel people in town. God Almighty, you was dumb enough to take Confederate scrip." He waved the large bills in the air. "Can't even pass these in card games."

Without a word, Rob left the house. Walking into the cool morning air, he was surprised that his father's wrath rolled off his back so easily. Pa had begun to play little part in his day-to- day life. He didn't even wonder much where Pa had started spending his time; he was just glad to be rid of him. Rob found the scythe in the shed and started down the hill toward the McKenny place. He'd promised them a day of haymaking and with so many men leaving to fight, it was hard to pull together a crew.

The sun beat down on the clear, sharply drawn horizon where the smoky blue hills met the sky. Rob felt safe surrounded by these mountains and the war was far away, but Billy was in the thick of it. Turning into the McKenny's lane, he met Nate and fell into step with him.

"Your pa said you'd gone this way, so I took a shortcut. He sure is a sore ass of a morning."

"Well, he ain't around much now. Truth is, I've started thinking of the farm as belonging to me. I'm the one works it and Millie knows my brother ain't coming back."

"Ain't coming back? Is that what the crazy witch woman said?"

"They say she's been seen walking abroad on the night of a death and she marked Billy."

They rounded a bend in the lane and saw that the haymaking was already underway. "You go right ahead and believe that," Nate said. "It's a fact that any soldier might not come home. As for me, I plan to be back in these hills after the war and I'll have a nice little stake to start me out in life." Grinning confidently, he ambled off toward the hay wagon.

After a good morning's work, the men stopped for lunch. Miss McKenny and her sisters, all thin, stern old ladies, dished out the food and led the grace praising the Lord with equal vigor. Rob found himself seated between Nate and Johnny McKenny, the sisters' nephew, who had been driving the hay wagon team.

"Can't say I'm sorry I banged up my knee," Johnny told the diners. "Otherwise I wouldn't have gotten no leave." He helped himself to another chicken leg. "Word has it that something big is coming up. All them boys under General Jackson are just spoiling for a fight. Me, I'm glad to see to my land."

"Have you run into my brother, Billy?" Rob asked.

"Matter of fact, I saw Billy last week. Said he couldn't wait to meet up with the Yankees. We talked about home, about the times I'd stop by to pick up your milk cans and he'd sneak out a jar of Tom's corn whiskey and ride with me for a bit. Matter of fact, that's when I got the taste for a little nip."

"Didn't the McKennys haul a lot more milk before the war?" Nate asked.

"Yeah, but now there's several farms not producing—men off in the army. One of the Union families shut up their place, sold their stock and headed north."

"Me, I'd never do that," Rob said. "Nobody's gonna come in and take what's mine."

Johnny studied his face. "I believe you'd put up a hellava fight." He reached in his pack and pulled out a letter. "Take this to the old man. It's from Billy."

* * * *

That evening, as Rob pushed through the farmhouse door he was surprised to find his father still there. Silently, he handed over Billy's letter. The old man's face lit up as he read the first few lines. "He just wrote this three days ago, on the seventeenth of July. Says they've been told to get ready to march. Yankees are on the move."

Pa finished reading the letter, moving his lips slowly to form the words. "He thinks General Jackson is close to a god." He passed the letter back to his younger son.

Reading it, Rob felt a sense of foreboding. Were these the words of a man already dead? Billy described the First Brigade of the 33rd Virginia as the best in the regiment. Most of the boys were from the Shenandoah Valley or the nearby mountains and knew what they were about. *They all welcome a fight, as I do*, he wrote. At the end of the brief letter, Billy said he missed the farm and often longed to be back home. He hoped that all was well with them and that the war would pass them by.

The next day Pa mended a few harnesses and repaired some broken tools. He was sober and his mood was surly. Rob was fitting a handle on an old hoe when he saw Nate sauntering toward them.

"Come to tell news of a big battle down at Manassas," Nate said. "Word reached Hancock an hour ago." He hunkered down on his heels and watched father and son. "Ain't that where Billy's regiment's likely to be?"

That night, July twenty-first, Rob stared out the window at the full moon. Sleep was impossible after hearing Nate's news, so he sat on his bed and waited. From the next room, Pa's rasping snores rose and fell in slow rhythm.

Ironically, this had been as close to a family evening as had happened for a long while. Pa had cut down the last ham from the smokehouse and cooked up a feast, even inviting Nate to eat with them. The old man had talked a lot about Billy, ignoring Nate's report of the battle. He'd even thrown a few crumbs of praise Rob's way.

"Rob works as hard as a man. Keeps things going here," Pa had said.

Then Nate had started to carry on about Fannie. When he'd minced around the kitchen switching his hips and holding up an imaginary skirt, Pa had roared with laughter. "Oh, Rob," Nate squealed, "just kill me a few of them Yankee boys and I'll love you all the more."

Brooding over the taunting he'd received, Rob knew his anger was what they'd enjoyed. He was awake far into the night and when he finally slept, he saw a figure silhouetted by the full moon standing on the ridge top. Rob shook himself awake and went to the window. There was a light moving on the ridge. Then the figure carrying the lantern stopped across from the Johnson farmhouse and the light was snuffed out.

The next morning he awoke in a cold sweat, certain that crazy Millie had held the light he'd seen and that his brother was dead on a faraway battlefield. There was no sign of Pa, so after taking care of the most urgent chores, Rob headed down the ridge road toward the Orrick farm.

"No, Rob," Mrs. Orrick said firmly. "None of my slaves was abroad last night. I lock them all in their quarters each evening. I don't want to be murdered in my sleep by my own Negras."

CHAPTER 2

BILLY JOHNSON

JULY 1861

"It was a rout," Pa said. "Word come up from Winchester that we chased the Yankees halfway to Washington. Them boys in Jackson's First Brigade was heroes."

"What about Billy?"

"The men I talked to in town said it was a damn bloody battle. It'll be some time before lists are made." Pa looked away.

As the days passed and there was still no word, Pa turned more sullen, but Rob grew angry. For the first time since the war began, he took sides. The army that had killed his brother was now his enemy.

On the evening of July twenty-sixth, the O'Ferralls' hired man, Evan Dow, knocked on the door. "I come as soon as I heard," he told Pa. "Miss Jane said I could take the rig." He fell silent.

"Who told you?" Pa demanded.

"Trip O'Ferrall. A soldier stopped by this morning with a letter from Trip. He knew about your son. The letter said Billy died at a place called Henry House Hill." Evan's watery blue eyes looked troubled. He had known Billy as a boy and was one of the few friends Pa had left. "I'm right sorry. The O'Ferralls, they send their condolences too." Evan produced a bottle. "Your boy died a hero," he said as he poured the whiskey.

Pa broke down and wept. Unnoticed, Rob left the house and headed for the Swann's place. He'd promised to let them know when he got word. In the morning he planned to find Nate and tell him he'd go along with anything that would make the Yankees pay.

* * * *

The next day there was no need to go hunting for Nate. Rob found him sitting on the porch steps. "Heard about Billy. I'm right sorry. Fannie told me you was in a state."

Rob nodded and mumbled his thanks. "I'm ready to take on the canal boat," he said.

A few hours later, Rob and Nate sat with Joe Fields in the lock-keeper's cottage. A heavily laden canal boat had just cleared the lock and was slowly making its way downstream toward Washington.

"There would have been a prize. Gotta chance to look inside when I turned the lock. Most of them carry coal, but this one was loaded with boxes of Yankee boots." Joe tapped tobacco into his pipe bowl. "You boys wanta do this, I can let you know when a boat ties up that's got something worth the taking. Mostly, the crews go into Hancock of an evening, sit in them bars for hours."

"What about the Union pickets?" Rob spoke up for the first time.

Joe drew on his pipe. "That won't be no problem. I got a couple bottles of moonshine."

Nate looked pleased. "What kinda signal can you send off to let us know the time's right?"

"Next couple of nights, you boys stay by the river bank. When something looks good, I'll set a blaze in the hearth here. That'll be the signal. Mind, I can't help you none. You're on your own, but I take a cut. Agreed?"

* * * *

The Swann kitchen was hot and airless in the July heat. Fannie served up large bowls of stew for her guests and called them to the table. "Here Rob, you sit over by me on the bench. Nate, come on in."

Nate slouched by the door. "You mind if I take my meal out here where there's a breath of air? Haveta keep an eye on the river in case Uncle Joe's chimney starts smoking."

"He's a strange one, your friend, Nate. Can he be trusted?"

The truth was that Rob didn't know for sure. "I reckon so, long as he gets his cut. He ain't no patriot."

"No, I can see that." Fannie handed him a thick slab of cornbread. "But I told Mary O'Ferrall we could count on you, though I'm afraid this scheme of Nate's may be dangerous."

At that moment, Rob knew no plan could ever be too dangerous and there would be nothing Fannie asked that he wouldn't do for her. He flashed a cocky grin. "Ain't nothing to worry about at all."

* * * *

The next night Uncle Joe's signal came and Rob found he had a lot to worry about. A steady rain fell as he and Nate poled the flatboat toward the Maryland shore. The C&O Canal, a main shipping artery between

Washington and areas to the northwest, ran near the shoreline. A barge was tied up by Joe's lock, though there was no sign of the old man.

The barge sat low in the water and seemed to be deserted, but when the boys approached, a large black dog appeared on deck and started barking. As they came nearer, the barking was replaced by low threatening growls. Rob could see the big mongrel's bared fangs. He hung back, but Nate walked right up the gangplank and knelt down by the animal. In moments, all was quiet. When Rob climbed aboard, he found the dog licking Nate's hand while he smoothed the mutt's black fur.

"Damn good dog," Nate said. "Oughta take him too." He fed the dog the last scrap of jerky from his pocket.

Rob looked around. "First, let's deal with Uncle Joe's cut. He must have taken care of the pickets since we ain't been challenged."

Nate led the way to the mules. "Here, help me get them to the gangplank." They sent the mules plodding down the canal towpath. Joe Fields had men waiting to herd off the animals. He said mules were easier to turn into cash money than other loot.

"Losing them mules is gonna make the captain madder than hell." Rob handed crates from the deck down to Nate.

"Yeah, captain don't give a damn for Union property, but he's gonna miss them mules."

The boys toted the crates down to the flatboat and loaded it as high as they dared before they poled across the river. They made two more trips back and forth to the Virginia shore, each time hauling crates of the Colt revolvers Nate had grabbed before. As they approached the canal for the fourth time, Rob noticed clouds of smoke drifting over the lock area. The black dog had abandoned the canal boat and stood yelping on the riverbank.

Nate let out a piercing whistle and the dog plunged into the Potomac and swam toward the flatboat.

"You ain't gonna haul that big mutt into this boat, are you? We'll sink," Rob said.

"Sink? Naw, this is a canal dog. He ain't gonna sink us." Nate leaned over the side and called the dog, encouraging him to swim alongside the boat.

By the time they tied up on the Virginia shore, the rainstorm had blown itself out over the mountains and a bright flare of orange was visible against the night sky. The canal boat was burning and the rest of the Yankee supplies with it.

"You were the last one off," Rob said. "How'd the fire start?"

"Accident." Nate was dragging crates of guns away from the shore. "The cook stove was still red hot and a pot of grease spilled while we was moving around. Didn't think nothing about it at the time, but there ain't gonna be no canal traffic going either way for a while."

The boys moved the guns a good distance from the flat boat, which they covered with brush. Then they pulled branches over the stash and ran through the woods to River Road.

"That fire's gonna rile the Yankees. They may send patrols over on the ferry." Rob looked back toward the river. "I'll have the wagon back here in two hours." The clanging fire bell from across the river drowned out Nate's reply.

Rob turned and headed up into the hills toward home. Nate and the big dog ran toward the Orrick farm. Johnson Orrick had to be informed so that he could work out how to transport the guns to Winchester.

* * * *

As he neared the farm, Rob hoped Pa would be gone. He saw three horses grazing in the yard and made a wide circle of the house. Drawing closer, he could hear voices. The door burst open and two blue-coated soldiers stepped onto the porch. Pa followed them.

"Don't worry, I'll take good care of your friend," Pa said.

The Yankee soldiers mounted their horses. The older one wearing sergeant's stripes called back, "We had bad luck running into the Rebel scouts, but it was good luck brought us to your door. Thanks for your help. We'll be back for Merrill." They rode off, leading the third horse behind them.

When the Union men were out of sight, Rob slipped into the house. A wounded soldier was lying on the floor by the fireplace. Pa entered the room with a bowl and a bottle of whiskey. "Here, see if you can spoon some broth into him. I gotta get me a drink."

The Yankee groaned and tried to move. His blue eyes were clouded with pain as he stared up at Rob. Setting the bowl on the floor, he knelt and studied the young soldier. His fair, curling hair reminded Rob of Billy.

"I'm sorry to put you out," the Yankee spoke softly. Rob raised the man's head with his left hand and tried to spoon broth into his mouth. "Thank you kindly," he whispered. After a few more sips of broth, he lapsed into unconsciousness.

"Here, let me see how he's doing. He has a right nasty wound." Pa hunkered down by the soldier. "I come across him on the ridge road. He'd lost a lot of blood, so I bound up his leg with old feed sacks and was hauling him to the wagon when them other Bluecoats rode up. They give me a Yankee dollar to keep him a few days."

Pa emptied the man's pockets. "Look here, a watch and two Yankee gold pieces. This soldier is a welcome guest. Hand me his pack." Pa dumped the contents on the floor. "Don't look at me that-a-way, boy. The Yankee don't need this stuff. Look here at these books. Imagine, him toting them to war with him." Pa pushed the well-worn volumes aside. "What do you know, there's a real prize in the bottom of the pack." He triumphantly produced a big plug of tobacco. "Damn, them Yankees know how to live. Here, boy, have some chaw. Reckon you earned it tonight." He looked expectantly at his son.

"The cargo's waiting on us. Need to get them crates over here and hid quick." Rob reached for the chaw. "Canal traffic's gonna stop for a good while. We left a burned out barge at the lock."

Rob never saw the blow coming. With one swift motion, his father slammed him up against the wall and stood over him. "Listen. You and that no-good Fields boy got this idea, but now you need my help. You ain't the general yet, understand? Firing a canal boat was plain stupid. Bluecoats gonna be crawling all over the shore. My cut's just gone up."

Rob helped Pa carry the Yankee soldier outside. He groaned as they loaded him onto the wagon bed. Rob knew this was wrong. The wounded man needed help, not a nighttime ride over mountain roads, but Pa was using him as an excuse to travel. Neither Pa nor Rob had a word to say as the wagon jolted down the ridge road and onto River Road. Sitting up front on the wagon seat, Pa cursed the squeaking wheels that even a bucket of tallow hadn't quieted.

Rob sat in the back and nursed his throbbing jaw. Damn small thanks he'd gotten for this night's work, for being a patriot. He and Nate had taken all the risks, and now Pa, just sober enough to drive the team, was trying to run things. As the wagon bounced along, Rob could hear the Yankee soldier moaning.

"Here, try to drink this," Rob said, as he held the canteen to the soldier's lips. "You're looking feverish."

Opening his eyes, the man looked at Rob. "Thank you. I heard you talking to the old man. Know how you feel about us Yankees. Sorry about Billy. Was he a relation?"

"Yeah, my brother. He was 20 years old."

"I'm only 22 myself. My name is Merrill Robinson, Private First Class, 13th Massachusetts Volunteers." His voice was low and hoarse. "What's your name?"

"I'm Rob Johnson. I'm almost 16 and I've lived hereabouts all my life," Rob whispered. "Don't mind my pa. Reckon you know he went through your pack."

"I owe you, you and your father both. Are the books still there?"

"Two books and a Bible."

"Can you read, boy?"

"Yes, sir."

"Good. Read those two books; they're about the West. I want to live and go out West." Merrill Robinson's head rolled to the side and he slept again.

Soon they were close enough to hear shouts from the Maryland side of the river. The sky was bright orange and smoke hung over the water. "Yankees ain't gonna let this go. Gonna be madder than hell," Pa rasped as he drew up the wagon and heaved himself onto the road. "Wouldn't have dragged this poor Yankee boy along if you hadn't been so damn stupid." Pa checked up and down the deserted road. "Now get going. Drag up as much as you can and wait in the brush. Holler out to me for all clear, but don't head toward the wagon 'til I say." Walking over to the side of the wagon, Pa stared down at the wounded man. "Sorry we had to carry you along, but you'll be all right. We need you, Yankee."

Rob worked steadily, but moving the heavy gun crates alone took time. Still, there was no sign of Nate. Could he have been picked up by a Yankee patrol, or had he lit out because things looked too risky?

When the final load was hidden in the loose straw of the wagon bed, Pa's manner became lighter. "Well, that's the last of it. Good boy." He clapped Rob on the shoulder and even offered him a pull from the bottle of corn whiskey. As they headed back toward the farm, Pa whistled softly. The soldier slept and Rob regretted trusting Nate Fields.

Merrill Robinson cried out in pain as the movement of the wagon threw him against the rough sideboards. Rob was trying to shove more straw around him when the team pulled up and the wagon jolted to a halt. Pa stood up and called to the horses. A thin, sickle moon shed pale light on the rider blocking the way ahead.

"A little late to be out with a farm wagon." The rider wore a Confederate officer's uniform and was well mounted.

"We're on an errand of mercy." Pa gestured toward the back of the wagon. "Got a wounded soldier here. On our way home." He picked up the reins.

"Not so fast." The officer moved closer. Four more men emerged from the shadows and surrounded the wagon. None of them wore uniforms, although some had Union caps and a couple wore dirty Confederate jackets. All were heavily armed.

"Errand of mercy, is it?" The leader maneuvered his horse closer and looked at the man in the wagon. Moonlight filtered through the clouds, revealing the soldier's face. The officer leaned down in the saddle and studied the wounded Yankee.

"True enough." He said and turned toward the silent, waiting men. "Go through the wagon. Wounded Yankee or dead Yankee, it's all the same to me. Somewhere on this road we'll find the loot from a burned-out canal barge. Why, I can almost smell it."

"You ain't got no right. You ain't soldiers in any army. I'm certain of that."

"I concede your point, sir. Major Joshua Bradley, Morgan Rangers, at your service." He removed his slouch hat in a sweeping bow.

"Rangers, my ass. You ain't nothing but bushwhackers. Outta my way. I got a wounded man here." Pa raised his whip.

The men moved forward. Major Bradley leveled a revolver at the wagon. "You're aiding the enemy, you old fool. If you want, I'll put another hole through your Bluecoat. Then there won't be no reason to rush off." He stepped closer to Merrill Robinson and cocked the revolver.

"No!" Rob threw his body over the soldier.

Suddenly, Merrill's eyes opened and his gaze was lucid. "Save yourself," he whispered. "I'm ready to die."

The wagon lurched forward as Pa applied the whip to the horses. A shot whistled by Rob's head and lodged in the wagon's side panel. Keeping his face pressed against the rough blue uniform, Rob prayed for the first time since his mother died.

He heard more gunshots, followed by the pounding of galloping horses. Three riders raced toward them, led by a huge black dog. Snarling, the dog leaped at Bradley's mount. The horse bolted, carrying its rider away into the darkness. His men spurred their horses and rode after him with the dog and its masters in pursuit. Rob recognized Johnson Orrick's big roan horse in the lead. Nate followed, screaming out a bloodcurdling Rebel yell. The third man could have been old Charles Swann.

Pa whipped up the tired team, then looked back at his passengers. "We'll make it now. Damn them bushwhackers to hell. Nothing but murdering thieves."

On the ride home, Rob watched the Yankee soldier sleep. He knew he should hate him, but he did not.

* * * *

In the shadowed light of the cave, Fannie ran her fingers over the smooth barrel of the Colt revolver. She looked up at Rob. Had he grown taller in the last few weeks? He really was a good-looking boy, with his wild black hair and earnest blue eyes. He would soon become a handsome man. The very fact that he and that crazy Nate Fields had taken these guns from under the noses of the Yankees was unbelievable. Blocking Federal canal traffic was a stroke of genius.

"You and Nate are the heroes of the day, Rob." Fannie handed him the revolver. "Everybody's talking about the canal boat fire. The Yankees are going crazy over it."

"It's gonna take the Yankees a while to clear the canal," Rob said. "I feel good about that." Carefully replacing the gun in the crate, he pulled down the cover and spread branches back over the cache, then the two left the shelter of the cave.

"The guns will be gone by morning. Mr. Orrick's gonna see that they're transported south," Rob said.

The pair stood for a moment looking down at the silver ribbon of the river far below, then they started down the steep mountain path. Stumbling over the last few feet to the pasture, Fannie slipped and fell to the ground. Trying to catch her, Rob managed to break her fall. They ended up in a tangled heap on the grass. Fannie felt his strong young body pressed into hers. His warm breath was against her cheek. Suddenly, his lips were on hers. She was surprised at the desire that shot through her. Breathless, Fannie tried to get up, but couldn't.

"Get off me!" She struggled, pushing him away.

For the space of several heartbeats nothing happened. Then he rolled away and stood up, not looking at her. She saw him heading back up the mountain path.

"Rob, Rob, wait," she cried. How dare he walk away from her? Fannie was furious, but Rob Johnson was already out of sight.

* * * *

The next day Pa left again. Rob mucked out the barn and spread manure over the nearest field. Ma used to say hard work cleared the mind, but images of Fannie Swann consumed him. Willing himself to forget her only made her rebuff more stinging.

When he went back to the house at noon, Rob could see that Merrill Robinson was stronger. He drank a little soup and managed to eat some dry cornbread. His fever was down and he became talkative.

"My leg is better. The wound is starting to heal, thanks to you and your Pa. He doctored me with some kind of salve he uses on the horses and it helped. Where is he?"

"He left this morning. Sorry, he gathered up some of your things."

"I know. I was awake more than you thought. I saw the way he knocked you around. It was wrong." Merrill stared at him. "Soon you'll be a man and you can leave here. Strike off on your own."

"I ain't the one who'll be leaving. I've thought on it. I've been working the place alone for a while now. Some of the fields have gone untended, but I've kept up the hotel deliveries. I don't need Pa."

"How long has your pa been like this?"

"He started drinking hard when Ma died. Then Billy was killed in the war. He ain't here much now and I've come to think of the farm as mine."

"It's only dirt and rocks, Rob. Hand me my Bible. I'll pray for you and your pa."

Rob rummaged through Merrill's pack and found the worn Bible. He wished he had the Yankee soldier's faith.

Merrill's friends returned that evening and carried him off. Rob found that the house was empty without him.

CHAPTER 3

THE CONSCRIPT GANG

AUGUST 1861

In August, hot muggy air settled in and there was seldom a hint of a breeze. This evening, the sun rode atop the dark mountains, still sending warmth along the ridges. Rob watched the cows plod down the path toward the barn and heard Bessie, the lead cow, bellowing in alarm. He waited at the barn door and wondered what was bothering the old girl. As the animals moved into the barn lot, he ran over to close the gate behind them. He had just herded them into their milking stalls when he heard horses approaching. Latching the barn door, he walked toward the house.

As the three riders drew near, Rob could see that they were dirty and unkempt. They wore Confederate uniforms and were heavily armed. The man in front was older than the others and spent some minutes sizing him up. His deep-set, black eyes scanned the boy, then the house. "You live here, boy?"

"Yes, sir." Rob saw that the two younger riders looked restless. Their horses danced impatiently.

"Where's your family?"

"They're at the neighbors."

The leader scowled at Rob. "I know of your pa, young Johnson. Don't believe he'll be back for a good while. Are you a patriotic family?"

"My brother died at Manassas." Slowly, Rob realized he was in trouble. "What do you want?"

The leader's broad smile was more menacing than his scowl. "We represent the 21st Virginia, the finest fighting men in the South. Glad to hear you folks are patriots, 'cause we've come to take you along with us, young Johnson. You're gonna have the honor of joining up with the 21st."

"I ain't interested." Rob started backing toward the door. The two younger men dismounted and walked toward him.

"Grab him," the leader ordered. "We wasted enough time."

Rob sidestepped the soldiers, made it inside and bolted the door. "Get the hell out of here," he shouted. Looking around for something to use as a weapon, he picked up the fireplace iron. Too late, he remembered the rifle hidden in the barn.

The door crashed inward, followed by the three soldiers. "I told you men to grab him. Now, gather up anything useable." The leader stomped back onto the porch, sat down on the steps and pulled out a plug of tobacco.

Rob swung the fire iron at his opponents, but it was all over quickly. The younger soldier circled behind and pinned down his arms, while the other man punched him in the stomach, then hit him in the face. One of the men prodded him back through the doorway with the barrel of his gun.

"You look old enough to be a soldier," the leader said.

"I got no intention of joining your army," Rob shouted. "I'm needed here on the farm." He wiped the blood away with his sleeve, but he wasn't going to give them the satisfaction of seeing his pain.

"Don't get excited, boy. There's no end of glory in the Confederate Army." The soldier with the rifle laughed. "Besides, our sergeant tells us we're short of quota this week."

Dragging out a sack of flour, the other man looked Rob over. "You best cut off them black curls, boy. Soldiers ain't supposed to be all that pretty. Of course, you ain't so pretty now." The two soldiers fell into fits of taunting laughter.

The leader heaved himself off the step. "Shut up, the lot of you. Brown and Burns, get something together to eat. Boy, go get them cattle from the barn. Remember, I'll be watching you every minute."

It took only seconds for Rob to pull the rifle from behind the corn bin. Loading it quickly, he crouched by the door. Pressing his hand against the wall, Rob was grateful to his grandfather for the solid construction of the old barn. Massive tree trunks had been used as posts and beams, and stout timbers reinforced the heavy door. Those soldiers weren't going to break in here.

Keeping watch through the slot carved into the door, Rob figured there must have always been trouble in these hills. The rifle slot was there for a reason. When they came, the Rebels shouted orders at him. He grinned. When they got closer, he pushed the rifle barrel through the slot and fired over their heads. Reloading, he fired near their feet.

Rob saw the leader hold up his hand. "Time to get out of here, men. We'll get the boy sooner or later."

As the conscript gang rode off, one of the soldiers shouted, "We'll be back, young Johnson. Best not shut your eyes."

The hayloft was dark and hot. Rob raked together the scatterings of hay that remained after the last raiders had hit the farm. A Yankee foraging party had been searching for horse feed and found the Johnson place. They had told him he'd be paid in Yankee dollars on the first of the month. What good would Yankee dollars do him? He needed the hay. Fortunately, the cattle had been out to pasture, or they would be gone also. Rob wondered how he'd be able to feed the cows through the winter. Old Bessie was with calf and he had never delivered a calf alone. He wasn't sure what to do. His father would have known; his brother would have known. But they weren't here.

Settling back on the hay, Rob thought about his situation. He was hiding from a Rebel conscript gang. Last week he'd been bullied and threatened by a Yankee foraging patrol. He hated both sides. Pa had been right about one thing; it wasn't their war. Neither side gave a damn about folks here in these mountains.

His thoughts drifted to Fannie Swann. Would he ever see her again? Or would he die in this war he didn't believe in? He knew it was just a matter of time before he would be run off the land, or dragged off. He couldn't survive alone and he was scared.

* * * *

As darkness closed in, a lone rider approached the Johnson farm. When Nate reached the house, the place looked deserted. He left his horse to graze and walked up on the porch. The front door was hanging on its hinges. The kitchen table was overturned and the fire iron lay in the middle of the floor. He looked into every room, but there was no sign of the Johnsons.

Nate paced on the porch. The mountains were now only blurred stretches of purple against the night sky. Where the hell was Rob? It was not surprising that old Tom wasn't around, but Rob was always here of an evening. The animals had to be looked to. He headed toward the barn.

Nate put his shoulder against the barn door but couldn't force it open. Soft rustling alerted him and his hand went to the Colt revolver at his belt. "Rob," Nate called. "It's me."

He hunkered down and waited. The pale moon was rising when the big door creaked open and a figure emerged.

Rob leaned his rifle against the barn door. "You ain't the first visitor today."

The cows heard familiar voices and started bellowing. It was way past their milking time. Back in the barn, Rob lit the lantern and Nate took a good look at his friend. "What happened?"

"Rebel conscript gang. They threatened to come back." Rob rubbed his bruised jaw and grinned. "I'm not about to be taken off my own land."

He surveyed his old pal. Nate's thin lanky frame adapted well to the Confederate gray uniform. His sandy hair fell to his shoulders and his long angular face was thinner also. "So, you finally joined up." He clapped Nate on the shoulder.

"Johnson Orrick didn't want no regular army routine, so he's forming his own ranger unit here in Morgan County and I signed on. He's Colonel Orrick now," Nate said.

Rob nodded. "Here, help me with the milking. It's all we'll have to eat."

Later, Nate pitched hay down to the manger. "You ain't got much feed left," he said.

"Yankee foragers took it. Don't know how I'll get these cows through 'til spring."

After storing the milk cans in the springhouse, Rob carried one can back to the house. Nate helped him prop the broken door in place with a bureau and then they sat on the kitchen floor drinking the warm milk.

"Them boys won't be back tonight." Nate broke off a piece of chewing tobacco and passed it down to Rob. "What you gonna do? Take on the lot of them?"

"If need be. I ain't being run off my land by either side."

"You're a stubborn fool. You're sitting right smack on the border here, a mile from the Potomac River. It's time to take sides. Join up with me. Orrick's Rangers will look out for your place here."

Rob was silent.

"There's talk that Stonewall Jackson is gonna march up here this winter and drive the Yankees back across the Potomac," Nate said.

Rob shook his head. "An army will never get through these mountains in winter."

"If Stonewall says he will do it, then he'll do it," Nate said.

"What about the Yankees? They won't just sit by."

"You ain't even thinking about going over to the Yankees?"

"I've thought on it," Rob said. "Truth is, I don't know what to do."

"Now I know you're crazy. They killed Billy at Manassas. Think of your old daddy."

"He's all but moved out. Pa don't give a damn about me or this farm. He's joined up with that gang of horse thieves over in Buck Valley."

"I was hoping you'd figure it was time to pull out and ride back to Colonel Orrick with me." Nate grinned at him.

"I'm not ready to leave here. Not yet."

"What are you gonna do? Die here and get buried over by your ma? That's the only way you're gonna stay."

Rob moved to the window and peered out into the darkness.

"I don't like this war no more than you do," Nate said. "I agree that Morgan County is stuck between two armies and set upon by every bushwhacker, cattle thief, and smuggler who can find his way here.

"You need to talk with Colonel Orrick. I know he needs more places to stash supplies. You got a root cellar and there's the cave up on the hillside. There's hiding places in the barn that we used as kids."

"Yeah," Rob's voice was flat. "And how would that help me? It would get me killed and the place burned to the ground."

Nate moved to the window beside Rob. "That's possible, but it don't have to be. Orrick's Rangers scout this area because we're local men and know the country. We could keep a good eye on your place here."

"Well, you ain't done the job so far."

"Don't be a fool, Rob. Colonel Orrick don't do nothing that ain't to his advantage. He needs a place for a family that was burned out over by Cherry Run. You got room."

"I'll think on it," Rob said at last.

The next morning the boys drove the cattle to the upper field, then set off to meet with Colonel Orrick. Rob turned and looked back at the farm, shrouded in mist and framed by blue banks of mountains. It would be all he'd have left at the end of the war and he aimed to hang on to it any way he could.

* * * *

Rob and Nate reached the high mountains by noon. In another half-hour they arrived at the smoky cave, which served as the rangers' main living quarters. His neighbor, Johnny McKenny, was the first to spot them.

"I quit my regiment and joined up with Colonel Orrick," Johnny said. "You'd be welcome here."

Rob looked around at the lean weathered faces and nodded. He knew them all. "I ain't ready yet. I come to talk to the colonel."

Colonel Orrick remembered Rob and affirmed that his men would look out for the Johnson farm. But the rangers were stretched thin as it was and Rob knew this most likely wouldn't happen. Making no promises in return, he left quickly. He was already working out plans to hide the few remaining valuables and stores of food.

* * * *

The next day Rob carried the milk cans from the springhouse and loaded them onto the wagon. The chickens were laying poorly, but he managed to gather up several dozen eggs. He picked anything ripe in the garden, mostly tomatoes, peppers and squash. The hotel folks in Bath wanted fresh vegetables.

The cows took their time plodding to the upper pasture. Rob's shouts and whistles were to no avail. From long habit, the two old horses met him at the pasture gate, even though he'd brought them no apples in months. They followed him docilely back to the barn but became skittish when he led them to the wagon. He rubbed their necks and talked quietly to them, so was able to harness the team and maneuver the wagon down the narrow lane onto the ridge road. Turning onto River Road, he glanced from left to right. He saw nothing but broad expanses of bottomland stretching to the Potomac.

The sun was climbing in the sky by the time Rob rode into Bath. At the Pavilion, Mabel McCabe stood by the kitchen door with arms crossed over her ample bosom. She glared at Rob. "You're late, boy. That no-good pa of yours has already been by wanting money for an order ain't even been delivered."

"Pa was here?"

"He was here. The man was skinny as Snyder's hound and tried to beg a meal."

Rob brooded over Pa while he carried the crates into the hotel. Pa showed up like a bad penny. Never came by the farm. Did he plan to?

CHAPTER 4

FANNIE SWANN

AUGUST 1861

Trying to catch the faintest breeze, Fannie and Mary sat on the long shady porch at O'Ferralls' Coffee House. There was little traffic on Fairfax Street. Even the stray dogs were lying in the shade.

"A terrible thing about old Colonel Strother." Mary looked over at the Pavilion Hotel. "He's a kind old man." She picked up her glass of iced tea and held it to her cheek.

"Is it true that Ashby's cavalry arrested him in the middle of the night?" Fannie asked.

"Shameful, but true. Ashby had the old colonel taken down to Winchester last Sunday. He'll be tried before a military court for treason, even though he was a war hero back in 1812." Mary set down her glass. "We hear that prisoners are being roughly handled and worry for John Strother's health."

"Mary, Colonel Strother has been charged with treason against the Confederacy. You know he's used his influence to sway many a young man into joining the Union Army." Fannie's voice rose in anger. "Look at Rob Johnson. I'm sure the old colonel has tried to coax him to join the Yankees."

"Where is Rob these days? You haven't seen him in a while, have you? What happened between you two?" Mary asked.

"Nothing."

"He isn't anxious to carry messages to you. Something went on."

"He's a boy. What could go on?" Fannie's fair complexion was flushed.

"He was man enough to take those guns from the Yankees; man enough to take over all the farm work. He's alone up there on the ridge now." Fannie looked away, so Mary continued, "You know, I was in love with Billy Johnson once. He was always ready for a lark, always joking—nothing like serious, brooding Rob. What does Rob brood about?"

It was true, Fannie realized, she had seen little enough of Rob since that evening at the cave. She wondered if he brooded over her. Well, that fantasy could be put to good use.

* * * *

The next day Fannie sent word to Rob that she must see him. There was no response. Three days later she took two loaves of freshly baked bread and started up the ridge road toward the farmhouse. She had taken care dressing, choosing an old dress that fit her tightly and clung to her small breasts. After the climb up to the ridge, she collapsed on the porch steps and watched the mist rise slowly up the mountains. Weak sunlight filtered down the deep blue ridges and all seemed peaceful. Fannie wondered if Rob would be happy to see her.

A slight movement behind her caught her attention. Startled, she turned to confront Nate Fields.

Scrambling up, Fannie rounded on him. "Don't you dare sneak up on me."

"What you doing here anyway, Fannie? Rob ain't got no time for you."

Fannie saw that Nate's gray uniform made him look older. Leaning on the porch rail, he watched her.

"How do you know what Rob Johnson wants? Where is he?"

"Colonel Orrick sent me to gather up some things old Colonel Strother needs down at the prison camp—clothes and such. Rob had to take the market goods to town anyway, so he offered to help out. The old colonel ain't too comfortable down in Winchester."

Fannie advanced on him. "Ain't too comfortable! John Strother is a traitor to Virginia. He will get a fair trial. That's all the comfort he should be afforded."

Nate backed up a step. "Well, I'm sure as hell sorry this don't suit you, Fannie, but you ain't running the army yet."

"You and Rob never did understand. The enemy is always the enemy—neighbors, kin folk, it doesn't matter."

"He's a sick old man. He come outta the War of 1812 a hero. Don't that mean nothing?"

"No. My father's an old man, but the Yankees have threatened to imprison him just for speaking his mind. No trial, just a jail cell."

"Yeah, well scream all you want. Some of us think different. You're one cold-blooded bitch." Nate turned and walked into the house, slamming the door.

"Go to hell, Nate Fields. And that goes for Rob, too. Tell him I said that." Fannie stumbled off the porch and started back down the lane at a run. She stopped once and looked back. The Johnson's door cracked open and Nate slipped out to gather up the loaves of bread.

"Damn thief!" She yelled.

* * * *

When Fannie reached home, she stopped only long enough to tell her mother that she must go to see her aunt Viola.

Reaching the Orrick home, Fannie found her aunt clipping day lilies in the garden. Following Viola around to the front of the house, Fannie spoke quickly, "Is Nate Fields under Uncle Johnson's command?"

Viola nodded as she studied the girl's rigid posture and the wild look in her eyes. "You're all het up, Fannie. Tell me what's wrong."

"People around here don't know what patriotism is." The girl faced her aunt. "That back country ruffian, Nate, had the nerve to tell me of Colonel Strother's discomfort in prison camp. Comfort for a traitor, while our boys are dying every day at the hands of the Yankees."

Viola set down her basket. "Fannie, I know you're sincere and the South has need of a young lady of your talents, but your real value to the cause has not yet been put to use."

Viola and her guest sat on rockers on the porch. While Viola poured tea, she watched her young niece closely. "You're a beauty, no doubt, Fannie, but headstrong and spoiled. Although, with proper direction you could be an asset to the Confederacy. How are your cousins in Hancock faring? Do you see them much?"

Shocked by her aunt's words, Fannie barely managed not to tell the old biddy what she thought of her—a plain, quarrelsome woman not good enough for her handsome husband. "I don't visit Hancock these days," she said "I don't choose to venture into enemy territory."

"There's where you're wrong, my girl. How better to know the enemy's intent than to meet him on his own ground, to attend dinner parties and social gatherings. This is where a man lets down his guard and tells secrets to pretty girls. The information you could gather would be invaluable." Viola stood and held out her hand to Fannie. "Come, I have something to show you."

Following her aunt up the dark staircase, Fannie wondered what Viola could possibly have to interest her. Looking at the paintings lining the walls, Fannie realized that these were Viola's family members and no kin to the Orricks or the Swanns. Viola was the rich relation and never let them forget it. They stopped at the door to Jessica Orrick's bedroom.

Viola threw open Jessica's wardrobe and laid out several dresses. She helped Fannie slip into a gown of fine blue damask. Fannie pirouetted before the long mirror, noting that the gown fit perfectly and made her look altogether the mature beauty. It was much more elegant than anything she had ever owned.

"Very becoming, my dear. You'll win the heart of every Yankee officer in Hancock. I'll write to Jessica that you've borrowed these." Viola gestured at the gaily-colored ball gowns draped over the bed coverlet. "After the baby, she realized her figure had changed forever."

Tracing the detailed beadwork on the bodice, Fannie tried to understand what she was agreeing to do. Dazzled by the image of the fashionable young lady in the mirror, she nodded. "You're right, Aunt Viola. In this gown I can torment the Yankees."

"Right now there is trouble from David Strother. He's so angry over his father's arrest that he's trying to talk the Union forces into occupying Morgan County. We must know what is planned. Talk with your parents and let me know what you decide."

Slipping out of the elegant gown, Fannie pulled on her own clothes and observed herself in the mirror. She saw a skinny country girl in a faded brown dress. "I know Ma will say no, so I'll talk to my father." Fannie held the ball gown against her body and swayed to unheard music. "I become a different person in this gown—a woman who can get whatever she wants."

"Fannie," Viola's voice was sharp again. "There are rules to follow in every game. First, you must be a sympathetic listener. The softer your voice and the sweeter your smile, the more you will be trusted." She smoothed the silk gown Fannie had tossed on the bed.

* * * *

Charles Swann kept the team at a slow plodding pace as he drove the wagon into Bath. Fannie fidgeted and fretted as she sat next to him. "I'm bone weary of your arguments," her father said.

"Pa, I've told you Aunt Viola made me a gift of the gowns. All I need are the bonnets and a new pair of shoes. How else can I attend the socials across the river? Can I dance in these farm boots?" Fannie's voice shrilled as she stamped her sturdy boots on the wagon bed.

Her father groaned. "Money is short, girl. You know the Union folks don't come into the store no more. They ain't bringing their logs into the sawmill either."

"This was Aunt Viola's idea. She wants me to make a difference. She believes I can be of help to the cause."

"Viola be damned. It ain't her girl she's sending into the viper's den all decked out like a Hagerstown whore. I've told you it's a dangerous undertaking." Arriving in town, Charles left Fannie at O'Ferrall's.

* * * *

Upstairs in Mary's bedroom, Fannie teetered unsteadily in her friend's high-heeled boots. She walked back to the mirror and admired her reflection. "They're a bit tight, but I can manage." She twirled and tried out a few dance steps. "Thanks, Mary."

Standing by the window, Mary wasn't listening. "Quick, Fannie. Come over here."

The girls looked down on the street below where Rebel cavalry herded three men toward the town square. They were roped together so tightly that they appeared to be partners in a clumsy dance. Their feet dragged, shuffled and kicked along the road.

"The tall one in the middle," Mary said, "is Rob Johnson."

"Those fools! Rob's no conscript. He's still a boy." Fannie leaned over the windowsill. "Stop! Where are you taking those men?" No one looked up or responded. "I'm talking to you, captain," Fannie screamed. "Turn them loose!"

The girls reached the street in seconds. Hearing the commotion, Jane O'Ferrall followed them outside. They found Rob and two older farmers surrounded by mounted soldiers.

Dismounting, the officer stepped forward and confronted the women. "Ladies, clear the way. This is a military matter."

The women stood their ground. "Captain," Jane O'Ferrall's voice was soft and pleasant, as if the assorted group had met at a social occasion. "The day is warm and oppressive. Please bring your men into O'Ferrall's for some refreshment."

The officer glanced uneasily at the girls, now smiling sweetly. Hesitating only briefly, he left one man to guard the conscripts and gratefully led the rest into the coffee house. The soldiers were taken to the kitchen, but the captain was invited into the dining room.

"The company couldn't be more charming and the beer is welcome," the captain said. He seemed to relax as he told the admiring ladies of his exploits at the Battle of Manassas. Later, he rambled on about his boyhood on a farm near Richmond. He addressed most of his remarks to Fannie, but when she left to fetch more beer, he began to describe his home place to Mary and her mother.

* * * *

Fannie stood in the dust of the road and looked down at the body of the Rebel guard. He had happily accepted the lemonade she'd offered, then collapsed after a few gulps. The empty tin cup lay near his hand. Helping the captives remove their bindings, she sensed their anxiety to be off.

"We best not head home," one of the older men said. "They'll be sure to look for us there."

"We could go to the McKenny place," Rob said. "They're neighbors of mine and will hide us for a few days. By then, this patrol will have moved on and we can go home."

Nodding agreement, the two older men turned to Fannie. They were so grateful that she blushed.

"You mustn't thank me so much. Old Delilah in O'Ferrall's kitchen knew what herb to mix into the guard's drink. I just carried the tray."

The men looked more and more nervous, so Rob waved them off. "I'll catch up with you," he said and smiled at Fannie.

Although she hadn't seen him for several months, the tall youth standing before her bore scant resemblance to the shy boy she remembered. Rob reached over the prone soldier and formally shook her hand.

"I'm beholden to you. If I do join this army, I want it to be on my own terms."

Before Fannie could reply, Rob was gone. She picked up the cup and started back toward the inn. This had not gone the way she'd expected. Her new plans were falling into place and she was beginning to worry about details. With a little prompting, her Maryland cousins had invited her to a small party planned for the next Saturday evening. Rob could have been useful in many ways, but he was proving less manageable and altogether less agreeable than before. She'd saved him from the conscript gang today and gotten meager thanks for her effort.

At the coffee house door, Fannie almost ran into the captain. He pushed past her and hurried out to the road where the groggy soldier was struggling to sit up. "What the hell happened here?" the captain yelled. "Where are the conscripts?"

"I don't know. This is how I found the guard." Fannie turned and walked into the inn. Calling for Mary and Mrs. O'Ferrall, she tried to sound alarmed. It was hard not to smile, not to outright laugh at the arrogant captain.

CHAPTER 5

PA

SEPTEMBER 1861

It was harvest time and Rob spent long days trying to bring in his crops with what help he could muster. Only old men and young boys were left around to give a hand. Many crops had rotted in the fields before he could harvest them, but he was pleased with what he had salvaged. Exhausted at the end of every day, he had little time to think of Fannie, but she still entered his dreams and he awoke with a raw longing.

Rob was pushing a wheelbarrow of corn to the barn when he saw Nate. Well-mounted and leading a pack-mule loaded with goods, he waved and yelled a greeting.

Rob dropped the wheelbarrow and grinned. "Nate, you're looking grander than General Lee." Nate wore a slouch hat and sported new corporal's stripes on his arm. "Now I got an excuse to quit for a while," Rob said.

Nate smiled and held up a stringer of bass. "I never come empty-handed. Is there a chance of dinner?"

After they ate, Nate asked, "Any more unwelcome visitors?"

"Things have been quiet, but I always keep my rifle handy."

"Colonel Orrick put the word out. Glad to hear it might have helped."

Out on the porch, they watched the sun sink down toward the purple hills. The sumac blazed orange along the fencerows and a chill was in the air. "All my ma's omens point to a bad winter," Rob said. "Will Lee fight on?"

"Hard to tell. There's a powerful lot of fighting going on up in Western Virginia, around Cheat Mountain and over to the Gauley River. I hear our boys routed the Yankees at a place called Cross Lanes in August."

Rob nodded. "In time, the fighting will turn back this way."

"It will," Nate agreed. "Except for the railroad, our small scrap of mountain land ain't worth much to the North, but we stand between them and the Valley. There'll be hell to pay for us then, no doubt about it." Nate stretched out his long legs and offered Rob a cigar. "Don't mind if I light up, do you?"

"Where'd you get these?" Rob asked.

"Some folks have more than they need. Others don't have enough. I'm evening it out."

Rob said nothing. It wasn't his concern. He told Nate a little about Fannie and how confused his feelings were. Nate looked at him steadily and finally said, "Fannie don't care nothing for you. She's just using you, Rob. She's got big ideas. Can you see her as a farmer's wife?"

"I don't guess she'd be much good at slopping the hogs." Rob grinned.

"Doubt she'd be much good at anything else, either," Nate said and snickered. "She's a bossy little bitch. You're well rid of her."

Rob nodded, but he didn't agree.

Nate confessed to an affair with a young 'grass widow' whose husband was off fighting the war. "That's one reason to join up," he said. "The ladies will love you. You need to find a nice, married woman who'll treat you right—some lonely lady who'll put a candle in the window and wait by the door." He puffed on the cigar. "My lady loves me, Rob. Her little ones call me 'Daddy.' They hardly remember their real daddy and neither does she."

"The war ain't been on that long. Are women really so fickle?" Rob asked.

"Some are, and they're the ones I'm looking for."

Rob threw his guest a blanket-roll. It was too late for him to head back to Colonel Orrick's headquarters.

* * * *

At dawn, Rob woke with a start. There were horses in the yard and Nate was already at the window. "Yankees," he said.

Silently, Rob joined his friend. "Looks like a cavalry troop. They're dragging something. Time to get out." Rob grabbed his rifle and headed to the back of the house. He pulled up a rug and opened the trap door to the cellar. Minutes later, he and Nate crawled through the narrow tunnel at the back of the cellar and emerged in a bramble thicket behind the house. As they watched, the Yankees led up a pack mule and cut loose a tattered bundle. Then the captain raised his arm and the soldiers filed out behind him, leaving the heap of rags behind.

Nate reached the yard first. Bending down to examine the rags, he was stopped by Rob's croaking yell, "No, get away." Flinging himself down, Rob wept. "Look, they're Pa's boots." He pointed to the worn pair of boots at one end of the bloody bundle.

Rob pushed the rags aside to reveal Pa's face. Still weeping, he tried to straighten his father's crumpled limbs—to make right what was left of Tom Johnson's torn body. "Why would they do this?"

"It's a warning. Most likely they caught him stealing Union horses." Nate walked toward the barn. "I'll get a shovel. We ain't got much time 'cause they'll be back. Otherwise, they'd have torched the place."

When Nate returned, he found Rob still sitting on the dirt beside his father. "I don't know if I loved him or hated him," Rob said.

* * * *

The boys left the farm just as the noon sun broke through the haze on the mountains. They took all they could: clothes, blankets, pots, pans, five dollars from the cash box, and a few mementos from a vanished life. Rob led the cows, and the old draft horses carried his small inheritance.

When they came to the McKenny place, Rob told the elderly sisters what had happened. "The animals are for you. I can't look after them now. Please ask the Reverend to say a word or two over Pa. We had to make a hasty burial."

The women regarded Rob stonily. But he knew no matter what they thought of Tom Johnson, they would carry out their Christian duty.

Rob and Nate reached the hillside cave by evening. The McKenny sisters had given them some food, which they ate quickly. "What you planning to do now, Rob? Ain't no point in staying around here." He pulled out a bottle of corn whiskey. "Here, let's drink to the old man."

Rob gulped the whiskey, sputtered, then answered, "I'm planning on getting clean away from Morgan County. Tomorrow I'm heading to Winchester to join up."

That night a large force of Yankees returned to the Johnson farm. Their campfires lit up the night and their rowdy songs and laughter filled the air. Nate stood watch while Rob, drunk on corn whiskey, slept through it all.

CHAPTER 6

48ᵀᴴ VIRGINIA INFANTRY
WINCHESTER, VIRGINIA

OCTOBER 1861

Rob lied about his age and joined the 48ᵗʰ Virginia Infantry. Now he'd been in the army less than three weeks and had already seen combat. He described the incident in a letter to Mary O'Ferrall:

> *I was sworn in with a large group of men and assigned to a squad. We got some training but mostly we were drilled on loading and firing our rifles. A soldier has to be able to load and fire up to four times a minute. I expected more training, but Sergeant Jarvis said a week of drilling and marching in formation was enough training for any man and the Confederacy had need of us. A few days later we were on picket duty north of Winchester when we ran into a Yankee patrol. Like a fool, one of our boys fired the first shot. I narrowly missed a bullet and the man next to me was hit. It was John Whitacre from over at Sleepy Creek Mountain. I hauled him to cover and kept firing. After the Yankees rode off, I left John propped against a tree and looked around for help.*

Rob left out the rest of the story. The other pickets had taken off. So, finding one of the Yankee horses grazing nearby, he had ridden toward camp. Almost at once he was surrounded by a group of armed men.

"Get off the horse, boy, and hand them reins here." The nearest rider grabbed for the reins, while another man rode up beside him and jerked him off his mount. Rob fell to his knees and found himself hemmed in by the other riders.

"We ain't gonna hurt you, soldier. We're Rebels same as you, just more independent like, but it wouldn't do to have all of Jackson's camp after us." The man who spoke had long yellow hair and wore a Yankee officer's hat. The others were dressed in an assortment of ragtag clothing.

"Let me go. I left a wounded man behind," Rob yelled.

"Too bad, son. We left a lot of wounded Yankees. They're in God's hands now."

The countryside they traveled through was heavily wooded, but they soon reached rolling farmland. Rob had been dragged up behind the lead rider and now hung onto the man's belt as they galloped toward a run-down farm. The man's jacket smelled of sweat and tobacco and the motion of the galloping horse threw them together as if they were old friends. Driving ten head of horses before them, the group raced toward the barnyard.

"You, boy, give a hand to rub down and feed them horses," the leader said. He was a big man with wide-set black eyes and a hawk-like nose. A thin scar ran from his left eye down to his neck.

The others weren't as menacing, but they were a surly lot. The youngest, a man about his brother Billy's age, snarled curses when Rob accidentally tipped over a water bucket. The horses, he noticed, were a mixture of Yankee and Confederate mounts. The Yankee horses were still saddled, and must have just been snatched from the hapless scouting party. Rob found blood on a saddle stirrup and figured that the firing had attracted this band of thieves.

* * * *

Later, the men sat around a table in the farmhouse kitchen. The room was spotlessly clean, but bare, save for the most basic items: cook stove, table, chairs and a tall cupboard in the corner. Rob hadn't eaten since daybreak` and the smell of food was overpowering. Watching the old woman stir the pot on the stove, he paid scant attention to the raucous laughter and loud conversation around him.

The tall man with the yellow hair pushed his chair back and walked over to the farmwife. "So, Auntie, where's little Laura?" He asked.

"She ain't here, Thad," the woman answered.

"I said where the hell is she?"

The old woman banged a pot lid down and Rob couldn't catch the rest of what was said. He turned his attention to the leader, called 'Big Earl,' who sat next to the old farmer.

"You can bring them horses into town by twos and threes. There's always a good price. Hell, who's gonna suspect an old codger like you?"

The old man's wife looked up sharply from the stove. A small, bent old woman, she moved quickly as she carried a pot of soup to the table. Across the room, rustling sounds by the cupboard caught Rob's attention.

The others appeared intent on the conversation, but Rob watched the cupboard. For an instant, he was sure he saw a pair of eyes watching through a gap in the lower doors.

"Well, it's risky, I tell you," the old man said. "I done made my final offer. If you don't like it, ride away and see how far you get with them horses."

The haggling dragged on, with the obstinate old man sticking to his guns. "Well, I see you're a man of principle," Big Earl said in a calm, even pleasant, voice, but the scar under his eye had turned bright red. Rob tensed, but Earl seemed perfectly at ease. He continued smiling as he watched the farmer.

The old man pounded the table. "It's mighty hard to make any kind of living now. First the Rebs take my crops and cheat me, then you boys come along and try to do me wrong."

The knife flashed quicker than the old man could react. Bright red blood spurted from his right forearm. Yowling in pain, he pushed back his chair and stood up. At the stove, his wife dropped a pan of cornbread. There were no other sounds in the room. Slowly, Big Earl lowered the knife and held his hands open, palm up. "What you think I'm gonna do? We're just talking a little business."

Glancing at the cupboard doors, Rob saw that the eyes had vanished. The men were quietly reaching for weapons in their belts. Rob had no weapon; they had taken his rifle and his prized Colt revolver. Knowing he had little chance of saving the old farmer, he figured if he threw himself under the table and scrambled toward the cupboard, he might be safe. The men weren't after him, but he could easily catch a stray bullet.

"You're right, grandpa. You've suffered enough." Big Earl started to rise from the table. His men followed suit. Rob watched the old man, who had realized his fate and bolted toward the door. As the first shot rang out, Rob flung himself down and rolled under the table toward the cupboard. Miraculously, the door opened and a terrified young girl shoved an old musket into his hands. She started pushing him back into the room.

"It's loaded and ready to fire," she whispered. "You ain't one of them. You gotta save my grandparents."

It was probably too late for the old man. As the firing continued, Rob saw him fall to the floor. But the old woman crouching by the stove looked unharmed. Rob crawled over to her and extended his left hand. She shied away and pressed herself against the wall. The kitchen was in chaos as Big Earl's men headed toward the door. They stumbled over the motionless old man who lay near the threshold.

Suddenly, the girl was by Rob's side. Speaking softly and soothingly, she was able to coax her grandmother to move toward the cupboard. The men were on the porch now. Rob could hear Big Earl shouting orders.

"Get them horses, then set a torch to this place. Folks around here need to know what happens if they cross me."

When the old woman had been taken to the safety of the cupboard, Rob and the girl turned their attention to the old man. Sobbing, she helped Rob pull her grandfather's body away from the door. They were covering the old man with the tablecloth when his wife ran, shrieking, across the room. Before they could stop her, she was out the door. Too late, Rob saw the kitchen knife in her hand. Moving faster than he could have imagined, she reached the knot of men in the barnyard. Grabbing the musket, Rob followed.

Intent on their tasks, the men were unaware of the crazed old woman until she was upon them. Raising the knife over her head like a battle axe, she rushed at Big Earl, screaming, "Murderer! Murderer!"

"Well, if this don't beat all." Earl looked amused as he grabbed the old woman's wrist. The knife clattered to the ground.

Now Rob was close enough to hear her cry of pain. Raising the gun, he aimed directly at Big Earl. "Let her go. She's a grieving old woman."

Amused, the other men watched. "Ain't you got no mercy, Earl?" The tall blond man called out.

The musket was shaking in Rob's hand, so he braced it with his other hand. "Let her go." His voice, at least, was steady.

"Let her go? I think we just might take her along with us." Earl must have twisted her wrist more, as the old woman cried out again. "We need a good cook, don't we, boys?"

Watching the scene before him, Rob didn't realize that the girl, armed with a shotgun, had come up from behind.

"Look boys, a pretty little girl. She's the one we oughta tote off," Big Earl said as he dragged granny toward the horses. "You want to save her, little girl? We'll make a trade."

The girl raised her shotgun, sighted down on Big Earl and fired. "Run, Granny!" she screamed.

Shot flew everywhere, but her aim was poor. Only a few stray shards of metal bit into Earl's arm. Blood spurted from his wound, but he kept moving with the old woman still in tow. Rob's aim was better. His bullet hit Earl in the left shoulder.

"Why, you little Reb sonnuvabitch," Earl shouted. But he released his grip on the woman. As his right hand went for a weapon, he stumbled and pitched forward to the ground.

Rob grabbed the girl's hand and dragged her toward the side of the barn. The old woman had run into the building. Peering around the corner, Rob was amazed to see that Big Earl's men were leaving. They drove the horses ahead of them and left their leader bleeding in the barn lot. Suddenly, the tall blond man turned and rode back, raised his pistol and shot Earl twice in the chest. Wheeling his horse, the shooter galloped off after the others.

They had trouble convincing the old woman to leave the barn, but the girl finally coaxed her to return to the house. Rob went back to Big Earl and took his gun and five Yankee dollars from his pockets. Now, at least, he had a weapon.

In the kitchen, the girl found a bottle of corn whiskey and forced her grandmother to drink. Then she poured shots for Rob and herself. Handing him the drink, she said, "Thanks. We'd have all been dead if not for you."

Bolting down the whiskey, Rob studied the girl. She was young, probably not much younger than himself. He placed the money on the table and asked, "Where'd you get the shotgun?"

"I had it hid in the cupboard." She looked at the coins on the table. "Big Earl's money?"

"It's yours now. You and your granny will need it. What's your name?" Rob poured himself another measure of whiskey and saw his hands were still shaking.

"Laura Meeks. What were you doing with them horse thieves?" She stared at him. Her pale blue eyes and yellow hair gave her a delicate beauty, and made Rob think of his mother.

"Sit down." He steered her to the table. "I'll tell you what happened. One of our pickets fired on a Yankee scouting party. So they commenced to fire back." He saw that the girl's gaze was fixed on her grandmother. Her breathing had become shallow, so he took her hands and rubbed them quickly between his own. Surprised, she looked up and gulped in a breath of air. Rob continued, "The man next to me got hit in the leg. After the Yankees rode off, I grabbed one of the horses and went for help."

"So, you're really a soldier? What's your name?"

Rob stiffened. "My name is Rob Johnson. What do you mean, am I really a soldier?"

"You look pretty young, is all. Did Big Earl's bunch capture you along with the Yankees?"

"They didn't capture no Yankees. They killed them all."

"I don't wonder," Laura said. "They're local men. The man with the yellow hair is kin. His name is Thad Meeks. His aim is to lead that gang of bushwhackers."

"What about your family? Is there anybody to help with the bury-ing?"

Laura looked over at her grandma huddled on the floor by her husband's body. "Ain't nobody but my Uncle Frank down at the next farm."

The sorrow in her eyes touched him. "I'll stop there on my way back to camp."

* * * *

Leaving the uncle's farm, Rob turned onto the Winchester Road. He was surprised by the couple's reaction to his news. Terrified of Thad Meeks, they seemed unwilling to get involved. Finally, the old man agreed to get word to the preacher and see to the burials of Laura's grandfather and Big Earl. They were a strange clan and he was glad to be done with them. He thought of Laura, growing up in this grim environment, but she still had a sweetness about her. She was a survivor.

The sound of approaching horses brought Rob back to his present situation: a lone soldier. He reached cover just as a Confederate cavalry troop came into sight. Walking back onto the roadway, he waited. He was tired and hungry and sorely needed a ride.

CHAPTER 7

LAURA MEEKS

NOVEMBER-DECEMBER 1861

Rob had been back at camp for two weeks and found that he was somewhat of a celebrity. John Whitacre had been rescued by patrolling Confederate troops and then told around camp that Rob had saved his life. Laura Meeks' grandmother had sent a letter to his commanding officer. She, too, credited Rob with keeping them alive. The Meeks had also written a letter to him inviting him to Thanksgiving dinner.

Leave didn't seem very likely. Rob had heard talk of a possible winter offensive up into the mountains, though he couldn't believe this would happen. He spent time cleaning his gun and repacking his gear. Like all the other young soldiers, he was spoiling for action. The skirmish and the attack at the Meeks' farm had shown him that no matter how scared he was, he would stand and fight the best he could.

In his spare moments, he dreamed of Fannie Swann, the beautiful girl who thought of him as a boy. Now, though, Laura Meeks had a way of intruding into his dreams. She was not as striking looking as Fannie— few girls were, but Laura was pretty and seemed to like him.

Cold weather brought good luck for Rob. Due to his valor during the Yankee attack, he was promoted to corporal and granted a two-day leave. He spent it with the Meeks.

* * * *

Astonished at the change in Laura, Rob could hardly take his eyes off her. She met him at the door wearing a very grown-up outfit. The dress of dark green fit her small body perfectly, showing off her tiny waist and fair coloring. Had he looked closely, he'd have seen that the gown had been cut down from a larger size and was worn in places. But with her hair piled high on her head, she presented a perfect picture. "Please come in. Granny will be down to join us presently."

Rob could detect little of the awkward girl of a few weeks ago. Even her speech seemed more sophisticated and her manner was that of a confident young woman. "Would you like some blackberry cordial? Granny and I made it last summer. Please, sit down by the fire." Laura busied herself with the bottle and glasses.

Rob wondered if he had also changed and now appeared more mature. After all, he had been promoted and, if not a seasoned soldier, he was no longer a raw recruit. This morning he had brushed his gray uniform and polished his boots. The army barber had trimmed his unruly hair and shaved the stubble off his chin. Yet, he had no idea of the image he presented and he was nervous.

After he downed half the glass, he felt the blackberry wine warming him. "You're such a pretty girl, Laura. I don't remember you being so pretty, but I do recall that you put up a hellava fight."

Laura smiled. "I didn't put up half the fight that Granny did."

"How's your grandma managing without the old man?"

"She ain't well—not her old self at all." Laura looked down, hesitated, then continued, "We've had a few problems."

"Problems? What kind of problems?"

"My cousin, Thad Meeks, has been calling on us. He walks in at dinner time and stays all evening."

Rob remembered the man with the long blond hair who had ridden with Big Earl. "Is Thad the man who shot Earl? What does he want here?"

"Yes, that's Thad. He seems to think he has some right to the farm. Says he took up for us. Now we owe him."

"What does your grandma say?"

"She don't say a thing. She's lost heart since grandpa died. It's left to me."

"Do you think you owe him?"

Laura got up to look at the roasting meat. Grabbing a fork, she jabbed furiously at the turkey. "We don't owe him nothing. I don't owe him, either."

Rob went over to the stove and stood beside her. "What do you mean?"

"I don't want to think about the things he says to me. He has no right." Laura set the fork down and took Rob's hand. "There ain't nothing you can do."

Laura's hand in his was small and roughened from hard work. Her touch caused him to throw out all caution. "I'll stay here a while longer. The army can fight on without me."

They walked, hand in hand, back to the blackberry cordial. "It ain't that easy," Laura said. "You don't know Thad Meeks. You'd have to kill him."

"Thad Meeks probably deserves to die more than most of them poor Yankee boys I'm set to kill." Rob drained his wine glass. "What about your family? Can they help out?"

"They're Thad's family, too." Laura looked unhappy. "He gives them things, things he steals. Now he's the boss of that gang of bushwhackers. They're afraid of him."

"They got good reason to be scared. But we can handle Thad Meeks if we plan it out."

"You're a good man, Rob. I didn't know where to turn." Impulsively, Laura kissed him on the lips.

Drawing her to him, Rob kissed her again. At first, Laura didn't respond. But by the time they heard old Mrs. Meeks descending the steps, they were both disheveled and red-cheeked. Demanding her dinner, the old lady hardly gave Rob a glance. Indeed, she did not seem to notice any of her surroundings. Mumbling to herself, Mrs. Meeks repeatedly asked that Laura save enough food for her grandpap.

"She won't admit that he's gone," Laura whispered.

Thanksgiving dinner was a tense, quiet affair. Mrs. Meeks did not speak at all and Laura and Rob didn't know what to say to each other.

The silence made Rob uneasy, so he asked, "Where did you manage to get the turkey? Birds have been scarce this fall."

"We traded with my Uncle Frank. He'd shot two birds, so he took a bottle of blackberry cordial for the hen." Laura passed heaping bowls of applesauce and sauerkraut. The potatoes were mashed and swam in gravy. After the pumpkin pie was served, the old lady left the table. They heard her making her way slowly back up the steps.

"How long has she been like this?" Rob asked.

"She hasn't been good since grandpap died. But a week ago she took a bad fall. Since then, she's just given up." Laura began to clear the table. "I'm alone now, Rob." She started to weep.

"Come here," Rob said softly, and pulled her down onto his lap. He brushed the hair from her face, then traced his fingers gently down the side of her cheek.

Tentatively, she ran her hands over his face and then kissed his mouth. The sensations this stirred in Rob were like nothing he'd ever felt before. He kissed her hungrily, his hands roaming over her firm young body. Laura started unbuttoning his shirt and then kissed his neck, his chest. His breath came in short gasps as he moved her off the chair onto the braided rug. She clutched at him and he fell on top of her. Her fancy dress was much harder to remove than his army uniform. The tiny buttons slipped through his clumsy fingers. Finally, Laura had to unbutton them herself. The firelight bathed her in a soft glow and he marveled at her perfection.

The urgency that gripped him now left no more time to admire Laura's beauty. He cupped her small breasts and knew this was the best thing that had ever happened to him. She was moving under him in a slow rhythmic way. He didn't know what he dared to do, so he kept kissing her. When he felt her hand guiding him, his whole body was on fire.

Later, Rob fell into an exhausted sleep with Laura in his arms. She had pulled the pillows and old quilt off Granny's chair and covered them. He woke her two more times that night and they made love. Now, he needed no encouragement from her, but he wondered at her knowledge. He was in love and that was all that mattered.

* * * *

As Rob rode back toward Winchester, guilt rode with him. He had been ready to stay at the Meeks; he was eager to stay. But Laura had taken a firm stand. Deserters were hunted down and shot and he would be no good to them dead. His helplessness made him angry. He'd never had a strong desire to fight for the Confederacy, but he felt compelled to help the Meeks women.

Back at camp, Rob notified his commanding officer of the plight of the Meeks women. Colonel Simms was sympathetic, but said there was little he could do. Rob was told that his regiment would move out soon. That evening he wrote to Mary O'Ferrall asking if she could find shelter for Laura and her granny. He was sealing the letter when Nate Fields found him.

"You got a soft job here. I just spent five days scouting for the army and I find you relaxing in camp. No wonder you don't want to do no scout duty with Colonel Orrick." Nate grinned broadly and hunkered down next to Rob. "Hear you're something of a hero."

"You're right, Nate. I'm a hero and just got promoted to corporal." Rob stood up and clapped his friend on the back.

"You ain't?" Nate grinned. "Tell me about it."

Rob related the story of the battle, the raid, and the threats to the Meeks women. Then he paused and said quietly, "I plan to kill Thad Meeks."

* * * *

Protected by bordering mountain ranges, the Shenandoah Valley offered up a cloudless mild day for Christmas Eve, 1861. Reining in his horse, Nate shrugged out of his jacket and pulled a canteen from the saddlebag. "Hey, Rob, want a drink?"

Rob's horse was an old military mount and plodded slowly ahead. Even so, he was grateful that Nate had known which groom in the cavalry stables to bribe, or he'd have been walking. When he finally reached his friend, Rob held out his hand for the canteen. As he drank, he watched the sky. A flock of crows swooped in and settled on a nearby oak tree. Bare of leaves, the tree was laden with dark forms.

"That there is a bad luck tree. My granny knew the omens." Nate looked unhappy.

Rob knew the tree as a marker. The Meeks' farm was over the next hill. "Your granny was old. Are you an old woman, too? Maybe you shouldn't have come, Nate."

"Maybe not, but I'm here now. So, what's the plan?"

"I ain't got a real plan, but Thad Meeks won't live out the day." Rob's tone was flat, his jaw set.

"You've changed, Rob. You ain't the same boy you was back home." Nate took the canteen and studied him critically. "A few months ago all you worried about was getting the hay in and making moon eyes at your red-haired girlfriend. Didn't want no part of the war. Now you got your own little war."

Rob didn't answer, but spurred his old horse forward. All seemed peaceful as they approached the Meeks' farmhouse. A thin wisp of smoke rose from the chimney, but the place looked deserted. Stopping in a grove of trees near the barn, Rob dismounted and threw the reins to Nate. "Wait here. I'll be back."

"Hold up," Nate said. "Wasn't you expected?"

"I didn't get no answer to my letter." Rob slipped into the pinewoods and was gone.

Entering the lower barn through a side door, Rob waited until his eyes grew accustomed to the dim light. He stared around at the empty stalls, which had housed two old draft horses, and realized that the Meeks had been raided. Clutching the revolver in his belt, he thanked God for Big Earl's gun. Rob's military issue Burnside carbine was cumbersome and not as accurate.

As he left the barn and began circling toward the back of the house, Rob found Nate at his side.

"Damn if I'm going to sit alone in the woods," Nate muttered.

Finding no signs of life in the back, Rob motioned Nate to go around the left side of the building; he headed around to the right. Reaching the front porch, Rob saw that the door stood open. He waited a moment, then threw his hat toward the front door.

The shot went wild, ricocheting off the porch rail. Running toward the door, Rob and Nate crashed into the house at almost the same moment. Granny Meeks, holding the rifle, screamed, "Run, Laura, he's back again. Run!"

Gently, Rob took the gun from the old woman and led her to a chair. "We won't hurt you, Mrs. Meeks. Don't you remember me? I'm Rob, Laura's friend. Where is Laura?"

"Laura?" Granny looked at him blankly. "She's gone. Not here. You must go and leave us alone. My husband will be home soon." Exhausted from the effort, her head slumped on the table.

Rob left Nate to look through the small downstairs rooms while he took the stairs two at a time. He found Laura in the front bedroom. At first he thought she was sleeping, but her eyes opened. She looked at him, then looked away.

He tried to take her hand, but she pulled it back. "It's too late for us now, Rob. You had best go."

"Laura, what are you talking about? What's happened?"

Laura started to weep and her sobs tore at his soul. Taking her in his arms, he spoke quietly. "It's all right. I'm here now. No one will hurt you again." Smoothing her soft golden hair, he felt the anger rising within him. She didn't need to tell him what happened. He knew. He traced the bruises on her face.

"Who did this?" His tone was grim.

"You know who." Seeing the look on Rob's face, Laura stopped crying. "But he's gone now."

"Gone?"

"Granny shot him. We dragged him to the smokehouse and hid him best we could. Neither of us had the strength to bury him. May God forgive us."

"God forgive you?" Rob shouted. "Thad Meeks don't deserve a Christian burial. He was an animal. I came here to kill him myself."

Laura started weeping again. Her harsh cries carried through the house. Cautiously, Nate entered the room to find Rob sitting with his head in his hands and Laura curled in a ball at the foot of the bed. Seeing a stranger, her cries rose to shrieks of fear.

"Ain't no cause for alarm, Miss. I'm Nate Fields, a friend of Rob's. Known him all my life." Kneeling down by Laura, Nate took her hands. "Rob says you're a brave, strong girl. You need to calm down now and tend to him. He blames himself for not being here."

* * * *

Outside, Rob put his rage into digging a deep narrow grave behind the smokehouse. He'd seen Nate head into the woods with a rifle, but had hardly noticed. The old woman had babbled on about Christmas pudding and Laura had taken to her bed again. Stabbing the shovel into the hard-packed earth, Rob tried to work out his anger. He hated Thad Meeks. He hated himself and he didn't know what to say to Laura. By the time the pit was deep enough and long enough, some of his anger had drained away. Sweating, he went to the house for water and found Laura and her granny busy in the kitchen. Busy, as though it were any other day.

"It's Christmas Eve, young man," Granny said gaily. Laura looked away and he went back outside.

To his amazement, Rob found that the grave was almost closed. Raw red earth was being heaped over it. Nate stood, shovel in hand, surveying his work. "Figured you could miss the ceremony. I told the devil Thad Meeks needed to rot in hell." He leaned on the shovel. "How did old Granny get that shot off? She hit him in the chest. Damned amazing."

"Maybe the omen tree was meant for him. I only wish I'd been here in time." Rob turned and walked toward the barn.

"Don't be too long, Rob. I got us a mess of squirrels for dinner. The old lady says she knows how to cook them."

* * * *

That evening Rob sat in the kitchen and watched in disbelief. Old Mrs. Meeks, who had just shot a man, and Nate, who had just put him in the ground, were now trailing popcorn strings over a small yellow pine tree. Nate had cut the tree in the woods and brought it inside with the skinned squirrels.

Laura poured out the last of the blackberry wine. She was pale and did not speak to Rob when she handed him his glass. The wine warmed him and he began to feel ashamed of his sullen behavior. So many strong emotions worked on his mind that he realized it would take time to sort through them all.

At dinner Granny Meeks and Nate kept up a spirited conversation. She seemed to have slipped into a time when she had been a young girl and her family had been homesteaders in the Valley of Virginia. Watching her, Rob was amazed at the change in her behavior. Happy in her memory world, she recounted stories of long ago Christmases. Her eyes sparkled as she called Laura "Sissy" and referred to Nate and himself as "the young men." Nate complimented her lavishly on the fine dinner and encouraged her stories. Rob and Laura sat in silence.

"Yes, we have had some fine Christmas times here," Granny said. Her eyes shone. "Tomorrow we'll have a grand feast. My man will be home soon with the Christmas turkey."

Laura hadn't touched her food and kept her eyes on her plate. Quietly, Rob excused himself and went out on the porch. Sitting on the steps, he looked up at the full moon. He heard the front door close behind him, but didn't turn.

"It will snow by week's end," Laura said softly. "My grandpap taught me to read the signs of the moon—the time to plant, time to harvest, time to batten down against the storm."

Rob felt her presence behind him, but he didn't know how to respond. Finally, he heard her move back toward the door. "Wait," he said. "Please, come and sit by me."

Night was coming on and it had turned colder. Rob realized that he was glad she was here next to him. He took her hand and the two sat quietly together.

* * * *

Christmas morning found Granny Meeks sulky and quarrelsome. Nate looked exasperated. "Laura, you have to explain to the old girl that there ain't no turkey for Christmas. She'd best start packing up because we gotta leave soon."

"She says she won't leave Grandpap."

Rob came down the steps carrying the bedding Laura had bundled together. "Tell her we'll meet him along the way. Tell her he's waiting for us."

Granny refused to leave the house and Nate had to carry her to the farm wagon. She beat on his back and screamed, but she was finally deposited atop the bedding. Rearing and prancing, the army mounts resisted pulling the loaded wagon. Finally, Rob had to lay on the whip to get them moving. Granny was still bawling when they left.

Nate had gone ahead and been lucky enough to bring down a young doe. So the Meeks women arrived at the home of Granny's brother-in-law with something to offer. Frank Meeks and his wife opened their house to the refugees once they heard that Thad was dead. The young soldiers helped to carry in the women's meager possessions, then declined the dinner invitation.

"We better get away from here before Granny figures out there ain't gonna be no reunion with the old man," Nate said quietly to Rob. "Say your goodbyes."

Rob found Laura waiting by the wagon. "I'm going to arrange a place for you and Granny with friends up in Morgan County. I'll do it, Laura."

In answer, Laura reached up and touched his cheek. Rob smoothed her hair. "I'll be back," he promised.

Riding away from the Meeks place, Nate and Rob said little. As they approached the main road, Nate asked, "What are you gonna do now? If it were me, I'd never look back. Them two women are trouble."

"I'll keep my promise," Rob said.

"You're crazy, then." Nate turned his horse and headed toward the mountains.

CHAPTER 8

JACKSON'S MARCH

JANUARY 1862

When Rob reached camp in Winchester, the first news he heard was that Sergeant Jarvis had been reassigned and the new sergeant was a madman. As he was unpacking his gear, he looked up to see a giant of a man come through the tent door. The men jumped to attention. Walking slowly to Rob's bunk, the man stood towering over him.

"I'm your new squad leader, Sergeant Williams. Where have you been keeping yourself, Corporal Johnson?" His short beard and mustache were brown, but his head was completely bald. A scar curved along the side of his right ear. Seeing that Rob was staring at the scar, the sergeant quickly replaced his cap.

"What the hell you looking at, boy? You're back late from leave. Why is that?" Williams' pale eyes never left Rob's face. There was a stillness in the sergeant's gaze that unnerved him.

"Sorry, Sergeant. On Christmas Eve my friend's home was raided and she was hurt. Her granny shot the man that done it."

"Sonny, don't lie to me." The hard uncompromising look in the sergeant's eyes stilled Rob's protests. Williams strode back and forth, staring down the young soldiers.

"This ain't an army, it's a social club. You men will never stand up in battle. You'll let your comrades down. You'll let General Jackson down." Williams turned back to Rob. "We're going to be marching soon and I hate to think of taking you men into a fight."

* * * *

A week before Christmas, Rob had gotten a letter from Mary O'Ferrall. He re-read it several times.

Dear Rob, I'm sending this letter by a friend of Trip's to be sure you receive it. I guess you've heard that the Yankees have set up camp at Alpine Station. The 13th Massachusetts arrived on December 13 and arrested Charles Swann as a dangerous Rebel. He's in the Hancock jail. Fannie and her mother are under house arrest and we are very worried for them. Fannie was able to send me a note. The Yankee doctor she met at one of the Hancock socials is now at Alpine. He's agreed to help her father get a Christmas parole. After all, he is a sick old man. Colonel Orrick's home has been renamed 'Fort Osborne' and serves as Union headquarters. Mrs. Orrick has headed to Richmond. We hear rumors that General Jackson will march north soon. It would be grand to see these Yankee scoundrels run back across the river. Stay safe. Your friend, Mary.

So, he thought, *the Union Army was camped a few miles from the farm*. He wondered what would be left to him if he ever got home.

* * * *

Rob began looking over his shoulder, because Sergeant Williams was always there. He came in as the men ate and assigned duties so that they couldn't finish their meals. He kept them on picket duty longer than other squads and harped on every small infraction. Their squad spent more time on work detail and their jobs were always the dirtiest. Rumor had it that the sergeant had gotten that nasty scar in the Battle of Manassas. His heroism had saved him from court martial for assaulting a soldier under his command.

Although Rob grew to hate the sergeant, he saw that Herman Jacobs, who had joined the squad before Christmas, took the worst abuse. Jacobs came from a farm near Harrisonburg and talked endlessly of a girl named Nelly. Rob was the only one who would listen to him. Jacobs rambled on about Nelly and about his grandpap, who made the best corn whiskey in the county. Small and wiry, Jacobs was quick on his feet and the first to volunteer for any duty. But his keenness did not impress Sergeant Williams, who had taken an instant dislike to the boy.

Two days before New Year's Eve Herman Jacobs was on picket duty. When he had not reported back by evening, Sergeant Williams sent Rob and another soldier to find him.

Half an hour into the woods, Rob stopped and held up his hand. He and his companion watched as Jacobs, carrying two rabbits, headed toward them. Catching sight of his friends, Jacobs waved and held up his catch. "Gonna be good eating tonight," he yelled. "I got a trap line going."

Sergeant Williams threw Jacobs in the guardhouse. He was only released when the army moved out.

* * * *

New Year's Day was so mild that many of the men left their coats and heavy blanket-rolls on the supply wagons. An army 8,500 strong, Jackson's soldiers marched smartly out of Winchester. The men had been told to draw five days' rations, but their destination was unknown. The soldiers in Rob's squad were lighthearted as they headed toward the mountains. Regimental flags waved in the breeze and the men around him started singing a rowdy marching song. He joined in the chorus.

It was late afternoon before the supply wagon caught up with Rob's squad. Joe Hardy, the driver, was a short dour man from Romney. He knew all the other drovers and kept his ear to the ground. Joe had it on good authority that the army was ultimately headed to his hometown, so he was in a congenial mood.

Halting briefly for a meal, the men picked up the march again and continued north. Now the blue line of mountains was clearly visible on the horizon and the soldiers felt a chill in the air. The weather was changing, but not for the better. The wind whipped up from the northwest and Rob thought it would snow before morning. When the men were finally allowed to stop for the night, they were met by a small patrol riding in from up the line. Rob watched as words were exchanged between his commanding officer and the patrol sergeant. Then they turned their horses and filed out, leaving an injured soldier behind. The soldier was Nate Fields.

"A cannon fell off one of them artillery wagons and I was in the detail sent to drag it back up to the road," Nate explained. "It rolled loose again halfway uphill and I took a nasty fall." Nate looked weary and held his injured arm awkwardly in its makeshift sling. "I had some friends in the group and they found your squad."

Rob stared at him. "I thought Orrick's men were scouts. What were you doing dragging wagons?"

"They grab anybody at hand when one of them wagons roll." Nate grinned.

Rob went in search of a bottle of corn whiskey for his friend. As the first wet snow flakes fell, most of the young soldiers were huddled around a fire. A few were playing cards. Even Nate had joined them, as he could never pass up a game of poker. The whiskey bottle passed stealthily from hand to hand. The men boasted that the snow squalls were a good omen, for now the Yankees would never expect an attack. Although Rob had not acquired a taste for whiskey, it was welcome on this night.

"You boys," Joe yelled to them, "best get a place under the wagon or we'll have to dig you out come morning."

Rob looked at Nate. They threw down their cards and dove for the wagon. "We know what can come tonight," Nate said. "Them boys by the fire are from the Valley. They're in for a hellava surprise."

* * * *

At dawn on January second snow was still falling. Men who hadn't found cover discovered that their blankets were mounded with snow. Nate groaned in pain as he dragged himself out from under the wagon. Rob had already been foraging for firewood. Finding dry wood was almost impossible, but he dragged in a few branches he'd taken from under a heap of pine needles. Soon he had a cooking fire going and called Nate and Jacobs over to share the meal.

While they ate corn cakes and drank coffee, Joe regaled them with the latest news. "The army stretches out at least seven miles long. Them boys at the front are in pitiful shape. They're further into the mountains where the snow is deeper. Some ain't had nothing to eat because the supply wagons are bogged down. You boys are pure lucky."

"Nobody at home would travel in weather like this. Old Jack is crazy," Nate complained.

* * * *

Later in the day the snow turned to sleet and progress was slow. A thin layer of ice proved to be much more treacherous than several inches of snow. The overloaded wagons slid on the slippery mountain road. Wagons and drovers collected at the base of hills, delaying movement even more.

A man named Bowen marched behind Rob. Bowen had developed a hacking cough and had trouble keeping up. He'd lost his cap and left his heavy coat on one of the long-lost supply wagons. Rob gave him his own blanket and offered to carry his pack. But when Sergeant Williams called a brief halt, Bowen fell to the ground and could go no further. Rob felt his forehead and realized that the man was burning with fever.

With the help of another soldier, Rob loaded Bowen onto the supply wagon with Nate. Old Joe turned in the wagon seat and studied the new man. "You boys best be on the lookout for a cabin. Bowen needs nursing and a warm bed, or he'll not live out the night."

A heavy freezing mist gathered at the base of the mountain. Looking upward, Rob saw that each tree branch glittered with a coating of ice. Suddenly, a sharp crack rang out and the soldiers around him threw themselves down in the snow. "Ain't no Yankees, you flatlanders," Joe yelled. "It's the damn tree branches breaking under the ice." Sheepishly, the men got up and resumed their uphill struggle.

As they continued to climb upward, Rob had some trouble keeping his footing. Ahead, the horses could barely stand. On the road above, a big roan horse crashed to the ground, pulling its wagon precariously close to the edge of the mountainside. Rob could hear the frantic, bellowed orders and see the soldiers trying to heave the poor animal up and stabilize the wagon. Thankfully, he was too far in the rear to be involved. Looking upward, he could see only a glare of ice where the road should have been.

"You men move smartly now." Sergeant Williams, sure footed as a mountain goat, moved down the line. Ice matted his beard and clung to his pack. Rob thought he looked like the mountain snow devil in his grandmother's stories. Williams stopped in front of him. "You again, Johnson. Throwing every mewling baby with a sniffle on the supply wagon. Them wagons can't make it uphill as it is. You and the three men in front," Williams said as he gestured to Jacobs and two others, "will be the rope detail for Joe's wagon."

Sergeant Williams walked over to another wagon and took lengths of stout rope from the back. He confronted the four soldiers. "Tie this rope to the top of the rear wagon bed. When Joe starts into a curve, you men grab a hold of the rope and swing to the upper side of the road. You're going to have to strain mightily to keep them horses upright and keep the wagon wheels on the road." He stared at each soldier in turn. "I don't want no overturned wagons. Is that understood?"

Falling out of line, Rob waited for Joe's wagon to wind its way up the slippery road toward him. "How is Bowen doing?" He called to Nate.

"He ain't good. Joe says there's a cabin up ahead. We should take him there."

By the time Rob found Sergeant Williams, ice was weighing down the tree limbs and the road ahead was more treacherous than ever. "Sergeant, we need to move Bowen. He's in a bad way and there's a cabin nearby. Do I have your permission?"

Williams regarded him steadily. "Do you know how serious a matter it is to abandon one of our own men? We don't know nothing about them people in that cabin. No. We'll be in Bath tomorrow, next day at the latest. Bowen is better off with us."

Heading back up the line, Rob wondered if Sergeant Williams had Bowen's best interests at heart, or only wanted to keep the line moving forward. Nearing Joe's wagon, he could see that the old man was agitated. He hurried ahead.

"We got a bad turn coming up," Joe yelled. "You boys take a hold of them ropes." Watching the wagon slowly move into the curve, Rob, Jacobs and the other two men each grabbed a rope and hauled the wagon to the upper side of the road.

"Put your backs into it," Sergeant Williams yelled. He moved quickly up from the rear of the line. "Jacobs, you ain't a little girl. Pull!" Williams darted in front of the wagon. "Pull your weight, Jacobs. If I have to do the job for you, you'll go before the captain."

Unsteadily, the wagon came around the turn and the horses didn't lose their footing. The men gave a ragged cheer and scrambled out of the way of the next team. Without a word, Sergeant Williams turned and moved back down the line.

"Bastard," Jacobs said to the others. "Didn't see him give a hand."

By afternoon, snow mixed with sleet fell on Jackson's army. Behind him, Rob could see a cavalry troop carefully walking their horses up the mountain road. "There ain't going be nothing to eat today," Jacobs complained. "I can't go much farther on an empty stomach." He shifted his pack and groaned. "I seen a few critters that would pass for supper if I could get off a shot."

"Remember what happened the last time you went missing to find supper?" Rob said. "You were in the guard house for three days." The grin Rob got in reply was not reassuring. He resolved to keep his eye on Jacobs.

As darkness set in, Joe pulled his wagon into the shelter of a grove of pines at the base of the mountain. The squad was also called to a halt and the men began making camp. Rob was exhausted, but knew he'd better try to set up a lean-to. The snow was still falling and there was no longer room under Joe's wagon. That area was reserved for the mounting numbers of sick and crippled.

"Give me a hand here, Jacobs," Rob shouted. "Jacobs?" Looking around, he realized that Jacobs was gone. Cursing under his breath, he continued to weave pine branches into a crude shelter.

"Where is Jacobs?" Sergeant Williams loomed over him.

Rob stood up and faced Williams. "I don't know, sergeant."

"You don't know? You are the corporal here." Rob studied the pine branches in his hand. The sergeant's face had turned a dark red. "Now, corporal, take two men and find Jacobs. Don't come back without him."

Following Jacobs' tracks in the snow was easy. The man must not have worried about being caught. Finally, they found him kneeling in a clearning, intent on skinning out a small doe. Looking up, he grinned broadly. "Boys, we're gonna have a good meal tonight."

"Jacobs, you damn fool, you ain't back on your daddy's farm. God knows who heard that shot. The sergeant's mad as hell." Rob walked toward him. "Come on, we got to get back."

"Not without my meal. I was just fixing to build a fire. Get me some kindling. Y'all are invited." Jacobs bent back over the doe.

Reaching him in three long strides, Rob grabbed him by the neck and yanked him up. Startled, Jacobs dropped the skinning knife and gasped, "What are you doing?"

"Stevens, drag that carcass off into the woods. O'Brien, give me a hand with Jacobs."

"You ain't taking away my deer meat?" Jacobs wailed.

When they reached camp, Sergeant Williams was waiting. "Jacobs, you were a poor excuse for a soldier and now you're a deserter. Take him to the captain."

No one saw Jacobs again that evening or, indeed, the next day. But Jacobs was forgotten as the army moved on toward Bath. It was the same night that Private Bowen died of fever.

* * * *

On January third, Rob's company had reached Johnson's Mill just a few miles south of Bath when a halt was called. A rider, leading an extra horse, approached Joe's wagon. Rob recognized the man as one of Colonel Orrick's Rangers. Although Nate's arm didn't look healed, his friend said goodbye and left them.

Private Jacobs had rejoined the army earlier that day and seemed more rebellious than ever. "If I started walking home now, I'd be there in less than two weeks. That would be just in time for Ma's birthday. I'm sick of this war."

Suddenly the sergeant appeared on the edge of the group. "You men, form up. General Jackson has ordered our company to march to the front. Move out."

On the outskirts of Bath the men were deployed as skirmishers. Rob could see the enemy on a nearby hill. When the Yankees commenced firing from behind a long fencerow, the Confederates got the order to fire. Rob picked his targets carefully, sighting in, aiming, and then squeezing the trigger. A blue-clad figure dropped, disappearing into the scrub. Had he hit the Yankee? Rob had never killed a man before and was surprised at his own reaction. He calmly reloaded and aimed again. *I don't have a choice*, he thought. Billy's dead and Pa's dead—killed by the Yankees.

Rob heard the man to his right cry out in pain. Turning, he saw that James Kensey had been hit in the leg and was starting to bleed heavily. Crawling over, Rob grabbed the man under the arms and dragged him to cover. "James, I'm going to get you help."

"No, stay here. Tie this bandanna around my leg and go back to firing. I don't want to be captured by them Yankees."

So Rob continued to load and fire. Fearing he would run out of ammunition, he began to choose his targets even more carefully. Suddenly, the Union skirmishers started running off down the ridge. Rob joined in the ear-splitting Rebel yell that rolled down the hillside and echoed back.

"Move out," Sergeant Williams shouted. "Well done, men."

Amazed at the sergeant's first words of praise, Rob followed the others back to the road. He found James Kensey on a makeshift stretcher. His face was drained of color.

"Johnson," he whispered, "I will die today. I've already lost too much blood." His eyes reflected his pain. Rob walked beside the stretcher until they made camp.

The main army was forced to remain outside Bath yet another day because General Loring's troops had still not arrived. Word had it that Stonewall was fuming at the delay. As night fell, it turned very cold and began to snow again. Camped on the outskirts of town, Rob could see the lights of Bath. He had survived the day, but it had just been a skirmish. Three men in his company had been wounded, eight captured, and James Kensey had died. Shivering in his thin bedroll, he tried to sleep.

CHAPTER 9

THE BATH-ROMNEY CAMPAIGN

JANUARY 1862

On the morning of January 4th, Rob's company moved along the road to Bath. He had heard that Colonel Ashby had already ridden into town with Samuel Meyer's cavalry and chased Union troops toward the Potomac. As Rob entered Bath, the place looked very different. Signs of the Northern occupation were everywhere. Union flags hung from many buildings and debris from the fleeing Yankees littered the streets. He could see the enemy strung out on Warm Springs Ridge. At first the Yankees were out of range, but soon he saw gray-coated sharpshooters take positions on the hillside. As the Southerners opened fire, the enemy retreated.

Hearing a commotion to the rear, Rob turned and saw that General Jackson himself had arrived with a small guard unit. The appearance of the man was not at all what Rob had expected. The general sat astride a small sorrel horse. He wore knee-high cavalry boots, a uniform jacket with gold stars on the high collar, an unbuttoned overcoat and a faded cap. Although hardly an elegant figure, his men gathered around him and listened respectfully.

"You men," the general said, "are going to drive the invaders out of Virginia today. I want you to move toward the Potomac at the double quick." He rode off and Rob's company followed him through the town of Bath.

As they marched on to Alpine, Rob thought of the many times he had driven the farm wagon over this road. His past life seemed far behind him, but he realized that he longed to see the farm again. He was only four miles away.

At the river, the artillerymen were digging in up on Orrick's Hill. The retreating Yankees had left much equipment behind, but a barrage of fire from across the river kept the Rebels away from the shore.

"Night will come soon enough," Sergeant Williams said. "Then we can take what we want. You men, step up for picket duty."

As Rob paced his picket line, he could see activity at the Swann house. Fannie and her mother were handing out food to passing Confederate soldiers. He wondered if they saw him. Just then, a Yankee shell landed between his position and the Swann's. Diving for cover, he looked up to see the front windows of the Swann house shattering. One of the outhouses lifted off its stone foundation and toppled over.

Staying close to the ground, Rob scuttled toward the house. He found Mrs. Swann lying on the ground near the front door. Moving closer, he could see that her face and arms were covered with blood, so he knelt down to feel her pulse and could see that she was breathing. As he was trying to drag her to safety, Fannie came running to them. Together, they carried her mother into the house and laid the injured woman on her bed.

"Is she hurt bad?" Fannie's tone was frantic.

"She's unconscious, but still breathing. I'll find help." Rob tried to sound confident. As he stepped outside, all was chaos. Troops were running toward the river and the big guns on both sides of the Potomac were hurling shells. It took him some time to make his way to a makeshift medical tent. He saw that most of the patients were suffering from fever or frostbite, but a few looked to be battle casualties.

"We don't have time to be making house calls," the young doctor said after he had listened to Rob's request.

An older doctor joined them. "You say it's Mrs. Swann?"

"Yes," Rob said. "I'm not sure how bad she's hurt. She wasn't conscious when I left."

"I'll come," he said.

When they got back to the Swann house, the old lady was still unconscious. Fannie wept as she bent over her. The doctor set down his bag and took Mrs. Swann's pulse.

"I need a little room, Miss," he told her.

"Come on, Fannie." Rob helped her up. "You need some air." Standing side by side on the porch, they watched the artillerymen moving around atop Orrick's Hill.

"Where's your pa? He should be here."

"He went to try to speak to General Jackson. Oh, my God," Fannie moaned.

"You need to send for him. Sorry, but I gotta go now. My sergeant ain't a forgiving man."

"Wait, Rob." Fannie turned toward him. "Thanks for your help. You're a decent boy."

"I'm still a boy to you?"

"Mary told me you had joined the army. You never came to say goodbye."

"You're right. I should have said a proper goodbye." Rob stepped toward her, encircling her waist with his arms. Her head slumped onto his shoulder and she wept.

"I'm losing everything, Rob. I've grown to hate this war."

Rob had no words of comfort, so he pulled her closer and kissed her. The soldiers marching by waved and whistled. Fannie pulled away and ran back into the house. But for just a moment, Rob knew she had returned his kiss. He picked up his gun and made his way back to the picket line.

"Rob," Jacobs called, "The sergeant is looking for you. There's a problem at the river." They neared the Potomac and stopped to load their rifles. "He's mad as hell that you left your post."

"My post got blown up. What's going on?"

"The Yankees are desperate to cross the river."

As they got closer, Rob saw Sergeant Williams' massive form surrounded by Union soldiers. They were pushing him ahead of them into the icy Potomac.

"You, Reb," the Yankee sergeant shouted, "We'll see how long you keep your head above water."

Rob and Jacobs moved back into the brush along the bank and watched Sergeant Williams wade into the river. "We've got to follow him," Rob said. "Come on. I know how we can cross." He led the way along the shore.

"The boat's still here." Rob gestured to Jacobs to hurry. He could hear the Bluecoats closing in behind them. The flat boat was just where he'd left it last summer. Pulling away the snow and driftwood, he motioned Jacobs to help drag it to the river. Hearing shouts and sporadic firing, they pushed off from shore. Ice floated on the water, but the strong current caught the boat and took them down river at a rapid clip.

"Is this the way we want to go?" Jacobs asked.

"Yeah, this is the direction the Yankees took Sergeant Williams." Rob started turning the boat toward the northern shore. The ice was thicker near the bank, forcing them to step out of the boat and drag it ashore. Their weight cracked the ice and though Rob was able to leap to high ground, Jacobs broke through the ice up to his knees.

"Oh, my God," Jacobs cried. "My feet are cold as hell."

Busy pulling branches over the flat boat, Rob turned, whispering, "Shut up, you fool. How many Yankees do you want on top of us?"

They started moving carefully through the woods toward the Yankee camp. Nearing Hancock, they saw shivering Yankees trying to warm themselves by a smoky fire. Most had swum the river and were soaking wet. Sergeant Williams was tied to a tree. He looked as wet and cold as his captors.

Edging forward, Rob thought he might be able to reach the sergeant from behind. He signaled Jacobs to follow. Rob fumbled under the snow, pulled out a good-sized rock and handed it to Jacobs. "When I give the signal, heave this as far away from here as you can."

Jacobs nodded sullenly.

They were so close now that Rob could hear the fire crackling and feel its warmth. Positioned behind Sergeant Williams, he studied the ropes binding him. Unsheathing his knife, Rob rapped the handle four times against his gun barrel, then rapped eight more times. The Forty-eighth Regiment. He thought he saw the sergeant's head turn slightly, but was not sure. Gently, he started working on the ropes. The sergeant didn't flinch. Placing the knife in Sergeant Williams' hands, Rob picked up his gun and signaled to Jacobs.

The rock fell short and landed in the midst of a group of Yankees on the far side of the fire. Throwing down their mess kits, they scrambled for weapons. Many had taken off their wet boots, and the confusion helped the Rebs melt into the woods.

Assuming that the Rebels would head back across the river, the Yankees didn't think to look inland. Free of pursuit, Rob led the group the long way around to Joe Fields' lock house. Smoke billowed from the chimney and Rob could see the old man sitting by the window. After the pickets passed, he ran to the door and slipped inside. Startled, Joe stood up and stepped toward him. "My God, boy, what're you doing here?"

"Running from the Yankees, Joe. We need a place to hide until they get tired of looking for us. Nate ain't with us."

"No, you can't stay here." Joe looked scared. "I ain't going to risk everything to hide you. Get out!"

They both turned as Sergeant Williams stepped through the doorway. His massive frame seemed to fill the small room. Jacobs came in after him.

"Is there a problem, corporal?" Williams asked.

"Yes, there's a problem." Joe's shrill voice betrayed his panic. "Get out!"

"Sit down, Joe," Rob said. "Between us we still have some Yankee dollars."

Joe sat down. Jacobs was already hanging his wet clothes around the small room.

CHAPTER 10

ORRICK'S RANGERS

WINTER 1862

The first rays of morning light found the exhausted soldiers still asleep. When Rob opened his eyes and sat up, he saw that old Joe was missing. Remembering that Sergeant Williams had told Jacobs to tie Joe to his bed, Rob shook his head as he looked over at the sleeping Jacobs. Rousing the sergeant, he was pulling on his boots when the door burst open. Five armed Yankees entered the room. Rob could see the rest of the squad waiting outside.

"We have to stick together," Sergeant Williams whispered to Rob as they were pushed through the door into the falling snow.

The Rebel soldiers were forced into a straggling line and prodded to move forward. Their Yankee captors were nervous and kept looking over their shoulders. During lulls in the artillery barrages, Rob could hear the soldiers talking among themselves about the Confederate raiding parties still in the area. The patrol was made up of men from the 21st Massachusetts. Rob watched as they stumbled and slid through the snow and thought they should have been used to this miserable, freezing weather. Their sergeant was a small wiry man who showed little pity for his captives. He drove them and his own men mercilessly.

"Got to get you boys back to camp. There's a special prison yard set up for you Rebs."

Sergeant Williams looked over at Rob and gestured with a slight tilt of his head at the right side of the trail. Rob caught a glimpse of movement and thought he saw the glint of a rifle barrel. The closer they got to Hancock, the thicker the cannon smoke became. It hung in black sheets amidst the falling snow. Visibility was so poor that the Rebel Rangers were upon them before the Yankees could move to defend themselves. They were quickly disarmed and forced to sit in the snow.

Rob recognized Colonel Orrick as he trotted toward them on his big roan horse. "We don't have time for these prisoners," the colonel said. "Take their arms and leave them. We have a job to do." Wheeling his horse, the colonel headed away from Hancock. "Move smartly now, men."

Falling in line, Rob and the other new recruits followed along behind the colonel. By evening the rangers joined up with a larger group. Leading five saddled horses, the new men were jubilant at their luck. "Yankee cavalry don't need them horses no more, so get mounted, boys." One of the men threw reins to Rob.

The group forded the river and found Orrick's men camped in one of the outbuildings on his farm. The main house had gone from Union headquarters to makeshift Confederate hospital. Rob, Sergeant Williams, and Jacobs followed the others into the kitchen. They found that all the seats at the long table were taken, so the newcomers stood along the wall. The room was warm and over-crowded. The smell of wet woolen clothing and sweat mixed with the tantalizing aroma of stew. When he got his bowl, Rob ate hungrily.

Several men claimed they had it on good authority that General Jackson planned to head for Romney in the morning. The men grumbled there'd be no time to gather up the Yankees' discarded supplies.

"Come on, boys. I brought dessert," Nate shouted from the doorway. Rob turned to see him hold up a can with his good hand. "Peaches in January. They're a gift from them running Yankees."

The men stumbled over each other getting to Nate. Seeing his old friend, he brought a can over to Rob. "I'm fit enough to rejoin the rangers, but I'll need to favor this arm for a bit," Nate said. "Why don't you stay with us? You know this is where you belong."

"We've got to get back to our company." Rob gestured across the room to Sergeant Williams and Jacobs.

"Word is that your company has already pulled out. You ain't going to catch up with them tonight."

Rob looked around the room. It was good to be here. Good to be home. If he stayed with Orrick's Rangers, he could look in on the farm from time to time. He might even be able to find Laura Meeks. The thought of Laura made up his mind. Making his way over to his comrades, he hunkered down beside them. "Nate says our company has already pulled out. We'd be hard put to catch them."

Jacobs looked relieved, but Sergeant Williams stood up. "We can sure as hell try."

"I'd like to stay here with the rangers. I know the countryside and could be useful," Rob said.

Sergeant Williams looked at Jacobs. "What about you?"

"I'm joining the rangers too," Jacobs replied.

"Well, the army won't miss you, Jacobs." The sergeant smiled wryly as he pulled on his overcoat and held out his hand. "Good luck, boys. Thanks for coming after me." He shook hands with both of his soldiers. His grip was powerful.

Rob looked Jacobs in the eye. "You've got to straighten up if you join the rangers. When you slack off or slip away from camp, they'll leave you on some tall mountain top with only the wolves for company."

* * * *

Rob found out quickly that life as a ranger was different from the routine of the regular army. That night the men settled down in the hayloft in Orrick's barn. After what seemed like minutes, they were up and moving. As they saddled their horses, Johnny McKenny handed each man two biscuits and a piece of venison jerky.

"Men," Colonel Orrick commanded from astride his horse, "your job is to cut telegraph wires below Hancock tonight. Follow me."

The rangers forded the Potomac downstream of the little town and immediately ran into Yankee pickets. A shot passed by close to Rob's horse's head and the animal reared up, throwing him to the ground. He could hear the Yankee pickets moving in when Jacobs raced toward him. Reaching down, Jacobs held out his hand. Rob grabbed the outstretched hand and pulled himself onto the horse behind Jacobs. The frenzied animal bolted and they lost their attackers. A short time later, they found Rob's horse grazing by the river.

By afternoon, the group found shelter in a densely wooded area. When darkness fell, they approached the telegraph lines on foot. The rangers had no sooner set to work when firing started from the wood line. Colonel Orrick deployed his men in the underbrush near the line of poles.

Jim Buck, a skinny man who could climb like a monkey, inched over to the pole on his belly and shimmied up quickly. At once, shots came from the nearby woods. The rangers fired back, keeping the Yankee pickets at bay long enough for Buck to cut the wires. He was back down on the snow-covered ground in minutes and the rangers withdrew into the woods.

They crossed the Potomac before the sun rose. Heading for the high ridges, the rangers made for their permanent camp. Colonel Orrick had stayed behind at Alpine to oversee the removal of any personal effects left in his home by the Union Army. Rob heard that Mrs. Swann had recovered enough to travel and the Swanns had left for Richmond. He knew now that Fannie was lost to him.

As the trail narrowed, the men rode single file. Rob found himself riding behind Jacobs' brown mare. Approaching a meadow, the land spread out and Rob was able to pull abreast of him.

"I've got to thank you," he said. "That was a generous thing you did. I could have been a prisoner again."

"Don't think nothing of it." Jacobs grinned.

Guiding their horses upward, the men reached a high field between pine-covered hills. Heading toward the hillside, Rob watched the lead rider disappear behind a grove of pines, which screened a lean-to shelter for the horses. After tending to his mount, Rob followed the others into the large cavern.

Johnny, who was second in command, came over and clapped him on the shoulder. "Glad to have you, boy. We need some new blood. Could you and your friend get us a fire going in the pit? We got a few rabbits to cook up."

Rob and Jacobs found a stash of dry wood near the cave entrance and soon had a fire blazing. Much of the smoke rose to the low ceiling, but must have escaped through many unseen crevices rather than one, as there was no smoke visible outside. The air in the cave carried the scent of a wood fire, but was not oppressive. Rob wondered how many men had found shelter here over time.

By noon, the men were roasting five scrawny rabbits over the fire pit. After the meal, Rob wandered outside and took a look around. From this high vantage point, he could see snow-covered ridges climbing atop one another into the distance. Looking at the ridge sheltering his farm, he felt at peace to be here, even in the middle of a war. He was home. It started to sleet and Rob returned to the cave to find the men were huddled around the fire swapping stories.

"Rob," Johnny called to him, "Your boy here, Jacobs, has been complaining that life in the mountains just don't suit him. Too damn cold, too much snow." Johnny's face looked flushed and his eyes bulged. "Why'd you drag him up here?"

Rob knew it was hard to reason with Johnny when he'd been drinking, so he didn't reply. He thought Johnny looked older and had a new relentless glint in his eyes.

Johnny looked over at Jacobs and nodded. "You're lucky to be here, boy. We eat good, we got good horses and we ain't sitting ducks like them poor bastards in the regular Confederate Army."

"I've thought on that," Jacobs said. "I hated the regular army. I hated the sergeant and his stupid rules."

The other men, lean and hardened by hours in the saddle, looked at him with amusement. "So you don't like taking orders, boy?" Olson asked. "You better not run afoul of McKenny here, 'cause he likes to give them. Kinda like your old sergeant."

"Well, you ain't too good at following orders." Johnny stood up and flexed the powerful muscles in his arms. "I need a picket posted, Olson. Take your fill of them rabbits and get to the lookout." Narrowing his eyes, Olson hesitated, then turned abruptly and left.

Watching Johnny through the haze of the fire, Rob wondered how long this conflict had been brewing between the two men. The colonel had left Johnny McKenny in charge, but it appeared that his control was continually challenged. In such close quarters, Rob figured that these flare-ups could cause real trouble, so he decided to give both men a wide berth. During the long afternoon the men tried to rest, and by evening they were ready to ride again.

The sleet had turned to snow and the horses had to be led down the steep mountain path. Even on the relatively flat areas near the river, the rangers had to walk their mounts. They made a wide detour around Alpine, as they expected that the enemy had re-taken the camp. When they reached the railroad, they set to work tearing up rails. Yankee pickets were nowhere in sight, so the work went quickly. Olson and Johnny McKenny took turns with the crowbar, while the others stood guard. The night was absolutely still, save for the hooting of an owl and the clink of the crowbar. Overcast skies afforded little light, but good cover. Working in freezing conditions took its toll, and soon another set of rangers manned the metal bar. They tore up the tracks at several locations before heavy driving snow forced them to quit.

Silently, the small band made its way back to the horses. Jacobs had been left as guard, but was asleep in his blanket-roll. Johnny reached him in three long strides. Kicking him awake, Johnny dragged him up. "What the hell are you doing, boy? You try this again and I'll shoot you myself."

* * * *

Three days later, Johnny led Rob, Nate, and Jacobs on a scouting expedition. The horses had a hard time keeping their footing on the snow-covered mountain trail and had to be led. Rob could see the ridge above his farm. "Johnny, is there any chance we could ride near my home-place?"

Sending Nate to scout ahead, Johnny signaled the group to remain within the tree line. "I don't see why not, but we'll have to stay out of sight."

From a distance, all looked as Rob remembered. The house and barn appeared peaceful under a blanket of snow. However, as they drew closer, he could see that the barn door stood wide open and that many of the fence posts had been dragged off, probably to fuel some Yankee's fire. Dismounting in back of the house, the men walked around to the front porch. Rob stood and surveyed the scene before him. Several of the porch floorboards had been ripped up and the door hung loosely on its hinges.

"I'll put this door to rights," Johnny said as the others entered the house.

The kitchen was bare. *The table and benches had probably become firewood*, Rob thought bitterly. Only the cook stove and the built-in corner-cupboard remained. A shard of blue pottery lay near the ash-filled hearth. As he stared into the fireplace, he could see the flames leaping and remembered the smell of roasting meat. He could feel the sense of safety the room had once provided. Picking up the sliver of blue, he realized that it was from his mother's teapot, a reminder of a lost life.

"Let's go," Nate said, turning to leave.

"Wait." Rob strode to the back of the room and knelt over the trapdoor. The rug was gone, but the door looked intact. Built by his grandfather, it blended skillfully into the tongue and groove flooring. Finding the release, Rob opened the door and climbed down to the cellar. Returning with two sacks of potatoes and a bag of onions, he grinned.

"Damned Yankees didn't find this." As the men left, Rob shut the front door carefully. No matter what damage the enemy had wrought, the house still stood. The food the farm had produced would feed Virginians, not Union soldiers, tonight.

The next morning Rob awoke to find another storm blowing wet snow and sleet in through the cave entrance. Colonel Orrick had still not returned and the men were in a quandary as to what to do.

"There ain't nothing we can do in this weather," Olson said. He was oiling his saddle and bridle by the fire.

"Sure hope Stonewall's army is settled in up at Romney by now," Joey Stanton, a young, baby-faced recruit, said. "I got kin up that way and they don't go nowhere in weather like this."

"Who's your kin? A bunch of old ladies?" Johnny's eyes narrowed. Rob thought he saw the bulge of a whiskey bottle in Johnny's jacket and wondered where he'd gotten it.

"You're right. My Aunt Lottie is almost 80 years old. I hear she pieced together a Confederate flag cut from old shirts and waved it as the Yankees rode up to her house. She'd sewn the initials 'J.D.' and 'S.C.' on the flag and flaunted it in their faces."

"What the hell do the initials mean?" Johnny growled.

"That's what the Yankees asked. Aunt Lottie said 'J.D' stood for Jefferson Davis and 'S. C.' meant Southern Confederacy—that's going to whip your ass, she told them."

The laughter that followed this story broke the tension. Nate pulled out his mouth organ and began to play "The Bonnie Blue Flag." Suddenly, a strong tenor voice came in at the chorus.

When the song ended, Rob looked over at Jacobs. "Where'd you learn to sing like that?"

"I sang in the church choir at home. All the ladies loved me."

"How come you ain't sung nothing before?" Johnny demanded.

"Ain't nobody ever asked me."

The men offered tobacco around and Jacobs, with Nate's accompaniment, started the first verse of "Lorena." Rob picked up the chorus, and soon all the men were singing, even Johnny McKenny.

* * * *

Days later, when the weather finally cleared, Colonel Orrick arrived at camp. Praising the men for their raids on the railroad track, he told them that General Jackson's army had suffered badly from icy conditions on the way to Romney. The enemy had tried to slow their advance, felling huge trees across roads and setting ambushes. He and Johnny spent some time talking together. Later Johnny told the men that the spring campaign was planned and they would serve as scouts.

* * * *

In mid-February the temperature spiked to sixty degrees and the roads turned to slushy mud. Rob was sent into Bath to get mail and supplies. Taking a roundabout route, he avoided Yankee pickets and left his horse at the edge of town. He knew all the back streets and soon arrived at the O'Ferrall's kitchen door.

Mary let him in and stood back to survey her young friend. "You look much older and you're much too thin. Sit down and have some dinner."

As Rob started in on a large plate of chicken and dumplings, he realized he was very hungry. When Mary got a minute to sit down with him, she brought more hot coffee. "How are things with Colonel Orrick's men?"

Rob shrugged. "We hit the Yankees when we can. I'm glad to be back home, but every time I pass the old farm it looks worse. There ain't a thing I can do about it."

"Nothing's like it used to be. The Yankees lord it over us, taking what they want." Mary's eyes darkened. "I'm sure the Swanns are better off away from here. I know it's best for Fannie, but I miss her."

Mary got up and went to the window. "You should go. Our wagon just turned into the street. Colonel Orrick's supplies will soon be waiting on you at the meeting place."

"You ain't heard from Fannie, then?" Rob asked as he got up and headed to the door.

"No. I think Fannie is gone for good."

"What about Laura Meeks? Is there word of her?"

"I haven't gotten any replies from my inquiries about Laura Meeks either. She seems to have disappeared."

* * * *

The rest of February passed quickly. Despite the return of bitter cold weather, Orrick's men continued to harass the Union Army. In early March, Rob asked Johnny if he could have a few days off to attend to a personal matter. The night before he was to leave, Rob and Nate sat up late around the fire.

"You sure you want to do this?" Nate asked. He watched Rob closely.

"Yeah, I been planning on this for some time. I need to know what's happened to Laura."

"You're a fool. I've told you before, them Meeks women are trouble."

"You're right, Nate." Rob continued to pack his gear.

"If you won't listen to me, then at least be careful. There's a lot of fighting going on around Winchester."

Rob studied his old friend. Nate was more confident than before. His long narrow face had lost its baby fat and had taken on a lean, tough cast. Nate's arm had healed badly and he held it awkwardly, but he looked every bit the soldier.

Loud voices caused Rob and Nate to look up. Olson and Johnny were playing cards nearby and both looked angry. Suddenly, Olson stood up.

"If you play that trick on me again, I'll kill you," he snarled, then turned and left.

"Them two are at it again," Nate said. "I sure hope Colonel Orrick gets back before they do each other in." He offered Rob a plug of tobacco. "Do you want me to go with you?"

"No, I need to do this myself." Even as he said the words, Rob realized it would have been good to have Nate with him. Nate was becoming a formidable fighter.

The next morning Rob rode south. He took little-known back roads, as Yankee scouts seemed to be everywhere. At the small town of Unger, he turned his horse onto a rough, overgrown trail. The ground was still saturated with recent snowmelt. He let his horse have its head, and the animal picked its way down the mountain.

It was evening by the time Rob reached the Meeks' place. He sat in the barn loft and watched the house. The front door hung loose on its hinges and made a mournful sound each time the wind forced it shut. He was leaving the barn as darkness gathered when he stubbed his toe. Rob rummaged on the floor and was surprised when he pulled a metal box out of the straw. Shaking it, he heard what sounded like the jingle of coins. Since it was found on the Meeks' property, the box should belong to Laura.

Inside the house, he stumbled from room to room. He felt uneasy and his concern for Laura soared. Rob couldn't leave the old house fast enough; it was like a tomb. Riding away, he thought of the metal box thrust deep in his saddlebag. It hadn't been well hidden, so perhaps the owner had meant to reclaim it soon. He remembered Thad Meeks, the man with the long yellow hair who Granny Meeks had shot dead.

Rob spent the rest of the night in pinewoods near Laura's uncle's place. At first light, he banged on the front door.

Roused out of bed, Frank Meeks seemed confused. "Laura? My sister? I don't know where Laura is, but my sister's buried in the family plot. She didn't survive a week here."

"I'm sorry, but what of Laura? You must have some idea where she is."

"Come in and have some coffee, boy."

Rob entered the warmth of the kitchen. Mrs. Meeks was feeding wood into the stove and nodded in recognition. "You're Laura's young man. Sit down."

The Meeks were silent while the coffee brewed. Rob sat uneasily. He had left Laura and her grandmother here after Christmas, but now the place looked different. The fancy dishes displayed on the sideboard looked costly. The old couple seemed nervous and neither would look at him. At last, Mrs. Meeks poured the coffee.

"Where is Laura?" Rob repeated.

"We don't know." Mr. Meeks spilled his coffee on the table. "She left here right after her grandma was buried. She said she had a job."

Rob watched them silently.

"We was worried, mister," the old woman continued. "What with the delicate state of her health. We tried to get her to stay."

"What delicate health?" Rob's eyes narrowed as he studied them. They were lying, but why?

"She was mighty upset, what with her grandparents dead, and you leaving her. She cried a lot," the old man said reasonably. "She wanted to get away, make some money."

"She needed money for the baby," Mrs. Meeks added, then clapped her hand over her mouth.

"Shut up, mother," the old man shouted. "We ain't supposed to say nothing."

"Baby?" Rob asked. "Is Laura expecting a baby?"

"It was early days, but she was right sick on her stomach of a morning and said she'd missed her moon phase. That's all we know." Mr. Meeks looked unhappily at Rob. "Guess you got a right to be told."

For a long while, the kitchen was quiet. Rob tried to sort through the fear, joy, and anger he felt. Finally he stood and walked toward the door. "How did she leave? Who took her away?"

"We told you enough. Now leave," Mr. Meeks said loudly.

Rob realized that Meeks must have picked up on his tone of desperation. Before the old man could react, Rob reached him and dragged him out of the chair. His voice was low.

"I want to know who took her." His grip tightened on Meeks' neck.

"Wait!" The old woman pleaded. "She went off with Thad Meeks' brother, Joshua. His family needed help in the house. That's all we know."

"Where does Joshua Meeks live?"

"They were moving to Richmond," Mrs. Meeks said.

Rob released his grip on the old man. As he left, he walked to the sideboard and threw all of the fine china to the floor. Riding away, he could still hear the old woman's shrieks of anguish. Too bad she hadn't valued her niece as highly as her new possessions.

* * * *

Rob reached Bath by nightfall and went on foot to O'Ferrall's. He found Mary in the kitchen.

"Rob, sit down. You look bone weary." Mary hurried to the stove and dished up a bowl of soup. "I'm sorry there's not more to offer you."

Rob ate while Mary told him the news of the town. She knew which neighbors had been hauled off by the Yankees and charged with crimes ranging from horse thieving to treason.

"I watch every word I say to certain people," Mary said. "Some folks are profiting from turning on their friends, and even their kin."

"I saw a good example of that today," Rob said. "Is there a way you could get word to your brother, Trip? I need his help to find a man named Joshua Meeks in Richmond. He's taken Laura."

* * * *

When Rob got back to camp, all was eerily quiet. Leaving his horse in the make-shift stable, he approached the cave. Hearing the murmur of voices, he hesitated. Nate met him at the entrance. He was carrying his pack and saddle.

"Rob, I'm glad you made it back. I wanted to say goodbye."

"You're leaving?"

"Got to." Nate gestured with a tilt of this head toward the fire pit.

Two men were laid out before the smoldering fire. As Rob moved closer, he recognized Johnny McKenny, who moaned and called for water. Jacobs hurried over and held a canteen to his lips. Olson was lying with his arms across his chest. Bending down to examine him, Rob noticed that there was very little blood, although it appeared that he'd been shot in the chest.

"What the hell happened here?" Rob asked.

Nate was still standing by the entrance. "I shot him. He tried to strangle Johnny, so I shot him. Sorry I ain't gonna be able to stay around for the wake. As soon as Olson's family gets word of this, I'll be a marked man." For the first time, Nate looked scared.

"All the Olsons have mean tempers. They may figure he asked for it," Rob said.

"I ain't waiting to learn the state of their thinking."

Outside, the moon had risen and threw pale light over the pine forest. In the distance, an owl called mournfully.

"That owl is calling Olson's soul," Nate said. "If he had a soul." He finished saddling his horse, tied on the pack, and slung his rifle over his shoulder.

"Where are you going now?"

"I'm heading toward Richmond. I'll make my fortune, then come back here and buy up every plot of land the Olson's own. I'll drive the bastards out of the county."

The two old friends shook hands. "Will you look out for Trip O'Ferrall? He may have news of Laura. Her uncle said that Thad Meeks' brother took her to Richmond. I mean to find her."

"I think you're crazy, but I'll do what you want. Goodbye, Rob." Nate turned his horse, then looked back. "You ain't gonna die in a brawl. Whether you get shot on the battlefield or on some mountaintop, you're gonna die 'cause you're too damn stubborn."

CHAPTER 11

MARY O'FERRALL

MAY 1862

"Miss Mary," the Yankee sergeant shouted, "this coffee ain't hot, and none of us will eat the grits. Ain't you got fried potatoes?"

Mary picked up the coffee pot. The dining room at the coffee house was full of muddy, unkempt Yankee soldiers. Without a word, she poured the coffee and turned back toward the kitchen.

"They ain't got no decent food down here, so don't bother to ask," a skinny boy in an oversized Union cap said. "She's not bad, though. I'd rather spend time with her than a dish of fried potatoes any day. Look there at the way she walks."

Mary slammed the kitchen door behind her. They could pour their own damn coffee. She slumped down on a chair at the kitchen table.

Jane O'Ferrall came up from the cellar carrying a sack of onions. "More trouble with the Northerners?" Mary nodded. "I'll handle them," her mother said.

Dumping the sack on the kitchen table, Jane stripped off her apron and headed toward the dining room. Mary went to the door, opened it a crack, and watched her mother advancing on the Yankee soldiers.

"Is there a problem, Sergeant?" Jane's tone was icy.

"No, ma'am. Sorry, ma'am." The sergeant stood and shuffled his feet. "My boys don't mean no harm."

"I will speak to your captain of this when I see him about your bill. Now, leave." Under the watchful eye of the sergeant, the Yankee soldiers left quietly.

Back in the kitchen, Jane busied herself making tea. "Bring the sugar bowl, Mary. Sweet tea is what we need."

"Maybe we should shut the coffee house, Mama, until things get better. We don't make a profit anyway."

"We're better off than many. So far we've suffered only insults and some minor thievery." Jane stood up and retied her starched apron. "We must start soup for the mid-day meal."

Both women turned at the sound of loud banging on the kitchen door. Mabel McCabe, looking close to tears, stood in the doorway.

"Come in, Mabel." Mary took her tattered carpetbag and led her to a chair. "What's wrong?"

Jane O'Ferrall rushed over and took Mabel's hands. "Sit down. You look like you've taken quite a fright. What's happened?"

A large woman with rough work-worn hands, Mabel sat gingerly on one of the small kitchen chairs. She folded her hands in her lap and stared straight ahead. "You know I've worked at Strother's Pavilion Hotel since I was fourteen years old. Well, today I quit."

"Why?" Jane asked.

"Since old Colonel Strother was jailed by the Yankees and then died, things haven't been the same." Mabel took a long drink of the hot tea Mary set before her. "David Strother is off in the Union Army and things have gone from bad to worse. Now the hotel is packed full of Yankees."

"What happened today?" Mary asked as she set a plate of cakes on the table. Mabel was a formidable woman who intimidated all the delivery men who stepped foot in the Pavilion. Mary couldn't imagine what had caused her to leave there in such a state.

Mabel nibbled a sugar cake, but didn't speak. The silence lengthened. It was broken when three Union soldiers crashed through the kitchen door and confronted Mabel.

"That's her!" the first invader shouted.

"Get up out of that chair, ma'am," the second soldier, a skinny blond boy, ordered. "You're coming with us."

"Grab her bag, Wilburn. Maybe she still has the stolen goods."

Flinging the chair aside, Mabel backed toward the wall. She started swinging her carpetbag like a battleax, warding off her attackers with loud shrieks. "Get away from me, you Yankee scum. Get away!"

The three soldiers were closing in when Jane O'Ferrall inserted herself into the fray. Mary ran over and stood beside her.

"What is going on?" Jane asked calmly.

"This woman's a thief," the first soldier said. "She took valuable Union documents."

"I never," Mabel screamed, landing a solid blow on her accuser's head.

"Grab her," the soldier shouted.

Jane, followed by Mary, moved in front of Mabel. "I demand to see your superior officer." Jane said firmly. "Get him."

The three men backed away. The soldier holding his head seemed to be in charge.

"Get the captain," he ordered and sat down facing the women. The others fled through the door.

When Mabel finally opened her bag, she was surrounded by a Yankee captain, three soldiers, and the O'Ferrall women. Her large rough hands fumbled with the clasp and finally the case opened. Grudgingly, she pulled out a shabby dress, a nightgown, and a pile of undergarments.

"Are you satisfied?" Mabel eyed the soldiers stonily.

"I believe, captain, that Miss McCabe is due an apology. She has been falsely accused and attacked by your troops." Jane O'Ferrall stared coldly at the Yankee officer.

"Yes, ma'am. I'm Captain James Hansen, 21st Indiana Volunteers. I apologize for my men. They will be reprimanded." The captain, a tall man with a mid-western twang, watched the women through his gold-framed spectacles. He wore his dark hair long under his slouch hat, which he quickly removed. After dismissing his men, he turned to the women and bowed slightly. "How may I make amends, ladies?"

Mary watched the young captain. He had a likeable face and she wondered what he did back in Indiana. She imagined meeting him under different circumstances.

Jane spoke softly, "Captain, we understand that you must do your duty and you seem a fair-minded man. Please join us for a cup of coffee and perhaps we can discuss some other problems we've had with Union soldiers. My daughter, Mary, will keep you company while Mabel and I make the coffee."

Sitting across the table from the Yankee officer, Mary smiled and hoped that her nervousness didn't show. She wasn't used to talking to Yankees and didn't have her mother's way with words.

Finally, Captain Hansen said, "Don't worry, I have no intention of arresting your friend. From what I've heard, she'd probably lay into me and my men with her carpetbag, and there wouldn't be a soldier left standing. How could I explain that to the colonel?"

He grinned, putting Mary at ease. She liked his easy manner and sense of humor. Sure she would never see him again, she said, "That's good to hear. We'd hate to have the coffee house cluttered with injured soldiers. Very bad for business."

"Perhaps I could return on Sunday for some of your establishment's fine cooking. Would I be welcome?"

Before she could stop herself, Mary answered, "Yes, you would be welcome."

When Captain Hansen left, the women sat together at the table. "Thank you, Miss Jane, Mary," Mabel said. "Them boys from the Indiana Regiment ain't bad. If they'd been from the 13th Massachusetts, them bastards would have found the papers and toted me off to jail." Mabel grinned.

"Papers?" Mary asked.

"Yes. I figured I'd be followed, so I slid them under the milk cans by the back door." Mabel got up and lumbered over to the door, returning with a large envelope. "I couldn't make heads or tails of them. I can't read much." She handed the envelope to Jane. "I knew they must be important 'cause the Yankee general hid them in his room. I found them when I was cleaning this morning."

"You did well, Mabel." Jane looked through the papers. "These are lists of Union sick, wounded, and dead. They show adjusted troop strengths. Our people can make good use of this information and we'll see they get it." Jane replaced the papers and took the envelope to the tall dish cupboard in the corner. "We use a loose panel in this cupboard to hide valuables. They'll be safe here for now."

Mabel looked relieved. "Thank you, Miss Jane. Now, I must go."

"Where will you go?" Mother and daughter asked together.

"I don't rightly know. I've lived at the Pavilion for most of my life. But that's all over."

"Stay here," Jane offered. "We need help, but can't pay much. You'd have a room and eat with the family."

The big woman started to cry.

* * * *

Mary sat in the shade of the spacious coffeehouse porch and waited for James Hansen. He had been a constant visitor over the past month and now he was to leave Bath. He'd promised he'd let her know when his regiment got marching orders. From their many earnest conversations, Mary knew James was not in favor of the war and only wished for its speedy end. He'd said many times that his main goal was to return to his small farm and his aging parents. Now he wanted these plans to include her.

At last Mary saw James striding toward her. She still found it hard to believe that she was keeping company with a Yankee officer—and not ashamed of it. Of course, there were many subtle benefits. The coffee house was no longer harassed by the Yankees. When they did patronize the restaurant, they were now courteous and paid their bills. Mary's Rebel neighbors were another matter. If it hadn't been for Jane O'Ferrall's reputation and Trip's war service, things might have gotten out of hand. Mary knew all of this, but she didn't care.

When James was seated beside her, Mary poured him a glass of tea and squeezed his hand. "I was afraid you wouldn't come."

"Nothing could have kept me away today. I don't know how much more time we'll have together. Now that your General Lee is in command of the Army of Northern Virginia, things have changed." James took a long drink of tea. "I want to stay here and be sure that you're safe, but I'm afraid my regiment will be sent to protect Washington. Stonewall Jackson's started to rampage in the Valley. He's had a string of victories, so we're forced to deal with him instead of reinforcing our troops around Richmond."

"I wish it would all end soon," Mary said. "I worry about my brother. We only know that Trip's captain of a company of irregular cavalry."

"Trip is part of an irregular cavalry company? You mean Rebel Rangers? If he's caught, it could go badly for him."

"What do you mean?"

"If he's in uniform, he may be all right. But many Union officers look on irregulars as bushwhackers and that's the way they'll treat those men." James looked uncomfortable.

"I worry for Trip."

"I worry for you and your mother. Do you have any weapons?"

Mary was startled. "Only kitchen knives and an old musket that hasn't been fired in years."

"I'll find a gun for you before I leave. These are bad times."

* * * *

James had been gone for ten days and Mary had no word from him. She couldn't sleep, but must have finally drifted off, because the noise woke her. Running to the window, she saw a dark figure in the back garden. The figure moved and another shower of pebbles hit her windowpane. As she ran downstairs, Mary thought that there was something very familiar about the shadowy figure. Peering through the kitchen window, she wasn't surprised to see Rob Johnson walking toward her. Opening the door, Mary pulled him inside quickly.

"Rob, thank God you're all right," she said.

"We've been away most of the month. Down in the Valley scouting for Stonewall. How are you and your mother?"

"Ma is resolute, and I'm in love. So the war washes around us."

Rob sat in the dark kitchen and drummed his fingers on the worn tabletop. "In love?"

"Yes. James is a captain in the Union Army. He's been very kind to us."

Rob said nothing. As the moon shone through the clouds, light filtered into the dark kitchen. She could see that his lips were set in a hard line. She didn't know what more to say, and Rob seemed lost in his own thoughts. He sat tilted back in the small kitchen chair, with his long legs stretched out before him. He seemed exhausted.

Starting to drum his fingers on the tabletop again, Rob looked up at Mary. "I killed a Yankee captain last week. He was the first man I've ever had to shoot at close range. I could see the terror in his eyes. He was young, probably less than twenty-five years old. I thought later about the man. I wondered about his family. I prayed for him, too, although I ain't religious." Rob got up and paced to the stove and back several times. "As for love, I don't know much about it. I just know you can't pick who you love or who loves you."

Mary jumped up and ran to hug the thin young soldier. "Thank you, Rob. That means a lot to me. That captain you shot, he wasn't from an Indiana regiment, was he?"

"No, he was from Pennsylvania. He was a brave man," Rob said in an uneven voice.

Slowly, he sat down and his head slumped on the table. Mary could see that he was crying. She smoothed his dark, unruly hair. He was still a boy, too young to be sitting here telling her he'd shot a man. Finally, she left him to gather up some leftovers from the pantry. That was at least something useful she could do for Rob. She was stirring up the embers in the cook stove so that she could make coffee when she heard his voice.

"Mary, I heard in camp that you had some mail for me."

The letter Mary handed him was torn and soiled, but still readable. It was from Nate Fields. Rob read the letter slowly, then balled it up and threw it across the room. For several moments he stood with his fists clenched, then walked over and picked up the crumpled letter.

"I've got to leave," he said, and started walking toward the door.

"But Rob," Mary called after him. "What about the food? Come back." She hurried behind him with a bundle.

At the door, he turned and she thrust the package into his hands. "Thanks, Mary. If I see your brother, Trip, I'll give him your greeting. Goodbye."

Mary watched Rob enter the darkness of the garden. Soon he was lost to sight.

CHAPTER 12

THE QUAKERS

UNGER, VIRGINIA

MAY 1862

It was nearly noon by the time Rob rode out of the hills. He avoided the Town of Bath and passed few travelers. The road was deserted, save for an old man working a nearby field. When he spotted Rob, the man turned and started running toward the wood line. Rob realized that the old grandfather looked on him as a stranger. Strangers were to be feared.

"Hey, mister," Rob yelled. "Seen any Yankees today?"

Winded, the old fellow stopped and turned around. "Not today. There was a passel of 'em by just two days ago."

Rob nodded. "Which way were they going?"

"Headed south, most likely to the Valley." The old man scuttled away toward the blue line of ridges.

Rob realized he was moving away from the safety of these mountains. He was a stranger and a target for both armies. It was best to keep moving. He saw only a few old men working the fields, although crops needed tending. Here and there, groups of women and young children worked the land, but didn't wave as he passed.

Stopping to rest his mount, he took out Nate's letter and read it over again:

Rob, I finally got to Richmond. I been shot at by both sides more times than I can count, and just glad to be living. Yesterday I saw Laura Meeks. She is with child. Laura asked after you, but we didn't get no chance to talk. The people she's with watch her all the time. She looked poorly and said she wanted to see you, but that it was too risky. Good luck. Your friend, Nate Fields

When Rob had first read this, he'd been angry. Now he worried for Laura.

* * * *

At sundown Rob moved off the road and found a sheltered rock overhang. Deciding not to build a fire, he finished off the rest of the food Mary had given him. He was just about to doze off when he heard a commotion on the road below. Silently making his way downward, he reached a place where he could see through the thick briar bushes. Two young children were trying to push a heavily laden wheelbarrow uphill. Moving closer, he could see that the wheelbarrow held what looked to be a heap of old clothes. Rob wondered how it could be so heavy. Then the heap moved.

"It's no use," a high voice called. "Stop! The barrow is too heavy. Help me get out."

The moon slid from behind the clouds, illuminating the road. A frail old woman sat in the wheelbarrow. A boy of about nine or ten held the handles and a small girl stood by the woman, clutching her hand.

"Thee cannot walk, Granny," the boy said.

"We best not stay here." The little girl looked frightened. "The soldiers will find us again." She started to cry.

"Don't cry, baby. Don't cry." The old lady tried to heave herself up, but fell back into the wheelbarrow.

"I'll go find help," the boy said.

The girl stopped crying and stood with her head down. "Will the panther scream tonight? Is he up there on the mountain?"

"We're making too much noise, Margaret. No panther's going to pounce on us." The boy tried to look confident.

Rob stripped off his uniform jacket and started making his way down to the huddled group. He was very near before they spotted him. The girl screamed and ran to her brother.

"Evening, ma'am." Rob addressed the old woman. "Do you need a hand?"

Drawing herself up with dignity, the grandmother looked him over. "We could use a little help, just up to the crest of this hill. We live near the village of Unger."

As Rob pushed the wheelbarrow up the road, he realized how little the passenger weighed. When he reached the top of the hill, he stopped. "Where are you folks headed?"

"A mile or so down this road." The old woman looked worn out, but she smiled. The boy gave Rob a suspicious look and the little girl grinned up at him.

"I can get you there. I'm Rob Johnson from over near Bath."

"We are Mae, Donald, and Margaret Clifford." The old woman's voice sounded stronger. "We were run off by of Rebel bushwhackers. My son and his wife died last year and we were packing up their belongings. Now their house is burned to the ground."

Rob nodded. "That's a terrible thing, ma'am." Turning to the boy, he asked, "Can you ride a horse, Donald?"

"Yes, I can."

"Wait here for a few minutes. I'll get my horse. Donald, you watch out for the ladies."

* * * *

When the small group arrived, they found the large stone farmhouse dark. Rob was surprised, as he hadn't expected such a grand place.

"Donald, go bang on the door," Mae directed. "Rob Johnson, please step out of sight for a minute. My husband is skittish of strangers in these times."

It took a while to rouse the household. After a long interval, Rob heard a window sliding open. "Mae?" a voice called.

"Yes, Thomas. Let us in. We've had a terrible time."

As the front door cracked open a few inches, Rob saw a thin, wary face peer out. Then an old man stepped onto the porch. "Mae, what's happened?"

"Raiders attacked us and set fire to Mark's house. We're lucky to be alive."

Thomas scuttled down the steps in his nightshirt and took his wife's hand. "Can thee get out of that barrow, Mae?"

"No, I'm poorly, but I've brought help. Rob Johnson, please come out."

Rob stepped into the moonlight. "Good evening, sir. I'm Rob Johnson, a traveler down from Bath." He tried to smile reassuringly.

Startled, old Thomas backed away. "Who is this man? Why is he here?" His alarm was apparent, as he glanced nervously into the shadows for more intruders.

"He helped us out, Thomas. We wouldn't be here if he hadn't come along. I trust him." Mae held out a hand to Rob. "Please help me a little farther. I'm bone weary."

Grudgingly, old Thomas let Rob into the house. Then, at Mae's prompting, asked him to share a late meal with them.

"Best take thy horse to the barn first," Thomas said. "It wouldn't do for anyone to see an extra mount about and ask questions."

The barn was also built of stone and had fine, large stalls. Rob unsaddled his horse, rubbed her down and gave her hay. As he left, he remembered that he needed to look over the map in his saddlebag. He slipped back inside. Startled by a dim glow filtering up through the floorboards, he headed toward the light. Voices and laughter rose up into the barn. Bending down, he tried to peer through the cracks between the boards, but could see nothing. Suddenly, the barn was dark and all was quiet.

Hearing the creaking of the barn door, Rob stood and moved toward his horse's stall.

"Rob Johnson?" Donald called.

Invited to a seat at Thomas Clifford's dining table, Rob heaped his plate with potato salad and thick slices of ham. He watched the Negro servants who passed platters of food. The meal had been cobbled together by a large, unsmiling woman called Betty. Two servers, a woman and a powerful-looking man, assisted her. The man caught Rob's attention and he watched him. Although his clothing was clean, the trousers were too short and the shirtsleeves ended a few inches below his elbows. He had the lean muscled look of a field hand, not the smooth appearance of a house servant. The young woman, on the other hand, was small and light complexioned. She looked as though she'd never done a day's work at all. Sent to get a tray, the pretty, doe-eyed girl returned empty-handed. Rob realized she was not familiar with the house. He wondered what connection these people had to the strange happenings in the barn.

Throughout the meal, Thomas listened intently to his wife's story of outrage and grief. "The leader of that band of outlaws told me I was a traitor to the Confederacy," Mae said tearfully, "just because I had tried to help a few unfortunate people."

Trying to follow the conversation, Rob realized he was very tired. The children had actually fallen asleep at the table and been carried upstairs by the servants.

"If you don't mind," Rob said as he stood up, "I'll take my leave. Thank you for the supper."

"Oh no, please stay with us," Mae said. "We owe thee so much. Besides, on the trip here thee mentioned knowing John Dawson, also of Bath. He is a friend and will be here tomorrow."

"Yes," Thomas said with less enthusiasm, "we have plenty of room. Please, be our guest."

Too tired to protest further, Rob followed the Negro manservant up the winding stairs. He barely remembered John Dawson, but Ma had known him well.

The next morning, Rob awoke with a start and stared around at his comfortable surroundings. It took a moment to remember where he was and how he'd gotten here. Although it was quite early, he heard sounds below his window. Getting up, he moved along the wall until he could look out. He watched Betty carry a tray of food to the barn and slip inside. So, the Cliffords, indeed, had a secret.

As he was dressing, Rob realized that his head hurt. He felt hot and every bone in his body ached. Disregarding the pain, he started down the stairs. As he reached the front door, he saw Thomas sitting calmly in a hall chair. He knew the old man had been waiting for him.

"Good morning. Thee is up quite early." Thomas stood. "Please join me for breakfast. I must apologize for my inhospitable behavior of last night." The slight old man held out his hand. "Thank thee for assisting my family."

"I was glad to help out. Now I've got to be on my way." He saw Betty enter the room with a large tray of eggs and sausage. As the aroma of the food reached him, his resolve to leave as quickly as possible melted away. He found himself again sitting at the table, which was covered with a lace cloth and set with fine china.

"We were expecting John Dawson to arrive this morning, but he sent a message that he's been delayed. Mae tells me that John knows thy family." Thomas's long, thin face was molded into a pleasant expression, almost a smile, but Rob sensed suspicion in the set of his shoulders and tone of his voice.

"Yes," Rob said as he helped himself to eggs and sausages. "Mr. Dawson and my mother were childhood friends."

"Ah, John Dawson is a good man. He is not of our persuasion, but he is a man of conscience."

"Yes, so my mother said." Rob buttered a biscuit and reached for the strawberry jam. He had no idea just what 'persuasion' John Dawson was, but planned to be well on his way before the man arrived. Looking at the food heaped on his plate, Rob realized he'd lost his appetite. The brief twinges of pain in his stomach had become insistent cramping. He tried to focus on what old Thomas was saying.

"Mae said thee was on thy way to Richmond to find a friend." Thomas smiled with polite interest. He had not touched his breakfast either. "I'm told that the Valley is a very dangerous place at present. Both armies are forming up near Richmond and civilians may not want to remain in that city."

"Yes, but I must go there, nevertheless. My friend is with child and needs help." Rob had thought of the problems involved in actually bringing Laura back with him, but now the trip looked more dangerous and difficult than he had imagined.

Thomas seemed to appraise this new twist in the situation. "My family and I are members of the Society of Friends and have many connections in Richmond. Perhaps I could assist thee in finding thy friend."

Puzzled, Rob remained silent. He wondered what Thomas wanted from him.

"If I may say so, thee does not look well."

"It's nothing," Rob said. Another jolt of pain hit him and he doubled over. The room spun around him.

When he awoke, he was back in his bedroom, attended by Mae.

"Thy fever is high. Thee must rest now." Her voice was firm.

* * * *

It was two days before he recognized his surroundings again and Mae was still sitting at his side. "Thee has been very ill. We were afraid for thy life." Mae tried to spoon soup into his mouth, but Rob brushed it away.

"I'm beholden, but I can't eat." He tried to sit up. "I gotta get to Richmond."

"Thee is weak. It will take many days of rest before thee will be well enough to travel."

When Mae left, Rob lay propped up on pillows and stared out the window. Gusting winds blew up dust swirls on the track leading to the back entrance. He watched the gray, cloud-shrouded sky and knew it would storm by evening. Several times he caught himself just at the edge of sleep. Images of the farm in summer flashed through his mind. Then Laura Meeks appeared. She held out her arms to him, but she was not smiling. Where was Laura? Like quicksilver, Laura's young pretty face turned into the lined face of his mother. Ma didn't look happy either and pointed in the direction of the small, green-clad figure walking away down the track. It was Laura in the green dress. He resolved to find her as soon as he could, since it was clear that she was his responsibility now. During periods of fitful sleep, Rob dreamed of Laura. He held her close to him through the long night.

* * * *

A week later, Rob had recovered much of his strength. Against Mae's advice, he saddled his horse and rode down to the creek. He returned exhausted. For the next few days, he spent his time mending harnesses and repairing tools for old Thomas. He wondered what had happened to the people he had heard in the barn. There was not a sign of them now. They had been hidden, then moved. Runaways—that was the only explanation.

Today, Rob waited behind a gnarled old apple tree at dusk. He knew that soon a small herd of deer would pass by on their way from the creek. He'd watched them many evenings from the window of his room. Tonight, he had his rifle ready. When he dragged the small doe to the kitchen door, he was met by Betty, who smiled at him for the first time.

"We been having trouble filling them cook pots. Thank you, Mister Rob."

That night at dinner Rob found that his appetite had returned and felt guilty eating more than his share. "I can bring in as much meat as you need," he told Thomas, "but I've got to think about getting on my way."

"We need to talk about thy trip south, Rob. We may be able to help each other."

"I owe you and your family a lot. I would have probably died if I'd been taken sick alone on the road. But I don't know how I can help you."

"Mae and I have seen that thee has spent thy time wisely by doing useful jobs. No one asked thee to undertake these tasks." Thomas paused and looked Rob in the eye. "We feel we can trust thee now. A gray army jacket with corporal's stripes was among thy things, so we know thee was a soldier. We need to know thy position on the war."

"I've never held with the war. All I've seen is the suffering that's come out of it. Where I live, both sides have attacked and robbed us."

Thomas leaned forward. "Let me be frank. Thee acted with compassion in aiding Mae and the children at some risk to thyself. My friends and I value compassion for others. We are peace-loving and don't believe in war. Even though our young men have been dragged from their homes and conscripted into the army, they have refused to fight. Now many of them have been imprisoned for their beliefs." Thomas's gaze was intent. He hesitated only a moment, then said, "Mr. Johnson, I have told thee that we are members of the Society of Friends, Quakers. Does thee understand what we undertake in these times?"

Now all the pieces of this strange puzzle were coming together. "You're moving slaves north?"

"Yes, with God's help, we are. We would like to engage thee for a special job."

Rob looked at the old man blankly. "I am beholden to you, but don't know what you mean."

"Things are quieter in the Valley now. Jackson has forced McClellen to withdraw south of Richmond." Thomas paused. "Here is our problem. We need six slaves escorted from Richmond to the Maryland border. Thee must find thy friend and bring her north. Quakers cannot pose as slave owners, but thee can escort thy household north. Can we work together?"

CHAPTER 13

ABIGAIL TREVERTON

PARIS, VIRGINIA

JUNE 1862

Two days later Rob sat in a comfortable carriage driven by the big Negro named Joseph. Lilly, the pretty, doe-eyed girl, sat beside Joseph on the front seat. Thomas Clifford had explained that Lilly knew something about birthing and could be of help on the return trip.

Rob kept fingering the fine broadcloth of the dark suit he wore. He also wore a wide-brimmed black hat. In fact, he looked every inch the well-off country gentleman. His clothing, he learned, had belonged to Thomas' son, Mark. Sickness had taken Mark and his wife in the winter. Rob hoped this was not a bad omen. He knew Nate would have had a cautionary tale for this turn of events. But, as Rob rode in style toward Richmond, he was filled with hope. He'd had to promise much, but now he was sure he would return with Laura.

Looking out the carriage window, Rob saw many signs that an army had passed this way. The roadside was littered with discarded belongings, wrecked military equipment and a few dead, bloated horses. Many farmsteads looked deserted. He figured that the families had left or were hiding from passing strangers.

Unused to inactivity, Rob spent time watching the couple in the front seat. He could see that they talked and laughed together from time-to-time. From their manner, he thought they might be more than friends. Suddenly, Rob felt very alone and wished he were anywhere but here, traveling in style and impersonating a rich man's son.

Surprisingly, they encountered only one patrol, a troop of Confederate cavalry. The captain looked into the carriage window, saluted Rob smartly and wished him a good journey. Watching the cavalry move off,

Rob was amazed at the treatment money and status could bring. He re-laxed into the comfortable seat and must have dozed off. Awaking with a start, he looked into Joseph's solemn face. The carriage sat before a stately brick house surrounded by many outbuildings.

"Mister Mark, we here."

Rob stared at him blankly.

"Mister Mark…. Robert Johnson, we stop for the night."

"Where are we?" Rob asked.

"We at a place called Paris, just south of Winchester."

Already, several somberly dressed people were coming out of the house and heading toward the carriage. Nervously, Rob tried to remem-ber what old Thomas had told him. 'All the stops on the way to Richmond will be at the homes of Quakers. Present this letter. They, of course, will all know that thee is not my son, Mark, but will call thee by that name. This is for thy own protection and thee must respond to this name.' Tears had come to the old man's eyes.

Holding the letter identifying him as Mark Clifford, Rob smiled at his puzzled host and hostess as he climbed down from the carriage.

After scanning the letter, the man smiled. "I am John Treverton, and this is my wife, Samantha. Please, come in, Mark."

They regarded Rob skeptically, but treated him well. He was ushered into a comfortable sitting room.

"Thee is most welcome here." Mrs. Treverton, a nervous woman with a sharp, beak-like nose, bade him sit down. She pulled a long tas-seled cord and a young Negro woman entered the room. "Molly, our maid servant, is emancipated. We pay her wages," Mrs. Treverton ex-plained to her guest. Turning to Molly, she asked for a refreshment tray.

"I understand that thee is on thy way to Richmond to pick up some freight headed up the line." Mr. Treverton nodded approvingly.

Rob shifted in his seat, feeling uneasy. Old Thomas had told him to expect railroading terms to be used when discussing the movement of slaves. Rob had heard the term *underground railroad,* but he had never thought he would find himself a *conductor* on the line.

Looking up at Mr. Treverton, he said, "Yes, sir. That's what I've been told."

"Please, Mark. We Quakers do not use titles of address. I am called simply John Treverton. We also address each other as 'thee.' When among us, thee will stand out if thee speaks otherwise."

Carrying a tray, a tall young woman entered the room. "Father, I brought the tea for Molly. I wanted to meet our guest."

Staring at the girl, Rob realized he had not expected that a woman could be so attractive when dressed in the plainest of clothing.

"This is my daughter, Abigail. She is also involved in the Abolitionist movement and the workings of the railroad. Now, I must excuse myself."

Standing, Rob smiled. Abigail sat down on the small settee and Rob sat opposite her. Mrs. Treverton, busying herself with sewing, sat near the window. Abigail smiled politely, but was quiet. He sensed that she was sizing him up. Just as he was beginning to feel uncomfortable, she spoke.

"I knew the first Mark. He was a kind young man and his death was a great loss to the community. Thee is much more handsome. I hope that thee is also as kind." She smiled, showing evenly spaced white teeth. Her brown hair was almost hidden beneath a starched white cap, but her smile seemed to promise a different Abigail, one who longed for adventure and laughter. "I am pleased to meet thee, Robert Johnson. I hear that thee is joining us in our endeavors."

Rob wasn't sure quite what he was joining, but smiled back at his companion. "Yes," he said firmly. "I am."

Later, as he tried to fall asleep, Rob reviewed the events of the evening. At dinner, John Treverton had talked at length about the fighting in the Valley. He'd emphasized how dangerous travel was in these times. Abigail had added that such turmoil seldom affected Quakers, who were usually given safe passage by both sides. But more than her words, Rob remembered her face and the softness of her voice. How could he think of Abigail Treverton? He was on his way to bring home Laura and his unborn child.

* * * *

Early the next morning, Rob climbed back into the carriage. Joseph drove and Lilly sat beside him. Everything was as it had been yesterday, but Rob realized that he had changed. He couldn't get Abigail out of his mind. There was something about her, a charm, an energy that made her different. He was still thinking of Abigail when he felt a crashing jolt. Heavy overnight rains had left the roads barely passable and the carriage had hit a gully in the roadway.

"Mister Mark," Joseph shouted. "This here front wheel is giving way." The carriage made a slow wobbling turn, rolled a few feet and stopped. Rob felt the compartment sway. He stepped down onto the road and found Joseph trying to calm the horses. The right front wheel slanted at a drunken angle and the carriage listed to the right.

"Sorry, Mister Mark. I'll be taking care of this, but it's gonna be afternoon now before we can set out again." Rob helped Joseph with the horses, then started walking back down the muddy road toward the Treverton farm.

The day was warm and cloudless. With time on his hands, Rob entered the woods and wandered beside a narrow stream. Eventually he reached a pond. Ferns clung to the banks and a blue heron stood motionless in the reeds. He watched the bird bend down and scoop up a small fish. Although a slight breeze stirred the pine forest, Rob was sweating. He took off the fine linen shirt, which had belonged to Mark Clifford, and hung it over a branch. Unused to wearing such fancy clothes, Rob looked down at the crisply creased trousers. The boots were now covered with mud. He wondered how Mark had ever enjoyed life dressed as such a gentleman. Kicking off the boots and pulling off the rest of his clothing, he jumped into the pond. All was quiet for a short time until, gradually, the frogs resumed their throbbing call. Rob floated aimlessly and the sweet earthy scent of water plants reminded him of swimming holes back home.

He gazed up at the clouds drifting toward the ridge tops and felt at peace. He shut his eyes and concentrated on the call of a red-winged blackbird. Its mate answered from the pine woods. Rob was so relaxed that he almost missed the sounds of cracking twigs and scattering stones. He was not alone here. Quickly, he slipped behind a cluster of tall cattails. A small brown dog bounded down to the water and started drinking thirstily. A sharp whistle from the woods brought the dog's head up. He turned and trotted away. Rob was calculating how far away his clothes were when the dog and Abigail Treverton arrived. She was laughing.

Startled, he pressed farther into the reeds. Abigail's deep throaty laughter kept on. From his hiding place, he saw that she was holding his shirt. "Is this Rob Johnson's shirt? Don't worry, I have thy knickers too. Come out, I know thee is here." She sat on the bank and giggled.

Rob swam over to her. "Do you often steal men's clothes?"

Abigail's hair fell loose around her face and her feet were bare. She grinned at him. "This is my first time. Does the water feel good against thy skin? I would so like to jump in."

"You're welcome. It's a big pond." Rob paddled closer. The dog came to the edge of the water and barked.

Abigail's face reddened. "I wish I could. I wish I could do many of the things men do." She bent over and ran her hands through the water. The sun glinted on her dark hair, bringing out glints of red. "I heard about the carriage wheel and I am glad thee is still here. I have wondered why thee is working with us on the Railroad."

"It's not right that one man should own another," Rob said.

"Thee does not support the South in this war?"

"No."

"What will thee do if the war ever ends?"

"Go back to my farm and try to pull together what may be left. I hear you help with the Railroad," Rob said. "That's needed work."

"Yes, I darn and mend so that the freed slaves will have clothes. That's all my father allows me to do." Anger flared in her hazel eyes.

"That's important too," Rob said.

"Thee sounds like my father. I can do more. I can do what thee will be doing."

"It's too dangerous. What about writing letters, keeping records? That must be done."

"Yes, those things must be done, but I doubt my father would think me capable." She moved closer to the water. "I like thee, Rob. Thee does not see me as other men do." Sunlight filtered through the tree branches, encasing the boy in the water and the girl on the bank in a golden circle of light. "Will thee come out of the water so that we can talk face to face?"

"I will if you hand me my things."

She handed him his clothes, then looked discreetly away. By the time Rob was dressed, a few dark clouds were sliding across the sun. As he approached Abigail, he saw that she was coiling her hair and pushing it under a white cap. She was no longer barefoot. "What happened to the beautiful pond spirit?" he asked as he sat down beside her.

"She is gone. While thee was in the water, our meeting seemed unreal. Now that thee is here beside me, I must be myself again."

"No more bold ideas, no more clothes stealing?"

"No," she said and looked down. "Each one of us has a course to follow. I have mine."

"What would you like to do, Abigail, if you were as free as a spirit?"

"I would like to kiss thee, Rob Johnson."

Smiling, Rob tilted his head toward hers. The kiss was light but lingering. The fact that he shouldn't be doing this at all nagged at the corners of his mind.

Abigail's response was wild and unexpected. She reached up and pulled him to her. Her lips were on his neck, on his mouth. Her eyes promised more than his dreams had imagined. His hands stroked her body and she responded with abandon. Abigail's passion and the suppleness and warmth of her young body overwhelmed him. Her hair fell lose from the Quaker cap and he kissed her hungrily.

Gradually, loud yelping barks entered his awareness. He tried to ignore them as he was beyond caution.

"Miss Abigail," a high-pitched voice called.

Abigail struggled away from him. "Bessie is coming. She is looking for me. We cannot be found this way. But oh, I do love thee, Rob."

Rob managed to pull himself together. "I love you too," he whispered, then turned and ran into the cover of the woods.

* * * *

A few hours later, Rob was once again seated in the carriage on his way south. He was too elated to consider the consequences of his meeting with Abigail, nor did Laura intrude on his happy memories of the morning at the pond.

The carriage proceeded without further incident until the group ran into a Union patrol. Yankee soldiers barred the way. The red-faced sergeant opened the carriage door and said sharply, "You must disembark, Sir. I need to see your papers."

"I can't do that. I'm in a hurry. Either step aside, or I'll report, eh, thee to thy superiors," Rob said.

Grudgingly, the Yankees made way and the carriage continued toward Richmond. Rob felt a surge of satisfaction. He was amazed at the change one good suit of clothes and a fine carriage could bring. He realized that he was actually beginning to enjoy his new role and felt confident that he would return home with Laura.

CHAPTER 14

LAURA FOUND

JUNE 1862

They approached Richmond on June twenty-fifth and found the road clogged with troops. Soldiers were working on the city's fortifications and teams of oxen were pulling supply wagons into the capitol. Pickets checked Rob's papers and waved the carriage into the city. The soldiers told him that the Federal advance had stalled to the south of the city at Oak Grove. The streets were in turmoil. Groups of drunken soldiers were clustered on street corners shouting of victory and glory, while a line of Northern prisoners shuffled by.

The carriage rolled to a halt before an elegant townhouse owned by Tobias Kulp, a relative of Thomas Clifford. News of Rob's arrival had preceded him. He was addressed as Mark Clifford by the large Kulp family.

"That is not Mark Clifford," a small boy said.

"Quiet, Toby. This is, indeed, Mark Clifford." Tobias Kulp glared at his son. "Welcome, welcome, Mark. We have waited dinner." Tobias was balding and his round face was creased in a perpetual smile. "Please come in and meet my family."

The house was filled with children. Mrs. Kulp, short and round like her husband, was also very friendly and talkative. "We had heard thee was coming, Mark. We have been awaiting thee." She ushered Rob into a formal dining room and seated him at the long table next to her husband.

"Thee has traveled a long way to reach us. Even though these are trying times in the city, I will have a welcome surprise by tomorrow," Tobias said, beaming at Rob.

"What do you...What does thee mean?" Rob asked cautiously.

"Why, thy wife, of course." Tobias looked pleased with himself.

Rob spent the evening talking with Tobias Kulp, who seemed unconcerned with the considerable risk he had undertaken by hiding six runaway slaves in his basement.

When the slaves were given their supper, the two men walked down the narrow cellar steps behind the servants. As they entered a large storage room, Rob looked around at the neat stacks of food and supplies. Tobias walked over to the far wall and pushed a row of bricks. Silently, a door opened on well-oiled hinges, revealing a large room. Torches flared along the walls, illuminating three men and three women sitting patiently at a long table. Large bowls of steaming rice and beans were served, followed by vegetables and fruit.

Tobias himself passed around the platter of cornbread. Addressing a few of the people by name, he smiled and urged them to eat. He and Rob sat at one end of the table and when the bowls were empty, Tobias stood.

"Good people," he looked over the group. "I would like thee to meet thy new conductor, Mark Clifford. He will lead you north in two days."

* * * *

Rob spent a sleepless night in the most elegant accommodations he had ever seen. The large, four-poster bed had fine coverings and the floor was laid with Turkey carpets. He had learned that the Quakers didn't believe in showiness, but, to him, this was luxury, indeed. Tossing in bed, Rob rehearsed again and again what he would say when he saw Laura tomorrow. He had asked Tobias Kulp how he had found her and how he had been sure she would come here in the morning.

"Black flesh is not all that's for sale in this town. Do not worry, she will be brought here. The price hangs in the balance." Tobias had looked confident.

Steeling himself for the fact that she would look quite different, Rob realized he was more afraid of how she would feel toward him. And how did he feel toward her? He finally fell into an exhausted sleep.

* * * *

At nine o'clock the next morning, a wagon drew up before the house. Tobias went out and spoke to the driver. Watching from the window, Rob saw money change hands. *The Meeks' would buy and sell anything*, he thought. Unbidden, the fact that Laura was a Meeks, and that the child would be half Meeks came to him.

Carrying a small bundle, Laura stood in the hall. As Rob approached her, he could see that she was ready to bolt. Reaching her, he was shocked at her appearance. He had known she would be large with child, but hadn't expected such drastic changes. Her threadbare dress barely covered her belly and her hair fell in lank masses to her waist. But she stood up straight and stared him in the eye.

"Laura," he said and pulled her awkwardly into his arms, "I've found you."

"Hello, Rob." She slumped into his embrace and dropped the bundle.

Tobias had disappeared and the rest of his boisterous family was also out of sight.

* * * *

In the bedroom, Rob coaxed Laura to sit down. "How are you?" he asked.

Looking at him carefully, Laura said, "I have survived, but not as well as you. I hardly know you."

Conscious of his fine clothes, Rob didn't reply. The silence lengthened. Finally, he said, "I'm the same man you knew, but things have changed."

"I can see that. I fell in love with a sweet boy, not a dark-clad man with no smile on his face. Why did it take you so long to find me?" Her voice rose to a shriek. "Now you finally walk in dressed like gentry. Who are you? How can I trust you? I don't want to stay here." Laura struggled up and started toward the door.

"No. I mean, don't be hasty. We have to talk."

Laura stopped and turned to him. "These people scare me. You scare me. It's plain I'll never fit in here. Now, leave me alone."

"Laura, wait. You need help and I can take care of you now. Things will work out."

"Whatever are you talking about? You have become one of them."

"What are you saying?"

"I'm saying that I want to leave here and go back to my own people."

Sitting down, Rob rubbed his forehead. Tempted to let her go, he tried one last time. "Laura, no matter what you think, I've spent months looking for you. I wouldn't be here with these people if it weren't for you. Look around. Where do you want the baby to be born? In a place like this or where you came from? These are good religious people. They'll help us."

They both turned as a discreet knock sounded on the door. The door opened a crack and Mrs. Kulp's plump face peered in. Holding a tray of steaming food, she stood uncertainly.

"Please, come in." Rob sprang up from the bed and held the door open. "Thank you," he said.

Mrs. Kulp left the tray and nearly ran from the room. Laura ate quickly and Rob realized just how desperate she was. "I'm going to leave you to rest. I'll be back in an hour." Quietly, he let himself out of the room.

* * * *

Later, when Rob went back to the bedroom, he stopped in the hallway and peered through the half-open door. He was surprised to see Laura sitting next to Tobias' wife on the bed, which was covered with tiny baby clothes. The women were both smiling and Laura laughed as she held up a little gown.

"Thee will need all these things soon." Mrs. Kulp handed the girl a pile of small blankets.

"Oh, no." Laura looked defensive. "I've got well over four weeks left."

"I think not," the older woman said, eyeing Laura's belly. "I've had much experience in these matters. Thy babe has dropped. It will be born in a week or so."

Rob stepped back into the shadows of the hallway. If Mrs. Kulp was right, then it was unlikely that Laura was carrying his child. Who should he believe?

* * * *

That night at dinner Laura appeared in a green gown that must have belonged to her hostess. Her hair had been washed and coiled on top of her head. Smiling nervously, she took her seat next to Rob and looked around in wonder at the fine china and silver serving pieces. Laura was transformed and her new appearance seemed to give her confidence. She ate well and even commented on the food.

"Mrs. Kulp, the chicken is very tender and the sauce is tasty."

"I thank thee, Laura, but please call me Julia. I am Julia Kulp. We don't use titles of address." Laura looked confused, but nodded.

After the meal, as she and Rob climbed the stairs to their bedroom, Rob took her hand.

"You look very beautiful tonight. Please say that you are a little happy to see me."

Panting, Laura stopped on the landing. "Yes, I'm happy to see you at last and, yes, these are kind people. But I feel as though I'm walking on broken glass and can't put a foot wrong."

"This is all new to you. It was strange for me at first." Rob took her arm and helped her up the rest of the stairs.

In their room, behind the closed door, Rob led her to the bed and sat next to her. "I've missed you, Laura," he said simply.

Leaning her head on his shoulder, Laura started to weep. "I don't deserve to be here with you. I ain't good enough." She sobbed loudly, gasping for air, and finally started to hiccup. "But the baby needs a chance in life." Still weeping, Laura slumped down on the bed.

"You don't know what I was forced to do," she whispered. "Them kinfolks who took me forced me to whore in a bordello until the baby started to show. They said I owed them." Sobbing, Laura hid her face in the bedding and motioned him away. "How can that ever be put right?"

Rob felt his anger rise at her godforsaken kin and at himself. He sat on the edge of the bed and tried to stroke her hair, but she pushed him away. "It doesn't matter. Shhh, don't cry," he said. "We'll work this out together. It will be all right."

At that moment, Rob believed they could work things out and that he would love the new child, no matter what. Tentatively, he placed his hand on her belly and immediately felt a kick.

He grinned down at her. "The little fellow is strong. He's going to make us proud."

Laura turned her head away and cried into the pillow.

* * * *

The next morning, Rob awoke with a start. He was lying on the floor next to the bed. Laura was still asleep, her blond hair falling over the pillow. Last night had been hard for them both and Rob had made a bed on the floor. Now that he had found Laura, he would put doubts about the baby out of his mind and make everything up to her.

Arriving late at the breakfast table, Rob noticed the older Kulp children looking at him and giggling behind their hands. He grinned at them as the Negro house servant set a full plate of eggs, sausage, and biscuits before him.

"Good morning, Mark." Tobias was also smiling broadly. "There is good news for thy trip tomorrow. Both armies are well to the south of Richmond. Lee is chasing the Yankees across the peninsula near Harrison's Landing. If thy group departs quickly, thee will not encounter fighting, but there will be other dangers. I hear that deserters are everywhere on the roads."

Rob had thought as much. "Yes," he said, "They'll be like vultures in the countryside."

"Thee must keep thy party together on the road. If the wagon falls behind, it will become fair game. But thee, thy wife and thy servants will go with God's blessing, Mark Clifford."

CHAPTER 15

THE NEW BABY

JULY 1862

At the end of the third day on the road north, Laura was feeling poorly. The jolting carriage ride over rough roads had been hard on her. She looked pale and refused to eat. Rapping on the side of the carriage, Rob saw Joseph look back, nod, and rein in the horses. The wagon behind also jolted to a halt. Stepping onto the road, Rob waited for Joseph to jump down from the driver's seat.

"My woman is not well. I think we should stop early for the night. What stations are nearby?"

"There ain't nothing near and it ain't safe to camp by the road. We best go on to Fredericksburg. It's only two more miles."

Even though the fighting was south of Richmond, Rob thought of the men he had seen running through the woods, but he knew they must go on. "Try to hurry, Joseph."

Back in the rocking carriage, Laura glared at him reprovingly. "You could have forced him to stop. You don't care if I drop this baby here and now." She gritted her teeth. "It's too soon. This bumpy road has made the baby come early." Laura started to sob and cried, "Who will help me? I need help!" She let out a long wail.

Rob rapped on the carriage door again. When Joseph approached, he called out, "I need Lilly here. Thomas Clifford said she knew about birthing. I need her now."

Slumping back on the seat, Laura stared at him coldly. Then her body convulsed and she cried out again.

Lilly tapped at the carriage door. "Do you need me, Mister Mark?" Her dark eyes darted over the plush carriage interior and came to rest on Laura.

"Yes," Rob was immensely relieved. "Come in. I'll just step out for a minute." Laura shot him a desperate look and moaned.

Walking back to the wagon, Rob nodded to the driver, a capable man who seemed up to the job. The women walked about nearby, but the three men stayed with the wagon. Rob knew they had thick wooden staffs and other homemade weapons hidden under the straw. The bordering woods seemed quiet, but he fingered the Colt revolver at his waist. He also had a rifle stashed with the luggage. Quakers did not carry guns, but he was not a Quaker.

Rob found Joseph leaning against a tree near the carriage. "Mister Mark, there's been a lot of screaming. Your woman's calling for you."

Tapping hesitantly on the carriage door, Rob tried to muster up some sympathy. Laura was young and this was hard on her. His mother had always said that some women went crazy during childbirth.

When he threw the door open, Laura tried to pull him inside. "She says it ain't my time. If that's true, why am I in such pain?"

"Can she travel?" Rob looked at Lilly.

"Yes, sir. This looks like false labor. She ain't ready yet."

Gently, Rob tried to pull away from Laura's clutching hands. Finally jerking away, he said, "Try to get some rest. We have only two more miles." Shutting the door, he joined Joseph on the driver's seat.

"Let's go." Rob stood and grabbed the rifle from the luggage rack as the carriage started moving. Scanning the hillsides, he couldn't see any movement.

Rounding a bend, four armed men blocked the road. Joseph laid the whip to the horses, and the carriage shot forward. Scattering as the frenzied horses bore down upon them, the men turned toward the slower moving wagon. As they rounded the next bend, Rob saw that the wagon was out of sight.

"Stop here," Rob shouted as he loaded the rifle. "Take my woman on to Fredericksburg. I'll meet you there." He jumped onto the ground and ran into the woods.

Reaching the wagon, Rob saw that the Negroes were lined up in the road, guarded by one of the attackers. The others were ransacking the wagon. His eyes went to the tall, sandy-haired leader wearing a ragged Confederate uniform. His back was turned, but there was something very familiar about him. Maybe it was the tilt of his head or the cocky set of his hat.

Rob stepped onto the road. "Nate Fields, turn around."

The man turned quickly, two guns leveled at Rob. Slowly, Nate grinned. "My God, can it be? Is this fancy gentlemen my old friend from Morgan County?"

Rob lowered the rifle and reached Nate in a few long strides. "It's me all right. I've fallen into a bit of luck. How about you?"

Lowering his weapons, Nate grinned. "Well, I can see that." He nodded approvingly. "Me and the boys are just trying to keep the roads safe for fine gentlemen such as yourself." He clapped Rob on the back and they shook hands. "Did you find Laura?"

* * * *

Later, Rob and Nate sat on the front seat of the wagon as the group headed to Fredericksburg. The rest of Nate's men scouted ahead. "Them boys ain't happy to lose such a prize as them slaves. Would have fetched a good price. But they understand. I told them you was almost family and had a pregnant woman along."

"I don't mind telling you I was relieved to see you. I figured it was my last day on earth."

"You were damned stupid to take us on. That's how I was sure it was you underneath all them fancy clothes. You're just as bull-headed as ever."

They were outside Fredericksburg when Rob finished his story. "Laura wasn't too happy to see me, truth be told. She even said she wanted to go back to her own people, the same folks who sold her to Tobias Kulp."

"I tried to tell you about the Meeks. Are you sure it's your baby?"

"I'm not sure of anything, Nate. I envy you your free and easy life. Mine is complicated."

"Let's drink on it." Nate pulled a flask from his jacket pocket. "My men and I can see you as far as Winchester. I'm sure your rich backers can supply a small fee."

* * * *

The carriage was drawn up before the next safe station, a stately brick home. Joseph ran toward the wagon as soon as they entered the driveway. "Thank God you're all here. It's a girl, Mister Mark. You're a daddy."

"Mister Mark? So your name's new too?" Nate followed Rob into the house. Directed by a Negro servant, Rob took the steps two at a time. In a small bedroom, he found the baby being fussed over by an old woman. Lying very still on the bed, Laura looked sweaty and limp as a rag-doll. She seemed exhausted. Turning first to the baby, Rob looked at the tiny form wrapped in blankets and wondered how it would survive. He felt totally inadequate.

The old woman looked at the two young men sharply. "Which one is the father?"

Rob stared at her, at the baby and at Laura, but said nothing. Finally, Nate punched him on the shoulder. "He is. I'm the favorite uncle."

From the bed, Laura whispered, "Nate, is that you? Is Rob here?"

* * * *

Traveling with an escort served to make the rest of the trip uneventful. Laura spent most of the time sleeping so Lilly took on the task of tending the baby. She woke Laura only long enough to nurse. Rob rode with Nate and had to admit that he was relieved to be away from the carriage, Laura, and the crying baby.

"You ain't much of a husband, or a daddy either." Nate grinned. "Are there problems?"

"No problems," Rob said shortly.

At Paris, the wagon lumbered down the tree-lined lane to the Treverton home. The household had been alerted by field hands who ran ahead with news of their arrival, so the family was assembled on the lawn. Abigail Treverton stood in the knot of people and waved when she saw Rob.

"Oh, my God," Rob muttered.

"Just what kind of mess are you in, Rob?" Nate's eyes followed Abigail as she ran toward them. "She's a fine-looking woman. Does she know about Laura and the baby?"

Rob winced and shook his head. "Not yet."

Just as Abigail reached them, the carriage door opened. Laura and Lilly, who carried the infant, slowly descended. Servants rushed to help them to the house.

"Rob, hello." Abigail smiled and reached up to take his hand.

"Abigail. I'm glad to see you. This is my friend, Nate Fields."

Removing his hat, Nate grinned broadly. "Pleased to meet you, ma'am." Both men dismounted and threw the reins to waiting servants.

Abigail turned at the sound of commotion by the house. "Is that a baby? Who is that woman?" She looked mildly interested. Receiving no answer, she asked again, "Did that woman and her child travel with thee?"

Finally, Rob nodded. "Yes, they did. That's my woman and my new baby. She was born on the trip."

Abigail Treverton looked at him for a long moment, then turned on her heel and left without a word.

"So, that's how it is." Nate grinned wolfishly. "You sure have changed since you left Morgan County."

* * * *

That night, in the privacy of their bedroom, Rob picked up the child for the first time. Her head was covered with wisps of light blond hair and her small legs kicked sturdily. He was overwhelmed with the sensation of holding her so closely. At that moment, he was sure he was her father. But from years of working with animals, he realized that she looked fully developed, brought to birth at the right time. This wasn't an early birth brought on by the jolting carriage ride, as Laura had insisted.

"She's beautiful," Rob said. "What shall we name her?"

Laura looked at him steadily. "How about Abigail?"

"That's a fine name."

"Fine name, indeed. It's the name of your new lady friend. I saw you together."

"Laura, you're wrong in this. I met Abigail Treverton on my trip south."

Laura didn't reply, but the suspicion in her eyes drove Rob from the room.

* * * *

"Going that well, is it?" Nate asked as Rob entered the barn.

"She's just excitable. It's natural."

"Is that so? And what does Abigail say?" Nate seemed to be enjoying himself.

"I haven't seen her. She wasn't at dinner."

"Well, if you ain't in a fine mess."

Rob grinned wryly. "Maybe I should have listened to you a year ago."

"No maybes about it." Nate produced tin cups and poured out corn whiskey. "We'll be leaving you tomorrow, so good luck to you and the family. Where're you headed?"

"I plan to leave Laura and the baby in Unger with the Cliffords and head to the border with the 'freight.' After that, I'm not sure." Rob drank the whiskey and coughed. "It's too dangerous to go back to the farm. I've even heard talk that the Union men back home want to take land away from anyone who served in the Confederate Army, but I don't believe it."

"If they don't win the war, they won't be taking nothing," Nate snorted. "Since the occupation, the Yankees can force you to take the oath. They can conscript you into the Union Army. It don't make sense to go home."

"If it weren't for Laura and the child, I'd go back to Colonel Orrick, or maybe even back into the army. I'd try to find Sergeant Williams." Rob gulped the rest of the whiskey.

"Yeah, the sergeant's most likely still alive. He's way too mean to die." Nate drained the whiskey bottle. "I'll probably head back home. Most of them boys I ride with are from the hills up in Hampshire County and they're hankering to go back. We'll probably offer our services up that way. You could join us."

"Frankly, I'm sick of this war. With things the way they are, I've been thinking of staying with the Underground Railroad, but I'm not sure they'll have me."

"Well, I don't know about that," Nate said thoughtfully. "But I ain't sure a fancy new dress would turn Laura into a respectable Quaker lady either." His laughter followed Rob out of the barn.

* * * *

Since Laura wasn't well enough to travel the next day, the Trevertons urged Rob to leave her and the baby with them while he continued north with the 'freight.' Laura was furious at being abandoned and vowed she wouldn't leave her room. Riding ahead on a borrowed mount, Rob felt almost lighthearted as the wagon once again headed north. Back in familiar territory, his optimism returned. All he and Laura needed was time. But Abigail Treverton's face was the one he saw floating on the blue haze over the hills.

The fighting was well to the south of Winchester and by taking back roads, Rob was able to avoid the Yankee lines. Feeling confident back in his home area, he relaxed. He knew the fall of the land and where the streams could be forded. He knew each mountain by name and which families lived in the hollows. By nightfall, the wagon reached the Clifford farm. Rushing out to greet them, the family and servants were jubilant.

"This is surely the work of God." Old Thomas beamed at Rob and the exhausted Negroes, who huddled beside the wagon. "We have been very worried and have prayed for thy deliverance. Thee has conducted thy part of the trip well."

"Where is thy wife?" Mae looked puzzled. "And where is the carriage?"

"Laura gave birth on the trip. I had to leave her and the baby at the Treverton's. I left Joseph, Lilly, and the carriage also. They'll bring her here as soon as she can travel."

"I hope the birthing went well." Mae led the way into the house. "Is it a boy or a girl?"

"It's a girl, and all is well now." He fervently wished this were true.

CHAPTER 16

THE SLAVE HUNTERS

JULY 1862

Three days later, Rob had delivered the slaves to a Pennsylvania conductor and was standing on the bank of the Potomac near Alpine Station. As the ferry docked, he could see the Reverend John Dawson among the passengers. Although in his mid-fifties, he was a big well-built man who looked capable of dealing with any situation. As he stepped off the ferry, he turned purposefully to the left and walked down the riverbank. Rob followed Reverend Dawson, falling into step with him some distance away from the ferry landing.

"The last time I saw you, you were delirious from fever. I see you've made a good recovery," the reverend said.

"Yes, and I have the Clifford family to thank for saving my life."

Stopping, Reverend Dawson watched the ferry start back toward Hancock. "We are careful of the conductors we recruit for the railroad. You are young, but the Cliffords recommended you and I know your family. We were pleased with the way you conducted the freight up the line from Richmond." He smiled approvingly. "It's good to have you aboard."

Back at the ferry landing, two riders left the dock and headed toward Bath. "Those men are fugitive slave hunters from the Carolinas." Reverend Dawson's eyes tracked the horsemen. "I wanted you to see them and know who they are. They are evil men and will stop at nothing." He looked steadily at Rob and continued, "The tall one is Hank Conner and the other man is his brother, Nick. I heard them brag about collecting a one thousand dollar reward for turning over four escaped slaves in Winchester. One was half-dead." He stared after the riders. "They joked that in another half-hour the man would have probably died and cost them over two hundred dollars."

Rob had heard of slave hunters, but realized he had underestimated men like the Conners. "I'll need to take on another man, someone to help out," he said.

The reverend looked doubtful. "Our organization is made up of volunteers, men of conviction. I understand you've made an arrangement with Thomas Clifford to care for your family in exchange for your services. This is acceptable, but there is little extra money."

Rob stared up toward the ridge above his farm. "In these times many men will agree to work for food and a place to sleep. I'll find someone," he said. "I'm beholden to the Cliffords. I have nowhere else for my family."

Reverend Dawson followed his gaze. "I think I have an idea what that land means to you."

* * * *

After saying goodbye to John Dawson, Rob headed up to the ridge. He could see that his fields had gone to seed and the pastures were overgrown. From this distance, he saw that the house and barn were still standing, but couldn't make out any details. Tempted to take a closer look, he changed his mind and turned toward the road to Bath. The farm was lost to him for now.

Rob left his horse in the livery stable and headed toward O'Ferrall's. So far, he had passed several old acquaintances, but had not been recognized. Walking through the front door at O'Ferrall's Coffee House, he spotted Mary sitting at the front table with a Yankee officer. They were in deep conversation and didn't look up as he entered.

Rob found a table in the back and started to relax. He heard the kitchen door swing open, but didn't realize that Mabel McCabe was bearing down on him until he heard her voice.

"Good afternoon. Dinner will not be served until one o'clock. Would you want a cup of coffee, Rob Johnson?"

He looked up at Mabel's ample form and was surprised. Despite his grand clothes and polished boots, she had recognized him immediately. "Yes, thank you, ma'am. I'll have coffee." Mabel didn't smile in welcome. She never had.

As the first dinner course was being served, Mary and her Yankee stood up and moved toward the door. The dining room was filling up with Union officers and Rob began to feel uneasy. In a few minutes, Mary re-entered the dining room and headed toward the kitchen. Speaking to various acquaintances, Mary reached Rob's table and stopped. Smiling tentatively, she looked at him and asked, "Have we met, sir?"

"We have." Rob stood.

"Oh, my God." Mary's hands flew to her face. "It's you. Follow me into the kitchen. We have much to talk about."

They passed by a scowling Mabel in the kitchen. Mary picked up a dinner tray and led the way to the family quarters. "Now, Rob, tell me how you've turned into such a fine handsome gentleman. And when you're finished with dinner, there's someone I want you to see."

At the small family table, Rob looked over at Mary. "A lot has happened. I'm helping a group of Quakers move runaway slaves north. Can you still be friends with someone working in the Underground Railroad?"

"I'm in no position to make judgments. But that is dangerous work. If you're caught in the South and your identity is revealed, it will go badly for you. Not even your fancy clothes and Quaker friends will save you." Mary poured out cups of coffee. "Have you thought on this?"

"I have. What you say is true, but there is no safe way to get through this war. You know I was never in favor of the war in the first place."

"Not like me. I had a romantic notion about war. Now, as you saw, I'm keeping company with a Yankee officer."

"Mary, I'm also in love, but not with the woman I must marry. She's just borne a child that I'm not even sure is mine." Rob pushed his plate away.

"So, you found Laura?"

"I've found her, but it hasn't gone well. Many things I've done, I've done for her, but she isn't happy."

Mary started piling the dinner plates on the tray. "What of the child?"

"She's a beautiful little girl. They're staying with Quaker friends in Unger."

"I see," Mary said. "You've gotten yourself tied down to an ungrateful girl who should be happy to have a roof over her head."

Rob could see that Mary had read the answer in his eyes and he felt ashamed. He had no right to sit in judgment of Laura. He could only guess at what she'd been through in Richmond. He looked away.

"I'm sorry, Rob. I'm prying. Let's talk of my brother, Trip. He's the hero of the family, although he doesn't approve of me."

Suddenly, a loud commotion at the back entrance had them on their feet and running toward the noise. A short, skinny man was holding up a garden hoe, trying to fend off two burly Yankee soldiers.

"Get off me. Get away."

The man turned toward him and Rob saw the startled recognition on his face.

"What is the meaning of this?" Mary demanded. "Let him go."

"We caught him trying to sneak in your back door, Miss Mary," the soldier with corporal's stripes said. "We're taking him to the colonel."

Rob stepped forward and confronted the soldiers. "Take your hands off him. He's my hired man and had been sent on an errand."

"He looks like a Rebel deserter to me." The corporal tightened his grip on Private Jacobs.

Rob advanced on the Yankees. "I require this man's services now. Let him go, or I'll file a formal complaint."

The two soldiers exchanged a look, pushed Jacobs forward and left without another word.

"Jacobs, what are you doing here?" Rob clapped him on the shoulder. "You're not going to believe this, but you're just the man I've been looking for."

* * * *

"A while back, I got a nasty leg wound," Jacobs said as he and Rob rode to Colonel Orrick's camp. "It got infected, so Johnny McKenny took me down to O'Ferrall's. Mrs. O'Ferrall takes our badly wounded and gets the doctor in."

"Why were you holding off two Yankees at the O'Ferrall's back door?"

"Oh, that. The O'Ferrall women don't know it, but I got a sweetie in town. I'm just about healed up and a man gets tired of living alone in the attic."

Rob shook his head and grinned. "You never change, Jacobs. Being shut up in an attic must have made it hard to meet the ladies."

"This one does the laundry at the coffee house. I just opened the attic window and sang a few songs. She fell in love with my voice."

"That explains it," Rob said as they approached the cave. They stopped only long enough for Jacobs to gather up his gear and tell Johnny he was leaving.

The two men could have reached Unger by nightfall, but Rob chose to ride on.

"Didn't you say your woman and child are staying in Unger?" Jacobs looked puzzled. "Don't you want no warm meal? What's going on?"

"I've got my reasons."

"If that don't beat all," Jacobs snorted. "You always said I was the crazy one, but I'd never turn down a woman and a hot meal."

"This woman sure don't act like she wants me. To make matters worse, I've let someone else down."

Jacobs looked at Rob inquiringly, but remained silent.

* * * *

After spending a rainy uncomfortable night in the woods, Rob and Jacobs reached the Treverton farm the next afternoon. The older Trevertons were pleased to see Rob and seemed to approve of Jacobs. However, after making a brief appearance, Abigail did not join the family at dinner.

"We must apologize for Abigail. She says she is unwell," Mrs. Treverton said. Then, looking at Rob, she asked, "How are thy wife and new baby?"

"They are both well. They are staying with the Cliffords."

"Thee must have preferred to stay with the Cliffords also. What brings thee here?" Mr. Treverton asked the one question Rob found hard to answer.

"Now that I work for you, I need to think about the next freight coming north."

"Due to the battles south of Richmond, it is unsafe to move at this time." Mr. Treverton looked puzzled. "I was hoping Thomas Clifford would have told thee."

* * * *

At dusk, Rob found himself walking alone in the woods bordering the Treverton home. Brooding over the events of the last week, he realized that his farm was lost, and now Abigail was lost to him also. If he lived through the war, he faced life with an ill-tempered girl and a child that wasn't his.

He smelled wood smoke and followed the scent until he heard banjo music and a voice he would have recognized anywhere. Jacobs stood in the middle of a clearing near a smoldering fire. A group of men, women and children sat in a semi-circle facing Jacobs, who was flanked by four large Negro women. The banjo player, a skinny man wearing a tattered high silk hat, sat on a log before the singers. He had just struck up the first chords of "Amazing Grace" when Rob stepped into the circle.

"Evening." Rob stood uncertainly. "I hope you don't mind if I listen for a bit. My mother used to sing this hymn."

No one said a word, but Rob knew he was intruding. As he looked over the group, he picked out a few of the Treverton's house servants and thought the others were field hands. Jacobs shot him a grin and led the singing. He carried the melody while the women sang harmony. Rob sat with his back against a tree trunk and stretched out his long legs. He looked up at the darkening sky and let the familiar music swell around him. The moon was rising over the treetops, and the war seemed far away.

After about an hour, Rob and Jacobs left the clearing and headed back toward the Trevertons. "You owe me." Jacobs looked over at Rob.

"What do you mean?"

"I thought on what you said about Laura. When Abigail didn't show her face today, you was sure unhappy. So I fixed it for you."

"What in the name of God are you talking about?" Rob stopped walking and grabbed Jacobs by the arm.

"Well, Abigail wouldn't speak to you. Wouldn't have nothing to do with you. So I had a word with Bessie."

"Bessie? Who's Bessie?" Rob was shaking the hapless Jacobs by this time. His head bobbed up and down as his feet came up off the ground.

"Put me down," Jacobs yelled. "Bessie is Abigail's maid. They're close." Jacobs rubbed his arm. "At first Bessie wouldn't hear nothing good about you, but I told her you were helping out a friend—a woman who was in trouble and most likely had lied to you."

Rob looked at him in disbelief. "You meddled in my business? What are you trying to do? Things are already enough of a mess."

"Bessie's going to talk to Abigail. Now she'll know you're not married. That matters, you fool. You've been trying to do the right thing. You're a decent God-fearing man."

"Jacobs, you've done some stupid things and I've come close to killing you before, but this time you've gone too far." Rob lunged for him, but the smaller man was too quick.

"You'll thank me some day," Jacobs shouted. His slight form was already out of sight in the woods.

When Rob reached the house, John Treverton was waiting for him. "There is trouble down in Richmond," he said. "I just got word from Tobias Kulp that fugitive slave hunters have been seen there. He has spotted them outside his business and lurking around his home."

Rob could see the concern in his host's eyes. He thought back to the men John Dawson had pointed out at the Potomac River ferry. "Does he know these men?"

"No, but Tobias is hiding thirty slaves in his cellar, so he is nervous. After the string of Confederate victories, we hear that the Valley is in turmoil."

"I know the dangers," Rob said. "But two men on horseback could make it through the lines. There may be some way we can help out Tobias Kulp."

* * * *

The first Yankees Rob and Jacobs saw were scouting near Warrenton. A lieutenant and two soldiers rode toward them.

"Good afternoon." The young officer saluted smartly. "What is your business?"

"Good afternoon." Gesturing to the somberly clad Jacobs, Rob said, "We are members of the Society of Friends on our way to aid a fellow member in distress. We must make haste."

The lieutenant waved them on, "Godspeed, gentlemen," he called after them.

"That was easy." Jacobs looked impressed. "Is this what a good suit of clothes does for you?"

"It is." Rob was still mad as hell. He should have known better than to ever take on Jacobs.

"Here." Jacobs handed an envelope over to Rob. "I was asked to give this to you."

Rob grunted and placed the envelope in his breast pocket. He didn't trust Jacobs.

* * * *

When they reached Richmond three days later, Rob was still going over the contents of Abigail's letter. The best part, as he remembered it, was: *I know thee to be a God-fearing man who is trying to do the right thing. I will wait for thee.* Rob couldn't believe his good fortune and he couldn't believe that he had Jacobs to thank.

Tobias Kulp was obviously glad to see them. His eyes darted nervously over the street as he bade them enter. "I am thankful that you have returned. We are in a bad way here."

Tobias' wife and children were hidden away, quite the opposite from Rob's first visit. Rob introduced Jacobs, then asked, "How can we help you?"

"I have thirty slaves hidden in my cellar and two evil men prowling outside. I am worried for my family's safety."

"Do you know who these bounty hunters are?"

"I only know they are the Conners." Tobias' voice reflected his concern. "Stonewall Jackson's victories only seem to embolden men like them."

"I've seen these men in Hancock, Maryland," Rob said. "They are well known in the slave trade and feared. But I know a man in Richmond who may be able to help."

* * * *

In the small hours of the morning, Rob made his way out the Kulp's back door. Skirting the kitchen garden, he slipped through a gate into the alley. The moon was full, so he easily avoided the piles of horse manure. Nothing stirred. Cutting through several alleys, he approached the seamier side of town near the river. Bursts of drunken laughter and song floated down from open windows.

The night was mild, almost balmy, and Rob enjoyed the walk. Glancing behind him, he saw no sign of pursuit. He wedged himself into a narrow slot between a carriage shed and a broken-down fence and waited. Soft rustling sounds filled the night, as cats stalked the rats feeding on the scattered garbage.

Pickets were posted on a nearby street and he caught bits of their conversation. "The sergeant ain't got no right to keep us on picket duty night after night." The man spoke with a twang and Rob knew that he was from the hill country.

"No, Williams ain't got no right. But that's never stopped him before." This man's speech was softer. He was probably from the Valley. "Just because he's such a big sonnovabitch, he knows he can treat us any way he wants. He's mean as a snake."

Confident that he had not been pursued into the alley, Rob stepped out of his hiding place and crept forward. Was this a coincidence, or could the big mean Sergeant Williams these men were grumbling about be his old sergeant? Rob was approaching the pickets when he saw a tall man bearing down on the two soldiers. Snapping to attention, the men saluted.

"Graves, Yost, this ain't no social club. You're to be patrolling, not leaning up against the lamppost. Anybody could sneak up on you."

Holding his hands high in the air, Rob stepped into the circle of light. "I'm living proof that Sergeant Williams is always right."

"Who are you?" Williams growled.

Rob noted that he was thinner, but no less menacing. The two pickets raised their rifles and moved toward him.

"I'm an old friend of the sergeant," Rob said. "I used to worry about him catching me up, just like you two."

"Rob Johnson, it can't be you?" Sergeant Williams looked at the well-dressed young man standing calmly as the soldiers confronted him.

"It's me, sir." Rob extended his hand, but the sergeant grabbed him in a bear hug.

"I thought sure you and Jacobs were dead. He ain't here with you, is he?"

"Yes, sir. Jacobs is in town, just not with me tonight."

"Where's your uniform, son?"

"It's a long story. Could we have a private talk?"

Glaring at the pickets, Sergeant Williams motioned them off.

Rob hoped he had judged the sergeant right. "I was on my way to the river tonight hoping to find your uncle. The man you said could move freight down-river to the bay in a week. I've got a problem."

The sun was rising by the time Rob had finished his story. The sergeant studied him and said, "You've made mistakes, but now you have to do the right thing by that girl." They started walking back toward the army camp. "As far as your slave business, it's damned risky. These slave hunters are ruthless men and hold themselves above the law. You could just walk away." Sergeant Williams watched Rob closely. "But I can see you ain't going to do that."

"I gave my word to these people. I told you because I remembered your story about slave hunters when you were living in Georgia. You know them for what they are."

"Dealing in human flesh is bad enough, but hunting men down like animals is a crime against God." The sergeant suddenly looked tired. "Staying loyal to the Confederacy has sorely tested my religion and my soul." He hesitated. "Your plan ain't going to work, but I may be able to help you."

* * * *

Rob returned to the Kulp's home about mid-day with the news that they had an ally and a plan. There was a price. If all went well, one hundred U.S. dollars were to be sent to the sergeant's mother in Georgia.

"How do you know we can trust the old sergeant?" Jacobs asked. "I never could figure him out." He and Rob were completing preparations for the coming evening.

Rob finished cleaning his Colt revolver and reached for the rifle. "I trust him," he said shortly. "Don't you remember his story about slave hunters in Georgia?"

"That tale? Yeah, I recall it." Jacobs scowled. "I sure hope you're right, 'cause our lives are in his hands."

"You can back out, find a uniform and go back into the army. Make up your mind."

Jacobs grinned. "I sure ain't going back to soldiering."

* * * *

As the sun began to set, Rob and Jacobs made their way through the city of Richmond. They were looking for the Silver Fiddle, a tavern near the river. Leading their mounts into an alley behind the tavern, they found the stable Sergeant Williams had described. The old man tending the stable was only too happy to put up their horses along with the only others he had, two black geldings belonging to brothers named Smith. Rob slipped the old fellow some change, and he shuffled out.

Digging in their saddlebags, Rob and Jacobs pulled out the sealed leather cases Sergeant Williams had given them. "How can we be sure these horses really belong to the Conners?" Jacobs looked uneasy.

"The sergeant's contacts swear by it." Rob started stuffing the cases into the geldings' saddlebags. "Hurry," he called over to Jacobs. "There ain't much time."

* * * *

The bar was hot and stuffy and smelled of spilled whiskey. Most of the clientele were soldiers who were gulping down beer and shouting verses of bawdy drinking songs. When Rob pushed his way to the bar, he saw the Conners sitting at a corner table. The tall one was deep in conversation with a buxom, blond barmaid, while the other one stared moodily into his beer.

Rob and Jacobs sat near the door and waited. A half hour passed and nothing happened. "Maybe the sergeant decided the plan was too dangerous." Jacobs was becoming nervous and took to peering out into the street.

"Settle down, he'll be here." Rob sipped his beer.

A mob of young soldiers jammed into the tavern. Jostling each other to get the attention of the bartender, they started pushing and shoving. Finally, a skinny private threw the first punch. "Get the hell outta my way," he shouted.

Roaring a warning, the big bartender reached under the bar for a club and began laying into the crowd. Rob and Jacobs watched as men ran past them into the street. The Conners were in the thick of things near the bar and Rob watched the short one lunge drunkenly at a scrawny boy, pulling him down.

"Get the sheriff," the bartender yelled.

When Rob caught sight of the Conners again, the tall one was dragging his brother toward the door. Rob and Jacobs got up and reached the entrance ahead of them. There was no sign of Sergeant Williams, but Rob realized he couldn't let these men get away. As the Conners left the tavern and turned into the alley, he and Jacobs stepped into their path. The sounds of the bar fight had faded away and they were alone.

"Good evening," Rob said pleasantly. "I think we have some business."

"Who the hell are you?" The taller Conner snarled. "Get outta the way."

The second man swayed a little and giggled. "They're swells, brother." His words were slurred. "They want us to relieve them of their money."

"Shut up, Nick." Turning to Rob, he said, "Move aside." His eyes held Rob's and the message they carried was clear. A handsome, well-built man in his middle years, Hank Conner looked confident, sure that he was in control of the situation. His hand went inside his jacket, and Rob knew he had a knife.

Glancing around quickly, Rob didn't see the sergeant anywhere in sight, but the buxom barmaid had just turned into the alley. Breaking into a run, she shrieked, "Where's my money, you sonnovabitch?"

Shouts came from the stable and the old man staggered toward them. "Help," he yelled.

Hesitating, Hank Conner backed toward the stable. "Get the horses," he ordered his brother.

Rooted to the ground, the brother swayed slightly but didn't move. With the blond woman almost upon him, Conner continued to move back.

"Stop," the woman shouted. "You owe me."

Rob gestured to Jacobs to stay with the drunken brother as he followed Hank Conner. He passed the old man, who was hobbling toward the street.

As he entered the stable, Rob heard scuffling noises in the darkness. The horses were stamping and whinnying loudly, then two soldiers emerged from the gloom dragging Hank Conner between them.

Sergeant Williams followed behind. "Get him and the other one down to the sheriff's office, men. Be sure you take the cases we recovered from the stage coach robbery outta their saddlebags."

Pausing, Sergeant Williams said, "We're lucky to have caught these two men. The rest of the gang was killed during the robbery." He smiled at Rob and walked after the Conners.

CHAPTER 17

FANNIE AND THE LAW

SUMMER 1862

As he and Jacobs rode back through the city to Tobias Kulp's home, Rob realized that thirty slaves still waited there and had to leave the city. Halted at a military checkpoint, Jacobs produced the pass issued by Sergeant Williams. As the wait lengthened, their mounts became uneasy. Stroking his horse and whispering calmly to her, Rob looked up as a commotion erupted at the picket post. He turned to see a woman being dragged from a carriage by several soldiers.

"Get your hands off me," she screamed. Struggling, she jerked away, freeing her long hair. It fell down her back in coils of fiery red-gold.

Although he couldn't see her face, Rob was sure he knew the woman. Dismounting, he motioned to Jacobs and the two approached the soldiers. "What's the meaning of this?" He demanded. "Can't you men see you're terrorizing a defenseless woman?"

At that moment the woman turned, and Rob came face to face with Fannie Swann. Shocked recognition flashed across her face, then she dropped her gaze and waited quietly.

A beefy, balding sergeant pushed forward. "Excuse me, sir. This is a military matter. Please step aside."

"What's the problem, sergeant?"

"As I said, this is military business."

"Well, then escort me to the officer in charge and I'll discuss the matter with him."

The sergeant hesitated, then moved aside. "Ask the lady yourself."

Fannie stared into his eyes with all her old intensity. She looked thin and weary, but she was still beautiful. Rob found himself tongue-tied, as though he was the scruffy farm boy again and she was the fine young lady.

"Fannie?"

"Rob?" she whispered.

"What's happened?"

"They've accused me of murder. They'll hang me."

"Murder?"

"Yes, I'm accused of killing a local businessman." She grabbed his hand. "I'm innocent, Rob. You've got to believe me."

* * * *

Through the intercession of Tobias Kulp, Fannie was paroled into Rob's custody and she moved into the Kulp home. No one saw her for the first two days. She said she was ill and remained in her bedroom.

During the day, Rob worked tirelessly trying to secure transport for the slaves. With Union troops overrunning the Valley, he and Jacobs were looking into water routes north. But at night, he thought about Fannie. Although he had asked Sergeant Williams to find out what he could about her, Rob had heard nothing. On the third morning, he received a message from the sergeant. Jamming the note into his pocket, he walked upstairs and knocked on Fannie's door. Receiving no answer, he knocked harder.

Finally, he heard the key turn in the lock. The door inched open and Fannie's tear-stained face peered out. "Rob?"

"Come out, Fannie. We need to talk."

"No, I'm just not up to it now."

"Then I'm coming in."

"You can't do that. How will it look?"

"It's a little late to put on fine manners, Fannie."

Entering the room, Rob was alarmed at Fannie's condition. Her long hair was lank and knotted and her eyes were red-rimmed. He stepped back. "What in tarnation has happened to you? You look awful."

"You look like a proper gentleman, Rob." She threw herself into his arms, but he held her at arm's length, as though she was on fire. "You must help me. I have nowhere else to turn." Standing back, she surveyed her visitor. "I always knew you'd grow into a handsome man and that you'd prosper. I hear you have a wife and child. Is this true?"

"I'm not sure of anything, Fannie. My life isn't as grand as the picture you paint."

"So, it is true. Don't you…" Fannie hesitated. The look on Rob's face must have given her warning. She collapsed on the edge of the bed and sat in silence for a while. "Things have not gone well for me since I left Morgan County. Here in Richmond people are mean-spirited. They probe until they find your weak spots."

Rob sat down next to her and took her hand. "What's happened?"

Fannie pulled up the sleeve of her dress, displaying large dark bruises. "I've been mistreated and I don't know where to turn. Will you help me?" Her eyes filled with tears and she turned her head away.

"Who did this?"

"The same man I'm accused of killing. But it wasn't me. He had many enemies."

Rob stood up and started pacing back and forth in the small room. "Who was this man? What was his name?"

"His name was Mason Brode. He owned a large mercantile store." Fannie slowly rose to her feet and faced Rob. "Mason gave me a job when I arrived in Richmond. At first he helped me, but then he turned hateful."

Watching her closely, Rob had a hard time reconciling this story with what he had learned from Sergeant Williams. Mason Brode had operated a high-class bordello and Fannie was a suspect in his murder.

"Couldn't you have just walked away, Fannie, and looked for a better job?"

"That's easy for you to say. Look at you. You're sleek and successful, though God knows how you have become so." She stepped closer. "But I haven't asked you. You are a friend and that's all that matters to me."

Backing up, Rob realized he was now seeing the old Fannie, the girl he remembered. He spoke calmly, "What of your family? What of your friends in Richmond? Can't you count on anyone here?"

"The fever carried away my entire family. They're all gone and now I find that I have no friends. I'm alone." Fannie turned away and began to weep.

Innocent or guilty, Rob knew he had to try to help her. He couldn't sit and wait for the judgment to come in. Walking toward the door, he turned. "I'll work something out, Fannie. I'll get you out of Richmond."

She ran toward him. "Thank you. I don't know how to thank you, Rob."

Turning the doorknob, he slipped out into the hall. "We must plan carefully, so that the Kulp family won't be involved."

Walking away, Rob knew he had to be careful around Fannie. Her touch still aroused the same old feelings. But now, after what he had learned from Sergeant Williams, he had to keep his distance. She was capable of more than he had ever imagined.

* * * *

"I've made promises to Fannie, promises to Tobias Kulp and silent promises to those thirty souls hiding in the cellar." Rob looked over at

Jacobs, who was stretched out on the grass by the Kulps' kitchen garden. "Now that the fighting has moved well away from Richmond, we should be able to slip out." He started pacing up and down the neat rows of vegetables.

"My ma has a garden like this." Jacobs, his eyes shut against the afternoon sun, seemed completely at ease.

"You ain't no help." Rob stopped pacing and stood looking down at him.

Yawning, Jacobs grinned at Rob. "Relax. You're just the hired hand. Can't be expected to make miracles." He pulled a few plump green beans off a nearby bush and popped them in his mouth. "Wish I was in ma's garden right now." His voice was muffled as he chewed the beans.

"You're worthless, Jacobs. I should have left you back in Morgan County."

Jacobs pulled himself up to a sitting position. "Well, just put me on a train. I'll head home."

Rob hunkered down next to him and smiled. "A train. That's it!"

John Dawson arrived by train four days later. He had brought thirty crates of supplies with him and had arranged for thirty crates to be shipped north. A slave would hide in each crate. John left the same day, as he had to arrange transport when the freight arrived in Winchester.

* * * *

Two days later, the train jolted up the grade heading north. Black smoke and soot billowed in through open windows, causing the only three passengers to cough and gasp for breath. "I should never have come with you," Fannie shouted over the roar of the locomotive.

"What did you aim to do?" Jacobs asked. "Stay and get hanged? A little humility wouldn't hurt you none."

"You stay out of this." Fannie's voice had taken on a frantic edge. "I'm talking to Rob."

"Fannie," Rob said quietly, "you need to figure out a way to re-pay Tobias Kulp. He put up two hundred dollars at my request. He doesn't know how it was spent."

"I told you I was innocent."

"I don't know whether you're innocent or not, but the Kulps' money bought you your freedom. You'll be all right if you stay away from Richmond."

"Well, of course I'm ever so grateful. But as to the money, I have no way to raise it."

"I can think of one way," Jacobs snickered.

Throwing herself at Jacobs, Fannie started clawing his face. "You scoundrel! How dare you?"

Pulling her off the hapless Jacobs, Rob glared at him. "Go check on the freight. Don't come back for a while." Then he turned to Fannie. "That two hundred dollars was contributed by trusting religious people who expected it would buy freedom for slaves, not murderers. You've got to find a way to pay it back."

Rob and Fannie traveled in silence until the train braked hard and they were thrown against the next row of seats. "Don't be alarmed, folks." The conductor entered the car and smiled reassuringly. "Damn Yankees tore up a section of track. Our men will fix it. We always carry guards and a work crew."

When the train pulled in to the small station south of Winchester, the 'freight' was divided into three groups of ten crates each and off-loaded onto the waiting wagons. Rob looked for Fannie, but she was gone. She had left the rail car and simply disappeared.

To hell with her, he thought as he watched the other drivers move away into the darkness. Laying on the whip, Jacobs tried to force the sulky horses to move. "Hurry up," Rob said. "As soon as we find cover, we've got to break open the crates and get those people out."

* * * *

Hours later, as dawn broke over distant blue hills, the wagon turned down Thomas Clifford's lane. The passengers, now sitting boldly in the wagon bed, cheered. Pulling pieces of straw from their tattered clothing, they were crying with relief at their escape.

"They think they're as good as free." Rob looked over at Jacobs and tilted his head back toward the wagon bed. "But we're still in Virginia."

Approaching the Clifford house, Rob thought how serene and peaceful the farm appeared, nestled in a small valley surrounded by rolling countryside. It was hard to believe that the war had even passed this way. As Jacobs drew the wagon up to the barn door, Rob jumped down and headed toward the house. He hadn't seen Laura and the child in months and wasn't sure how this reunion would go.

It was strange that no one was around. Even the dogs were out of sight. No one ran out of the house and called a greeting. Instinctively, Rob knew what had happened. Turning, he started running back toward the wagon. "Run! Hide!" he yelled.

Jacobs threw himself to the ground and motioned the slaves to run, but the warning was too late. Four armed men burst out of the barn and started rounding up the Negroes. Jacobs was held at gunpoint and two of the men advanced toward Rob.

"Get your hands up in the air," the first man shouted.

Rob ducked behind a watering trough and reached for his pistol. Rising up, he fired a shot near the lead man's foot. "I'd have killed you if I'd wanted to," he yelled. "Let those people go."

"Can't do that. Why don't you make it easy on yourself. We don't have no quarrel with you."

Rob answered with another near miss, the bullet thudding into the earth beside his pursuer. Sensing movement, Rob half-turned and saw a fifth man close behind him. The man was big and heavyset, and the gun he pointed downward was only inches from Rob's head.

"She said not to kill him," the man near the barn yelled. "Tie him up."

Rob could see the blow coming and tried to roll out of the way, but he wasn't quick enough.

* * * *

When he came to, he saw old Mae's face hovering above him. "Is thee awake?" She asked. "We have been worried."

Attempting to sit up, Rob collapsed again on the pillows. "What day is it?"

"Thee arrived here yesterday. It is now noon on Friday. The doctor says thee has suffered a concussion and must rest."

"What happened?"

"Those bandits lay in wait and then took the ten slaves. They knew thee and the others were expected here."

Rob must have lost consciousness for a minute, because when he focused on Mae again, she was weeping. "Two men hit Thomas; they even pushed me out of the way. Then they kept guard on all of us, so we could not warn thee. I have brought thee some beef broth. But first, it is time for thy medicine."

Holding his throbbing head, Rob tried to push away the spoonful of syrup with his free hand. Intent on shoving the liquid into his mouth, Mae finally won out.

Rob gagged on the bitter syrup. When he could speak again, he asked, "Where is Laura? What's happened to Jacobs?"

"Your friend has ridden off with John Dawson. They are searching for those poor, missing souls." Fixing her gaze intently on Rob, she continued, "Laura is going about her daily tasks, as a good woman should. She has been in to see thee several times, but was unable to rouse thee."

Mae stood abruptly. "Laura has been a great help to us here. Although thee has not asked after thy babe, I will tell thee that she is healthy and delights the entire household." Mae picked up her cane and hobbled to the door. Even in Rob's dazed state, the change in her manner was hard not to miss.

When he next awoke, his head felt clearer and his thoughts were more lucid. But the sequence of events he reconstructed was disturbing: The approximate arrival time of the slaves had been known. The leader of the slave hunters had instructed the man threatening Rob, 'She said not to kill him.' Who were these men? What woman had enough control to dictate the terms of engagement?

Drifting off into sleep, Rob didn't awake again until evening. As he lay trying to piece together what had happened, he heard soft laughter and the murmur of voices coming through the open window. Struggling upright on the bed, he could see the garden below.

A man and woman stood under the massive chestnut oak. Although their backs were turned, he thought the woman was Laura. But this woman wore severe Quaker attire and a white cap covered her hair. The man wore Confederate gray. Rob watched as the soldier offered his arm to her and the two strolled toward the orchard. He stared out the window until they were lost among the trees, then fell back on the bed. Suddenly it was clear to him just how lonely his life had become.

It must have been near midnight when Rob sensed another presence in the room. He had been dozing, dreaming that he was lying in a field of fresh-mown hay. Breathing in the clean earthy scent, he had felt at peace. He had been home.

Now movement in the darkened room alerted him. Tensing, he realized that he had no weapon. Slowly the panic subsided and his thoughts started to drift back to the hay field when he heard his name. Opening his eyes, he made out Laura's face. Her golden hair was framed by the moonlight filtering in through the window.

"Rob, are you awake?" Her voice was soft.

He groaned and felt her take his hand in hers.

"You don't need to talk. I just wanted to sit with you for a while."

Some part of his mind tried to hold him back, but he said, "Will you stay?"

* * * *

In two days Rob felt well enough to get out of bed. Troubled that Laura had not visited him again, he determined to find her. He was in the kitchen trying to get a second helping of breakfast from Big Betty when he saw a woman standing at the back door. She carried a bundle wrapped in blankets, and seemed startled to see him there. He recognized Lilly, the doe-eyed girl who had delivered Laura's baby on the road. Bobbing her head in his direction, she came into the large kitchen and spoke quietly to Betty.

"Show him. Show the man, even though he ain't had much interest," Betty ordered.

Timidly, Lilly pulled the blankets apart to reveal a sleeping baby. Blond curls gave the child an angelic look.

"This Melinda, Mister Rob. Here, you hold her." Lilly thrust the bundle into his arms, and fled the room.

The movement roused Melinda and her round blue eyes flickered open. *She looks like Ma*, Rob thought. Then the tiny girl made a cooing sound and he realized that his eyes were starting to fill with tears.

"She a fine, healthy girl." Betty moved closer. "We all love her."

Rob handed the baby to Betty and escaped into the garden.

* * * *

Trying to sort out his feelings, he wandered through the small herb garden and finally sat down on a bench. Looking up at the blue haze over the mountains, he thought of home. This brought him full circle back to Laura and the baby girl. They were all the family he had left.

Hearing voices, he got up and walked toward the front of the house. As he rounded the corner, he saw Mae and Laura sitting on the porch with a large mending basket between them.

Slowly, he approached the women. Mae looked up and spotted him first. Gathering the work in her lap, she nodded at Laura and moved as quickly as she could to the door. Laura sat very still, holding her needle poised above the garment she was mending.

Rob smiled what he hoped was his old easy smile. "It was good of you to visit me the other night."

"How are you feeling?"

"Much better. Do you mind if I sit down?"

"I don't mind." Her expression was watchful. "I hear you saw Melinda earlier."

"She's a beautiful child. She looks like my mother."

Laura smiled for the first time. "Melinda is a great comfort to me."

Watching her, Rob thought she seemed like the girl he had first met, but he well knew that she had a way of fitting in, of surviving. Then he remembered the Confederate officer he had seen. He thought of the ambush and the missing slaves. He had never considered that this could have been Laura's doing, but could she have arranged it? She would have been well paid for this treachery. Did the blame lay with Laura?

"Are you and the child happy here?" he asked pointedly.

"As happy as we can be in these times. I must see that the baby is safe, and I must look where I can for help."

Rob was silent. What could he say? That he would marry her tomorrow? That he loved her? He realized that he did, in fact, feel something for the tiny girl, whether she was his child or not. But what should he say to a woman he could never trust? He thought she was as guilty as the gang who had stolen the slaves. She was a Meeks, after all.

CHAPTER 18

LAURA AND THE DESERTERS

FALL 1862

Rob was gone. Laura knew that he'd found it awkward to say good-bye. When he'd held the baby, she had watched him smooth Melinda's fine light hair and smile down at her. He was a strange man.

The next day Laura sat at the end of the back porch with a pile of mending. Melinda slept nearby in a large wicker laundry basket, which was convenient to carry about the house. Mae's two grandchildren, Donald and Margaret, played ball in the garden. The warmth of the sun and the peacefulness of the surroundings only served to make Laura more depressed.

Musing over Rob's short visit, Laura thought again that she should take Big Betty's advice and look for another man. There was the Clifford's neighbor, Captain Ramsey Collins, who sometimes walked with her in the evening. Ramsey seemed interested, but he, of course, thought she was a married woman. She had never been a married woman and now she was abandoned. She had always known Rob wouldn't forgive her for what she'd had to do in Richmond, but she and the baby had survived. Hearing the Clifford children running toward her, Laura stood and held out her arms. She caught Margaret and pulled the little girl into her lap.

"We want a story," Margaret demanded.

Smoothing back the girl's long hair, Laura knew that life was good. She thought of Rob and her disappointment at his cold distant manner and now, for the first time, she realized that she didn't need him. She and Melinda had a place here. She was useful and would soon make herself indispensable to this good Quaker family.

* * * *

A few days later, Captain Ramsey Collins sent a scout to warn the Cliffords that after the defeat at Sharpsburg, bands of Rebel deserters were roaming the area. He advised them to mount a defense. The scout handed a bulky package to Laura and rode off. Pulling away the paper covering, she found a pistol.

"We have no way of defending ourselves. We trust in the Lord," Thomas Clifford said.

Mae moved slowly to stand beside her husband and said, "Our family will not bear arms, but what of the others?" She looked at the group of people crowding into the kitchen. Laura, Big Betty, Lilly, and Joseph were surrounded by the house servants. Even a few field hands clustered near the door.

"We must defend ourselves." Laura's voice was high-pitched. "Think of the children."

"Do what thee wishes," Thomas said resignedly. "Mae and I will have no part of it."

Laura, with the help of Big Betty and Lilly, spent the rest of the day instructing every man, woman, and child on the farm, some twenty souls in all, where to hide if they were attacked by deserters.

"Spread them folks out as much as possible, Miss Laura," Big Betty advised. "It ain't good to have more than two or three together." The servants, all free Negroes, knew what would happen if they were found. They would be brought to slave traders and sold south.

In the early evening, the women and two field hands started moving the food stores. They chose three locations, hoping that at least one would remain undiscovered.

"These here shelly beans are from my kitchen garden. I done planted every one of them, and I ain't gonna stand by and see them toted off by some scoundrel of a white man, North or South." Big Betty shook her head vigorously and grabbed another sack of beans. "No, sir, I ain't."

As darkness closed in, Laura knew they must stop working for the night. Lantern light would attract the interest of anyone passing on the road.

"What we to do if they come here?" Lilly looked tired and scared.

"Are there any weapons?" Laura asked.

The women stirred uncomfortably, but did not reply. Laura realized that purpose had drawn them together, but they wouldn't answer this question. "I mean to protect my child any way I can. What about the rest of you?"

"We got kitchen knives and there's plenty of sharp farm tools in the sheds." Big Betty looked sullen. "There's picks and hoes. Our people have used them before if they had to."

"Picks and hoes," Laura repeated. "Are there no guns?"

"Where would we get guns?" Betty snorted.

Lilly stood up and faced Betty. "We got two rifles and shells off them dead Yankees last spring. Joseph, he have them."

* * * *

That night was quiet and the next day dawned clear and brisk. In the afternoon Laura and the children were gathering fallen apples in the yard. She kept them close to the house and constantly scanned the wood line.

"Should we take the wormy ones, Laura?" Donald asked.

"Yes, we'll use them today."

Turning to put more apples in the basket, Laura came face to face with a ragged soldier.

"Ma'am, don't be scared. I ain't going to hurt you or your young 'uns." He was very thin, and Laura could see that he held his right arm awkwardly.

"Could you spare a bit of food? I ain't had nothing to eat but apples for days." He was young, probably near her own age.

"Are you alone?" she asked.

"Yes, ma'am. I been lost for a few days, but I'm aiming to find my regiment."

Laura looked directly into his light blue eyes. Having learned how to read a man's intent from her time at the bordello, she saw that he didn't try to evade her gaze.

"I'm telling the truth, missus. This happened at Sharpsburg, and I couldn't keep up." He held out his arm. "I had to stop for a while, then I got lost."

"Follow me." Laura led the way to the house. The children cast curious glances at the soldier as they ran along behind.

In the kitchen, Big Betty wrinkled her nose at the newcomer, but ladled up a bowl of soup at Laura's direction.

"That soldier need a bath," Betty muttered as she cut off thick slices of bread to go with the soup.

"Thank you, thank you. I ain't had nothing this good in months." The boy ate quickly. After his meal, the young soldier was in good spirits and became talkative. "My name's John O'Day. I'm a Georgia boy. Is there something I can do for y'all, you being so kind and all."

Laura could see that John O'Day was thinking up ways to spin out his stay. "We got workers," she answered, looking at the awkward angle his right arm had assumed.

"My arm's bad, but I can still work."

Something in the tilt of the boy's head and his defiant tone reminded Laura of Rob Johnson. "Can you read and write?"

John O'Day brightened. "Yes, ma'am. My daddy has a general store outside Atlanta. "I've helped him out for years."

"We have two children in need of lessons until their grandmother is well enough to teach them again."

"I'd be proud to be their teacher, just for a few days, of course."

Laura was ashamed that she had no book learning, a fact she'd hidden from Rob and the Cliffords. She knew Quakers put a lot of weight on education. She wasn't sure how an illiterate backwoods girl would be accepted. Laura had worked hard to look like a Quaker woman, but doubted she'd ever be good enough to become one.

The next morning John O'Day's class went well. Laura, with Melinda in her lap, sat in the back of the small room. She knew most of the letters John was writing across the blackboard. Granny had known how to read, but had never taught her, as Grandpap hadn't held with book learning. She hoped she'd learn as fast as little Margaret.

When John called a short recess, the children ran outside. He came to the back of the room and sat opposite Laura. "You people have been good to me." He fingered the fine cotton shirt that Thomas Clifford had taken from the store of his dead son's clothes. "It was decent of Mr. Clifford to give me this shirt. My uniform was in tatters."

"The Cliffords are good people. They've treated me well also."

"You're not one of them?"

"No."

"Then maybe I can reason with you. Old Mr. Clifford wouldn't hear of taking steps to defend his property."

"The Quakers won't bear arms."

"So he said." John O'Day looked unsure of himself. "Here's the thing. Yesterday, before I came here, I ran into a band of deserters—maybe ten to twelve men. They were making their way south after taking a whipping from the Yankees in Maryland. Said they were done with the war. They wanted to know where I'd been and which farms would be easy picking. They mentioned Oakleigh Manor and this place."

"We've heard that there are bands of armed men around."

"It's nothing to ignore. These are dangerous men." John's young face became serious. "You may not have fancy furnishings like some of the grander homes, but you have a wealth of slaves here."

"These people aren't slaves. They're free." Laura rocked the baby, who had awakened and started to fuss. "But I understand what you're saying. I'm not going to watch calmly as thieves tote off these folks."

* * * *

It was almost midnight and all was still. John O'Day had advised posting sentries and had volunteered to take the first watch along the road. Three owl calls would be the alarm. Laura fingered the smooth barrel of Ramsey Collins' pistol. She felt relieved that the house was secured and the Negroes were hidden well out of sight. Smiling, she remembered Thomas Clifford's outrage at the prospect of an attack by men who had been Confederate soldiers. But she had not been surprised. She'd been the victim of southern men for years.

Unable to sleep, Laura tossed in the soft feather bed. She wondered if John O'Day was still keeping watch on the road, or if he'd high-tailed it. Last evening, when he and Joseph had made plans for dealing with the deserters, she had been sure she could count on him. Now, she could see that this wasn't his fight. Finally, Laura got up, dressed quickly, and stood over her sleeping baby. Moving the child to the carry basket, she tucked the pistol under the pillow.

Starting down the dark hallway, Laura held up the oil lamp and balanced the heavy basket on her left hip. She moved slowly down the steps, not wanting to wake Melinda. Reaching the front hall, she set down the basket and was just straightening up when she heard the hooting of an owl. It called three times. Turning out the lamp, she took the baby to the relative safety of the parlor and edged over to a window. All was still.

"That is the warning." Thomas Clifford's voice rose up from the large wing chair. "Pray with me, Laura."

"My word, Thomas, you scared me." Making her way over to Thomas, she dropped to her knees beside his chair. Never very religious, Laura found herself praying.

She was still kneeling when the front door was kicked open and three armed men burst into the house. The one in the rear pulled a cover off the lantern he carried, filling the room with light. Old Thomas stood unsteadily. Laura jumped up and ran over to Melinda.

"Get back over here, girl, where I can see you," the big man in front ordered.

Bending down, Laura scooped up the baby, then hesitated.

"Get over there with the old man."

As Laura slowly crossed the room, she could see his narrow dark eyes following her. The other two men stayed close to the doorway. The door dangled on its hinges and the younger man tried to prop it up. He looked ill at ease as he brushed the yellow hair from his eyes.

"Murray, stand guard outside. The other boys will be here soon." The leader never took his eyes from Thomas Clifford and Laura. "Jenkins, come here and keep an eye on these two. I want to look around."

"I must protest," Thomas took a step forward. "We are peaceful people and have little of any value here."

"You have much of great value, old man." The leader turned his dark eyes on Laura.

"We are members of the Society of Friends and do not believe in violence, nor do we bear arms." Thomas's voice was resolute. "I must ask thee to leave my home."

"Can't oblige just yet. Jenkins, be sure they stay put." The leader left the room.

"Is Mae all right?" Thomas asked softly.

"Yes, Lilly is with her and the children." Melinda had awakened and was starting to fuss. As Laura tried to comfort the baby, she saw the young deserter watching them.

"I'm sorry, ma'am. I know it ain't right busting into folks' homes." He was hardly more than a boy. His ragged uniform was much too large, giving him a bedraggled, almost humorous appearance.

Laura stared at him coldly. "What are you doing with this bunch of outlaws? I can tell by the way you talk that you're from this part of the country." She moved closer, confronting Jenkins. "You don't belong with these men. You weren't brought up to treat women and children this way."

"No, ma'am, I ain't like them." His eyes began to water. "It's only that I'm scared and hungry and now I'm afraid to leave. Rufus, the boss man, says the army shoots deserters."

"If you help us, I'll see to it that you don't go hungry. It's the right thing to do." Laura could see that the boy was wavering. "You're been put in a bad spot, but you can make it right. Help us."

"What's that commotion?" Thomas looked toward the hall. Slumping back into his chair, he looked fearful for the first time.

Shrieks and scuffling sounds came from the stairway. Then Lilly fell the last few feet down the stairs and lay sprawled on the floor. The man Jenkins had called Rufus followed close behind. "Get up, you bitch," he shouted.

Handing the baby to Thomas, Laura ran toward the girl.

"Get back, woman. Jenkins, drag her back." Rufus pointed his pistol at Lilly.

Jenkins didn't move as Laura passed him. "Threatening woman and children, is that the way you act back in the Carolinas?" she said defiantly. "Yes, I know that way of talking. I've heard it from men like you in Richmond." When Laura reached the girl, she was alarmed to see the blood on Lilly's face. "Let her go!"

"She's going with us, all right. This one will fetch a pretty price." Rufus smiled. "Once I have money, I won't look so bad to you. You ain't no Quaker woman, I can see that."

Turning on the man, Laura yelled, "Get out. You can't come in here and treat us this way." She helped Lilly to her feet and dragged her back toward Thomas and the baby, who was now screaming long ragged sobs.

Rufus watched them with amusement. "Stop that damn brat from bawling."

Laura took the screaming child and tried to calm her. Lilly sank down on the floor and Laura could see the terror in her eyes. The girl knew what could lie ahead for her. Thomas looked alarmingly pale, but nodded firmly to the women. Laura caught his slight glance toward the door. Alert, she watched Rufus.

He never took his eyes from his huddled captives as he strode toward the door. "You got to take a stronger hand with the women. Keep them here," he ordered Jenkins.

Laura could hear him hollering for the lookout, Murray. Then she heard an owl call three times. "What's your first name?" She asked Jenkins.

"Sam, Samuel after my grandfather."

"What would your grandpap think of you now?" She hoped he couldn't sense her panic.

Not meeting her gaze, the young soldier hung his head.

"Sam, go over to the fireplace and pick up the fire iron, then stand behind the front door." Laura fought to keep her tone firm. "When Rufus comes back, hit him so he goes down."

Thomas looked at her pleadingly, then started to pray. They watched as Sam Jenkins slowly followed her directions. Laura handed Melinda to Thomas, then knelt down and took the pistol hidden in the basket. She ran over to Sam. "You're doing the right thing. I'll tell the army you're a hero," she assured him.

Faint rustling sounds outside caught Laura's attention. Her hands shook as she primed the pistol. Seconds later, Rufus slammed through the damaged door.

"Where the hell's that idiot Jenkins?" He roared. The fire iron came down neatly on the side of the big man's head and he slumped to the floor. Blood spurted from his wound and soaked into the braided rug.

"Keep watch on him." Laura turned her back and started ripping off strips from her petticoat. "We have to tie him up."

As they were finishing the job, Rufus moaned. "You bitch. I knew you wasn't no Quaker woman."

"Laura!" Thomas called from the window.

Outside, John O'Day, Joseph, and two of the other Negroes were herding a group of men toward the barn. The lookout, Murray, was among them.

Sam Jenkins looked increasingly nervous. Edging toward the door, he said, "I wish you all a safe way through this war. As for me, I'm on my way home now." He pushed the broken door aside and was gone.

"We will pray for thee," Thomas called after him.

"Sonnuvabitch traitor," Rufus muttered and tested the strength of his bindings.

The crack of a rifle sounded in the still night, then John O'Day entered the house. "We got the last one of them, a young kid lingering outside."

"Oh, my God," Laura cried, and rushed out. A few feet up the lane, Sam Jenkins lay crumpled on the ground. She knelt beside him and found he had no pulse. This boy had told her about his grandpap and now he was dead. Brushing the fair hair from his eyes, she knew that she was responsible. Laura doubled over and wept.

"Violence begets violence," Thomas cried from the doorway.

The next morning, Joseph and his men arrived with the coffin. They had worked through the night to build it, as Quaker tradition required a timely burial. The raw red earth had been opened to receive Sam Jenkins. Laura stood with John O'Day and the Negroes as Thomas read from the Bible. His words droned on, but all Laura could hear was the voice of the boy who had died because of her.

* * * *

Captain Ramsey Collins arrived the next afternoon. John O'Day had ridden all night to find him and deliver Laura's message. While his men rounded up the deserters in the barn, Captain Collins took tea with Laura and the Clifford family. A tall lanky man, Ramsey was soft-spoken but confident. His relaxed manner put those about him at ease. When he and Laura had a brief moment alone, he put his arm around her and told her how brave she had been.

"The Cliffords are good Quakers and their attitude against bearing arms is well-meaning, but were it not for you and Mr. O'Day, none of your people would be left. You saved them, Laura."

Still shaken by Sam Jenkins' death, Laura ignored Ramsey's smile and the hopeful look in his light blue eyes. "I'm in need of a favor," she said.

"You have only to ask."

"Could you get word to Private Jenkins' commanding officer and to his family that he died trying to help others. He was a good person." She broke into tears.

"I'll do my best," Captain Collins said. Then he joined his men and led the prisoners away.

* * * *

Laura found it difficult to meet the Cliffords' accusing glances, so she took to spending much time in the schoolroom with John O'Day and the children. Soon she surprised herself by sounding out some of the words in Mae's cookbook. A week later, she was able to read a few words from an old Richmond newspaper she'd found in the study. Elated, she wished there was someone who could share her news.

And, of course, there was Lilly. Silent and skittish since the deserters' attack, Lilly performed her daily tasks, but seldom smiled or sought Laura out to laugh or share a bit of gossip. She left off slipping out to meet Joseph in the evening and disappeared into her attic room in her free time.

Laura found her there, curled up in her bed with the covers drawn over her head. "Lilly, wake up. It's Laura."

"I ain't wanting to see no one," came the muffled reply. "Please, I want to be alone."

Gently, Laura eased the sheet down so that she could see the girl's head. Her face was turned to the wall. "It's hot and stuffy up here, but the sun is shining outside and Melinda needs some fresh air." She smiled hopefully as Lilly turned her head. The expression in her large dark eyes was remote.

"I need to talk to you, Lilly. I've been trying hard to please the Cliffords since that poor boy's death. I feel guilty enough, but they look at me differently now. I've lost their respect. They know I'm not worthy of it."

"That ain't so." Lilly sat up. "The Cliffords don't judge folks. You ought not to think that." She slid out of bed and dressed quickly.

"We'll see this through together," Laura said. She took Lilly's hand and urged her toward the steps. "Come downstairs. I've got a surprise and there's no one else I can tell. I can read!"

It was the second week in December and the first light snowfall had turned the Cliffords' garden into a glistening kingdom. Laura and Lilly put Melinda in her basket, covered her with a blanket, and took her out into the swirling flakes. They danced and twirled along the garden path, singing "Jingle Bells." Lilly didn't know the words, so Laura sang the verses and Lilly picked up the chorus.

CHAPTER 19

CHRISTMAS AT THE CLIFFORDS

DECEMBER 1862

Ramsey Collins arrived the next day. He brought cured hams and a large white pine tree. "It's near Christmas." He grinned at Laura and the assembled Clifford family. "We need to celebrate."

Laura watched him. If not a handsome man, he was a healthy, vibrant man with a flair for life. She listened as old Thomas thanked him for his kindness. Ramsey looked lean and fit in his new uniform with the major's braid on the shoulders. She must congratulate him on his promotion.

Walking over to the baby's basket, Ramsey knelt and touched the sleeping child's cheek, then placed something on the blanket. He beckoned to Laura.

"Come outside a moment. I need a word with you."

Bundled up against the cold, Laura stood on the porch and watched Ramsey as he seemed to be trying to gather his thoughts.

"Laura," he finally began. "I don't know your situation with Rob Johnson and I don't mean to pry." He hesitated. Reaching into his breast pocket, Ramsey pulled out a small box. "This is a Christmas gift, but it could be much more if you want it to be."

As she slowly extended her hand, Laura knew she shouldn't take the box.

"Open it." Ramsey's smile made him almost handsome.

The box held a small golden ring set with an opal. The initials 'L.M. and R.C.' were engraved inside the band. "Try it on," Ramsey said.

Laura hesitated, so he took the ring and slipped it on her finger. "It's a gift of friendship. We are friends?"

"Yes, of course we are. But it's too grand for me to accept."

"No, Laura. I want you to have the ring. If you wear it, I will have something to hang on to when I go back." He looked away. "I never told you, but I was wounded at Sharpsburg. That's why I got the promotion. Now I'm ordered to the defense of Fredericksburg." He still held her hand tightly as he continued. "If I don't come back, I've made provisions for you and Melinda. I came into a small amount of money when my mother died. It will go to you."

Laura looked up at him in disbelief. He hardly knew her. In comparison, Rob, who knew her well, hadn't contacted her in months.

* * * *

On Christmas Eve, Mae joined the family at dinner for the first time in weeks. Although she looked thin and pale, her laughter was genuine. "It is Christmas after all," she said, "and I must play a few songs on the piano. We have gifts for all of you."

Laura had helped Big Betty cook the dinner, so she took pleasure in watching the family attack the mounds of ham, sweet potatoes, and vegetables weighing down the table. Compared with the horrors of last Christmas at her grandparent's farm, Laura counted herself very lucky to be here. Fleetingly, she thought of Thad Meeks, the relative who had used her so badly, and shuddered. He was dead and she had Melinda.

Later, Thomas handed out gifts. Donald and Margaret each received tops carved by John O'Day. Laura gave knitted socks as gifts and the Cliffords presented everyone with Yankee dollars.

When Thomas bestowed two coins on her, Laura protested. "Thank you, but this is too much."

"My dear, thee has a family of two, so two it shall be."

Laura placed the shiny coins in her pocket. She would add them to the one Ramsey had left on Melinda's blanket. Then there were the fifty coins in the tin box from her family's barn. Rob had given her the box in Richmond. She knew it was blood money that Thad and his gang had hidden there, but she and Melinda needed a secure future independent of the whims of others.

Thomas had invited the entire household in for sweets and punch. Led by Joseph, they sang several spirituals, which added a deeper sadder note to the evening.

"Come and join me." Mae gestured to Laura and the children as she seated herself at the piano. She played a few opening notes. "This is a Quaker hymn from North Carolina. In this holy season we must never forget our oppressed brethren." She started singing in a high reedy voice and the children joined in.

My life flows on in endless song above earth's lamentation
I hear the real though far-off hymn that hails a new creation.

Through all the tumult and the strife I hear that music ringing.
It sounds an echo in my soul. How can I keep from singing?

When tyrants tremble as they hear the bells of freedom ringing
When friends rejoice both far and near, how can I keep from
singing?
In prison cell and dungeon vile our thoughts to them are wing-
ing.
When friends by shame are undefiled how can I keep from
singing?

As the hymn ended, the room remained very quiet. Laura remembered that Mae had told her about the persecution of North Carolina Quakers for their opposition to slavery. The music moved Laura as no amount of preaching ever had. She realized that she would probably never reach this level of faith.

"Now, we must sing a Christmas song," Mae said and pounded out the first jubilant notes of *Oh, Come All Ye Faithful.*

They were still singing when a sharp knock sounded on the door. Immediately fearful, Laura looked down at her baby sleeping in the wicker basket. When had desired guests arrived at this time of night? Thomas motioned Joseph to answer the door, while John slipped out of the room. Laura knew he had gone after his weapon. Lilly, who was standing next to her, grabbed Laura's hand.

Three men stood on the threshold. The tall man wearing a ragged Confederate uniform, with his slouch hat pushed at a jaunty angle, was Nate Fields. The other two were gaunt and rough looking, but all smiled broadly.

"Merry Christmas," Nate and his companions called out. Each man held a dressed turkey. "We're friends of Laura," Nate said.

Laura jumped up. Dismay must have shown on her face, as Nate winked at her from across the room.

"Come in. You are welcome here." Thomas gestured toward the punch bowl. "Betty, pour punch for these gentlemen."

Removing his hat, Nate smiled at the old man. "Thank you, sir. I'm Nate Fields, late of Orrick's Rangers in Morgan County. This here is John McCord and the man with the guitar is Joe Tate."

As the men exchanged greetings, Joseph took the proffered birds. The other men walked to the punch table and Nate turned toward Laura.

"Hello, girl. You look well."

"Nate! I'm surprised to see you."

"We were in the area," Nate answered. "Rob told me you were here." He knelt down by the baby's basket. "I've got a gift for the little one."

Reaching into his pocket, he brought out a small gold locket. "She's a beautiful baby, Laura. Rob is a lucky man."

Laura stiffened. "I haven't seen or heard from him in months." *He's the only one who hasn't brought a gift for the child*, she thought.

"I've known Rob all his life. Believe me, he's always been a fool." Nate grinned.

"Anyway, I thought you should be with an old friend on Christmas Eve."

Laura looked into Nate's eyes and judged that he was sincere. She noted that the war had honed him. Leaner than ever, he had acquired a hard edge. It was obvious that he was no longer the clumsy country boy she had met a year ago.

"Do you remember last Christmas, Nate?"

"I do. It was the strangest time I ever spent."

Thoughts of Rob came rushing back. "You and Rob looked out for me then. I'll never forget it."

Nate looked thoughtful, "So you haven't seen Rob?" He stood, stretching his long legs. "It's Christmas Eve, so I wish him well," Nate said. "Can I get you a cup of punch?"

Laura looked up at him. "Yes," she said. "I'd love some punch. It was generous of you to bring the turkeys."

Nate nodded and sauntered over to the punch bowl.

As he moved away, Lilly came up behind Laura. "That man, the one with the thin, bony face, he likes you."

"He's an old friend of Rob's." Laura noted that although the other Negroes had melted away when the soldiers came, Lilly had stayed close to her.

"He ain't no friend of Rob. He has a hungry look in his eye, that one."

"He does seem to have changed," Laura said, as she watched the newcomers. The man Nate had called Joe was tuning his guitar and laughing with Mae and the children. Near the stairs, she saw John O'Day watching the new guests also.

As Nate returned with the punch, Mae took her seat at the piano and the new two-piece band struck up *I Saw Three Ships Come Sailing In*. Nate grinned at her. "The boys need me at the piano. We're gonna sing a few old Christmas songs. But I'll be back; I need to talk with you."

The men's voices blended together sweetly and Laura realized that they might often sing for their supper, perhaps to other lonely women. They sang *Silent Night*. Then they launched into a medley of old songs, including *Lorena*, which Nate dedicated to her. She didn't like the name or the song, but he couldn't have known that. As the singing became louder and more boisterous, she noticed that they were quietly topping off their punch cups from hip flasks, but their harmony only seemed to improve.

Fascinated with the vital young soldiers, the children begged for another song. After a brief consultation, Mae left the piano, saying she didn't know the piece. Joe Tate grinned at the children and struck up *Christmas is a'Coming*. As they sang, the firelight played on the faces of the three young men. Although none were classically handsome, they all appeared beautiful to Laura. They were like Sam Jenkins, who would have no more Christmases. She silently prayed that these soldiers would make it through the war alive.

Joe played the next verse and the group sang *Snow Flakes a'Falling, Hound Dogs a'Calling*. At this point they moved in closer and all three looked upward, howling in unison. Delighted, the children clapped and joined in the howling. Laughing, Laura covered her ears. Next, Joe sang an old Christmas carol. His voice reached for the high notes, but he was in total control of the melody. Using spoons to beat time on the tabletop, his comrades joined in the chorus.

Catching herself actually giggling and tapping her feet, Laura realized that she hadn't had so much fun in a long time. She hated to end it, but she could see that the children's eyes were too bright and their faces too flushed. Motioning to Lilly, she gathered Donald, Margaret and Melinda and headed toward the stairs. She was surprised to find Nate Fields behind her.

"Wait just a minute, Laura. We must be off at first light and I need a word with you."

Handing the baby's basket to Lilly, she nodded and turned to face Nate.

"You've become a proper Quaker woman. I never thought you could do it, but you have." Nate impulsively took her hand. "Remember, I was the one who found you in Richmond, so I know things went badly for you there. But you survived. You're one hell of a woman."

He shifted his weight and for the first time seemed nervous. "The old gentleman told me you have been taking care of things here. They couldn't do without you."

Laura stared at him. "What?"

"Yes, you have no more to prove here. The question is, where do you see yourself, say, on Christmas five years from now? The war has got to end someday."

Laura moved squarely in front of him. "I see myself as an independent woman, living in my own home, surrounded by my own family," she said firmly.

Nate grinned and Laura did see the hunger in his eyes.

"I've had a lot of time to think about this. I want to be with you after the war and be part of that family. Think on it." He turned quickly and walked back down the stairs.

* * * *

At first light, Laura was up with Melinda and watched through the window as the three men rode away. They had slept in the barn and now headed up the lane at a brisk trot. She was glad they had come. It had felt good to laugh and sing and be complimented. She reflected that Nate Fields knew more about her than either Ramsey Collins or Rob. Yet he had still sought her out. Had he proposed marriage? Smiling, she picked up the locket and turned it to catch the early rays of the sun. When she opened it, she was surprised to find a picture of Nate dressed in a handsome uniform. The man wouldn't let himself be forgotten.

When the baby was settled, Laura went down to the kitchen and found Big Betty stuffing the turkeys. The room was already filled with the aroma of baking bread and spices. Nodding a greeting, Betty kept on working. Laura tied on her apron and joined in.

"That was a good dinner yesterday," Laura said. "The soldiers enjoyed the leftovers you brought out." She spooned mounds of dressing into one of the large birds.

"Them men knew how to sing. They friends of yours?"

"I know one of them, the tall one." Laura felt herself blushing. She knew the big woman's eyes were on her.

"You're too good for that Rob Johnson, Miss Laura. He don't deserve you, or the baby neither."

Surprised, Laura turned to face her. "I thought you all liked Rob."

"He got troubles, but he don't try to solve none of them."

* * * *

Later, Laura watched the children play by the big fireplace in the parlor. Hearing the sound of drums, Donald and Margaret ran to the window. Outside, Laura saw that the Negroes were gathered on the front lawn. It was a mild day for late December and many wore no coats.

"They come here to offer their Christmas to the Cliffords," Lilly said as she entered the room.

Excited, the children rushed to the door. "You must wear your wraps," Laura called after them.

Thomas came in from his study. Mae, although unsteady, was helped down the stairs by John O'Day. Assembled on the porch, the Cliffords waved and called out greetings.

Laura watched as four brightly dressed women separated from the group and started dancing. At first, the drums beat slowly, but then the tempo quickened and the women moved faster. The dancers and the insistent rhythm of the drums transformed the stark winter landscape into a foreign place. Fascinated, she watched as the others swayed with the drum beat and started to sing a low plaintive song. Although she couldn't make out the words, she thought the whole performance beautiful in its simplicity. As the drumbeat slowed, the dancers moved slower also, finally ending in a deep bow.

Everyone on the porch clapped loudly. Thomas moved down onto the lawn to congratulate the performers. The children and John followed. Laura left Melinda on the porch with Mae and Lilly and went from group to group. Many asked about the baby. Laura was standing in the middle of the lawn when the dancers approached her. Laura saw that their costumes were much more elaborate than she had thought. Bright orange and blue and green cloths were wrapped cleverly and tucked to form a long skirt and loose over-blouse.

"Your dancing was a joy to watch," she said. Smiling shyly, the women held out their hands to her.

A commotion in the center of the group drew everyone's attention. Joseph and two other men walked toward Thomas. Each man carried an object wrapped in cloth. As Laura and the dancers edged forward to see, they heard Joseph speaking softly. But Thomas's words of thanks were clear, as he held up two beautifully carved wooden walking sticks.

The children received an inlaid wooden game board and checker set. John O'Day was given a chess set and then Joseph moved toward Laura. Setting the largest package in front of her, he said, "This is for the little one."

Carefully removing the covering cloth, Laura found a miniature bed for Melinda. Fashioned from walnut wood, the crib had been fitted with a feather pillow mattress.

"It is beautiful. Thank you." Taking Joseph's hand, she smiled. "You and the others do fine work and I'm sure that the cabinet shop will prosper."

"We owe everything to Thomas Clifford. He has given us a chance," Joseph said.

* * * *

Late that night, after the turkey had been eaten and games of checkers played, Laura slipped out of the house. The weather had changed, bringing a brisk north wind and light snow. On her way up the lane toward the Clifford burial ground, Laura pulled down several evergreen branches. When she reached Sam Jenkins' grave, the snow had covered the newly heaped earth. Kneeling, she began to weave a garland to place on the plain wooden cross.

CHAPTER 20

THE BLACKSMITH'S COTTAGE

SPRING 1863

By spring, Rob saw that their Quaker employers were concerned about how to proceed with the Underground Railroad work. In April, Lee had won a great victory at Chancellorsville even though his right hand, Stonewall Jackson, had been wounded there and later died. Now rumors persisted that the South planned to invade Pennsylvania.

If this happened, troops would be scattered along the freedom routes and there'd be no safe transit north. Although there was much elation over Lincoln's emancipation of the slaves, most were still trapped in the south. Since there was no hope of moving freight up the line, Rob and Jacobs had time off. Their work had been appreciated and John Treverton offered them the use of an old cottage at the edge of the farm.

* * * *

Rob hadn't seen Abigail for almost a year and he had no idea how she would greet him. Jacobs had arranged this meeting and now Rob waited. He realized that the last time he'd actually seen Abigail was the day he'd arrived at her door with Laura, the new baby, and six fugitive slaves.

The marsh grass was filled with tree frogs throbbing their insistent song. The dense thicket gave off a sweet earthy scent, which combined with the fresh smell of water running into the pond. He and Abigail had spent time at this pond before. He'd fallen in love with her here. Sitting with his back against an old hickory tree, Rob watched the path. Every time a rabbit slipped through the underbrush, he tensed. The sun was swinging lower in the sky, sending filtered light through the surrounding pine forest. When he heard footsteps, he moved into the protection of the pines.

Abigail stepped into the clearing and called his name. Even her severely cut gray garb could not make her plain. Her hair escaped in wisps and tendrils from under the Quaker bonnet. Her color was high and her hazel eyes were guarded.

"Rob Johnson," she called. "Has thee not come?"

Rob entered the clearing. Running to him, she wrapped her arms around his waist and buried her head on his shoulder. He held her close and the feel of her in his arms was as sweet as he had imagined on all those long cold nights.

"It's so good to see you, Abigail, but I must talk to you," Rob said. "I know it stands between us, so I need to explain about the woman and the baby I brought to your home."

Abigail moved away and stared up at him. "Yes," she said quietly. "I remember."

"I knew Laura before I met you and I wanted to help her."

"Was thee in love with her? Is thee wed?"

Rob's mind raced for some remnant of his rehearsed confession. "I have tried to love her, but I don't trust her. We are not wed."

"Is thee the child's father?"

"I don't know. Laura says the child is mine, but I doubt it. I do have some feeling for the little girl."

Abigail moved away, sat down on the grass, and watched him.

"I'm so sorry. I never meant to hurt you. The day I brought Laura and the baby to your door was the worst day of my life. I never wanted to stop there, but Laura's health was poor and we had no choice." He looked into Abigail's eyes. "Now Laura and the child are doing well at the Clifford's and I plan to send them money." Rob spread out his hands, beseeching her. "How can I have feelings for her when I love you? Will you give me another chance?" He sat down on the grass near Abigail.

Abigail started to cry and this was too much for Rob. He moved closer and gathered her to him. The scent of her hair filled his senses and the feel of her breasts through the layers of cloth was overpowering. Rob bent down and kissed her neck, slowly moving his lips up to her face. Her cheek was soft to his kisses and her lips on his were insistent.

"I was afraid thee did not love me," she clung to him.

"I was afraid I'd never see you again. Abigail, I'll love you forever."

She tightened her arms around his body. "My father said that I must forget thee. He's vowing to marry me off to a church elder with full purses and cold eyes."

Rob caressed her hair. "He won't do that. In time, when this war is over, I'll be back for you. Wait for me."

In response, Abigail started covering his face with kisses and pulling him down to the soft grass.

"No," Rob whispered. Then there were no more words between them.

The sun was traveling down the sky to the west when Rob and Abigail left the pond. They made plans to meet the next day and walked hand-in-hand back toward her home. Stopping at the edge of the woods, he drew her to him. "Promise that you'll wait for me."

The next day word came that Abigail had been sent to visit relatives.

* * * *

In mid-June, Ewell and his Rebels recaptured Winchester and moved north. Life continued on the Treverton farm, unaffected by the devastation unleashed around it. The old man set Rob and Jacobs to mending fences, but they quickly tired of the monotonous work. Although the regular army stayed to the main roads, bands of armed men often roamed the back roads near the Treverton place.

Today, they were working at the north end of the farm when Jacobs pointed to a group of riders on the road. "Them poor sods could be us," he said. "Just a piece of luck you landed us this job." He set down his hammer and gazed at the road. "Wouldn't you think them men would raid this place? It's ripe for the plucking."

"I've been wondering that myself," Rob said.

"There's hungry armed men everywhere, but they leave this place alone. Why?"

"I don't know. Maybe they respect Quakers," Rob muttered, but he knew that many of these men respected nothing at all.

* * * *

In July, word of the terrible defeat at Gettysburg reached the Treverton farm. "You and me would surely be dead by now," Jacobs said.

Rob could hardly believe that so many had died in one battle. He mumbled agreement and wondered just when his time would come.

By August, hot, humid air had settled over the farm. John Treverton had chosen this stifling day to start to enlarge the basement beneath his home. He planned to add a secret room to hide runaway slaves. Abigail watched from her bedroom window as Rob and a group of black men carried stout beams from the barn to the back of the house. Sweat glistened on their bare backs as they strained under the weight of the lumber. Her eyes lingered on Rob. His skin had turned brown from the sun and his body was as heavily muscled as the black workers.

Although Abigail had been home for over a week, she'd hardly seen him. Now she found that Rob and his friend were no longer invited to the family dinner table. "They are hired help," her father had said, when she asked why the soldiers must eat in the kitchen. "They are not of our persuasion," he had continued. "It is said that Rob Johnson has a wife and child that he does not acknowledge. No, Abigail, thee will not be supping with a man like that."

Abigail sent Rob several notes asking him to meet her at the pond. He did not reply, so today she decided she would find a way to see him. Her father was off attending to Meeting business and her mother had taken to her bed with a sick headache.

At dinnertime, Abigail waited at the kitchen table, despite loud muttering from Emma, the cook. "Your daddy ain't gonna like you being here. He tell me keep you away." Emma banged pots and stomped over to the cook stove. She was a large, heavy-set woman unused to trouble in her kitchen. "Gotta feed these here white boys. They eat like horses, then they still hungry."

Abigail listened to the cook's long list of the misdeeds committed by the two soldiers. Emma ended with, "and them two don't even say no blessing over the food."

Noise outside brought both women to the kitchen door. Jacobs came in carrying two skinned rabbits.

"Here, Emma," he said. "I brought you a little gift, being you're so good to us." Startled to see Abigail, he looked confused. "Sorry, miss, we ain't to be in your company. The old man said."

"Where's Rob?" Abigail demanded.

"He'll be along." Jacobs sniffed the pungent kitchen air. "Chicken for dinner, is it?"

Shoving her way past Jacobs, Abigail went outside and waited on the porch. When Rob did arrive, he smiled at first, then backed away.

"I want to be with you, Abigail, but I promised your father I'd stay away." Rob looked down. "I know this is hard, but I'm on your daddy's land and these are his wishes." He looked at her helplessly.

"They are not my wishes," the girl said. "Thee has disappointed me. Has thee not gotten any of my letters?"

"Yes, but I promised your father not to see you. What was I to do?"

"This." Abigail reached up and kissed him on the mouth. "Come," she said, "I know where we can go."

* * * *

The small shed hadn't been used for years. It had been built by Abigail's grandfather for the resident blacksmith, but after one of the old man's horses trampled the smith to death the place had never been used again. Vines had grown over the structure so that it almost blended into the wood line. The door gave in when Rob put his weight against it and the two found themselves in a small room used as living quarters by the smith. A layer of dust covered the sparse furnishings: a narrow bed, a chair and a small table.

"The Negras call this place jinxed because the smith died here. They won't go near it. Now we send the horses to the neighboring farm to be shod," Abigail said. She took Rob's hand and they stood quietly in the middle of the small room. She looked up at him and saw the hunger and the fear in his eyes.

"This is not a good idea. We should leave," Rob said. "I don't know if I can…" He stopped talking and watched her.

Abigail was unbuttoning her blouse with her free hand. "It's the only good idea I've ever had. Here, help me with the buttons." Rob pulled away. "Thee can leave me now, but thee will not," she said.

He stood inches from her, but didn't move. His dark blue eyes held a dreamlike expression as he watched her movements. The plain gray dress fell from her shoulders and slipped down her slim body to her ankles. She reached up and removed the prim Quaker bonnet, freeing her long dark hair.

"You are so beautiful," he said. "Your daddy can horsewhip me and set the hounds on me, I don't care. But what about you?"

"I believe that one day thee and I will wed and never part."

Rob reached out and drew her to him. He slowly lowered himself into the chair and pulled Abigail onto his lap.

* * * *

Ten days later Abigail's marriage to Carl Dowd, a wealthy Quaker Elder, was announced. The bridegroom was a pinched old man who owned adjoining land.

Rob heard from Emma that Abigail had cried, fought with her father, and refused to leave her room. On their next appointed meeting date, he swept out the small room at the smithy and filled it with cut roses. He waited but she did not come. Finally, as the moon started to climb above the ridges, he accepted the fact that he would never see Abigail again. Indeed, she was married within the month.

* * * *

By September the weather had turned dry and cooler. Rob tried to keep busy so he'd have no time to think of Abigail. Twilight was settling in as he entered the Treverton stable and made his way to the back. Since

Rob's mare was quartered in one of the narrow back stalls, he had to wedge himself into a corner to apply medication to her right front leg. The horse must have liked the warmth of the salve, for she held still and nuzzled his neck.

Hidden in the gloom of the stable, Rob heard movement near the door. Angry voices broke through the quiet peace of the place. Rob couldn't hear what was said, so he eased the mare's leg down and moved to the front of the stall.

"I'm telling you that ain't enough money. I got expenses and what I do for you is risky."

"Thee is not the only brigand around, Harvey. Many men would take the job on." Rob recognized John Treverton's voice.

"They'd take the job, but would they do it? Since you hired me your farm ain't been attacked. You ain't lost a single heifer or servant. I'll have the money now or you can find yourself a new crew."

The silence lengthened. Rob could hear the horses moving restlessly in their stalls.

"That's it, old man. I got no time for this." The newcomer turned to leave.

"Wait!" Treverton said. "I understand the urgency of the times. Would thee take trade rather than Yankee dollars?"

"Trade? Why not? A young field hand should buy a month of my services. A comely woman would double that."

"Absolutely out of the question. I don't deal in trading slaves. However, might thee have use for a couple of able-bodied deserters?"

"Done," the other man said. "I'll be back for them in a few days and we'll be square for the next two months."

The stable door shut behind the two men and Rob was left in the darkness. "That two-faced bastard," he muttered.

* * * *

Rob left the stables and set out in search of Jacobs. The two of them would have little time to pack their belongings and leave. If he'd run into John Treverton, Rob would have thrown him to the ground and called him out for the lying treacherous sonnuvabitch he was. But Jacobs found Rob first.

"We gotta pack our gear and get outta here!" Jacobs told him. "Tobias Kulp needs help in Richmond. A rider just brought this letter."

Tobias Kulp had written to Rob, begging for assistance.

Rats sell for a dollar a piece in Richmond and housewives riot in the streets. The Northern blockade has driven up prices for everything, especially salt and medical supplies. Many refugees have sought protection here, creating an impossible situation. My family suffers and the children of the poor suffer much more. I have enclosed money for the purchases. Any food I receive will be shared with these unfortunates.

Rob scribbled a note to Mr. Treverton on the back of Tobias's letter, stating that he must take the wagon and horses. Then he and Jacobs went to the kitchen to leave this message with Emma and say goodbye. She promised to let Abigail know what had happened to them.

CHAPTER 21

THE 21ˢᵗ VIRGINIA INFANTRY

FALL 1863

After buying sacks of rice, beans and other provisions, Rob and Jacobs headed south to Richmond. Still traveling as Quakers, they were not stopped, but it was a long, slow trip. By the time they reached Richmond, defeat and desperation were in the air. Jacobs carefully maneuvered the Treverton farm wagon through the narrow city streets. Turning a corner, they found themselves surrounded by an angry mob. Skinny dirty children and gaunt determined women grabbed at the sides of the wagon.

"Food," they screamed. "We need food!"

Rob tried to fend them off and ended up shoving them aside.

"You look well-fed, young mister," one wild-eyed woman shouted. "We know you got food and we will have it!"

The children's rail-thin bodies told the tale of their hunger and Rob hesitated. He heard something fly past his left ear. From the corner of his eye, he saw a large rock fall on the cobblestones. Suddenly, the horses reared, dragging the wagon to the side of the road. He watched helplessly as Jacobs slumped over in the driver's seat. He moaned and blood trickled down the back of his neck. A bloody rock lay on the floorboards. Stepping over him, Rob grabbed the reins and tried to turn the team back onto the road. He saw people carrying off crates that had been cargo on the wagon.

"Stop!" Rob jumped down and ran to the back. Sacks of rice lay scattered on the ground. A small boy darted around him and ran off with a heavy bag of beans. His bare feet slapped on the cobblestones. Rob saw a large group of people coming down the street toward them. He wore a pistol at his waist and had a shotgun under the seat, but he had no stomach for shooting down hungry women and children.

Going back to the wagon seat, he found that Jacobs was trying to sit up. "We need to get out of here. More are coming." Rob tried to turn the horses back onto the road, but gunfire cracked behind them and spooked the team. Turning, he saw infantrymen running toward the mob. "See what you can do with the horses," Rob said and started up the street at a run. He spotted the same small boy crouched in a doorway. He still clutched the sack.

"You. You there, stop!" Rob stopped. The infantrymen had formed up in a ragged line and stood with their weapons at the ready. Stepping forward, the sergeant confronted Rob.

"You turn up in the damnest places, Corporal," Sergeant Williams said.

"I could sure use some help, sergeant." The two men shook hands. "My employer needs these supplies, but I can see that these folks are in a bad way." He noticed that the crowd had already thinned to just a few poor souls too feeble to make a hasty retreat.

"We shoot over their heads. What else can we do? There are bread lines for them, but I admit, there ain't much bread to go around."

"Things are that hard in the city?"

"We got people coming in from all over Virginia. The fighting sends them scurrying to the capitol. They may be safer here, but we can't feed them." He slapped Rob on the back. "I'll see you to your destination. Then we'll talk."

* * * *

Tobias Kulp was grateful for the supplies, but handed Rob a letter from his Quaker employers. They no longer had need of his services unless he got himself wed to Laura Meeks in a timely manner. Tobias was unhappy about this decision, but said Abigail's father was adamant that Rob must go.

That evening Rob and Jacobs sat in the Kulps' back garden and shared a pitcher of beer from the local tavern. "What now?" Jacobs asked.

"We'd have a hard time heading north. We'd either be prisoners or Confederate soldiers by nightfall."

"Or dead," Jacobs said morosely. "What can we do?"

"We might as well choose our fate. Pack up."

* * * *

By October 1863, Rob and Jacobs were back in the Confederate Army with Sergeant Williams. He had been charged with insubordination again and transferred to the 21st Virginia Infantry. The sergeant said that only his war record had saved him.

Rob was reluctant to join up. He remembered the conscript gang from the 21st that attacked him back in 1861, but now he found that he was among men from the mountains and the Shenandoah Valley and felt at home.

In early October they joined Lee's defensive line behind the Rapidan River. Still reeling from defeat at Gettysburg, Lee needed a decisive victory in Virginia. On October tenth, the Confederates crossed the river. Sergeant Williams' squad used a make-shift raft which soon took on water. The men stood ankle-deep by the time they reached the other side.

"We could easier have walked across," Jacobs grumbled.

"Come on, men," the sergeant called back over his shoulder. "We're gonna whip them at Centreville."

Rob was skeptical and wished he'd been able to steer clear of the army. He figured he was on his way to die. In fact, luck was not with the South that day. Lee's advance ran into the Federals at Bristoe Station. General Warren's Second Corps appeared on the side of the tracks and pounced on A.P. Hill's Confederates.

Rob heard shouted orders, cries of pain, and the yelping Rebel yell. The acrid smell of exploding shells hung in the air. He could taste the smoke. Trees splintered by cannon fire crashed around him. His ears rang and he could only see a few feet ahead. There was little cover; the only option was to face the enemy head-on.

Finding himself in a press of several men, Rob saw fear in the tall Yankee's eyes as the man lunged at him. Rob managed to swerve and missed the bayonet blade. All around him, Confederate soldiers began a pell-mell retreat.

"Form up, form up!" the officer shouted. But the Rebels were falling back. Rob saw the young lieutenant take careful aim. The only men he shot down were his own running troops.

Managing to gain a bit of higher ground, Rob fought his way to a large oak. With his back pressed against the tree, he slashed out with his bayonet, as there was no time to reload. He could see more retreating graycoats and hear the screams of the fallen. A young boy, no more than fifteen, ran past him. Rob had seen the same panic in the eyes of treed raccoons when the dogs leapt at them.

"Help me," the boy cried. The next moment he fell to the ground. Blood ran from a gaping wound in his chest.

Looking up, Rob saw a Yankee soldier raise his gun and sight in on him. Moving quickly to the left, Rob felt a searing pain. The bullet had missed his chest and lodged in his shoulder. Trying to close the wound with his hand, he watched blood seep down and stain his gray jacket. His legs wobbled and he felt his body slowly slide to the ground at the base of the tree. He was lying very close to the boy, whose eyes still reflected the terror of his last moments on earth.

* * * *

At first, Rob was counted among the dead. Had it not been for Jacobs, he would surely have died. Rob found out later that Jacobs had asked among the wounded until he'd found someone who'd known Rob and seen him fall. Searching near the big oak tree, Jacobs found a man about Rob's size lying in the mud. As Jacobs turned him over, Rob remembered looking into his terrified face.

Alarmed at his pallor and blood-soaked jacket, Jacobs wrapped Rob in a saddle blanket and dragged him to the field hospital. At first the haggard doctor had said they must wait, but after Jacobs slipped the nurse a Yankee dollar, they'd moved to the head of the line. The doctor warned that Rob had lost much blood. He had just finished dressing Rob's wound when Federal troops swarmed into the hospital tent. They were now all Yankee prisoners.

CHAPTER 22

POINT LOOKOUT PRISON CAMP

WINTER 1863

Rob heard the crash of waves and the cry of gulls and realized that he was lying in sand. He sifted the fine grains through his fingers. Cold blasts of air swept through openings in the faded tent walls. He tried to raise his head, but the pain stopped him. The last thing he remembered was the stench of death in the boxcar and the jolting motion of the train.

The train ride and the sand faded away and he was back on his family's land in the mountains. Resting on his back in a field of new-mown hay, he breathed in the clean sweet scent and felt the sun warm his body. Slowly, he became aware of voices.

"This Reb ain't going to make it. He's lost too much blood." The man spoke in a clipped northern accent.

"That may be, but the Doc's wanting him up in the infirmary. Here, take his feet." The second man spoke like the Irishmen Rob knew back home.

Pain seared through the wound in his shoulder as the men moved him to a stretcher. They carried him into a building smelling of carbolic. At last he was stretched out on a cot in a large room. All around him, men were moaning and crying out. The place was packed with the wounded and dying. Detached, he wondered which category he fell into. He felt very peaceful. His spirit lifted up and moved away from this hellish place.

Hearing the church bells toll in the Town of Bath, he saw Laura and a small blonde girl hurrying toward the service. Inside, a long narrow coffin was set before the altar. Fannie Swann stood at one end and Abigail Treverton stood at the other. Rob looked down at his own body in the coffin. His dark hair lay long and curling on the collar of the gray uniform. He looked composed in death and younger than his nineteen years.

The women started to weep. Reverend Dawson approached them and said solemnly, "We are here today to lay Robert Johnson in the ground. He was a devil in life and did each one of you wrong. Where should he rest ladies, in heaven or in hell?" They surged toward the coffin.

Rob woke up screaming.

Bending over him, the Irishman spoke softly, "Don't fear, lad. You're well out of battle and your wound is looking better."

"I'm meant to die," Rob mumbled. "Before this war is over, I'm meant to die."

"We're all born to die. This life is fleeting." The man had a long bony face and sad pale eyes. "My name is Tim Foley. I'll try to look after you, lad. I know what it's like to be on the wrong side of powerful folk." As Tim Foley moved away, Rob saw that he walked with a limp.

It must have been near midnight when Rob woke again. The small high window threw light from the full moon into the room. Looking around at the men on the many other cots, he saw that some were still, while others thrashed and cried out. He realized that he must have been here several days, since the moon had been waxing the night he and the others were captured. He wondered what had happened to the sergeant and Jacobs. Despite the throbbing wound in his left shoulder, he lapsed into a fitful sleep.

The next morning, Rob woke to find Tim Foley staring down at him. "You need to start eating or, sure, you will die." Easing himself down on the side of Rob's cot, Foley stretched his left leg out and grimaced. "Here, young Johnson, eat this gruel," he said as he shoved the thin, gray mush into Rob's mouth.

"You're not a Yankee soldier, are you?" Rob looked at Foley's nondescript clothing. "How did you get here?"

"I came over from Ireland with the holy sisters who nurse at this place. I've been with them since the bad times, when they found me dying in the street. They took me in and saved me life, those sainted women did." Foley crossed himself and grinned. "You see, I'm meant for a purpose. Now eat your food. It's scarce enough here."

"Where am I?"

"This is Point Lookout Prison Camp. It's on a great body of water called the Chesapeake in Maryland." Foley looked away. "Me brother died in just such a place in Ireland. He was stolen from me, don't you see. But you have the look of him, young Johnson, and I'll do me best to see you survive."

Rob went through periods of troubled haunted sleep and painful wakefulness. Near evening, an older man, also a prisoner, moved among the cots and talked quietly with each man. "Take this. It's sent by the

Yankee doctor." He lingered at Rob's bedside. Slipping a potion into the patient's tin cup, he smiled. "This is from the Irishman. Sweet dreams, soldier."

Soon Rob's torn body began to relax, and his mind drifted again. He saw purple rows of hills sloping down to the river. As he walked along the lane to the farm, he caught the scent of wild roses. His mother's face floated before him. "Now, boy, now is the time to repent," she told him. Weak and listless, he turned his face to the wall.

* * * *

A week later, Rob was escorted back to his tent. Clinging to Tim Foley's arm, he walked slowly but steadily. A guard followed close behind. The first night in the tent Rob found that he was far too weak to move. But others were restless and tossed constantly. Lenny, a short gawky boy from the back country of Georgia, shot up from his place on the sandy floor and ran out the door.

"Get him," one of the men shouted. He and another prisoner ran after Lenny.

They called softly, "Get back here, boy. They'll shoot you."

Alert, Rob tried to pick up every sound. Shuffling noises and low whispers came from the rear of the tent.

"Oh, good Lord," the man next to him muttered. "Lenny's gone crazy again. Might as well let them guards shoot him and be done with it."

"Shut up, Fritz," a deep voice said. "The boy is sick. You want him to shit in the tent?"

When the shot rang out into the cold, damp darkness, even those who had expected it looked shocked. The one called Fritz started praying in German, while others ran to the door. The men who had known Lenny sat in stunned silence. Rob realized now that he might not survive here.

The next morning, the men divided up Lenny's meager belongings and someone threw Rob a small book. The book turned out to be a journal, never used by the unfortunate Lenny.

"Why was he shot?" Rob asked.

"Damn fool got too close to the deadline," was the terse reply. Later, Rob found out that this was a ten-foot strip starting at the parapet wall. Any prisoner crossing it, or even getting near it, was shot.

At roll call, three men were assigned to burial detail. "Who's gonna say a few words over him?" Fritz asked.

"Shut up," the guard ordered.

Rob didn't hear any more. His legs collapsed under him as he lost consciousness. Later, he found that he had escaped a work detail yet one more day.

It took Rob a few days to comprehend his surroundings. The camp, packed beyond capacity with hopeless fearful men, was enclosed on three sides by a five-foot parapet wall. The fourth border was the Chesapeake Bay. The common soldiers were held in a large guarded area consisting of about 30 acres of barren sand. Tents were pitched in rows, divided by mucky paths. A large latrine area spread to the rear of the tents. When necessity forced Rob into that area, the sour, cloying smell almost choked him.

That night, fog rolled in from the bay and it turned much colder, with a bitter northeast wind bringing sleet. Tim Foley came into the tent and found Rob huddled in his blankets. "Your Sergeant Williams and Private Jacobs are here. They've been put on roadwork. You'll likely be joining them soon." Foley looked critically at the bone-thin prisoner. "Here's my advice. Catch anything that runs, crawls, or flies near your tent. I hear the rations are to be cut again."

In the days to come, Rob was to remember Foley's words.

* * * *

"You'd be living the good life if you'd stayed with the Quakers," Sergeant Williams said as he dumped a wheelbarrow of oyster shells. Rob started raking them onto the roadway.

"They told me to leave due to my immoral ways. 'Get thee wed, or get thee gone.'" Rob shrugged.

Under the watchful eye of the guard, Williams nodded as he turned the wheelbarrow, making way for Jacobs with the next load.

"Tim Foley says to tell you you've got mail. We're betting on which woman's sent you a love note."

"You've got a wicked tongue, Jacobs." Rob continued raking, although his left shoulder was throbbing with pain.

As the sergeant moved slowly back to the road, Rob noted how thin and haggard he had become. "Rob," he spoke quietly. "Foley has a clean-up detail for us in the church. He's a good man."

Later that night, Foley directed the three men as to what needed to be done in the church. The sweeping and scrubbing was easy work, and Tim Foley had promised them some supper.

"So, who was the letter from?" Jacobs asked.

"It's none of your concern." Rob looked irritated. "But the lady promised to send a food parcel."

"The guards will take it," Tim said. "They're a thieving lot, but I've saved up a few treats for you boys."

Back in Tim's small cubbyhole off the nun's quarters, the men sat on the floor and gorged themselves on fresh oysters and cabbage soup.

"How did you come by all this?" Sergeant Williams seemed amazed.

"I know the right people, oystermen and farm folk who'll trade with me. They can see I'm not a Yankee."

"What do you have to trade?" Jacobs asked.

"I'm a poor man, sure. But I have friends. I can get the key to the contraband quarters and the dear nuns never inventory the altar wine." Foley winked. "I'm trusted, you see."

"Trust is a good thing," Sergeant Williams said.

* * * *

The mounds of oyster shells regulated Rob's days. They either had to be loaded or spread out. This cold December morning the wind was coming from the east, pushing white caps up the bay. Working near the prison gates, he could see the stacks of waiting coffins. Even in the short time he'd been here, many had died of fever and dysentery. Many more were sick. He watched the flocks of gulls soaring overhead. Their sharp cries chilled his bones. He knew he was going to die here in this alien place.

Ignoring the pain in his shoulder, he raked faster. The letter he had received from Abigail Treverton ran through his mind. He could remember every word.

> *Dear Rob, Please thank Sister Mary Teresa for getting thy letter to me. She said a mutual friend at the prison arranged it. I feel responsible that thee is now in a Union prison. If it were not for me and all the problems I caused, thee would never have gone back into the army and would still be safe here among us.*
>
> *Although I do not regret that sweet time we spent together, I know that I was selfish to seek thee out. I hope that the war will soon end and I will see thee again. My new husband is a cold, old man who won't let me out of his sight. His grand home was all but destroyed by the Rebels billeted there, so we've had to move to my parent's farmhouse. Please keep thyself safe and know that I send thee my love. Abigail.*

Smiling, Rob leaned on the rake and stared out at the bay.

"Get busy, Reb," the guard shouted down from the watchtower.

* * * *

The long days ran one into another and Rob started writing sporadically in the journal.

> *Christmas at Point Lookout —The holy day passed with little notice. The prisoners got the day off and could attend*

church services. Some of the men received packages from home and shared out the treats. Jacobs was assigned to my tent, which is good, but he talks too much. I was weary and slept most of the day.

Spring 1864—My shoulder wound has healed, but I've gotten skinnier than Snyder's hound. Rations have been cut again. It's hard to survive on two cups of beans and a handful of rice a day. One of the guards told me this was done in retaliation for ration cuts at Confederate prisons. A boy from South Carolina was brought in yesterday. He says there ain't no food left in the South for anybody. Here, one of the prisoners I know dies almost every day.

June—I received a letter from Mary O'Ferrall: Dear Rob, I hope you get this letter and you are surviving. We hear that the camps are brutal. We manage here at home, but live under martial law and are constantly beset by the Yankee town folks. They are worse than the Union Army. All of us here think of you and wish you well. Stay strong. Your friend, Mary O'Ferrall.

I thought of what she could not say since the Union guards censor our mail. A recently captured sergeant from the 21st Virginia Infantry told me that in March, Trip O'Ferrall and his cavalry had stolen horses from the Union Leaguers in Bath and taken prisoners. He said there was much bitterness over this.

July—The guards say that Atlanta is under attack. It's long been told around camp that Jeff Davis believes if the South can hold Atlanta, the North will give up the fight. I ain't so sure of this. We are nearing the end. The sergeant's not well and we see little of him. Tim says he's been moved to the infirmary. Jacobs fell and cut himself up on the oyster shells he was raking. He's been moaning like a baby.

August—The heat has gotten unbearable. I long to swim in the brackish bay water, but we are not allowed. I see schools of fish pass near shore, but our meals include little meat of any kind. Tim Foley keeps up with us and slips us food when he can. He's also been able to find me a few books left by those who no longer need them. Right now I'm reading 'Moby Dick.' It's hard for me to understand the life at sea, but it's a good story. I've tried to pass the books on to Jacobs, but he ain't interested. The sergeant is still in the infirmary. It doesn't look good for him.

September—We've heard that Atlanta has fallen. One of the new boys in the tent says that our troops destroyed their own supply wagons when the Yankees were set to enter the city. What a waste. Yesterday, he refused to go on work detail and has been thrown in the lock-up. I don't look for him to last long here.

Laura hasn't answered my letters at all. There has been no mail from Abigail in months. When I sleep, I dream of her. Then I see my mother's face. She calls out the name of Laura's child, Melinda. My dreams bring me back to the farm, the land that will be waiting for me when this war is over. I walk every foot of it during the long desperate nights.

October—I figure that my days on earth are numbered. Jacobs and I are among the few remaining soldiers who started out the year in this tent. Many of the others have departed, some to the infirmary, some to the prisoners' graveyard and new men keep arriving. News travels fast. We know that Petersburg has fallen and, finally, that Richmond has fallen. We hear tales of Sheridan's rampage in the Shenandoah Valley. I'm glad that it will all be over soon.

November—I have been at Point Lookout Prison for over a year. So much has changed around me. So many have died, but I'm still alive. I often wonder why. God help me.

Rob shut the journal and watched the snow drift silently over the steel-gray water. The flurries obscured the outline of the *Minnesota*, a 60-gun Union warship anchored offshore. All sixty guns were aimed at the prison camp. He had heard that only forty prisoners had ever escaped this hellhole.

* * * *

Rob shuffled along with the work detail. He could see that wind-driven snow was piling up on the roadway. At the pier, a large skipjack, the *Lorena*, was waiting to be unloaded.

Standing on deck, the short barrel-chested captain barked orders. "Be quick. I'm in a hurry to be off." Moving to the gangplank, he spoke to the guards. "These men don't have proper shoes. Some have sacks wrapped around their feet. If they slip and drop my oysters, there'll be hell to pay. You hear?"

Staring at the captain sullenly, the corporal stepped forward. "This is the crap we got to work with. But they ain't going to drop nothing. They ain't that stupid."

As Rob made his way down the gangplank, he could feel his feet slipping on the icy boards. He shifted his weight to accommodate the heavy crate of oysters. Reaching solid ground, he drew a deep breath of relief as he set the crate on the waiting wagon. A sharp scream behind him was met with shouts and curses from the guards and the captain. Turning, Rob saw that Jacobs and his crate of oysters had landed at the foot of the gangplank. Oysters were scattered everywhere. Quickly covered by the snow, they would soon disappear. When Rob reached him, Jacobs was trying to dodge the kicks and blows delivered by the guards. No one complained when Rob started helping to scoop up the oysters.

"Here, what's going on?" Tim Foley's voice rose above the furor. He limped through the snow and stood over Jacobs and Rob.

"This stupid Reb sunnavabitch dropped a crate of oysters. He's going to pay with his hide," the corporal shouted.

"Is he, now? Then let me deal with him. I need men to clean out the smallpox stockade."

Grudgingly, the corporal nodded and walked back toward the ship. Turning, he said, "Good you showed up, Foley. Whatever these dumb bastards can scoop out of the snow is your nuns' crate of oysters. Now, get these men out of my sight."

The snow was swirling in thick gusts, bringing with it the salt smell of the bay. Tim Foley grumbled and cursed the Union Army as he limped back to Hammond Hospital. Rob and Jacobs followed close behind, sliding and stumbling as they carried the crate of oysters between them. An unhappy-looking guard trailed them about halfway, then turned back.

When they reached the shelter of the nun's quarters, Rob and Jacobs collapsed on the floor. "Come, lads. We must get this crate to the cook, then head for the stockade." Foley urged them on. Numbed by the cold, they followed. Grabbing what food he could as they passed through the large kitchen, Tim led them back into the storm.

CHAPTER 23

THE PEST HOUSE

WINTER 1864

The smallpox stockade consisted of a fifteen-foot-high log parapet wall, which enclosed a small shabby wooden building. Inside, Rob looked around at the empty cots, which filled the two mean rooms. Inhaling the sharp rank smell of illness and carbolic, Rob felt the desolation and despair of the place pass through him.

Making the sign of the cross, Tim Foley muttered, "Poor sods. The southern lads they send here don't have much of a chance." He limped toward a closet. "Here, we must get started. New patients could come through the door at any time." After he handed out buckets, brooms and mops, Tim set about making a fire in the stove. "You boys scoop snow into them buckets, and we'll melt it here."

As Rob was sweeping up the litter, a large rat raced across the floor in front of him. Jacobs moved in on the rat and slammed his bucket down, narrowly missing his prey. "Damn," he shouted. "I almost had the little bugger. Could've sold him for a Yankee dollar back at camp."

"Or, you could stew him up with a little seaweed," Rob said in disgust.

"Boys, it will soon come to that." Foley's sad face took on an even more forlorn expression. "That's why we need to talk."

Alerted by voices, Tim moved to the door and edged it open. "A detail is bringing in two patients. We must move lively, now." Pointing to a pile of sheets and thin worn blankets, he indicated that his helpers should make up two cots.

Although the new arrivals were waiting at the door, Rob could hear Tim arguing with the litter-bearers. "I'll be needing written orders to take in these men. Where is Doctor Hodges?"

"He ain't around, Mick. And we ain't allowed to bring these two back into camp. They won't trouble you for long. Be dead by tomorrow." Laughing, the soldiers walked out the door.

"Wait. Who's in charge of the smallpox ward? I can't admit them."

"Damn you, man. You're here, so you're in charge. They're your problem." The parapet gate banged shut behind the Union soldiers.

Indeed, the first patient looked close to death. Large pustules were scattered across his face and arms. He was an older man, and stared up at them in resignation. Stepping backward, Jacobs shook his head.

Kneeling down beside the man, Rob stared into his eyes. "What can we do for you? Do you need a letter sent?"

Nodding his head, the man spoke in the soft twang of the hill country. "My name is Jett Marshall, 2nd Virginia Cavalry. I'm from Jefferson County, near Charles Town. Please send word to my wife." He fell back on the cot and closed his eyes.

Tim was bending over the other patient, who was younger, stronger, and in the earlier stages of the disease. "There is a chance for this lad. Says his name is Mason Rowe from Maryland." He smiled down at the man. "See, his rash is just developing." Tim indicated the small red bumps forming on the young soldier's face.

* * * *

The next day, Rob and Jacobs found themselves assigned to the Smallpox Stockade. Tim Foley had also been pressed into service, as the nuns had been unable to save him from this fate.

Squaring his shoulders, Tim faced his unhappy helpers. "I'm sorry, lads. I hadn't planned on this." He limped over to the supply closet and found towels and bedpans. "Seems the regular man here went on leave and came down with the fever. His crew has gone over the fence, as they say."

"But we don't know nothing about doctoring," Jacobs moaned.

"I only know the little the nuns have taught me. But, look on the bright side. You'll get more to eat." Tim looked serious. "I hear the rations for prisoners are to be cut again."

"Hey, Rob, would you rather die slow of starvation or quick of fever?" Jacobs asked.

"Shut up, Jacobs. This ain't Foley's fault. Maybe there's some way it can work to our advantage."

Tim Foley motioned for the others to sit on one of the sagging cots. "I've been thinking on that very thing. I've got the mists of a plan forming. How would you lads like to get out of this place? I'll be coming with you, of course."

"I'd like to be home for Christmas." Jacobs smiled wistfully.

"The grand plan needs some arranging. Just say your prayers, lads."

Rob looked away. He put little faith in Foley's plans, as the man was a dreamer. Besides, Rob had seen his destiny in several harrowing nightmares. He knew one of the stacked coffins at the camp gate had his name on it. With whatever short time was left to him, he felt he had to concentrate on getting a message out to Abigail. He owed her that much.

* * * *

It snowed again overnight, giving the prison camp a pristine look. At six in the morning the clanging of the parapet gate alerted them and Tim limped over to the window.

"Lads, be quick. Bring stretchers to the yard. We have a wagonload of new patients to sort out."

As the first of the fevered prisoners was lifted off the wagon, Tim Foley confronted the sergeant in charge. "Here," he shouted, "We'll be needing the doctor present to admit patients."

"The doctors are all busy. Just do what you usually do, Mick." The sergeant turned toward the wagon, then hesitated. "Look, I'm sorry for these poor bastards. I'm a Christian man myself. But they're in God's hands now, not yours." He supervised the unloading of the prisoners, then moved his detail off through the snow.

By nightfall, two of the twelve patients had died. Their wasted, pock-marked bodies were shrouded and placed near the door. One of the dead was Jett Marshall from Jefferson County. Rob had written a letter to Mrs. Marshall, but Jett had been too weak to sign it. Rob had heard stories in camp that the Yankee armies led by General Sheridan were burning and pillaging in the Valley. Jett Marshall would have had little left to go home to, and now he'd be buried here in this foreign land.

Including his own letter to Abigail in the mail pouch, Rob hoped it would reach her. Rumor had it that prisoners' mail was routinely destroyed, but he thought that even the Yankees would send on deathbed letters. Afraid his writing would convey his mournful mood, Rob had tried to focus on the time they had spent together and his feelings for her. If he did, indeed, die in this Godforsaken place, she should know that he had truly loved her.

Late at night, several more men seemed close to death. Rob and Jacobs worked to keep their fevers down. Applying cold wet compresses was only a token comfort, but these men were dying far from home and any scant attention was appreciated. Tim Foley had sent word to Dr. Hodges that there were men in need of a doctor and a priest, and that he must have more supplies.

Carrying a teapot, Tim limped toward the men. He smiled encouragingly and poured out a small amount for everyone. "This might do some good for all of us. It's a tincture brewed from the pitcher plant, a weed that grows in marshy bogs to the north." He drank his portion and grinned. "I feel far better already. The Indians used it to cure the pox."

"How did you come by it?" Jacobs looked puzzled.

"How, indeed? One of the fishermen was able to get it for me. A mate of his brought it south down the coast as far as Annapolis." Tim refilled the cups. "A waterman aboard the *Lorena* brought the parcel. I had to trade dear for this plant, but the nuns were willing to pay. It was their idea, you see."

"The nuns?" Finally paying attention to the conversation, Rob was confused. "How could Irish nuns know of Indian cures?"

"The good sisters to the north, of course. They minister to the heathen savages and call this Indian Cup Tea."

"Does it work?" Rob was now interested.

"Who's to know? I pray to Mother Mary and all the saints it does, as we have little else to offer."

* * * *

Toward morning, some of the sickest men looked close to death. Others were retching and suffering from high fevers. Tim kept the stove stoked and gave his tea to anyone strong enough to sip the brew. The warmth spreading from the stove heightened the cloying odor of sickness and unwashed bodies. Rob wished he could breathe in fresh air and escape the moans and cries of the afflicted. He was as trapped as they were.

"How did you get the extra load of wood?" he asked. "There's little enough firewood in the tents."

"Even the Union Army dare not let men freeze before they die of the pox." Tim smiled grimly.

Steeping a new batch of Indian Cup Tea, Rob poured a small amount of honey into the pot. It was going to be a long day.

"When are we going to get the pox?" Jacobs had come up behind him.

Rob straightened up and faced him. "I wonder about that all the time. I figure that's how I'll leave this world." Rob couldn't see any sense in lying. "I'll never see my baby daughter again."

"Thought you said she wasn't your child."

"These days, I think a lot about Laura and the little girl. Laura never had a chance in life."

"Don't tell me you're twisting in the wind again. What about Abigail? And what about the parcel you been looking to get?"

"Abigail? She's much too good for me. Besides, she's a married woman now." Rob started pouring the tea into beakers. "I doubt the parcel will ever find us here."

Trying to get patients to drink the dark liquid was a tedious task. Rob tried cajoling the men, telling them jokes, giving them the hope he, himself, didn't have. Mason Rowe, the soldier from Maryland who had shown improvement, was now fighting the outbreak of large pustules.

"There ain't no cure, so get that nasty tea away from me." Mason tried to shove away the beaker.

"The nuns think this is a cure. They've prayed over it." Tim Foley joined the group.

"They can pray for me when I'm dead. Now I want to be left alone." Mason Rowe turned toward the wall.

"He's feverish. We'll leave the lad for now." Tim limped toward the next cot. Carrying a tray of supplies, Jacobs followed him.

The next patient was too weak to complain. "I want to be showing you how to dress these sores." Tim reached for a weak vinegar solution. Jacobs backed away as Tim gently dabbed at the pustules on the man's face. "We're wanting these to dry out. Hand me that jar of limp seed ointment."

"I can't do this." Jacobs looked away. "I'll get the pox for sure."

"Listen, lad, if you were meant to get the smallpox, you would already have it. You told me that a man in your tent took sick two weeks ago. The pox is passed from man to man and the incubation time is twelve days."

Seeing the horror in Jacobs' eyes, Rob added, "Not everyone gets the disease. You and I grew up on farms. Doc Hodges says years of milking cows can keep people from getting the disease, even though they ain't been pin-pricked with a vaccination."

"I'm the one who should be worrying." Tim didn't look at all worried. "I grew up in a city, not in the midst of a dairy herd. But the nuns have given me enough saints' medals to weigh meself down." He motioned them on to the next cot. "Besides, over half of pox victims recover, especially the strong healthy ones."

Jacobs handed Tim the tray. "I'll help out, but I won't touch those sores."

Rob stepped in and picked up the vinegar wash. "No need, Jacobs. Tim and I can handle it." He grinned at the terrified man.

"Jacobs, there's a good lad," Tim said, "Sweep up a bit, then mop with hot water and carbolic."

Toward evening, Rob found Jacobs reading a tattered Bible left by the nuns. He looked up. "I ain't had much time for religion, but there's not much else left."

Most of the men had fallen into fitful sleep when Jacobs started to sing. At first, he concentrated on old-time hymns, then he sang Christmas carols. His clear tenor voice carried into the night. Sometimes Tim and Rob joined in the chorus. Rob was amazed to see that several of the men tried to sit up and sing along, but weren't strong enough. Hope was still alive, even here in this place.

No one noticed Dr. Hodges standing in the doorway. A small, heavyset man, he appeared transfixed at the scene before him. The sick men, all stricken with fever and some near death, were focused on the young man who sang like an angel.

By morning, the young soldier, Mason Rowe from Maryland, had started to improve. Whether this was due to Tim's tea or Jacobs' singing was hard to say. Tim had also lit candles to the Virgin, so he knew who to thank for this miracle.

That afternoon Dr. Hodges returned and sought out Tim Foley. The two men walked outside and were gone for some time. Finding Jacobs hovering near the door, Rob knew he was trying to catch bits of conversation.

"So, what's going on?"

"I've heard my name a few times and something about Christmas," Jacobs said. "I hope I won't be sent to the big hospital."

"You might live longer there."

Jacobs pulled a long face, limped over to Rob and said in a thick brogue, "We're all in this life to die, lad. Say your prayers."

Rob found himself actually smiling. "You'd best not let himself catch you making light of religion." Rob's smile broadened as he saw the flicker of concern on Jacobs' face. He scuttled back to work just as the door opened.

"Ah, Rob." Tim Foley looked quite pleased. "Where is Jacobs?"

Passing them, Dr. Hodges started on his rounds and finally caught up with Jacobs in the back room. Watching the two in conversation, Rob could see Jacobs nodding his head in agreement.

As he left, the doctor shook Tim's hand. "You and your men are doing a fine job under difficult conditions. I'm most pleased that the young Maryland soldier is holding his own. The disease will run its course, but he has a chance."

As soon as the parapet gate shut, Jacobs let out a yell. "Boys, we'll have a good Christmas now. The doc has promised a real feast with roast turkey for everyone here." His eyes gleamed with pure delight. "And all for the singing of a few songs at General Marston's Christmas party."

Tim also seemed excited. "Why, this fits right into the grand plan. It couldn't be better."

Dark winter days stretched on toward Christmas. The nuns managed to send a tub of applesauce and several containers of sauerkraut to the smallpox stockade. Tim traded altar wine to local farmers for some smoked sausage, but overall, the patients' diet was poor. Eight of the men survived and Tim Foley vowed he would not lose one more.

* * * *

On December twenty-first, the shortest day of the year, a new patient was brought in. Rob noticed immediately that the man appeared alert. His eyes tracked Rob as he moved around the room. At suppertime, Tim called Rob and Jacobs into the back room he had set aside for the latest arrival.

"Lads, I want you to meet Isaac Pryor, out newest guest." Rob realized that this gesture was unusual in itself, as most new arrivals were too ill and fevered to meet anyone.

Propped up on pillows, Isaac Pryor looked relaxed, not ill. Young and wiry, he looked like he was ready for a day on an oyster boat, not a turn in the Smallpox Stockade. Moreover, the skin on his face was clear, save for several small red marks, which were already melting away in the heat of the room. Isaac mopped his cheeks with a red kerchief. "Damn stuff's dripping, Tim. You ain't much of an artist."

Tim nodded solemnly. "You passed the test, though. You're here." Turning to the others, Tim said, "This lad is the best waterman on the bay. He's crewed on blockade runners. The Yankees captured him sailing up the Potomac in a boat loaded with medical supplies. We're honored to have him among us."

Grinning, Isaac extended his hard calloused hand. "Pleased to meet you. I hear you're tired of this prison camp. So am I." His speech was slow and accented with the local waterman's dialect.

"Lads, things are fitting into place, now that we have Isaac." Tim looked at each man in turn. "The Christmas caroling will give the three of us a reason to be out and about. Isaac's mate, Mike, will land a small boat on the beach."

"The *Minnesota* is waiting off-shore," Jacobs grumbled.

* * * *

By Christmas Eve, neither of the "Pest House lads," as Tim called his helpers, had come down with smallpox. Jacobs' mood seemed to lighten as the day drew on. Dragging in scrub pine branches, he tied them around the window frames. Several of the patients, including Mason Rowe, were showing signs of recovery. When Tim came through the door dragging a small Christmas tree, the men gave out a ragged cheer. Pulling sand and various-sized shells from his pockets, Tim motioned to Jacobs. Using the yellow twine meant to cordon off quarantines, they tied shells on the scraggly tree, topping it with a corncob angel Mason had fashioned.

Praying that the weather would hold, Rob stared out the window at the gathering clouds. He was committed to going along with Tim's crazy plan. He had nothing to lose. As he was gathering up his few belongings, he thought about the chance they would be taking on this night. If all went well, they would slip away after the Christmas caroling.

Night fell early, and Rob was thankful for the cold dense fog that shrouded Point Lookout. He found Tim Foley walking in the yard.

"All is ready, lad. Soon you'll be a free man."

Nodding uneasily, Rob asked, "What about Sergeant Williams? Is there any way we can take him?"

"The man is suffering from malaria fever. He's far too sick to travel."

"I feel bad about leaving him. But you, Tim, why do you go with us? It's a risk you don't have to take."

"In a way, you're right. But what future do I have, with little money and nowhere to go? Besides, you're me mates."

"What of the dear nuns?"

"Sure, and they'll understand. I've left them a note."

Both men looked up at the sound of jangling harnesses and the creak of wagon wheels. The gate swung open, allowing Dr. Hodges and a group of Union soldiers to ride into the yard. A heavily laden wagon followed.

"Merry Christmas, men," the doctor called. "I've brought you the promised Christmas feast. Your replacements are with me and will begin duty tonight. Quite a Christmas present, eh?" He beamed down at Rob and Tim. "You men have done an excellent job, and will be commended to the superintendent. You'll leave here tonight and report back to the tents."

"Thank you, sir, but we have no wish to leave." Tim looked confused. "Most of the patients are gaining strength."

"That may be, Foley, but these soldiers are trained. This is work for the Union Army." Dr. Hodges wished everyone a merry Christmas and left.

The new Yankee medical team did not look happy to be spending Christmas Eve in the pest house. After inspecting the small rooms, the heavy-set sergeant sought out Tim.

"This place don't even have necessary supplies." The sergeant breathed heavily as he confronted his predecessor. "Are you sure you Johnnies weren't out peddling Union medical supplies or, worse yet, passing them on to blockade runners?"

"Begging your pardon, sergeant." Tim looked offended. "I'm a civilian and these men have not left the stockade. We found little enough here when we arrived."

"I have my men doing a count now." The sergeant carefully wiped his glasses with a large bandana. "The Union Army's got standards."

"Yes, to be sure," Tim said. "Will you be taking Christmas Eve dinner with us?"

"Hell, no. We got a job to do." He walked away, then turned. "Before your grand feast, Foley, you and your men get rid of that corpse lying at the entrance. Enter time of death and follow all other U.S. Army procedures. You hear?"

* * * *

Tim and Rob carefully loaded the blanket-covered body into the new wagon brought by the Yankees. As Rob guided the horses through the stockade gate, a loud thumping sound came from the back of the wagon.

"Pipe down, Isaac," Tim called softly. "You're supposed to be in the next world with the angels."

Arriving at the nuns' quarters, the two men carried Isaac into Tim's small room. "Don't make a sound," Tim cautioned. "We'll be back for you."

Returning to the wagon, Rob looked doubtful. "What if the Yankee sergeant looks into Isaac's whereabouts?"

"Don't worry, lad. He's too busy supervising the bandage counting." Tim grinned. "Besides, he's a cold-hearted bastard. What does he care about a dead Reb?"

"The whole thing is riskier now than ever. What if he won't let us go with Jacobs?" Rob looked narrowly at Tim Foley. "What about the guards on the palisade catwalk? This fog could lift and we'd be sitting ducks."

"I've given much thought to the guards, lad. It will work out. As for Jacobs, he has a command performance, and we are part of his act." Tim grinned confidently. "It's now or never, me boy. Just say your prayers."

* * * *

Back at the smallpox stockade, the warmth and the aroma of food made the place almost welcoming. Rob knew that he'd had it much better than those poor fellows in the tents, although they hadn't risked catching the pox. He and Tim ate quickly. At the other side of the room, Jacobs had finished his meal and was trying to brush and clean his random pieces of clothing. With the Yankees away stacking supplies in the back room, the atmosphere was almost peaceful.

"I'm going to sing one last song for you boys," Jacobs called out to the patients. He grinned the old devilish grin that Rob had learned to view with caution. "This is for Mason Rowe." Then Jacobs launched into a stirring rendition of *Maryland, my Maryland*. His tenor voice hit all the high notes, and Rob could see that the men were moved. Mason Rowe looked close to tears. Just as Jacobs finished the first verse, the Yankee sergeant charged into the room.

"Stop! This ain't the music Dr. Hodges wants to hear." The sergeant's double chins shook and his pale eyes bulged. "Reynolds," he shouted, "Escort these men out of here. Stay with them and see them back to the tents later." Turning to Jacobs, he assumed a hard, commanding tone. "Out of here, you Rebel scum. You men ain't got no appreciation for the good turn you been done." He stomped off.

Shouldering their packs, the men followed Tim through the stockade gate and none of them looked back. Private Reynolds, gun at the ready, followed close behind. They stumbled along the path through the thick fog.

"We need to be going to the home of General Marston," Tim called back to Reynolds. There was no response. Tim shot Rob a worried look.

As the group headed to General Marston's quarters, they passed soldiers in groups of two and threes headed to the service at the Yankee chapel. Approaching them through the fog, the Yankees called out "Merry Christmas," unaware they were passing prisoners under escort.

Entering the general's home by the back door, the men were confronted by a small gray-haired woman. Wrinkling her nose, she addressed Private Reynolds, "These men ain't going to be allowed anywheres near the general in this condition." She surveyed the three men. "Take them to General Marston's personal servant, William Baker. He'll know what to do."

Private Reynolds stood his ground and stared back at the tiny woman.

"Did you hear me, boy? Lower that rifle and do what I tell you." Reynolds stood motionless. "Go through that door." The woman waved her arm toward the door. "Now, get this bunch out of here."

Private Reynolds finally turned toward the door.

"Begging your pardon, ma'am," Tim said. "Is Maggie Murray working here this night?"

"What would the likes of you want with Maggie? She has nothing to do with prisoners."

"My name is Tim Foley. I traveled here with the Irish nuns and have been working with the sick and wounded. I see Maggie at mass and found that she comes from a village near my home." Tim looked deeply offended. "I only wanted to wish her a good Christmas."

"I see." The small woman seemed to weigh his story. "I ain't promising, but I'll try to find her. We're all busy tonight." Turning her attention to the Yankee private, she pointed again at the door. "Get out of here, you idiot, or I'll set the general himself on you."

* * * *

When Rob and his companions entered the brightly lit hall, they were clad as seamen. This was the only clothing available in the former homeowner's sea chest. Richly dressed women and their blue-clad escorts were grouped around the room. Few noticed as the small band of seamen took their places near the Christmas tree. While Jacobs conferred with the piano player, Rob noticed that both Tim and Private Reynolds had disappeared. He took the moment to look over the audience. Most of the women were dowdy and middle-aged. Here and there, a few young women were talking and laughing with the junior officers.

For just an instant, Rob glimpsed a slim girl with coils of red hair piled high on her head. He would have known her anywhere. Years ago, Fannie Swann had told him she would dress in silk gowns and dance at fancy balls.

She must have felt his gaze on her, because she turned and looked directly at him. Smiling, Fannie left her group of admirers and walked toward the Christmas tree. "Rob Johnson, you turn up in the most surprising places. What happened to the fine Richmond gentleman?" She was wearing a sky-blue gown. Her smile was radiant.

"Fannie, you look beautiful." He grinned at her. "Are you the same skinny country girl I knew back in Morgan County?"

Fannie threw back her head and laughed. He remembered her laughter. "I've always told you I have big dreams, Rob. You know that."

"I had no idea what had happened to you. Why did you run away that night on the train out of Richmond?"

"I saw an opportunity and I needed money. I always need money."

Rob stared at her. "It was you who sold the Negroes to that gang of slave hunters?" He felt his anger rise. "How could you do that?"

"You weren't hurt, were you? That was on my orders. Don't look at me that way." Casually, she glanced over his seaman's outfit. "I heard that prisoners were to perform tonight. First I spotted that little hellion, Jacobs, then I saw you. Fate keeps throwing us together."

"I see fate's been good to you. Where's your Southern patriotism?"

Still smiling, Fannie turned to go. "The ship is sinking, Rob. Now, you may need my help."

He stared as Fannie moved gracefully away, meeting a tall Union officer and taking his arm. Rob wondered how he could despise her and still want her. Worse yet, Fannie had done the deed that he had blamed Laura for all this time.

"We're ready." Jacobs had come up behind him. "I see that your red-headed tart is here entertaining the Yankees."

Rob rounded on him. "Shut your mouth, Jacobs, or I'll toss your ass into that fancy Christmas tree and there won't be no concert."

Tim was grinning broadly as he joined them. "Where have you been?" Rob asked.

"Never you fear, lad. Things are going nicely."

"Where's the Yankee private?"

"Reynolds is enjoying a bit of Christmas cheer back in the kitchen. I'm thinking he won't be a problem."

The audience hushed as Jacobs sang the first clear notes of *Silent Night*. Standing a discreet distance away, Rob and Tim sang harmony. People crowded forward with requests, mostly for old-time Christmas songs. Jacobs' strong voice filled the room.

Next, he and Tim sang *The Girl I Left Behind Me*, which ended with a standing ovation from the audience. As the show ended, people shook Jacobs' hand and gave him money. *It was ironic*, Rob thought, *that this young prisoner, capable of causing such an outpouring of emotion by these people, would soon be risking his life to escape from them.*

Following Tim through the cluttered kitchen toward the back door, Rob realized that Private Reynolds was nowhere to be seen. As they started down the driveway, Rob touched Tim's shoulder. "Where's Reynolds?"

"He took a liking to Maggie Murray and he wasn't turning down a drink of whiskey either."

Jacobs was in high spirits. "I'll buy you all a drink when we get out of this God awful place," he promised.

Tim looked back at him. "Don't worry, lad, we're working up a mighty thirst."

CHAPTER 24

THE ESCAPE

CHRISTMAS 1864

The fog was still thick as pea soup when the group arrived at the nuns' quarters. They found Isaac waiting by the door. "The tide will turn soon. We need to get out of here." He grabbed his pack and headed to the door.

"Hold up, lad. Let me have a look around outside." Tim slipped through the door.

While they waited, Rob watched as Isaac paced the floor in the tiny room. He wondered again what chance they really had of making it to freedom.

When Tim returned, he, too, seemed to have a sense of urgency. "The wind has picked up. If we don't start moving now, the fog may lift before we're in the clear."

Outside, heavy mist swirled around them, but breaks in the dense masses were starting to appear. The men moved quickly as they headed toward the shore. Tim limped behind the others and Rob hung back to help him along. Isaac seemed to know the area and guided them to the palisade wall. Rob could see guards walking on the catwalk and heard some of their conversation.

Motioning the others to wait in the shadows, Tim approached the wall. "Merry Christmas to you, lads," he called up to the two soldiers.

Stopping to peer down at him, the guards hollered a greeting. Tim stepped closer to the wall. "All seems quiet enough. Have the Johnnies been on their good behavior, then?"

"They have, Mr. Foley. No trouble at all. Have you brought us that bit of Christmas cheer you promised?"

"To be sure, lads. Pass down the basket," Tim said. The others moved on and Rob stumbled after them. He could barely hear Tim's voice. The sound of waves hitting the sandy shore became louder and soon the men were scrambling along the beach.

The thought of Fannie's treachery galled Rob. As he tried to concentrate on keeping his balance in the sand, he saw Fannie's pretty face and heard her laugh. He saw the guile in her eyes. His mouth went dry and he had to force himself forward through the darkness. Ahead, Jacobs staggered and fell, letting out of cry of pain.

"Halt! Who goes there?" The voice sounded very close. Moments passed in silence. "I say, who goes there?"

Off to the left, Rob heard the rasp of a rifle being loaded. He could feel his heart begin to race and could barely resist the urge to run out into the blackness.

"Simmons, there may be intruders here," the voice called again. "Get the sergeant."

"Is it you, Private O'Malley?" Tim called. "Here, lad, I've brought you some Christmas cheer. It's a sad thing to guard a lonely beachfront on Holy Night."

Rob could hear Tim approaching off to the right. He had started singing and banging out the beat on a tin canteen. Rob and the others slipped away toward the sound of the crashing waves and headed to the left parapet wall, as Isaac had instructed. Gusts of wind were hitting the beach and lifting the blanket of fog. Moonlight broke through the clouds and revealed the outline of a small boat drawn up at the water's edge. Rob could make out movement aboard. As he drew closer, an arm reached out and hauled him into the boat.

"Get in quick," a voice ordered. "Where's Isaac?"

"Behind me," Rob whispered. "He stayed back to wait for Tim." Rob lowered his long frame onto a plank seat and waited.

Jacobs clamored on board next. The whites of his eyes shone in the darkness and his breath came in short gasps. "Ain't never liked water or boats," he whispered. "I can't swim."

When the others arrived, they shoved off. With Isaac and Rob rowing mightily, they cleared the surf.

"Can't raise the sail until we're well away from that damn gunboat," the boatman muttered. "Fog's lifting. We'd best be quick. Here, boys, take the other set of oars." He gestured at Tim and Jacobs.

The wind was shifting to the southeast, making the bay choppy and throwing briny spray over the group. "I'm chilled through to me bones," Tim said mournfully.

As the boatman steered the small craft around the Minnesota, laughter and verses of song drifted across the water. Expertly, he brought the boat past the hulking frigate and out into the open water.

"Well done, Mike," Isaac spoke into the freshening breeze, "and just in time." As he and Rob raised the ragged sail, shouts were heard from the *Minnesota*.

"Sail, ho. To starboard."

The men in the small boat still rowed, waiting for wind to catch the sail.

"Escapees. Get the first mate." The voices from the frigate became fainter.

By now, Mike had maneuvered his craft into the bay and the boat was racing toward Virginia's eastern shore. "We're almost out of range. We made it, boys!" Mike shouted, and a cheer went up from the men.

Jacobs was busy losing his fine dinner over the side when a cannon ball hit the water just feet away. Deftly, Mike brought the boat about and headed back toward the western shore. "Now things are getting interesting, so we'll have to tack more," he shouted.

Several more shots were fired, but the small sailboat was running away at a good clip. Jacobs, scared and thoroughly drenched, huddled on the floorboards and mumbled bits of Bible verse.

"They ain't gonna set out after us," Mike said. "It's Christmas."

* * * *

When the boat slipped around Walnut Point into Coan River, the men knew they were safe. Yankee patrol boats wouldn't venture into these shallow tidewater creeks and inlets. Traveling mostly at night, it took the men a week to reach Port Royal on the Rappahannock River. They dragged the boat ashore in a sheltered cove and hid it in marsh grass.

"We're near my home." Isaac looked toward the pine woods. "Wait here. I'll be back with food."

Black clouds were gathering to the east and light rain had begun to fall while they waited for Isaac. "It's shaping up to storm by evening, maybe even turn into a nor'easter," Mike observed. "I'm aiming to point this out to Isaac." Rob could see the worry in his eyes.

Isaac returned with a bulging sea bag. He didn't seem concerned about the weather and passed out tin plates heaped with oysters and cornbread.

"We've made it up this river many a time, Mike. Let's ask the boys how they feel."

"It suits me fine to get off the water," Jacobs said.

Rob had hoped to get further up-river toward Fredericksburg, but he was concerned about the weather. He said nothing.

Tim shook his head sadly. "Does this mean we must walk, then?"

"No, we've got three horses for you." Isaac said.

"We ain't got much money." Jacobs looked stricken.

"No need. I owe you. My family recently came by some Yankee mounts. Have the uniforms too, if you want them."

Rob looked over his seaman's garb. "These clothes will do."

Isaac nodded. "Be on the lookout for troop movements. My daddy got word from local watermen that the big Yankee fleet has reached Fort Fisher. Both sides will most likely be sending more men there."

* * * *

While the storm raged around them, the three travelers spent a cold, sleepless night in Isaac Pryor's barn. At dawn, they forded the river. There were no roads, so they rode through woods and frozen farmland. Rob would always remember the flocks of geese and swans feeding in the fields or flying in to settle on the waterways.

"We ain't going hungry with all these here birds around." Jacobs brightened and looked over the landscape with anticipation. "Matter-of-fact, there's a mighty lot of food in these swamps."

"You can have all this." Rob gazed around at the soggy, treacherous salt-marsh and breathed in the rank smell of decaying vegetation. "I can't wait to get back to the hills."

"We had places like this in Ireland," Tim said. "People went in and many didn't come out. There are stories told about the bogs." He shook his head.

Riding in front, Rob raised his hand. They had entered dense woods and were slowly making their way through a large grove of oaks. Jumping down onto the soggy ground, he led his horse to cover. The others followed and, within minutes, a Yankee patrol rode by. Looking back, Rob saw Tim crossing himself.

They had almost reached the small town of New Post when they next came upon the enemy. Cresting a small hill, they almost rode into a Union encampment. *The Bluecoats must have felt secure,* Rob thought, *as they had no sentry posted.* Racing their mounts back downhill, they heard the Yankees hollering orders. As they headed back into the marsh, their pursuers were right behind them. At the first bend in the trail, Rob jumped down and led his horse behind a thicket. Hunkered down with the others, he realized that the bare branches offered little cover. He fingered the old musket he had gotten from Isaac. But, amazingly, it didn't matter, as the Yankees galloped by and headed into the swamp at breakneck speed.

That night, they reached the small farm of Isaac's grandparents. The old man eyed them narrowly, but Mrs. Pryor invited them into her kitchen.

"If you helped our boy to escape from that hateful prison, you're very welcome here." She busied herself at the stove.

Mr. Pryor passed around a jug of whiskey and all three men took a big swig. "You're from foreign parts, ain't you?" he asked.

"We are, sir." Tim seemed relaxed and motioned toward the jug again. "Don't mind if I do," he said and smiled at the host.

Sleeping in real beds made all the difference in the world. The next day, Rob felt good. He was on his way to see Abigail Treverton.

* * * *

Starting out at dawn, the three men skirted around Fredericksburg. Although they could have traveled on the road, Rob thought it best to stay to the woods. The area was devastated. Many farmhouses were burned to the ground, and barn doors sagged on rusty hinges.

Suddenly, they found themselves surrounded by a troop of Confederate cavalry, who seemed to have materialized out of nowhere. Ragged and gaunt, the Rebels eyed them suspiciously.

"Good afternoon." The young lieutenant smiled, showing jagged, yellowed teeth.

Tim spoke up quickly. "I'm bringing me nephews to me own dear sister's funeral. I just hope they wait for us." He cast the officer his most doleful look. "So you see, we must be off."

"A funeral, is it?" The lieutenant flashed his shark-like grin. "You're all seamen?"

"We are. Now, if you don't mind, we're in a bit of a hurry."

"Are you?" The lieutenant eyed them critically. "You have the look of deserters to me. What do you think, men?" The soldiers nodded and moved to block off any retreat.

An hour later, the men found themselves standing before a Confederate colonel. The man took his time looking them over. Finally he said, "The regiment you mentioned has not been in these parts for months. You're lying."

"You're right, sir. Here's the truth." Rob looked into the eyes of the short, balding colonel. "We escaped from Point Lookout Prison on Christmas. We're trying to get home."

The Rebel colonel surveyed them shrewdly. "Very few men escape from that hell hole and live to tell about it." He closed his eyes and said nothing for at least two minutes. "What is the name of the prison camp cook?"

"Albie Ringer," Jacobs spoke up. "He ain't a bad cook if he has food for the pot."

Again, the colonel seemed to meditate. Then he turned abruptly to Rob. "Who are you?"

"My name is Rob Johnson. I was with the 21st Virginia Infantry."

"Johnson, what's the name of the camp doctor?"

Rob grinned. "Doc Hodges. We worked for him in the Smallpox Stockade."

"The pest house?" The colonel waved his hand. "That's enough reason to send you on your way. I'll write you a safe passage through our lines." He lapsed into silence again. "I spent six months at Point Lookout last winter. My wife bought my way out, so I, too, was one of the lucky ones."

CHAPTER 25

THE TRIP NORTH

WINTER 1865

The weather had turned cold and gusts of snow battered the travelers. Tim had developed a rasping cough, and Jacobs complained that his belly was empty. Rob calculated that this was the third day since they had left the Rebel colonel. The small bag of beans he had given them was gone and they were hungry.

Recognizing many landmarks, Rob knew they were getting close to the Treverton farm and he needed to concentrate on what he would say to Abigail. When they crossed an icy stream, he called a halt and tried to clean up his ragged appearance.

"You'll do, lad." Tim looked him over.

"Ask about dinner," Jacobs said.

As they rode down the lane toward the house, Rob hoped that Abigail and her husband were still living with her parents. The place looked largely untouched by years of war, unlike many of the neighboring farms. He realized that he was sweating, even though the temperature was below freezing. When they reached the barn, Rob left the others and approached the large pillared front porch. Clenching and unclenching his fists, he waited at the door. He had to knock twice before an elderly Negro servant appeared.

In response to Rob's request, the man shook his head. "I'm sorry, Mr. Johnson, Miss Abigail don't wish to see you." He tried to push the door shut.

"Wait, I only want a brief word."

"Miss Abigail left instructions after she returned from the Clifford farm. Now, I must ask you to leave."

"The Cliffords?"

"Yes, they're distant relations. Good day." The heavy door banged shut.

Seeing a curtain move at an upstairs window, Rob shouted, "Abigail, please, Abigail come out. I just want to talk to you." Starting to circle the house, he tried all the doors.

Rob found that the kitchen door swung open easily. Abigail's father was standing stiffly in the hallway. "Thee is not welcome here, Rob Johnson." His tone was uncompromising.

"I'm sorry for my mistakes in the past. I take full responsibility, but I must speak with Abigail," Rob said. He remembered that this man had been ready to trade him and Jacobs to bandits to ensure the farm's safety.

"That is not possible. She is a married woman." He looked coldly at Rob. "I believe she wrote to thee and asked thee to stay away." Staring hard at Rob, he tried to slam the door.

Rob managed to hold the door open. "Please, I don't understand. I never got that letter. "

"Don't come here again." The door shut.

When Rob rejoined the others, he was crying, but he didn't care.

* * * *

That night, the group stayed in an abandoned cabin and feasted on potatoes, onions, and beans they found in the root cellar. "If them folks hadn't pushed brush over the cellar door, there wouldn't have been nothing left. Damned soldiers were too stupid to find it." Jacobs looked pleased.

Tim went into a fit of coughing and Rob stared into the fire. As far as he was concerned, the best find was a jug of corn whiskey hidden under the floorboards near the hearth.

Jacobs poured another round of drinks. "I can't go no further north with you," he said. "I gotta go home tomorrow. I ain't heard from my folks in months and I'm worried."

Rob nodded. "I understand the urge to go home, but things won't be the same without you."

"You'll miss me, then? I knew you would."

The fire burned low and the group lapsed into silence. Jacobs dozed and Rob stared into the glowing embers. "Rob," Tim's voice was loud in the silence. "Being turned away is a terrible thing. It's happened to me more than once."

Rob looked up at him. "You've been in love?"

"I know it's hard to believe, but I've been madly in love." When Rob didn't answer, he continued, "What of the blond girl and the baby? What of them?"

Stillness settled over the small cabin. Finally, Rob replied, "I owe Laura an apology. I've been wrong about her and have treated her badly. She should hate me."

* * * *

The next day, Rob felt a strange elation as he neared the Clifford farm. The people there had always treated him well. He found himself looking forward to seeing Laura and little Melinda.

This time, the Cliffords' front door was thrown open and Rob was fairly yanked inside. Joseph motioned him to hurry. "Follow me, Mister Rob. We have a sick Yankee here. His friends may come back anytime."

When they reached the kitchen, Joseph spoke quietly to Big Betty, then turned to Rob. "I must go and hide your friend in the barn." He left the room quickly.

Enduring Big Betty's hostile stare, Rob wondered if coming here had been a good idea. Suddenly, Lilly ran into the room. She glanced at him and whispered to Betty.

"Miss Laura, she see you now," Lilly said and motioned for Rob to follow her.

In the parlor, Rob found a handsome woman clad in black. A starched white bonnet covered her yellow hair. As he entered, she nodded and regarded him with a cool, direct stare.

"Laura, you look well," he stammered.

"And you, Rob."

The silence drew out and Rob found himself shuffling his feet uneasily. "How is Melinda? Is she well?"

"She is."

"And the Cliffords? I heard that Mae Clifford had passed."

"Yes, she died shortly after Christmas. We are in mourning."

"She was a good woman. What of Thomas?"

"He is poorly and not up to seeing anyone."

"Can I see Melinda?"

"She's sleeping."

Amazed at the presence of the woman standing calmly in this Quaker home, Rob realized that Laura had finally found her place in life. "Did you get any of the mail I sent from Point Lookout?"

"I received a few letters, yes."

"I said a lot in those letters that I'd never told you before, but you never wrote back."

"No, I heard that you got enough mail."

Rob looked away. "I'm sorry for a lot of things, Laura. I've made mistakes."

"You have. But, I have you to thank for bringing me here. Do you have plans to see Miss Treverton?"

Her composure unnerved him. "Abigail has married a Quaker."

For the first time, Laura smiled. "I'm happy for Abigail. She was very confused when I met her. She has finally found her way."

Rob grimaced. "Did you tell Abigail of every wrong I had done you?"

"I tried to be fair. Others have wronged me far more, and you gave me Melinda."

Here it was, Rob thought, *the old bone of contention.* "When can I see her?"

"She should wake soon." Laura walked over to a chair and sat down, motioning Rob to do the same.

Rob relaxed a little. He saw that Laura still moved in the old, sensual way, swinging her hips in the black skirt. Underneath the severe Quaker garb, she was the same girl he had known. He sat opposite her.

"I will not trouble you long. When I can, I'll try to send you something for Melinda. Can I see you again?" Unsure of what he really wanted, Rob smiled at her.

"I know things have been hard for you, Rob. The prison must have been an awful place. Times have been hard here, too, but I don't need your money."

"Is your position that secure here?"

"Yes, probably, but I have been engaged twice since I last saw you." She turned calmly toward him. "The first man was a neighbor who, sadly, died in the war. He loved me and left me his inheritance." She hesitated and looked at Rob levelly. "The other man has promised to marry me in a few months' time." Laura took the gold chain from around her neck and handed it to Rob. "Open it."

Rob held the small locket like a red-hot ember. Gingerly, he slid it open. "Oh, my God, girl." Rob hooted with laughter. "You can't be serious."

"I am. Nate and I are to wed soon. You might as well know."

"You say you recently came into some money? Well, I guess that makes you all the more beautiful in Nate's eyes." Rob's head began to pound and he realized that what he was feeling was rage—jealousy and rage. He stood abruptly.

"Get out, Rob. You haven't changed, you selfish bastard. Get out." Laura ran at him, her nails clawing at his face.

"What happened to the proper Quaker lady?" Rob was laughing as he held her off, which infuriated Laura more. Finally, he caught her arms and pulled her closer. He found himself kissing her. Her mouth was soft and, for an instant, she responded.

Then, she bit his lip and wriggled out of his grasp. "You bastard, leave me alone. I hate you!" Her cap fell off, loosing her long, blond hair. "You've looked down on me all these years. You've ignored me. You've deserted me. Why are you here now?"

"Momma," A small hand pulled at Laura's skirt. "Are you all right?"

Both adults stood motionless. Still dabbing at his lips with a bandanna, Rob smiled down at the little girl. She studied him from behind her mother's skirts and said, "My name is Melinda. Who are you?"

Noting her uncanny resemblance to his mother, Rob eased himself down on one knee and held out his hand. "I'm happy to meet you, Melinda. I'm Rob Johnson, your daddy."

The child took a few tentative steps toward him, then looked up at Laura. "Is he my daddy? Do I really have a daddy?"

"Mr. Johnson is an old friend."

"An old friend and your father," Rob finished firmly.

Melinda ran to him and he scooped her up and held her close. Her silky curls brushed his cheek and he breathed in the fresh scent of soap and bath powder. Rob knew at that moment that little Melinda was important to him. She was a sweet, innocent child and the thought of Nate Fields taking her and Laura away from him sealed his resolve.

"I'll be back, child," he whispered. Handing Melinda to her mother, he took Laura's hand. She didn't pull away, so he bent down and kissed her. "Forgive me," he said.

Joseph came to the door. "You must go now. Yankees up on the road. Hurry."

CHAPTER 26

HOMECOMING

MARCH 1865

Snow started to fall as Rob and Tim continued north. Wet and cold, they stopped for the night at the Harkins' farm. Lark Harkins was a distant Johnson cousin, but had been guarded in his welcome.

"It ain't safe for you here, Rob. You're a fugitive now." He met them on the porch. "Some of my wife's kin are Union men." Lark ushered them quickly inside his small cabin.

"It's only for tonight. We got no place else to go." Rob gestured to Tim. "This is Tim Foley. He's ailing. He ain't a soldier, so he won't bring trouble down on your head."

"Well, only for tonight, then. I'll get my wife to dish up some stew. Sit down." Tim sat stiffly and stretched out his bad leg. Rob was alarmed at the Irishman's drawn pale face.

As he watched them eat, Lark became agitated. "Things have changed since you been gone. Morgan County got throwed into a new state they call West Virginia. Folks say that Union men rigged the statehood election and now they're riding high." Lark's eyes darted away from his two guests. "So it ain't a good idea for you to head home. My uncle came home last month. He just wanted to get back to farming and take care of his family, but they grabbed him and forced him to take the Union oath."

"Who grabbed him?" Rob asked.

"A bunch of Bluebelly-leaning town folks. Had soldiers with them."

"Was that it?"

"Hell, no. They hauled him into the courthouse and told him if he didn't put up a thousand dollar surety bond, they'd throw him in jail. He had to borrow from his father-in-law."

Rob stood up and started pacing around the small room. "Why didn't your uncle put up his own land for surety?"

"He wanted to, but they told him his farm would likely be taken soon, confiscated."

Rob stopped pacing. "What in hell are you talking about, Harkins?"

The small man got to his feet and took a step backward. "From what I done made out, a new law was passed while you was off fighting. Rebels who come home can't vote no more. Their land can be taken. A few been jailed."

"I heard rumors." His food untouched, Rob sat staring out the window at the swirling snow. "It ain't gonna happen with my land."

* * * *

The next morning, Tim was not well enough to continue the trip and stayed on with the Harkins. Lark promised to bring him to the farm within the week.

A few hours later, Rob rode down the lane to the farm and saw tracks in the snow. A thin spiral of smoke drifted up from the chimney. Curiosity quickly changed to anger as he spurred his horse down the slippery lane. Whoever was in the house had no right to be there. Harkins' words came back to haunt him. Confiscation. How could it be possible here in Morgan County?

His anger sustained him as he rode into the yard. Hesitating on the porch, he decided he needn't knock on his own door and pushed it open. The place was deserted, although it appeared that someone had just made a hasty departure. A pot of beans simmering on the cook stove filled the room with a well-remembered homey aroma. Running up the stairs, Rob glanced into the two small bedrooms and saw a blanket roll and clothes scattered in Pa's old room.

"Damn, it takes nerve to invade a man's house," Rob yelled. "Why don't you come out, you thief?"

Back in the kitchen, Rob reasoned that there was only one place the intruder could be hiding. He must have found the hidden trapdoor leading to the cellar. Rob released the lock and yanked the trapdoor open, then made his way down the steps into the blackness. He knew he had the advantage, as he was familiar with every inch of the small cellar. He started walking around the stonewall and heard movement in the corner.

"Stay where you are," he ordered.

"Don't shoot. I'll come out." Rob followed the bone-thin man as he climbed up the ladder slowly. Although he was a young man, he had the look of someone much older. His ragged, blue uniform hung on him and he seemed near collapse. His pale eyes had sunk back into his face, but Rob sensed something familiar about him.

"I know you," Rob said. "The last time I saw you was at the beginning of the war and you were sick then, too."

"Yes, I'm Merrill Robinson, sergeant, 13th Massachusetts Volunteers, and you're Rob Johnson. You and your pa took me in and saved my life back then."

"What's happened to you?"

"I been through a long war."

* * * *

After Rob walked his horse into the barn and gave him feed from his saddlebag, he looked the other horse over. The old gelding was bone-thin as his master, so Rob poured out feed for him also.

Back in the house, Rob found that Merrill Robinson had dished up two bowls of beans. "Sorry it ain't too grand a meal." He handed Rob a bowl.

Sitting on the floor by the fire, the two men ate hungrily. "That sack of beans in your cellar saved me." Merrill smiled for the first time. "I considered it a gift from you and your pa."

"Pa's dead. Union cavalry dumped his body in the front yard." Even after all this time, Rob was surprised at the loss he felt. Although his pa hadn't been much of a father at the end, Rob remembered the good times. Sitting in this house again had a powerful effect on him.

"I'm sorry." Merrill looked at Rob closely. "I remember your father and I expect you think of the happier days. That's what I do with my father. I got word at Andersonville that both my parents were dead."

"Andersonville." Now Rob understood. "How long were you there?"

"Almost a year. If I hadn't gotten out, I'd be dead now." He smiled again. "I see you think I'm close to dead anyway."

"I spent over a year and a half at Point Lookout. I guess I was lucky that the Yankees detailed me to the Smallpox Stockade. They had to feed me enough to keep me mopping floors and killing rats."

"I've seen men with smallpox. I don't know if I'd call that luck. How did you get out?"

"A friend helped me. I owe him a mighty debt. How about you?"

"Friends helped me, too. My sister's husband was related to one of the guards. Money changed hands and I escaped. I've been making my way north ever since." Merrill's drawn face reflected his exhaustion. "Two days ago I found myself near your place. I couldn't go any further."

"Any Union patrol would have helped you." Rob couldn't see the logic in Merrill's story.

"Yes, and I'd be back in the army sooner or later. This war is wearing itself out, but it ain't over yet."

Rob nodded. "No, it's not. But with Fort Fisher and Wilmington lost, it won't be long 'til the end. With no more supplies coming in, the South can't go on." He looked at Merrill, the man who had wanted to go West. "Why don't you rest up here until you get your strength back."

"Thank you kindly."

"I hear that returning Rebels are treated like fugitives." Rob stood up and went to the window. "Have you seen anyone around scouting the place?"

"No. Who are you looking to come here?"

"Yankee soldiers, Union-leaning people from Bath, I don't know." Rob walked over to the cellar trapdoor, knelt down and examined the perfectly aligned floorboards. "How did you find this door? My grand-pap was a craftsman and these boards are joined without trace of a seam. He rigged the door lock to that tiny lever over on the cupboard." Rob waved his arm in the direction of the built-in corner cupboard, the only piece of furniture left in the room. "No one else has ever found it."

Merrill looked up at him and actually laughed. "Remember. I was here before. You thought I was sleeping, but I watched you and your pa open that door many times."

Rob grinned. "I'm glad no other scoundrel of a Yankee found out the Johnson secret."

Merrill dozed off and Rob sat looking into the fire. He was still buoyed up with the feeling of homecoming, but he knew he was not done fighting. He realized that the threat he faced now could not be fought off with a gun. He could only save the farm by outsmarting the bastards who were enforcing this Confiscation Act. He planned to do just that. Nobody was going to run him off his land again.

* * * *

The second day Rob was home the McKenny sisters arrived with his milk cows. The two younger ones had been skinny heifers when he'd left for the war. They told him sadly that the draft horses had been stolen right out of their barn. The old women also brought a ham and four loaves of bread, so that night the men ate well.

"This is the grandest meal I've had in years." Merrill took a third helping of ham and beans. "How did those old women get those cows through the war?" he asked. "Bushwhackers and gangs of deserters are everywhere."

Rob grinned. "Women in these parts do whatever needs done. They can be a fierce lot." Alerted by noise in the yard, Rob drew his pistol and went to the door.

"Please, sir," a voice carried into the house. "We're hungry. Ain't had a meal in days. Could you spare a bit of food?"

Rob opened the door a crack and saw three men on the porch. Two more stood in the yard. Looking at them, he knew the signs. They were close to starvation. Throwing open the door, he called, "You're welcome here."

Rob filled their tin cups with food. He had been in their shoes not long ago.

"The roads are clogged with Rebel soldiers like us, trying to get home. I guess we're deserters, but the war ain't gonna last much longer." The man who had asked for food spoke up.

"We hear you, brother," Merrill Robinson said. "We need to look after ourselves now."

* * * *

The next morning, weak winter sunlight filtered through the bare tree branches into the farmyard. Rob watched as Lark Harkins' wagon rumbled toward the house. Tim climbed down slowly and looked around at the muddy yard and ramshackle buildings.

"Sure, this is a bloody paradise, lad, just like you always said it was." Tim called in greeting. He still appeared weak, but the color had returned to his face.

That afternoon Rob stood in the barnyard and watched dark clouds climb over the bleak mountains. It would probably snow by evening. He had spent the morning tearing rough boards off an old roofless shed and dragging them into the barn. He was determined to put together a table for the kitchen. Engrossed in the task, he was slow to pick up the sound of an approaching rider. Rob dropped the tools and grabbed his gun. In the yard, he saw that a horseman had crested the hill and was riding toward him.

"Rob," the man shouted. "It's John Dawson. I need to talk with you."

Leading the way into the house, Rob gestured to the men sleeping on the floor. "One man came with me. One was already here and the others stopped for food."

"These are troubled times." John nodded to the men and lowered his large frame onto the floor. "I see you don't have much left."

"I still got the farm. Knowing I had this place helped me get through hard days."

"You're bone-thin, Rob. I heard you'd been at Point Lookout."

"Yes, sir. I was there. It's good of you to come."

"I came to warn you. Trouble is brewing for you returning Rebs. There's talk of retribution. Stay well away from Johnny McKenny and that bunch. If you're seen in their company, you'll be branded a trouble maker." John got to his feet and headed to the door. "Go into town and take the oath. The Union folks will be looking for a scapegoat in a confiscation court case. They're out for blood." As he left, the reverend handed Rob a Colt pistol. "Take this. You may need it."

"Thanks, sir. The old musket the waterman gave me can't hit a toad on a tree trunk."

CHAPTER 27

LEE SURRENDERS

APRIL 1865

News of Lee's surrender at Appomattox reached Bath quickly. The O'Ferralls heard the news from Mabel McCabe, who'd been shopping at the farmers' market.

"General Lee did all he could for his men. He treated them soldiers like his own sons, but they couldn't go on. It was over on April ninth." She blew her nose loudly. "The Yankees gave them boys three days rations and turned them loose."

Jane O'Ferrall wept, and Mary shouted, "Thank God it's over."

Jane raised her head. "I'm glad the fighting's over, but the country's torn apart. Many a man won't be coming home and those who do will never be the same." She went after the sherry decanter and poured drinks all around. "I worry for Trip and for your man, Mary. It won't be over for me until they're back."

"Them Yankee folks in town are running wild," Mabel said, "I seen more coming in from the farms and hollers. I don't like the look of it."

"They're here to celebrate," Jane said. "I only hope they don't prowl the streets."

By nightfall, the women heard cheering and random gunfire. The celebration centered around a big bonfire in the town park. Toward midnight, the O'Ferralls heard loud banging on the front door.

"Rebel sluts," a deep voice yelled.

The banging on the door grew louder. Suddenly, flames flared upward near the entrance. Mabel McCabe, screaming like a banshee, ran out the back door and careened around the side of the building. She held a large iron frying pan above her head as she ran toward the attackers. The same men who had called for "the damn Rebels to clear outta town," now melted away into the darkness. No one was left to face Mabel's fury.

"Cowards," she screamed.

Mary ran out the front door and poured a bucket of water on the blaze, which smoldered and died. Coughing and tearing from the smoke, the two women ran back into the coffee house. Jane handed them shots of whiskey.

"What's wrong with those people?" Mary cried.

"They're just a few drunks. Don't judge the whole town by them," Jane said. "Union troops are marching toward the square. I saw them from an upstairs window." She poured another round of whiskey. "The Union Army is the only law we have now."

"I never thought I'd be saying this, but thank God for them Blue-coats," Mabel said.

* * * *

In the next weeks, the roads were clogged with returning soldiers. The O'Ferralls gave out as much food as they could and often had a dozen men sleeping on the kitchen floor. Many needed medical attention, so Jane applied her store of salves and herbal potions.

They heard bits of news from Trip's friends. He was alive, he was sick, he'd been promoted on the battlefield. They did not hear from him. There was no news at all from Captain James Hansen. By June, the women had resorted to praying.

* * * *

Mary and Mabel McCabe were folding linens in the kitchen when a commotion drew them out to the dining room. They watched as an elegantly dressed woman directed the placement of her luggage. Her dark blue traveling outfit set off her fair complexion and red hair. Walking toward her, Mary thought there was something familiar about the new arrival.

"Mary," the woman cried, "It's so good to see you. I've dreamed of home."

"Fannie? Is it you? You're such a fine lady."

Fannie hugged her, saying, "I hope you have a room for me. I'm so glad to be here."

Mary signaled Mabel to collect the luggage. "Come this way."

At dinner, Fannie regaled Mary and Jane O'Ferrall with stories of her fairytale life in Richmond. "You wouldn't believe how courtly the officers were. I was invited to every party."

"You were lucky to escape Richmond," Mary said. Her sharp eye noted the fine, embroidered detail on Fannie's stylish jacket.

"Oh, I left Richmond last December and went to Mama's relatives in Maryland." Fannie picked up another piece of fried chicken. "The Northern officers were charming and quite kind to a homeless refugee."

"Fannie, I can't believe you socialized with the Yankees. You were such a patriot."

"After Mama and Daddy died, I learned to survive. Patriotism is a luxury." Fannie folded her napkin and placed it carefully on the table. "What do you hear of Rob Johnson? I saw him at Christmas time down at Point Lookout. There was talk later that he'd escaped." Even Fannie's new lacquer of lady-like composure couldn't hide her curiosity.

"He made it home. But things don't go well for returning Southern soldiers. Rob's worried he'll lose his farm."

"No." Fannie looked surprised. "How could that happen?"

"Confiscation." Jane could not keep the bitterness from her voice.

"What? That farm has been in the Johnson family for generations. Who's behind this?"

Mary measured her response. "The men running the county now are seeking vengeance. Rob isn't the only one. If a man fought for the Confederacy, he's lost his civil rights, and his property can be taken." She felt the old anger returning. "That's why many men, like my brother Trip, don't come back home. There's still a warrant out for Trip's arrest here."

"Poor Rob. All he ever cared about were those rocky fields of his."

"He has a child now," Mary said. "A little girl he says looks like his mother."

"A child? So he has a wife?" A sharp tone had entered Fannie's carefully modulated speech.

Mabel, who was busy collecting the dinner dishes and setting out the dessert course, stopped her work and eyed Fannie. "Oh, he's got a couple of women, so I hear it told."

Watching her guest, Mary caught a flicker of anger in her blue eyes.

"Well, I guess Rob Johnson has finally grown up." Fannie's tone was cold. Rummaging in her purse, she brought out a small tintype which she handed to the O'Ferrall women. "This is the man I plan to marry. He owns a large farm near Chicago. I'm on my way there now."

"He has a kind face. Have you known him long?" Jane asked.

Mary studied the picture again. An elegantly dressed Fannie stood with a short, balding Yankee colonel. He did, indeed, have a kind face, a face she had seen before.

"I met him at the start of the war. Do you remember Charles Clark, Mary? He was a physician with the 39th Illinois. Charles helped my Daddy out when he was a prisoner in the Hancock jail. We've kept in touch ever since."

"Congratulations, Fannie, I do remember Dr. Clark." Mary's smile was sincere. "You and I are both engaged to Yankee officers, but I haven't heard from my man in over four weeks."

"A month is not long in these times," her mother said. "Let me add my congratulations, Fannie. Now I must leave you girls to catch up on all the news."

Alone, the two girls fell silent. Then Fannie reached out and took Mary's hand. "Remember how we hated the Yankees. We spied and schemed against them. Now we're both to become Yankee brides."

"It wasn't an easy decision for me," Mary said, "My family was not happy at first. But it was Rob Johnson who told me that you can't choose who you love."

* * * *

Strong noonday sun beat down on the two riders. A blue haze hung over the mountains, and the air barely stirred. Riding ahead, Fannie set a fast pace. Mary still didn't know how she had been talked into this trip. As they neared the ruins of the Orrick place, Mary bowed her head. Johnson Orrick had been killed by a sharpshooter back in 1863. They rode past what was left of the Swann's old home. Fannie gave the place a passing glance and raced on toward the Johnson farm.

As they turned into the lane leading to the farmhouse, a man stepped out onto the road. His long, dark hair gave him a wild appearance. He held a pistol loosely in his right hand. When they drew closer, Rob lowered the gun.

"Hello, ladies. I don't get much company."

"That's obvious." Fannie flung herself off her horse and ran to him. "I've been worried for you. Mary says you have legal trouble."

Rob held her at arm's length. "Things are complicated here. Why did you come?"

Fannie spun away. Watching her, Mary read the surprise and anger reflected in her eyes.

"I'm on my way to Illinois, but I took the time to see you. I must say you don't seem pleased that I've come." Fannie's voice was shrill.

Rob stood looking at her. "It's dangerous for you here. I've had threats against myself and my property." Turning to Mary, he continued. "She don't understand what's going on. Have you told her what happened to James Gill?"

Mary shook her head. "No, there's been no time."

"After Gill got home from the war, the Unionist hardliners in county government served a fugitive warrant on him. His property confiscation suit is dragging through the court and James has had to hide out across the river. He's only dared visit his family once." Rob's jaw tightened and his eyes narrowed. "He took their oath, but that wasn't enough. They want revenge."

"I know his wife," Mary said. "The Gills are decent people."

"Why didn't James Gill just put up bond until his case went to court?" Fannie asked.

"He's got no money and no right to sue in court." Rob's voice was so low that Mary had to strain to hear the words. "I'm in the same mess, but I ain't running."

A look of dismay spread over Fannie's face. "You were a soldier, not a spy or a bushwhacker." She sounded indignant. "They have no right."

"They've got new laws on the books and they want to settle old scores." Rob turned to look back over his fields. "I've taken their oath. That should be enough."

"You're in danger, Rob." Fannie tried to move toward him, but Mary grabbed her arm.

"Thanks for coming, but you ladies shouldn't be here. Be careful riding back." He started walking back up the lane toward the farmhouse.

"Wait, Rob. I want to help you," Fannie called after him. "Wait." But Rob kept on walking.

* * * *

When Fannie left the next morning, she looked close to tears. Mary knew things hadn't gone as Fannie had hoped. She had handed Mary an envelope addressed to Rob and asked that she deliver it.

That night, Mary was sitting at the kitchen table writing out menus when Rob slipped in through the kitchen door. John Dawson was already waiting for him in the family parlor, so Mary hurried Rob up the back steps. Returning a little later with a pot of tea, she noted that he looked tired and uneasy.

"I've seen many confiscation notices in the Wheeling newspaper," Reverend Dawson was saying. "That's what these people do; they think no one here will see the notices and catch on to their schemes." He shook his head. "All they need to do is publish in any West Virginia newspaper. They're shrewd."

Watching him, Mary saw that the reverend had aged during the war years. A preacher and Justice of the Peace, John Dawson was one of the most respected men in the county. Sitting across the table, Rob clenched his glass tightly. The veins in his temples throbbed.

"What do you advise me to do, sir? I could be next."

"There's nothing you can do unless you can post bond, but don't run and don't fight."

"I can't put up bond, but I won't go to jail."

John Dawson nodded. "I understand." He rose to leave. "I'll go by the courthouse and remind these men that you worked with the Underground Railroad. You risked your life to help slaves to freedom. Yours is a special case."

Mary could find no more reason to linger in the room, but left the door ajar as she entered the hallway.

"Thank you, Reverend Dawson." she heard Rob's voice. "Do you think they'll listen?"

"I can't say. I've angered a few people by defending some of my own family who fought with the South. That's why I can't offer to post your bond. I have no ready cash left."

As Mary went down the stairs, she could already think of several local men who would make rock bottom bids on the Johnson farm. She headed outside to the back porch and sat in the shadows. Soon the reverend left and then Rob stepped out on the porch. Quietly, she called his name. He sat down next to her.

"Fannie left this for you," Mary said as she handed him the letter. "I hope your luck will change." She stood and moved toward the door.

"And you, Mary. Your mother told me that your man is missing. I hope you hear some good news." He stood also. "I had hoped I'd have a home to offer Laura and the little girl, but now I have nothing." He walked off into the night.

CHAPTER 28

REVENGE

JUNE 1865

The heat had lifted as Rob made his way home with the supplies from town. A strong west wind blew over the mountains, driving away the cloud cover. The stars glittered blue-white, and the moon hung heavy above the purple ridges. Nearing the farm, he hoped that Tim had put a pot of beans on the stove. Since there was scarce little coming from the vegetable plot, they foraged for field greens and threw them into the stew.

Approaching the farmhouse, he could make out several men on the porch. Drawing his pistol, he left his mount behind the barn. As he drew nearer, he heard singing. Breaking into a run, he reached the porch just as Jacobs finished the last verse of *Lorena*.

Grabbing him in a bear hug, Rob pounded him on the back. "I was sure you'd be dead by now, without me and Tim keeping an eye on you."

"That there is close to the truth." Jacobs looked Rob over. "You don't look a hellava lot better than you did back at Point Lookout. What's wrong?"

"I'll tell you later. It ain't a pretty story. How were things at your home place?"

"There ain't no more home place." Jacobs' tone was sober. "I was telling Tim and your Yank friend that the house and barn got burned to the ground and the livestock was gone."

"And your folks?" Too late, Rob caught the warning look Tim sent him.

"My parents were both dead and buried by the time I got back. My oldest brother and his family are trying to rebuild, but there ain't nothing left for me there. So, here I am."

"My God, Jacobs, it's good to see you. You got more troubles than I do. Let's see if there's any corn whiskey left."

The next day dawned hot and dry, with the wind blowing hard from the west. Taking his coffee onto the porch, Rob opened Fannie's letter. It read: Dear Rob, I am sad to find you in such a desperate state. I hope the enclosed will help. If you could meet me in Chicago, I would make the trip well worth your while. I have a line of credit on a bank in that city. After all, we are old friends and should care for one another. With Love, Fannie

A one hundred dollar bill was folded inside the envelope. Rob carefully replaced the thin stationary and turned the bill over in his hands. Could this be part of the blood money made from betraying slaves? The same slaves who had hidden in crates on the train north from Richmond? No, that money was spent long ago. But Rob remembered the look of excitement in Fannie's eyes as she'd sat in the railcar. She'd had it planned all along. He went toward the barn to saddle his horse.

As he rode out of the yard, he saw Jacobs dragging a deer carcass out of the woods. "I thought you'd need that stew pot filled up," he shouted. "Where are you off to?"

"I'm on my way over to James Gill's farm. I have a gift for his family."

* * * *

That evening at supper, Rob had to listen to Tim's tirade. "When you drove into the yard with the Gill's wagon I knew something was amiss, lad. Filled to the brim it was, with them broken-down chairs and bedsteads." Tim's voice had taken on a high, plaintive tone.

"You sound like a wronged woman," Jacobs observed, seeming to enjoy the show.

"Mrs. Gill didn't need that old furniture. She had it stored in the barn." Rob was on the defensive. "She knew we didn't have nothing left here."

"When her and her boys brought that wagonload of junk, I heard her praising you for a generous man. Weeping with joy, she was." Tim shoved a loaf of bread toward the men. "And we're having such a fine meal too, courtesy of Mrs. Gill."

Looking down at their plates, the group ate in silence. Getting up to limp back to the stove, Tim rounded on Rob. "You needed that money yourself, you damn fool. You're in just as dire straits as the Gills."

"It's blood money. I won't touch it."

"Ah, the high principles. You won't take the money. You won't run. You won't hide. Where the hell does that leave you?"

Rob grinned at the agitated little Irishman. "You're right, Tim. I'm a damn fool, and I'll deserve what I get."

* * * *

The next day was so clear that the deep purple of the distant Maryland mountains stood out starkly against the cloudless sky. Swinging the scythe in rhythm with the other haymakers, Rob worked his way down the field. It was almost like old times, but he'd only been able to muster a few workers. The old man moving along beside him was Carl McKenny, the McKenny sisters' youngest brother. The twelve-year-old Gill twins and Jacobs made up the crew.

Although laced through with weeds, the grass was high and he drank in its sweet heady scent. Since Rob knew each tree line, stump and pile of rocks, he barely had to look up as he swung the scythe. His mind raced ahead over the choices of what to plant next year. He'd found a cache of seeds in the cellar and wondered if they'd yield a crop.

The sun hung directly above them as they ate the lunch Tim had prepared. The fare was plain, but filling. Heading back to the field, Carl McKenny shot Rob a toothless grin. A spare, weathered old man, he had spent his life on the land.

"You ain't got no fence posts left and your fields are running to weeds. That ain't bad for four years of neglect," Carl said.

"I plan to bring this place back better than it was."

"That's if you still own the place." Johnny McKenny had silently joined the group. "I hear you're in a bind, Rob. I come to help with the haying, then you and me need to talk business."

It was dark by the time Rob and Johnny were able to sit on the porch and share a drink of whiskey. Although Johnny had been drinking, he wasn't drunk and his tone was serious.

"I agree that John Dawson would have done what he could for you, but there's a powerful lot of bad feeling around here against returning Rebs. There're some men who are after profit, power and revenge." He passed the jug over to Rob. "If you gotta post bond, you'll need money."

"I hope it won't come to that. I got friends here, people who will stand up for me." As Rob said this, he believed it was true.

"Who are your friends? Other Reb families? Don't forget that your pa made some powerful enemies when he joined up with that gang of horse thieves. People around here don't forget."

Rob started pacing the length of the porch. "I only want to keep what's rightfully mine."

* * * *

The next day Rob was on the barn roof trying to mend several gaping holes. He needed to keep the new hay dry, as he hoped to sell part of it. From his perch, he spotted the visitor long before his wagon reached the yard. As the rig drew near, Rob was able to make out all manner of goods hanging from the canopy. He figured he should be honored that a peddler thought he'd have the money to be a customer. By the time he'd finished the job and climbed down, Tim, Jacobs, and Merrill were clustered around the wagon.

When Rob reached them, the peddler smiled broadly. "My name is Timmons. I've brought a letter from one of my best customers for Mr. Johnson." He handed Rob an envelope. Rob would have recognized the hand writing anywhere. The man brought a message from Abigail Treverton.

Dear Rob, I know I should not contact thee, but I miss thee so terribly. My husband is an old man who only wants someone to listen to his long, boring stories and hang on his arm at Meeting. There is no love between us and I cannot live my life this way. I remember the time we spent in each other's arms and would run to thee in an instant if thee would only say the word. Thy adoring Abigail.

Folding the letter, Rob realized that he felt more guilty than elated. What did he have to offer Abigail?

That night he slept badly. The full moon cast long shadows in the yard and threw an eerie half-light over the black outlines of the mountains. Rob had abandoned the heat of the upstairs bedroom and had spread a thin blanket on the porch floor. There was no breeze and even the fireflies seemed to hang suspended in the still air. He spent hours going over the contents of Abigail's letter. He thought of the suppleness of her young body and the scent of her hair. She was too young and too passionate to spend her life with an old man. He knew she wouldn't have been forced into this marriage had it not been for him, so he owed her. But what did he owe her?

* * * *

After a day of thunderstorms battering the ridges, the wind blew from the north bringing dry cool air. The hills stood out in shades of deep blue against the cloudless sky. Rob had spread his tools out on the ground near the barn. The old two-man saw was dull as butter and he was trying to hone it to a workable edge. Jacobs was going to help him cut firewood up on the mountain. Rob had his eye on several large trees that were dying and ready to fall.

They were headed into the woods when Carl McKenny's rickety wagon lumbered up the lane. Moving quickly for a man of his age, Carl climbed down from the wagon seat and approached the two men. He looked at them sadly.

"I have news. My nephew, Johnny, died this morning. His friends tried to get him into town to the doctor, but he didn't make it." Carl started to cry.

Rob went over and put his hand on the old man's shoulder. "Come in, Carl. I'm sorry to hear this. Johnny was always good to me. How did he die?"

"You know he had a little drinking problem, but it was his heart, most likely. He'll be buried in two days' time."

In the kitchen, Tim joined them at the table with the last of the whiskey. The men listened quietly as Carl told of his nephew's last few days. Slowly, Rob grappled with the reality that Johnny was gone.

When Carl was able, Rob helped him out to his wagon. "Oh," Carl said, "I have a note for you from John Dawson."

Leaning on the porch rail, Rob watched the wagon drive slowly down the lane. Jacobs brought his cup of whiskey outside and sat on the step. "Johnny had a big drinking problem when I knew him. It ain't no surprise he's met his reward."

Rob hardly heard him as he re-read the note.

I have heard from my Quaker friends that small pox fever has been plaguing the Valley this summer. It is said that the Clifford farm has been hard hit. I'm sorry to tell you that your woman and child are very ill. Sincerely, John Dawson.

* * * *

"I ain't sure how long I'll be gone," Rob said as he stuffed a few belongings into his saddlebags.

"You know how to deal with the pox. You'll be fine." Jacobs shook Rob's hand.

Merrill handed him a worn Bible. "I'll pray for Laura and the child," he said.

Tim gave Rob a small cloth bag. "I kept this. It's dried Indian Cup plant."

Smiling at the thin, weather-beaten Irishman, Rob felt a thin thread of hope. "You're a good lad, Tim Foley," he said in a thick brogue. "I won't forget to say me prayers."

CHAPTER 29

THE FEVER

JULY 1865

The road rose up to meet the moonlight and Rob let the horse have its head. He conjured up little Melinda's round, baby face covered in welts. Bending over her child, Laura was weeping.

At dawn, small groups of men wearing rag-tag remnants of Confederate uniforms started passing him on the road. Most threw up their hands in greeting. A wagon filled with gaunt ragged men rolled by. Rob could see their canes and crutches stacked neatly in the back.

"Where're you headed?" He shouted in greeting.

"We're on our way up to Hampshire County. We're finally headed home," the driver called back.

Ruined homes and derelict fields stood out forlornly in the morning light. Rob realized that these people had lost everything. Maybe he should count himself lucky that he still had anything left. Although he was tired, Rob wanted to press on to the Clifford farm, but his horse needed rest. Finding an overgrown meadow, he put the horse out to graze and lay under a tree with his head propped on the saddle.

By late morning, the steady stream of refugees on the road had not slackened. Whole families seemed to be on the move. Groups of Negroes were also traveling. Not that long ago, Rob had risked his own life and the lives of runaway slaves while traveling up this same road. He thought about this as he saddled the horse. Ready to move out, he heard a familiar voice.

"Mister Rob, there you be. I been looking for you," Joseph said. The tall, powerfully-built Negro pulled his wagon off the road.

"How are things at the Cliffords?"

"We got a lot of folks down with the fever. Miss Laura and the little girl, they bad off. You need to come."

Nodding, Rob tied his horse to the back of the wagon and jumped up on the seat with Joseph.

"I heard and was headed there. Tell me about my family."

"Miss Laura, she done for everybody else until she and Melinda took sick. Now, Lilly tries to help, but she ain't strong. She's eight months with child. I'm a worried man, Mister Rob."

"Why wasn't I sent for earlier?"

Joseph looked away. "She said not to."

"Not to? Why in heaven not?"

Looking uncomfortable, Joseph answered, "Miss Laura say you don't claim her and the little girl as kin. You don't want the girl."

"That isn't true." Rob was starting to sweat. "Is this because of Nate?"

"Mister Nate ain't been around. He say he has business to tend to, but he send money."

"What did Laura say?" Rob felt his anger rising.

"She say Mister Nate, he scared of sickness."

Rob fought down the frustration he felt. "Everybody's scared of sickness, but that don't mean you let people die. Nate's always been a sonnuvabitch. I hope Laura can see that now."

* * * *

When Rob arrived at the Cliffords, old Thomas was waiting to greet him. Focusing on the old man, Rob noticed how much he had changed since they last met. "I'm so sorry to hear of Mae's passing," Rob said.

"I thank thee." Tears welled up in Thomas's eyes. "I pray for thee and thy loved ones at this time." He bowed his head and wept.

Rob nodded and quietly left in search of Laura. When he found her, he was alarmed to see the change in her. Her long, fair hair hung in damp masses around her face and several red pustules were scattered across her cheeks. Although she seemed to be sleeping, he saw her eyelids flutter. In the corner, Melinda slept on a little cot. Rob could see that her small frail body looked feverish, although no welts had yet appeared. Kneeling down by her bed, he wept.

"What you doing, Mister Rob?" Big Betty, hands on her wide hips, stood over him menacingly. "Can't you see there's work to be done? Ain't no time for tears, tears you should have shed long ago. Now, get up."

When Rob tried to coax Laura to drink a little water, her eyes opened and she looked up at him. "It's you. Thank God. Help Melinda." Exhausted from the effort, Laura's eyes closed again and she drifted off.

"That's the first time she's said a word since she be like this," Big Betty looked pleased. "Maybe you will be of some account."

"I know a little about smallpox."

"So I hear tell. You better save them." Big Betty's dark eyes held contempt as she stared at him. "Lilly ain't helping no more. I in charge here."

"We need some cold water to bring down the fever. Where can I get it?" Rob asked quietly.

"Joseph get it. You look after the child." Big Betty turned and left the room.

Melinda's small hands clutched a rag doll. Rob brushed the soft hair away from her face and was alarmed at how hot she was. At his touch, she tossed and whimpered.

I don't know if I can do this, Rob thought. *What if they die?* I couldn't stand it. He cradled the child in his arms and she whispered, "Momma?"

Rob was in tears again when Betty, followed by Joseph, entered the room. "Pull yourself together, man, or you ain't gonna be no use at all." Dumping a pile of towels on the dresser, she turned to Joseph. "Open them windows and get more water."

Setting down two large buckets, Joseph quietly followed Betty's directions, then left the room. As the night wore on, Rob and Betty bathed both patients several times, then applied wet cloths to their foreheads. Rob also dosed them with Indian Cup tea. The first time the cold water hit Melinda, her eyes flashed open and she cried out. Looking intently at Rob, she reached out her hand.

"It hurts," she said.

Holding Melinda's small hand, Rob felt true fear. She and Laura must survive. Silently, he cursed himself for a fool. He had lost three years with them. He vowed he would not lose them again. Smiling down at the child, he saw that a tiny pustule had erupted on her face. Now he knew that if she was strong enough to survive the fever, she had a chance. If the pox didn't break out, the victim was doomed.

"Don't worry, Melinda. I'm here now." Rob put the rag doll back in her arms.

By nightfall, little Melinda was covered with angry red pustules. Her fever had broken and she had taken a little broth.

"Where is my momma?" she cried. "I want my momma."

* * * *

Since the little girl was continuing to gain strength, Betty moved her back to her own room the next day. Laura questioned this, but didn't object. During her short periods of consciousness, Rob could see that she was not improving. She clutched his hand.

"Don't leave me, Rob." Her eyes held his. "I'm going to die, so it won't be long."

"No, Laura. I'm going to take you and Melinda back home with me. You won't die."

She smiled weakly. "Take Melinda. There's no one else to look after her."

He saw the glint of Nate's gold locket around her neck. "What of Nate?"

"He says he loves me, but I've never loved him." Laura paused. "How could I, when you're the man I love." She collapsed back on the bed.

"Forgive me, Laura, for the way I've treated you. I'm so sorry." He held her hand. "Can you forgive me?"

"I've never understood you. But, yes, I forgive you." She gasped for breath. "Promise me that you will take Melinda."

"She will go with me. I swear."

Laura's head fell back on the pillows and Rob prayed for the first time in years. Late in the day, she awoke and rallied a bit. She seemed surprised to find Rob still by her bed.

He held out a cup of water. "You need to drink as much as you can." Watching her sip from the cup, he said, "Not too fast." He held her hand again. "I was just thinking of your crazy, old granny. Remember when she went after Big Earl with a butcher knife? She could run pretty fast."

"She ran like a rabbit." Laura laughed with Rob until she started choking.

Alarmed, Rob propped her up higher on the pillows and reached for the basin. She would need it soon. He had no way to stop the vomiting, which embarrassed Laura so. After each bout, she grew weaker.

Melinda was brought to visit her mother several times each day. She usually chattered on about the tabby cat that had just given birth to six kittens and the peach pies the women were making down in the kitchen. But today Laura tossed fitfully and seemed not to know that Melinda was there.

"What's wrong with momma?" She demanded of Rob. "I want her to talk to me."

The child's round, blue eyes stared at him and he could sense the fear she was feeling. When Betty returned, he motioned toward Laura and led the little girl from the room. Hand-in-hand, they walked to the orchard where they found several empty baskets stacked under the trees.

"If I pick the peaches and hand them down to you, can you put them in the basket?" Rob reached up and picked a perfect peach.

Melinda took it from him and carefully turned it over in her small hands. She sniffed tentatively. "It smells good. Can I eat this one?"

Later, Rob carried the heavy basket to the kitchen. Melinda had filled her apron with fruit and held it up by the corners. They found Lilly waiting for them.

"Betty say to leave the child with me," she said. "Her momma ain't good."

* * * *

Sitting with Laura again, Rob could tell that she was losing strength. He had seen too many smallpox victims not to recognize the signs. He urged her to drink more of the Indian Cup tea. She waved it away and shut her eyes.

Sensing another presence in the room, he looked up, expecting to see that Big Betty had returned. Instead, he found two sets of frightened eyes staring at him from the doorway. Thomas Clifford's grandson, Donald, had become a tall, stocky young man. His sister, Margaret, had grown into a plain child who looked to be about ten years old. She tried to enter the room, but Donald held her back.

"Our friend Jill died last week," Margaret said as her solemn eyes surveyed the patient. "Will Laura die too?"

"I hope not. Melinda has started to improve."

"What about Laura? She's been like a mother to us. She can't die."

"It's in the Lord's hands now," Big Betty said. She gently pushed the children aside as she entered the room.

"They're building coffins in the wood shop. I've seen them." Margaret started to cry.

"Donald," Rob spoke softly. "You need to take Margaret away and try to comfort her. That's a man's job."

* * * *

Lilly's baby was born the same day Laura died. A fine baby boy, he was named Meeks.

That morning Big Betty ordered Rob out of the room so that the women could prepare Laura for burial. Betty handed him the same dark suit he'd worn during his Underground Railroad days. It was the suit that had belonged to Mark Clifford.

Thomas Clifford found Rob waiting in the hall. "I just heard about Laura," the old man said. "I am so sorry. She was a fine woman."

"Thank you." Rob turned his face away. *I can't stand this*, he thought. Laura was barely more than a girl. Now she'd never see her child grow up. "I should have come earlier," he said, "Maybe I could have saved her."

Thomas put a hand on his shoulder. "It was her time. Some have no chance with the pox. It is God's will."

Anger overwhelmed him. Rob didn't dare look at Thomas or make a reply. What kind of God could do this?

"The child is recovering. She's been a blessing to this house." Thomas hesitated. "She will always have a home here."

Sometime later, Rob heard the door shut. He was alone again with Laura, the woman he had betrayed and deserted. He should have been able to save her. He had seen sicker patients survive the pox.

* * * *

The day of the funeral dawned hot and dreary. Betty and little Melinda found Rob sitting by Laura's coffin, where he'd spent the night. He looked at them vacantly.

"Take the child's hand, Mister Rob. Can't you see she scared?"

Rob took the child's hand and they looked down at Laura. She was dressed in a white beaded gown. A garland of small white flowers adorned her hair and the welts on her face had been artfully covered. She looked serene.

"Momma," Melinda whispered, "is it you? You look like a princess." Touching Laura's folded hands, she looked alarmed. "She's cold. We need a blanket for my momma." Breaking into tears, the little girl ran from the room. Betty followed her.

Looking at Laura one last time, Rob saw the glint of gold in the folds of cloth lining the coffin. Carefully reaching in, he pulled out Nate's locket. Not reasoning why, he slipped it into his pocket. It should not have been there.

He found Melinda by the stairs and scooped her up in his arms. Hugging her tightly, he said, "It's going to be all right. I'm taking you home with me." Melinda still wept long wracking sobs. Sitting on the steps, Rob held her in his arms. He had no idea how much time had passed, but finally the child stopped crying. He had thought she was asleep when her head popped up.

"Why are you taking me away? I want to stay here."

"I'm taking you home with me because that's where you belong. I'm your father." Once the words were out, Rob knew they were true, no matter whether his blood ran in her veins, or not.

* * * *

The local Methodist minister came to the Clifford farm to perform the simple graveside service. Rob was surprised at the large crowd gathered at the family cemetery. Quaker friends and neighbors of the Cliffords, as well as the entire Negro farm community, waited quietly. Jacobs, Tim, and Merrill had been sent for and they carried the casket, alongside John O'Day and two Quaker men. Rob and Melinda walked behind the pallbearers, followed by Thomas, Donald, and Margaret Clifford. Betty and Lilly made up the procession. No longer crying, the little girl clutched Rob's hand as they neared the gravesite.

Apart from the others, Nate Fields stood with his head bowed. He wore a dark suit of good quality and held a broad-brimmed hat. As the reverend droned on, Rob found himself standing at the graveside between Thomas and Melinda. Nate was on the other side of the little girl. His legs were braced wide apart and his fists were clenched.

Jacobs' clear high tenor sang out the first words of *Amazing Grace* and the rest of the mourners joined in. The hymn drifted over the hills, giving Rob no comfort and no hope. Melinda started crying softly and he took her hand again. He kept his eyes on the flower-covered coffin. He felt grief for Laura and contempt for himself. She had been a good woman and he had never treated her right.

Sensing movement from the corner of his eye, Rob saw that Nate had taken hold of Melinda's other hand. Now the guilt turned to rage. Where had Nate Fields been when Laura needed him? Rob dropped Melinda's hand. He scooped up a clump of raw red earth and threw it on the casket. The child followed suit. When the third lump of earth hit the wooden casket, Rob's body tensed. It was only Thomas's restraining arm on his shoulder and the girl's small hand in his that kept him from springing at his old friend and bringing him to the ground. He watched Nate through narrowed eyes and his heart raced. Even in the war, Rob had not felt such a powerful urge to do another man harm.

Invited by Thomas, most of the mourners went back to the Clifford home to pay their respects. The Clifford children lured Melinda off with the promise of cake and Nate disappeared into the crowd. Rob sat by the grave until a light rain began to fall. He knew Laura would have been pleased to be laid to rest near Mae Clifford in the family plot. The grave to her right was the final resting place of a young Confederate soldier, Sam Jenkins, who had died in the winter of 1862. He wondered if Laura had known him.

Walking back toward the house, he saw a light in the barn. Slipping in through a side door, he found Nate Fields saddling his horse. Rob stood in the shadows watching him. As he was tightening the girth, the horse nuzzled him. *So Nate still had a way with animals*, Rob thought. They had been friends and he should leave it at that. As he turned to go, Nate's voice cut into the silence.

"I know you're there, Rob. You can't fool another mountain man. Why don't you step out here? I can see you got something to say."

Facing him, Rob realized that his old friend was now taller and must out-weigh him by twenty-five pounds. "Leaving so soon?" Rob asked. His voice was low.

"I got scarce little welcome here—from anyone. I'll mourn in my own way."

"Maybe if you'd bothered to come when she was dying and needed help, you might have gotten a different welcome."

In one swift motion, Nate sent his horse back into the stall and turned. His face was only inches from Rob's.

"I loved her. You never did. She was wearing the wedding dress I sent her."

"You saw her in the casket?"

"Big Betty let me in to see her one last time. I had the right." A warning flashed from Nate's eyes. "Don't make me forget that we were friends." He moved back toward his horse. "Now, if you'll get the hell out of the way, I'm leaving."

"Don't go without this, you sonnuvabitch." Rob threw the shiny gold locket at Nate's feet.

Slowly, Nate bent down and picked up the little locket. Turning it over in his hands, it gleamed in the lantern light. "So, now you're a grave robber. The fair-haired boy is nothing but a grave robber. What did you ever give her?" Nate took a step closer. "Oh, that's right, you gave her the child that you don't want."

Rob's first punch landed on Nate's jaw, throwing him into the barn wall. Recovering quickly, Nate went after Rob's mid-section, jabbing and pounding unmercifully. But the attack cleared Rob's mind and he started calculating his movements. He was able to feint and avoid some of Nate's blows, while landing his own punches.

"Stay away from Melinda," Rob growled. "I'm taking her home with me."

Nate danced around, giving Rob fewer chances to get in a telling blow. "Finally doing the right thing, are you? I can't believe I looked up to you when we were kids."

"I never trusted you then, and I don't trust you now," Rob said. His next assault brought Nate down to his knees. Rob was on top of him instantly, hitting and jabbing until he felt strong hands pulling him off.

Tim and Jacobs stood looking down at the bloodied men. They helped Rob to a standing position, but he collapsed back onto the floor.

Tim clucked over Nate. "This lad got the worst of it. What's wrong with you two? The lady deserves to rest in peace, not have brawlers at her wake." He knelt by Nate. "Jacobs, go after the medical bag and a bottle of whiskey. Be quick about it."

Tim had said that he had no broken bones, but Rob wasn't sure. His whole body ached and he was bleeding from several cuts. Nursing his throbbing jaw, he made an effort to get up and hobble toward the door.

"What in the name of God is the matter with you, lad? Wait for the whiskey," Tim ordered. "This man says he could have killed you if he'd wanted you dead. Instead, he took a beating. The least you can do is have a drink with him. After all, you're old friends," Tim said as he tried to drag Nate into a sitting position.

The fury was gone and Rob felt weak. There was nothing to replace the anger but emptiness. "I'll have a drink," he said.

When Jacobs returned, Tim poured out whiskey all around. "I'd like to make a toast to Laura, may the saints preserve her."

"To Laura," the men shouted, and drained their glasses.

As Nate prepared to leave, Rob went over to him. "Nate, I want to apologize."

"These are bad times," Nate said. "We all have regrets." He extended his hand. "We won't meet again. I'm heading West. There's nothing for me here anymore, but I wish you well with the little girl." The two men shook hands formally.

"Good luck," Rob said. He walked out with Nate and watched him ride off into the still evening. Now that his senses were returning, he felt a heavy sadness. Nate had been his childhood friend and Laura had been his first real love. They were both gone.

CHAPTER 30

REPARATIONS OF WAR

SEPTEMBER 1865

A day later Rob made his goodbyes to the Cliffords and the group set out for the farm. The trip was made easier for Melinda and Tim as Thomas Clifford had lent his carriage, with Joseph as driver. Rain fell in the morning and the roadway became a muddy quagmire, forcing the carriage to proceed slowly. Melinda had been quiet and withdrawn since the funeral and Rob was worried for her, but now her small face appeared at the carriage window and Rob saw her waving. Waving back, he wondered if he could be mother and father to this child.

By noon, the rain had cleared and the temperature was climbing. The hilltops were a deep green, shading almost to black as the clouds covered portions of the mountain. As they neared the farm, the summer heat and monotonous drone of crickets had a lulling effect. When the small group approached the lane up to the farm, Rob relaxed and felt safe for the first time. They were almost home.

Riding out in front, Rob was the first to crest the hill and get a view of the farmyard and the house. He stopped short, holding up his hand to signal the others. An old wagon sat in front of the house. A woman and half-grown boy were busy unloading washtubs and other household goods. They struggled to move a heavy bedstead, but couldn't get it as far as the porch steps. Two small children played in the yard. Looking up, the boy spotted Rob and waved. The woman shaded her eyes and stared up at him.

Shock turned to anger and then to fear as Rob tried to fathom the scene below. When he reached the yard, he saw that the woman was standing by the empty wagon. She was rail-thin and her graying hair was pulled back severely from her face. Her fingers plucked repeatedly at the folds of her apron. She smiled at the newcomers, but her pale eyes darted from Rob to the fancy carriage.

"Hello," she said. The small children ran over and she pushed them behind her. "I'm Opal Blackburn. Who might you be?"

"Rob Johnson, ma'am. This is my farm. What are you doing here?"

The woman clutched the side of the wagon. "The landlord said this might happen."

"Landlord?"

"Yes, sir, we're tenant farmers down from Pennsylvania. Our house burned to the ground. We had nothing left there." Opal released her hold on the wagon. "We needed a place to live and Mr. Fields offered us this house in trade for farm work."

"My farm belongs to Mr. Fields?"

"Yeah, Joe Fields from over at Hancock. He paid cash at the sale."

The reality of what this woman was saying began to sink in. The rumors about confiscation and auction had been true. They had waited until the place was left unguarded and then made their move. Rob jumped down off the horse, threw the reins over the porch rail and confronted Opal Blackburn.

"This is my farm. It's been in the Johnson family for generations—since this land was Indian country. You have to leave."

The woman wailed and sank to her knees in the mud. Her children huddled around her. "We ain't got no place to go," she sobbed. The older boy, a sturdy-looking child of about ten, balled his fists and glared at Rob.

"Where's your man?" Rob's voice cracked. He was still trying to sort out the situation.

Standing up, Mrs. Blackburn looked at him steadily and gestured off toward the pasture. "Him and Jeremiah are mending fences."

Feeling an arm on his shoulder, he turned to find Tim standing behind him.

"I heard," Tim said. "We need to go into town, lad, and try to find out what's happened. It ain't this poor woman's fault."

"Take the others to O'Ferrall's." Rob turned away. "I'll find Blackburn." He watched the carriage turn down the lane.

He found Blackburn and an older boy in the back pasture. The man looked up from his work and waited for Rob to reach him. Dressed in patched clothes that hung on his bony frame, he set down his hammer and motioned to the boy to collect the other tools.

"I'm Jasper Blackburn. Are you looking for me?" He didn't turn to face Rob.

"My name's Rob Johnson. I'm the owner of this farm."

"Pleased to meet you. This is my oldest son, Jeremiah." As he extended his hand, the man turned his head.

Rob reached for Blackburn's hand, then fell back a step. The man had no right eye, and his right cheek was reduced to a sunken twisted mass of flesh.

"I was a gunnery sergeant with the 139th Pennsylvania at Petersburg," Blackburn explained.

Rob shook the man's hand. "I'm sorry." He saw that Blackburn had barely survived the war and now had nothing left. Rob knew he could have been this man.

"The war was a sorry business, Mr. Johnson. It don't seem right that a man should lose his land because he was a soldier. Mr. Fields told us you might be back. Have you talked to him?"

"No, but I will."

"We've packed up your personal goods. Ask Opal for them."

"Thank you." Rob felt stunned, like he'd taken a blow to the head. He headed back to the farmhouse.

As he drew near the house, Rob saw that the younger Blackburn children were playing with several kittens near the barn door. Their mother stood on the porch and held up an envelope as he approached.

"A peddler brought this yesterday. We'll keep the rest of your belongings 'till you can get them."

Rob took the letter and felt a spark of hope. Abigail had sent a message. He turned to go, then hesitated. "Could your children spare one of the kittens?" he asked Opal Blackburn. "My daughter had kittens at her old home."

Before he left, Opal handed him a small, wiggling sack. "For your girl," she said and smiled shyly.

As he rode down the lane, Rob was still trying to sort out what had just happened. He knew that without money, he wouldn't be able to fight this and his sense of despair deepened. He turned and looked back at the farm, framed by the blue banks of mountains. He had thought that it would be all he'd have left at the end of the war, but now he knew that wasn't true. Like Jasper Blackburn, he had his family. Rob vowed he'd be back.

* * * *

Night was falling when Rob reached Bath. At O'Ferrall's, Mabel met him at the door. "Where is Melinda?" Rob asked. "I've got something for her." He was carrying the wriggling sack.

"Ellie's putting her to bed. She's been asking for you. Sorry about your woman, Rob."

Following Mabel up two flights of steps, Rob entered a small, plain room. He realized that this was the bedroom where Ellie slept. The child was curled up on a mattress beside the narrow bed. Her yellow curls fell over the pillow and she clutched the corncob doll Rob had made for her. As he knelt beside her, he opened the sack and the kitten jumped out. Sniffing tentatively at the child, the little cat turned and started for the door. Melinda's hand shot out and grabbed it.

"Kitty," she said softly, "stay here." Looking up, she saw Rob and smiled. "Did you bring the kitty, daddy? Is it mine? My momma liked kitties."

Bending down, Rob kissed her forehead. "Yes, it's yours to keep."

Ellie came into the room quietly and set a bowl of milk down near the kitten.

"Thanks," Rob said. Although she was older and a few pounds heavier, he recognized Ellie as the girl Jacobs had been sweet on early in the war.

"Mabel told me to bring you the milk. It's funny, 'cause she hates cats." Ellie grinned. "But I like them. Don't worry, I'll see it gets outside." Ellie pulled the kitten away from the milk and headed to the door. "I'll just say goodnight to Mr. Jacobs. Oh, Mr. Rob, Miss Jane wants you in the family parlor."

He saw that Melinda had fallen back to sleep, so he quietly left the room.

Jane O'Ferrall and Reverend Dawson were waiting as Rob entered the small sitting room filled with dark heavy furniture. Jane ran over and hugged him. "I'm so sorry, Rob. There was nothing we could do."

"Thanks. It wasn't the homecoming I'd planned for my little girl, but without your kindness we wouldn't have a roof over our heads tonight. I'm grateful."

Reverend Dawson stood up and extended his hand. "It's not a homecoming any man would want. Sorry, son, that I wasn't able to put a stop to the sale."

As the men shook hands, Reverend Dawson continued. "The auction was a surprise to me, although there's been talk of Rebel land being confiscated since the end of the war and others are still awaiting confiscation hearings."

"I didn't have a hearing."

"Someone knew that you were away. If enough money was spread around, that could have been arranged." The reverend looked weary. "I asked Charles Faulkner, a friend and a lawyer from Berkeley County to look into the matter. He was puzzled, as your farm isn't rich bottomland, it's just a few rocky acres in hill country. Faulkner says that somebody filed a complaint against you as a non-citizen. Somebody wanted your place."

"Joe Fields, the uncle of an old friend, bought the farm. How did he even know it was up for auction?"

"Yes, Fields. He probably paid someone inside the courthouse to notify him of upcoming sales. He got it at a low price. Only one man bid against him."

"Was this unusual?" Rob asked.

"There is no such thing as business as usual now. Our county is in the grip of those who want revenge, and those who act out of bitterness and greed."

"What can I do?"

"Without ready cash to hire a lawyer, there's nothing you can do. In time, things will settle down here. You'll be restored to citizenship and can make a claim."

Rob slumped in the chair. "I never believed this could happen."

"Move on, son. You have a child to consider now. Many Rebels haven't come back here at all. They've headed West. Have you thought about that?"

"No, sir, I've never wanted to leave my home, but there is nothing here for me now."

That night Rob sat in a rocker on the O'Ferrall's porch and watched the full moon rise. He had almost memorized the words in Abigail's short letter. They ran through his mind and soothed his troubled spirit.

Dear Rob, I was so deeply sorry to hear of Laura's death. I met her once and believe her to have been a good woman. I have heard that thee has taken the child. That was the right thing to do. My husband is very ill, and I cannot leave his bedside. The long, lonely days stretch on here. I think of thee often and long to see thee again. Please do not forget me. Abigail.

Was there hope that he'd see Abigail again? Should he wish for another man's death?

"Rob." Tim sat down next to him. "Joseph needs to see you. He's leaving at first light tomorrow."

Rob stood up. "Tim, how do you feel about heading West?"

"I'm here to see the country, lad, and folks are none too hospitable here." He settled back into the rocker and looked up at the orange harvest moon. "This is lovely country, so it is, but they'll be no harvest this year. Do you not think you can get your land back?"

"No, not now. Maybe not ever. But I mean to find Nate Fields and he's headed West."

Joseph was cleaning mud off the carriage wheels when Rob found him. "I wanted to say goodbye, Mister Rob. I leave tomorrow."

"Thanks for your help, and thanks for being a friend to Laura and the child. Tell Lilly and Big Betty I'm grateful to them as well." Rob extended his hand. "I'm thinking of heading West."

As they shook hands, a slow grin spread over the big black man's face. "You doing the right thing. Good luck to you and little Melinda." He opened the carriage door and retrieved a leather pouch from under the seat. "Mr. Clifford wanted you to have this." He handed Rob the pouch.

Thomas Clifford had sent a brief note and two bank drafts, one in Rob's name for one hundred dollars, and one in Melinda's name for three hundred dollars. A small box in the bottom of the pouch contained an opal ring with the initials 'L.M.' and 'R.C.' engraved on the inside. Incredulous, he read the note.

Rob Johnson, This was Laura's money, most of it left to her at the death of a friend. I know thee will use it to start a new life for thyself and the child. Thomas Clifford.

Now, Rob thought, he could hire a lawyer to fight for his land, or he could afford the trip West. But it was not his money. What would Laura have wanted? And who was 'R.C.?'

* * * *

The next morning Rob left Melinda with Mary and he, Tim, and Jacobs headed for Hancock. Fording the Potomac near Colonel Orrick's once grand home, Rob shouted back at Jacobs, "Remember when Stonewall fired on Hancock from up on Orrick's Hill?"

Jacobs guided his horse along-side Rob's mount. "Yeah, that was the day we tried to snatch Sergeant Williams back from the Yankees and we all got captured."

"That was the day Joe Fields turned us over to the Bluecoats." Rob's jaw was set. "Joe knows I'll come looking for him now."

When they reached Joe's old lock house, they found that a new man was tending the lock and had no idea where Joe Fields had gone. In town, they came up empty in the first riverfront bar. The skinny bartender said he'd never heard of Joe Fields.

As they walked along Hancock's main street, Rob noted that the town had a prosperous air. The war had left a far heavier mark on Bath. Here in Maryland, canal men filled the barber shops, cheaper restaurants, and bars. In the third bar they tried, the heavy sweetish scent of tobacco and spilled beer filled the small close room. The bartender was a big jovial Irishman, who told Tim he hailed from County Cork.

"I miss my homeland." A plaintive note crept into Tim's voice. "But here I have a lad who can sing like a true Irish tenor. His voice only needs a little lubrication."

The barman poured three glasses of beer and Jacobs launched into the first verse of *Lorena*. The song had a hypnotic effect on the big barkeep. Smiling, he poured another round and Jacobs continued to sing in high sweet tones.

Rob moved around quietly, questioning the drinkers lining the bar. In a corner seat, he found a shriveled old man nursing a glass of beer. The old fellow had been watching him since he'd walked through the door.

"You're a Johnson from across the river, ain't you? I knew your daddy and a right scoundrel he was." The old man looked at him through watery eyes. "I heard you asking for Joe Fields. He sold me a stolen mule once. The law come and took it away the next day. Joe was a worse crook than your daddy." The old man let out a dry hacking cough. "I need a drink, boy."

"Do you know where Fields is?"

"I might."

Rob went back to the bartender and ordered a beer. "I think that old grandfather knows where Joe is," he whispered to Tim.

When the bartender brought the beer, he winked at Rob. "Tell the good lad what he wants to know, Marley, or you'll no longer be welcome in me establishment."

Marley gulped the beer, then wiped his mouth with the back of his dirty cuff. He seemed to be weighing his chances of prying more drinks out of Rob. "I'm a poor man, as you see. I didn't know Fields too good."

"Look, Mr. Marley." Rob stepped closer. "I came home from my woman's funeral to find that Joe Fields had stolen my farm. I mean to get it back."

Marley shrunk back into the corner. His attention seemed to shift to the bar behind Rob. The burley Irishman stood there and hefted a stout wooden bat in his right hand.

"Fields only told me he was headed to Wheeling to meet up with his nephew."

"When did he leave?"

"He rode the train yesterday. Them two are heading west."

* * * *

It was late afternoon by the time the group returned to Bath and the men parted at the livery stable. Tim and Jacobs headed to O'Ferrall's and Rob went on to the Court House. The day's court session was just ending as he strode up the Court House steps. Pointing to the 'closed' sign, the clerk tried to slam the office door in his face. Rob didn't recognize the man.

"Please. I need information on a recent land confiscation."

"You'll have to come back tomorrow. I need to close up."

"Wait. Did Charles Faulkner try a case today? Where can I find him?" Rob wedged his foot in the circuit clerk's door.

The man gestured toward the courtroom. "Look for yourself."

Faulkner was preparing to leave when Rob found him in one of the anterooms. The lawyer, a dapper man in his middle years, looked up as Rob entered and introduced himself.

"Pleased to meet you, Mr. Johnson. Reverend Dawson has spoken highly of you." Faulkner watched him through narrow, dark eyes.

"I need to know how I lost my farm."

"Indeed. I was surprised that the case moved so quickly through the court. There is a large backlog to be dealt with, especially with those cases involving the Confiscation Act of November, '63." Charles Faulkner pulled two cigars from his jacket pocket and offered one to Rob. "At Reverend Dawson's request, I did a little digging. Just as I suspected, someone had a special interest in obtaining your land. Informer's oaths were in the record, but informers can be bought."

"Why me?"

"Again, I wondered the same thing. Although it's tempting to confiscate rich properties, yours is not especially valuable." Faulkner rolled the cigar between his thumb and forefinger. "Does your family have enemies, Mr. Johnson?"

Startled, Rob shook his head. "No. I mean, I don't know." He began to pace back and forth in the small room. "My father made enemies. He was a drunk, a gambler, and a horse thief. But you say the Confiscation Act was passed in November, '63? My pa was dead by then. How can he be held accountable by a law that was passed after his death?"

"Good point, Mr. Johnson." Faulkner looked at Rob sharply. "I couldn't have put it better myself. As I see it, you've run afoul of someone with money, power, and influence. A lawyer from Winchester handled the matter. His client's name was protected. Think harder, young Johnson."

"I've been away for the last four years."

Faulkner studied Rob closely. "Someone went to a lot of trouble and expense to see that this case was pushed through during your absence. Someone who wanted to see you broken."

"A lawyer from Winchester," Rob mused. "That doesn't make any sense. Joe Fields bought the farm at auction. He's from Hancock."

"Was there bad blood with this Joe Fields?" Charles Faulkner asked.

"Yes, I had a disagreement with his nephew, Nate. I never thought much of Joe either."

"What kind of disagreement?" Faulkner's tone was even, but his gaze was intent.

"We had an argument over a woman."

"I'm not surprised. You're a handsome young devil." The lawyer smiled, displaying even white teeth. "Any other skeletons in your closet? Other women, perhaps?"

It was then that Rob saw the truth. The same man he had thought might conveniently die of illness had wanted him gone, gone from this part of the country entirely. How better to accomplish this than to take his land? Abigail's husband had reason to hate him.

"The man who had real cause to do me harm didn't buy the land," Rob said carefully.

"No, but it was sold. You no longer have it. Maybe this was an even better outcome. The manipulator has remained anonymous."

"What can I do?"

"Move on, son." Charles Faulkner closed his briefcase. "Right now, the cards are stacked against you. You backed the wrong horse in the war." He placed the cigar back in the pocket of his finely tailored suit coat. "I understand you've taken the oath."

"Yes, sir."

"That's the first step. Returning Southern soldiers are non-citizens here. They can't vote, hold any kind of license, or plead a case in court. But in time, these things will pass and you'll be restored to citizenship. Then you can fight for your land." Charles Faulkner stood and extended his hand to Rob. "Visit me at my office in Martinsburg. I may have an interesting proposition for you."

* * * *

Mabel McCabe was hard at work filling dinner orders when Rob slipped into O'Ferrall's kitchen. The aroma of simmering meat filled the room. "Rob Johnson." She looked up as he closed the door. "It ain't right what they done to you at the Court House. I never thought I'd live to see such crookery blessed by the law."

"Thanks, Mabel. I still can't believe it."

"You don't deserve this. You was only doing your duty. Here, have a bowl of stew and some cornbread." Mabel brought over a tray. "Keep me company, boy. The others are already done with their meals."

As Rob dug into the food, she returned and placed a telegram on the table. "I almost forgot. This came for you."

Reading the words in the telegram, Rob was dumbfounded. *Rob, The deed to the farm is at the bank. It shouldn't have gone to strangers. Nate Fields.* The telegram had been sent from Wheeling.

Nate, his childhood friend, the man he was ready to hunt down, had handed him back his land. Had Nate done it for him or for Laura's child? Did it matter? Would he have done the same for Nate? He didn't have any answers.

"Oh my God, Mabel, I got it back. I got my land back." Jumping up, Rob ran over and grabbed the startled cook. Planting a kiss on her cheek, he slapped her on the back. "I've got to tell the others. Is Melinda asleep yet? I've got to tell Melinda." He headed to the back stairs.

The little girl was sound asleep. Rob brushed the fair hair from her forehead. "It's going to be all right," he said. Rousing, the child clutched at his hand, then fell back asleep.

Rob found his friends on O'Ferrall's spacious front porch. After he broke the news, Tim wept. Merrill said he knew the Lord was watching over them and Jacobs went in search of a bottle of whiskey. Jane O'Ferrall came out and joined them for a drink. Mary brought out a tray of glasses and joined in the toast.

"To Rob," Tim said. "May he and his family live long and prosper." Amid the cheers and well wishes, Tim asked, "So lad, what will become of the Blackburn family, now living so cozy in your house?"

* * * *

At dawn the next morning Rob rode out of Bath. He had meant to stop by the bank first, but couldn't sit idle, waiting for that institution to open. Fired with energy, he had to get moving. The morning was cool and wind whipped down the valleys. Pulling up the collar of his jacket, he realized that fall was almost upon them. He needed to cut more firewood and mend the farmhouse roof.

Rob found that he had trouble sorting out his thoughts. Events of the last few days crowded his mind. If Abigail's husband had gone to this much trouble to get rid of his rival, what revenge might he take out on a wife he thought was unfaithful? Rob knew he had to get word to Abigail.

Turning up the lane to the farm, he could see movement near the wood line. As he drew closer, he heard the rasp of a saw. Framed by the blue banks of mountains, two figures moved methodically to and fro in the early sunlight. Each cut of the saw bit deeper into the huge oak. Struck by lightning years ago, the old tree had died a little more each year.

"Good morning," Rob called over to Jasper Blackburn and his son. "I always meant to take that tree down."

"You're up early, Mr. Johnson." Blackburn looked wary as he set down his end of the saw.

Rob dismounted and looped his horse's reins around a nearby sapling. The sharp smell of fresh wood chips filled the air. "You folks are hard-working. I can see that." The Blackburns watched him silently. "I got some good news yesterday," Rob continued. "Joe Fields' nephew, Nate, who actually put up the money for the farm, sent me a telegram. He's left me the deed at the bank in town. Said the farm shouldn't go to strangers."

Jasper's good eye surveyed him skeptically. "Have you seen the deed yet?"

"I had no time this morning." Rob saw that the son looked increasingly anxious. "Look, Mr. Blackburn, I ain't here to throw you out. I just wanted to see the old place. We can work something out for you and your family. You have my word."

"It's good of you to say that." Blackburn hesitated. "You see, I was at the auction and things may not be what they seem."

"The auction at the Court House? What do you remember?"

Jasper Blackburn sat down on a tree stump. "Jeremiah, go on back to the house and get breakfast." Unwillingly, the boy turned to go. Turning back to Rob, Jasper said, "Hope you don't mind me taking a little rest. Some days this old body works better than others." He stretched out his bad leg. "I was hanging around at the auction, hoping that someone would offer a day's work. At first there were two bidders on your farm, but the man in the fancy suit of clothes backed out, and the old fellow got it." Blackburn stood and faced Rob. "I asked Mr. Fields if he needed any work done. Fields said that the new owner wouldn't be able to claim the farm for a number of years and it would need to be kept up. After some bargaining, I got put on as tenant."

* * * *

By the time Rob got back to Bath it was mid-morning. He found Jacobs at the livery stable. "I need a favor," Rob said.

Setting down the grooming brush, Jacobs grinned. "That ain't nothing new."

"I've got to get a message to Abigail. If you carry it as far as the Clifford farm, Joseph will bring it to her. He won't be suspected."

"What are you talking about?"

"I think the peddler who delivered Abigail's messages was paid twice, once by her and once by her husband. The old man knew what he was about. He saw to it that I lost the farm."

"I think you're crazy," Jacobs said. "But I'll do it."

Back at O'Ferrall's, Rob wrote a short note to Abigail and handed Jacobs two silver dollars. "Give the other dollar to Joseph and tell him thanks. And Jacobs, it's good of you to help."

Going in search of Melinda, Rob found her in the kitchen watching Mabel make bread. The child was playing with odds and ends of dough, but looked up when he stepped into the warm, yeast-scented room. She ran to him and hugged him. Holding up her small dough-covered hands, she grinned. "Miss Mabel lets me help."

Rob picked her up and swung her into the air. "You're a lucky little girl that Miss Mabel likes you. It took her years to warm up to me."

"That ain't true, Rob Johnson." Mabel looked indignant. "Have you had a bite to eat yet today?"

"No, ma'am. I'm starved."

* * * *

By the time Rob got to the bank, it was close to noon. "Ah, Mr. Johnson," the manager grabbed his hand. "I've been expecting you. If you'll just wait a moment, I have something for you from Mr. Fields." He hurried off and returned shortly with an envelope. "You'll probably need to consult a lawyer to record this deed." His eyes slid away from Rob.

With the envelope safe in his jacket pocket, Rob walked over to a bench in the park. The business of the town flowed around him. Women intent on errands walked briskly past, and farm wagons lumbered along Washington Street. *It must be market day*, Rob thought as he unfolded the deed.

The property described was his. It had been deeded by Nathan J. Fields to Melinda Meeks, a minor, on September 5, 1865. At first, Rob was dismayed. His confusion was tinged with anger. But, the longer he sat there in the warm early autumn sun, the more resigned he became. Nate had held the cards and he had played them. That was Nate's way. Rob knew he could have lost the place altogether. He pondered the bank manager's remark about needing a lawyer. Melinda was a minor, so recording the deed might be tricky. As he got up and headed back to O'Ferrall's, he thought of Charles Faulkner. Faulkner would give him a straight answer.

CHAPTER 31

THE LAW

FALL 1865

The following day Rob rode toward Martinsburg. He mulled over what he'd heard about Charles Faulkner. Jane O'Ferrall had told him that Faulkner had spent time in two Yankee prisons during the war. Reverend Dawson had told him that Faulkner was now widely sought after for legal representation, especially by returning Rebels. He was relentless and won most of his cases.

Later, as he waited in Faulkner's office, Rob appraised the Turkey carpets and old hunting scenes hanging on the walls. One bookcase must have held over 100 books. Drawn to a volume entitled 'Land Disputes,' he was leafing through it when Charles Faulkner entered the room.

"Mr. Johnson, what a surprise."

Rob was impressed again by Faulkner's easy manner. "I need some advice, sir. Do you have a minute?"

"Of course, sit down. What's the problem?"

Handing him the deed, Rob outlined the facts.

Faulkner nodded and studied the paper. "The way I see it, you've been hornswaggled and there's nothing you can do about it." He propped his hand-tooled calfskin boots up on the desk. "You say the child has no birth certificate that you know of, so you can't prove parentage. Do you plan to raise her?"

"Yes, sir, I do."

"Then there's no problem. We'll get you set up as guardian and you can have the deed recorded." He hesitated. "By the way, I saw a colleague from Winchester recently. He knew who pushed for the confiscation of your land. Does the name Carl Dowd mean anything to you?"

"Yes, I've heard the name," Rob answered, but his heart raced. He had been right about Abigail's husband, Carl Dowd.

Invited to the Faulkner home for a meal, Rob walked with his host to a large brick house on a quiet tree-lined street. The entrance hall was even larger than the front hall at the Clifford home. The men sat at one end of a long table in the formal dining room. As the family was away visiting relatives, a simple supper was served by an elderly Negro servant. Faulkner regaled his guest with stories of the war and the time he'd spent imprisoned by the Yankees. As he listened, Rob's eyes roved over the rich furnishings. Dark velvet drapes hung at the windows and silver gleamed on the sideboard. He could picture Abigail at home in such surroundings.

"So, Mr. Johnson," Faulkner said. "What do you plan to do with the land? Will you continue to farm?"

"That's what I've always wanted, but the tenant family there now has nowhere else to go. The man was badly injured in the war. I don't know how I can turn him out, and the land can barely feed one family, much less two."

Faulkner nodded. "I see your problem, although in time it can probably be worked out." He smiled. "Unless, of course, you follow another course altogether."

After supper, they retired to the study where Rob's attention was drawn to the number of books filling the tall bookcases. Watching him, Faulkner said, "Borrow anything you like. Many of these books deal with the law." He looked pleased. "As a matter of fact, I was hoping you'd take an interest in legal matters. You see, I find myself in need of a law clerk. My last clerk passed the bar exam and moved on to greener pastures. Have you ever considered reading for the law?"

Rob studied Faulkner's face. He seemed serious, his offer genuine. "No, sir, I've never given that any thought. I haven't had much schooling."

"You can read, write, and cipher. You have an agile mind and a determined nature. That's all that is needed." Charles reached for the brandy decanter. "You could do worse in life. In a few years, you could find yourself well set up. The war has left a scarcity of lawyers everywhere, especially up in Morgan County. The courts there are clogged with cases like yours, many involving Trip O'Ferrall's raid in '64. Remember, Rob, when cases come to trial, it's not what law was broken, it's who was angered."

Charles poured out two glasses of brandy. "I take pride in my ability to size up a man. It's invaluable in my business. I feel you'd become a commanding presence in the courtroom." Faulkner raised his glass. "To the future, Mr. Johnson. Think about my offer; I'll require an answer soon."

The two men drank down the brandy. "I take your offer as a kindness, Mr. Faulkner. I'm poorly equipped for the job, but I'd like to try it. In my present situation, how could I ever be licensed to practice law?"

His host poured more brandy. "I've been around for a while and I'll wager that your situation won't last forever. If you have a problem with a law license, move down here. There are no witch hunts for returning Rebels in Berkeley County. There are too many of us." He flashed his wolfish grin.

"You're right, sir. I have to look ahead. I've got my little girl to look after."

"You need a wife, boy. I'm sure my Thelma will have no end of cousins vying for an introduction."

Rob grinned. "I've had someone in mind for a long time."

* * * *

Having accepted Charles Faulkner's invitation to spend the night at his home, Rob didn't reach Bath until the next afternoon. Even from a distance he recognized the tall ramrod-straight figure standing on O'Ferrall's porch. Dismounting, he broke into a run, taking the steps two at a time. "Sergeant, I knew you were too tough to die down at Point Lookout."

Sergeant Williams grabbed him in a bear hug. "It's good to see you, corporal."

As the two men sat in the big porch rockers and talked, Rob realized that the sergeant was not in as good health as he tried to make out. He'd admitted that an old wound acted up and that his bouts with dysentery and fever still returned from time to time.

"I'm headed west," Sergeant Williams said resolutely, "but thought I'd stop by to see what had become of my soldiers. I took a room here at O'Ferrall's and then ran into Tim. He says he's a bartender now." The sergeant's sharp blue eyes scanned Rob's face. "Tim told me about Laura's death and your problems with the land. I'm sorry, son."

"I think about Laura a lot. I never valued her as I should have. I have a load of regrets, but I also have Melinda."

At that moment, shrieks and shouts erupted from the back of the building. "Get outta my kitchen, you lumbering fool. You're clumsy as a pig in a parlor, Jacobs."

A child's sobs mixed into the uproar. Jumping up, Rob led the way back to the kitchen. Mabel was jabbing a broom at heaps of flour scattered on the floor. The kitchen was quickly filling with white dust.

"I just done what you told me," Jacobs shouted. "Do I still get them corncakes?"

Yelling like a banshee, Mabel leveled the broom at him and charged. At the kitchen door, Rob was nearly flattened by the fleeing Jacobs. Mabel was hard on his heels.

Melinda ran over to him. "Daddy, Miss Mabel's yelling 'cause we messed up her kitchen." The child's large eyes filled with tears.

"Get this lout outta here," Mabel shook her fist at Jacobs, who now appeared to be rooted to the spot.

Sergeant Williams grabbed the startled man and shoved him toward the door. "Let's go. We need a drink. Smile at the old harpy on your way out."

Rob gave Melinda a kiss and thankfully handed her over to Ellie, who had run in from the dining room. Quickly, he followed the others through the back door.

"You've got a pretty little girl," Sergeant Williams called back to Rob. "You're a lucky man."

* * * *

On Washington Street, the group entered one of the smaller, quieter bars in town and ordered beer. "There's nothing so soothing as the smell of tobacco smoke and spilled whiskey," the sergeant said. "And the distance between us and that screaming woman is a bonus." Looking at the two young men sitting across from him, he grinned at Jacobs. "My God, boy, you need to pick your fights better. I'd rather mess with a dozen Yankees than that crazy old girl."

"Your hair's turned white, Jacobs. Did Mabel scare you that much?" Rob nodded at the sergeant and the two men laughed.

"That's right, have a good laugh on me." Jacobs tried to brush off his jacket. "Just like old times."

"What happened?" Rob asked in as sympathetic a tone as he could muster.

"The old woman wanted help filling the flour bin. A little spilled and I slipped. That floor was slippery as ice." This remark brought on more laughter. Even Jacobs grinned. "You should have seen the look on her face."

"This reminds me of the time you boys helped the Yankees off-load oysters at Point Lookout," Sergeant Williams said.

"Yeah, old Mabel doesn't know about them oysters all scattered in the snow or she wouldn't have asked our boy here for a hand." Rob slapped Jacobs on the back.

Standing, the sergeant asked, "Who wants another round?" He headed toward the bar.

"I hope Ellie ain't mad," Jacobs said. "She's just about promised to head west with me."

"Congratulations. Will there be a wedding soon?" Rob grinned.

Considering the idea, Jacobs shrugged. "Maybe." He reached into his jacket pocket and brought out an envelope. "I'm surprised you ain't more interested in hearing from your lady than poking fun at me."

Rob sobered. "I'm fearful for her. I'm afraid of what she may be faced with." He took the envelope and left the table. "Thanks, Jacobs. I'll be back."

Leaning on a porch column near the bar entrance, Rob read Abigail's letter.

> *My dearest Rob, Thanks for thy letter. I will not trust the peddler again. He is a deceitful man. My husband is also deceitful. He carries on as if nothing has happened. He is colder and more aloof than formerly, but it is hard to believe that he has done what thee says. His health is poor, so I try to look kindly on him. I am so sorry about the farm, but glad that it has stayed in the family. I have not told thee before, but I am with child. I should give birth in about three months. Because of this, I feel that I will be safe here. Thee need not worry. I will send word when the babe is born. I miss thee every day and hope that someday we will be together. Love, Abigail.*

When Rob went back into the bar, he found that plates of meat and cheese had been brought to the table. Sergeant Williams was cutting thick slices of bread and Jacobs was already eating. Looking up as Rob joined them, he gestured to the food. "It's all on the sergeant. Guess he figured old Mabel wouldn't fix us much for dinner today."

"Sit down and eat, Rob." The sergeant pushed a plate toward him.

"I can't eat right now." Rob waved away the food. "Abigail's note said that she is six months pregnant. Now she's stuck there."

"Nobody's ever stuck who doesn't want to be." Sergeant Williams piled his plate high with food. "You need to plan for the future. You gotta trust that Abigail will come to you one day."

"I've made a start. Next week I begin work as law clerk for a lawyer in Martinsburg. I hope to God that I can do it."

"That's good news." Jacobs reached over and shook Rob's hand. "I always knew you was too smart to stay on the farm."

"Congratulations, son. I know you'll do well." The sergeant looked relieved. "Where will you live—you and the child?"

"I thought I'd start to build a small cabin on the farm—up on the mountainside where you can see for miles. I plan to talk with the

Blackburns about looking after Melinda while I'm away, but I'd like someone there keeping an eye on things." Rob took a slice of ham. "I know Jacobs has made his travel plans. Merrill, too. They plan to head west together. Tim spends most of his time at the bar in Hancock, but what about you, Sergeant? Will you stay a while and give me a hand?"

"I'd like that," Sergeant Williams said.

* * * *

Jacobs was anxious to set out for Wheeling before winter, so the wedding date was pushed up. Jane O'Ferrall had offered the Coffee House for the wedding party, but when the day arrived Jacobs got as skittish as a mule.

"I don't know if I can go through with it. What if it don't work out?"

Squeezed into one of the O'Ferrall's small upstairs rooms, Tim and Rob were trying to get the nervous groom into his new suit of clothes. "It's a little late for them worries now, me boy. So get dressed," Tim said firmly.

Slicking his wiry brown hair down as he looked in the mirror, Jacobs admired the dark suit that did a pretty good job of filling out his skinny frame. "Whadaya think? Will Ellie like it?" He grinned.

"You're a proper dandy," Tim told him. "You look grand."

"What do you mean?" Rob took over the job of adjusting Jacob's tie. "He looks like a Black Jack dealer to me."

"Don't even make them cracks," Jacobs said. "Ellie's family is very religious. I'm just glad they live too far away to get here."

Merrill stuck his head in the door. "Miss Jane says the minister's ready. Why ain't you downstairs? Mabel says if I can't get you, she will." The men headed for the door.

Ellie, wearing a frilly white dress, stood by the mantel in the large parlor. A sturdy country girl with a sweet, round face, she held out her hand to Jacobs as he approached. The minister commenced the ceremony and in a few short minutes they were man and wife. Bashfully, they accepted congratulations from the guests and opened the few gifts they'd received. Rob, Tim, and Merrill had scraped together a small sum of money for the new couple. Jane O'Ferrall had presented them with a ten dollar gold piece and a set of bed linens. Mabel gave them a quilt of her own design, and Sergeant Williams hired a photographer to take their wedding picture.

Taking Melinda by the hand, Rob helped her fill a plate at the sideboard and sat her down between Tim and Jane O'Ferrall.

"Rob," Jane put her hand on his arm. "I have some good news. There's to be another wedding in two months time. Mary's Yankee soldier will arrive soon and they will marry here. I wanted you to know."

"I'm happy for them, Jane. I wish them well."

Rob headed over to the bar and asked Mabel for a shot of whiskey. "Tell me about Mary's Yankee," he said.

"He's a fine young man. Lost a leg in the war—such a shame."

"Merrill and Jasper Blackburn were both wounded also. Both fought for the North and are decent men." Rob raised his glass. "I salute them. All of them."

"And what of your Sergeant Williams? He ain't so well. And what of you, Rob Johnson? How has the war left you? No woman, no land, not a cent in your pocket." She leaned close. "You better pull yourself together. You got that little girl to think of."

"You're right." Rob watched Melinda as Jane tied her hair bows and Tim cut her meat. The child had already been through many changes in her short life. She still cried for her mother and didn't understand why she was gone. He wondered if she would be able to adjust to losing Ellie, Jane, Mary, and Mabel. She was pampered here, but would soon be one of five children at the Blackburns.

* * * *

The next morning, Rob made a bundle of Melinda's clothes and sat her and Ellie on the front seat of the O'Ferrall's wagon. Jacobs, Merrill, and their luggage rode in the back. When they reached Alpine Station they had to wait for the train. Although Rob had always thought of Merrill as a quiet shy man, he launched into a lengthy speech at the station.

"It's hard to say goodbye, Rob, to you and your little daughter. You've been good to me. Twice you've saved my life. The first time, you were only a boy. The second time you gave me a home when I was a sick Yankee soldier and had no place to go." Merrill smiled, and reminded Rob again of his brother, Billy. Billy, who had had the same fair hair and blue eyes, had been dead for the past five years.

As the train approached and slowed to a stop, the two men embraced and Merrill climbed aboard. "Good luck," was all Rob managed to say.

Jacobs broke down and wept as he and Rob said their goodbyes. "We been through a lot together," he said. "You've always looked out for me."

"You're the man who kept me alive at Bristoe Station," Rob told him. "I'll never forget that." He grabbed Jacobs in a bear hug. "Good luck to you and Ellie. I'll miss you."

Little Melinda clung to Ellie and sobbed. As the train pulled out, the child continued to wail. Rob tried to comfort her, but his heart wasn't in it. He realized he had lost two good friends. They had moved on, just as he must. Resolutely, he headed the wagon team toward the farm and told the red-eyed little girl how much fun she'd have with her new playmates.

"I've even brought kitty," he said, as he reached under the seat and pulled out a wriggling sack. "Kitty's going back home and so are we."

As he watched the cloudbanks forming over the high ridge tops, he knew he'd never envisioned a time when this wouldn't be his home. Sergeant Williams planned to meet him at noon to begin work on the new cabin.

CHAPTER 32

MARY'S WEDDING

NOVEMBER 1865

Two months later, light snow fell as Rob carried Melinda out the cabin door and down the steep hill to the buggy. She squealed with delight as he skidded down the icy path. When they reached the farmyard, he set her down and watched her slide happily in the fresh snow. After settling her on the seat under the carriage blanket, he guided the horse and buggy down the lane to the slick ridge road. In no time, Melinda had fallen asleep at his side. Every so often he reached over and smoothed her fair curls.

"We've made it, little girl. We've survived and it's almost Thanksgiving."

Rob's voice broke the silence that had settled over the snow-covered woods. Tall pine trees stood sentinel at the top of the ridge and broke the white landscape in dark jagged thrusts toward the sky. Brush and low scrub lining the sides of the narrow road were already sagging beneath the weight of the snow. The icy weather made him glad he'd bought the buggy. It wouldn't do to carry the child with him on horseback. Charles Faulkner had found the small buggy at an estate sale and convinced Rob to buy it. He'd had to use some of the money from Melinda's account, but he'd vowed to replace it as soon as he could.

Rob counted himself lucky. Although law clerks made little money, Charles and his wife had gone out of their way to see that he got by. When he worked at the office, he stayed in their home and took meals with the family. Thelma Faulkner had pressed odds and ends of furniture on him for use in the new cabin. Even the fancy dress Melinda was wearing today was a hand-me-down from the Faulkner girls. He was pleased that he'd been able to dress up the little girl for her first Sunday at church. Rob realized that at an earlier time, he would have turned down all of these offers of help. Had he grown up, or was he just more desperate? He didn't know.

Melinda awakened when they reached Bath. As they walked into the small church house, Rob realized uncomfortably that many eyes were on them. He had never been a churchgoer, but thought it was the right thing to do for the child. He felt guilty that she got little enough of his time, although she'd settled in well at the Blackburns. The child sat quietly, awed by the crush of people and the lusty hymn singing. She had brought the small corncob doll and placed it next to her in the pew. Then she turned her attention to the minister and the white-robed choir members.

"Is that God and the angels?" she asked.

A well-dressed woman in the row behind them leaned forward and smiled. "They only think they are, little one." The woman was Fannie Swann.

As soon as the last hymn was sung, Rob picked up Melinda and walked quickly to the door.

"Mr. Johnson," a high-pitched, female voice called. "Over here. It's Missy Stokes."

Turning, Rob saw a tall, bony matron bearing down on him. With her skinny daughter in tow, Mrs. Stokes moved with alarming speed.

"I remember your mother," she said, as she cut Rob off at the door. "She was a good Christian woman, God rest her soul. The little girl favors her."

"Thank you," Rob turned toward the minister, who was greeting the faithful as they left. "Good morning, reverend. Melinda has enjoyed her first Sunday at church."

Glancing behind him, he saw another mother steering her homely daughter toward him. None of them had given him the time of day before. Perplexed, he made it to the steps and strode toward the buggy. The layer of snow made the ground treacherous and he almost slipped.

"Careful," a familiar voice said. "You mustn't let that precious little girl fall." Fannie came up behind them. "I can see why all the mothers with eligible daughters pursue you, Rob. You're more handsome than ever, and the little one is adorable. You make an appealing pair." She held out her arms to Melinda, who squirmed and asked to be put down. Fannie stroked her long curls. "Good-looking and reading for the law. Maybe they'll forget you're a dirt-poor Reb now that you have prospects."

Fannie wore her red-gold hair piled high on her head. Her smart blue dress, cut very low at the neckline and nipped in tightly at the waist, draped softly over her small body. When she smiled at him, Rob became a tongue-tied sixteen-year-old again. She still held powerful sway over his emotions. Even though he knew what she was capable of, her sensuality drew him to her. He swallowed hard and mumbled, "I'm surprised to see you here, Fannie."

Her cool blue eyes appraised him. "I'm here for the wedding. Mary has asked me to stand up for her. I hear that you will be the best man. We always did make a handsome couple."

* * * *

Mary's wedding was as grand as Jane O'Ferrall could manage in the sparse days after the war. The groom's family was not represented, but the O'Ferralls and family friends had gathered to celebrate the event. Trip O'Ferrall was the notable exception. It wasn't safe for him to return to Morgan County, as there was still a warrant out for his arrest. Local outrage had yet to die down over his March '64 raid in Bath.

Rob, Tim, and the sergeant were out on the porch, even though a chill was in the air. Tim looked in through the door and said, "They're not ready yet, but shouldn't you be in there, lad? You are to stand up for the groom, are you not?"

Looking away, Rob muttered, "Not yet. I gotta stay away from that woman."

"You mean Miss Fannie? I agree she looks like she could be a handful." Sergeant Williams grinned wickedly. "Why are you running so fast?"

"Because I scare him." Fannie came up behind them.

"My God, woman, you scare all of us. How'd you get here? I never heard the door shut," Tim said.

"Miss Fannie, or should I say Miss Francine, learned the art of stealth in Richmond. I knew her there." The sergeant winked at Fannie and continued, "Why, I remember…"

"Excuse me," Fannie cut in. "I came to tell you it's time for the ceremony. After all, Rob, we are a part of it."

Fannie grabbed his arm and led him to the door. Rob looked back at his companions and winced. He heard Tim ask how the sergeant knew Fannie in Richmond.

Jane and Mabel had made the parlor as festive as possible, hanging pine garlands and wreathes made from laurel leaves and bittersweet berries. Mary was a radiant bride. She and Captain James Hansen, who had to support his body with crutches, exchanged vows and became man and wife. Jane O'Ferrall wept throughout the ceremony and Mabel blew her nose loudly.

When Rob offered his congratulations, Mary took his hand. "I hope you find the happiness we have found," she said.

James had a firm handshake and a quick smile. "Mary tells me you're an old friend. She's told me about your time at Point Lookout. Even our boys say it was a hellish place."

Rob felt an immediate bond with this man who had fought for the North and left his leg on some southern battlefield. Later, Rob saw Sergeant Williams talking quietly with him. There was a connection, Rob realized, between men who had been through the war. Brooding over the years that he had lost, years that all these men had lost, Rob sat alone over a glass of whiskey. Hearing laughter, he looked up and couldn't help noticing that Fannie was attracting more attention than the bride, at least from the men present. The energy she generated was hard to resist.

"Rob," Fannie was walking toward him. She held a sleepy Melinda by the hand. "Isn't it time for this little girl to go to bed? Jane says to put her down in Ellie's old room."

"Thanks, I'll take her." Rob picked up the child and headed for the stairs. At the landing, he turned to find Fannie right behind him. "Enjoy the evening. I'll take care of her." But he heard Fannie's footsteps continuing upward.

"Damn woman," Rob muttered under his breath. He knew he needed to keep his distance, but there seemed to be no way to discourage her.

"You're not very sociable these days," Fannie said as she watched him put Melinda to bed. "Mabel tells me you're in love with a married woman. Is this true?"

Rob looked up at her. Her hair had escaped its bindings and was trailing over her shoulders. "Yes, it's true. What of your husband, Fannie? Why isn't he here?"

"His medical practice keeps him very busy. He has no time for weddings." She handed him an extra blanket from the dresser. "Here, it will be cold tonight."

He knelt down next to Melinda's cot and tucked the blanket around her. The child was already asleep.

"I'm tired of the Midwest, Rob. The women are plain and stuffy and the men are dull. I miss life here." Fannie sat down next to him on the floor. "I miss my old friends."

"How did you know Sergeant Williams in Richmond?"

Fannie looked up quickly. Her eyes slid away from him. She stood and looked out the window into the back garden. "I'd fallen on hard times. I was broke and had to find work." She turned back toward him.

Watching her, Rob could see that she was uncomfortable. "Look, Fannie, it doesn't matter. It's your business."

"I've never told my husband, but I need to tell you." She hesitated, then said, "I was forced to work in a brothel. It was a terrible time in my life."

Rob fell silent. He never knew when to believe her. Would she lie about this? He couldn't even contemplate how awful this time must have been for her. "I'm sorry," he said.

"You're sorry." He could see the color rising in her face. "You have no idea—none." She took a step toward him. "Did you know that your precious Laura Meeks was there with me? She was called 'Miss Lorena.'"

"She told me." Rob could see that she savored the look on his face.

"Her own family sold her to the bordello. Ask Nate. He knew her there."

"Nate? He never said."

"Nate was the one who brokered her release to the Quakers. After all, she wasn't much use to Madam when she reached her eighth month." Fannie's voice rose. "Nate tried to help Laura and me. He didn't turn away. He was willing to marry Laura. Nate had his faults, but at least he stood up and was a man. You sit and judge us. I can see it in your eyes. Laura was a victim, but I'm a whore."

Standing, Rob started backing up in the small room. Whirling toward him, Fannie screamed, "Maybe Nate's a better friend than you deserve. Maybe we all are. You're a fool, Rob. I sent you money and I hear that you gave it away. You're a fool and deserve what you get." She balled her small hands into fists and charged.

Rob grabbed her arms and stared down at her. He no longer felt desire, only anger. "What about the slaves we were moving north on that train? You sold them like cattle."

"Ask Nate about the stolen slaves. I only got a small finder's fee. Ask your friend, Nate." She struggled free. "Go to hell, Rob Johnson, and I hope you rot there." Fannie walked out of the room, slamming the door behind her.

Melinda stretched out her arms. "Daddy," she cried.

Rob picked up the child and the blanket and walked downstairs. He had failed her mother, but he wouldn't fail Melinda. It was time to take her home.

CHAPTER 33

A BEAUTIFUL PLACE

CHRISTMAS 1865-SPRING 1866

Work in the law office proved easier than Rob had expected. He spent much time in county court houses researching old deeds and other civil documents. Although gaps in legal records existed due to the war, he still dug up deeds and certificates. Charles Faulkner complimented him on his thoroughness.

Today, while Rob pored over dusty land deed books, unbidden thoughts disturbed his concentration. Was Fannie right? Was he a shallow judgmental man, a poor friend? He knew he owed a big debt to Laura, but Fannie? Fannie was a married woman, but she didn't act like one. He was in love with Abigail, another married woman. Who held the moral high ground here?

* * * *

On Christmas Eve, Rob walked on the mountain that overlooked the farm. A coating of snow covered the pine trees and a cold wind blew over the ridges. He knew more snow was on the way. From this distance, the cabin seemed to cling to the hillside and looked even smaller than it was. He watched smoke spiraling from the stone chimney and caught the scent of burning oak logs. This was the way his ancestors had homesteaded on this lonely mountain ridge. The Johnson farmhouse had acquired several additions over the years, but it had started out as a cabin.

He thought of Pa and hunting trips they had made together. He remembered the time at the beginning of the war when Pa had doctored Merrill Robinson, even though he was a Yankee soldier. He also remembered Pa's drinking bouts and his flashes of anger. But it was Christmas, so Rob concentrated on the good times.

Rob made his way back down the mountainside as new snow started to fall. Throwing open the cabin door, he entered the warm room filled with the aroma of roasting turkey. Intent on hanging popcorn strings on the small pine tree, Melinda looked up as he entered.

"Daddy," she cried and ran to him. He picked her up and twirled her around, anticipating her excitement in the morning when she found the new doll under the tree.

Tim left off stirring his pots on the cook stove and limped over. "Here you are, lad. We've been waiting dinner."

Sergeant Williams produced a bottle of good brandy and poured drinks all around. "To Father Christmas and to good friends," he said.

Still holding the child, Rob took the glass with his left hand.

"To my family," he said.

* * * *

When Rob returned to the law office in the new year, he found a letter awaiting him. Recognizing the handwriting, he knew it was a message from Abigail.

Dear Rob, I am writing to tell thee that I've given birth to a fine baby boy. My husband has recovered and takes great joy in the child. I miss thee, but see no way that we can be together. Don't forget me. Love, Abigail.

That evening Rob went to a bar in the city of Martinsburg and got drunk. He was barely able to find his way back to the Faulkner's house.

Almost every night during that long lonely winter, Rob wrote a letter to Abigail. He told her how much he loved her. He told her he thought of her during the day and through the endless cold nights. He rambled on about every detail of the short sweet time they'd spent together. Then he rewrote most of the letter. He knew his tone had been too stark, his feelings too raw. Finally, each night he tore the letter to shreds. Abigail was far beyond his reach. Married to a wealthy man and the mother of a son, she would soon forget him. What did he have to offer her?

* * * *

By spring, Charles Faulkner praised Rob on the thoroughness and accuracy of his work. He worked long hours, but the rest of his life was a shambles. Looking through the law office window day by day, Rob watched the cherry tree in the yard bud then bloom, but he felt no surge of hope. He had no fields to plough, no crops to plant. He was a lowly clerk in the city.

Rob got home on weekends only to see Melinda being raised by other people. She had now started calling Opal Blackburn 'momma,' and sometimes cried when he came to fetch her. Tim had rented rooms above the tavern in Hancock and Sergeant Williams had started spending more time there. Rob realized that his own life had become a solitary existence.

Turning back to the job at hand, Rob's concentration was broken by the insistent wailing of a baby. Trying to ignore the noise, he continued to make notations from pertinent sections of the legal text. He wondered how Charles could stand the squalling, then remembered that he was gone for the day. Finally, Rob pushed the law book away, got up and walked toward the anteroom. Throwing the door open, he saw a young woman bending over a screaming infant. At that moment the child quieted and the woman looked up.

"Rob," Abigail said. "I came to find thee. I need advice regarding a will, as I'm a recent widow."

He reached her in three long strides and pulled her up into his arms. Holding her close, he kissed her, feeling the warmth of her body and the softness of her lips on his. He felt giddy, almost light-headed. The baby started crying again and Rob scooped up the child from its blankets. "He's a beautiful boy, Abigail. A boy to be proud of."

The baby boy looked round-eyed at Rob and broke into a smile. "You see, he likes me."

"Samuel will learn to love thee, Rob, as I do." Abigail took his hand and led him to a chair. "Sit down, there is much I need to tell thee."

He kissed her again and held her hand. The baby lay quietly on his lap.

"My husband is dead and buried," Abigail began. "His heart was weak and finally gave out. Before he died, he confessed many things to his God and to me. Thee lost thy farm by his design. He paid dearly to have it confiscated and sold at auction. His lawyer bid the property up, then let another buy it." She looked down. "He hated thee, Rob. In the end, he hated me. He died a bitter man."

Rob smoothed the tendrils of dark hair from her face. "Now that we're together, none of it matters. Look outside, it's springtime. I want you to see the farm. It's the most beautiful place in the world in spring. I want to take you and the baby home with me. Melinda's waiting there."

"I will go with thee. I made up my mind to this before I boarded the train." She reached out and took his face in her hands. "We have waited long enough."

* * * *

Rob ran all the way to the Faulkner home. Along the way, he called out greetings to everyone he met. He burst into the house and found the family eating a late breakfast.

"Charles, Thelma," he shouted. "I'm getting married!" He was breathless and felt a little drunk.

Lavish with their congratulations, the Faulkners insisted that he take their carriage for the trip to Morgan County. A half-hour later, Rob maneuvered the fine team and carriage down narrow streets to the law office. The weather was good and he hoped to reach the farm by evening.

Abigail and the child slept in the back of the carriage while Rob kept the horses moving briskly. When they reached the outskirts of Bath, the sun was sinking over the ridgetops. He guided the horses to the Ridge Road and headed toward the farm. His excitement grew as the deep purple hills folded around them. The new green of the high meadows burst with life. He felt at peace for the first time in years. He was bringing Abigail home.

When Rob opened the carriage door and she stepped out, he held his breath. She handed him the sleeping child and gazed at the cabin nestled on the rugged hillside. "Thee was right, Rob. This is a beautiful place."

He took her hand. The small cabin was not the home he had envisioned for Abigail, but when she walked through the door she seemed delighted. "I feel free here, Rob. I feel safe with thee by my side."

The baby, now awake, stared wide-eyed at his surroundings and reached toward his mother. Rob gathered Abigail to him with his free arm and kissed her.

Melinda found them embracing when she ran through the door. "Daddy, you got me a baby." She touched Samuel's little foot tentatively.

Rob knelt down beside her, hugging her with his free arm. He still held the baby. Melinda watched the little boy reach for her long curls. "He likes me," she said.

"Melinda, this is Abigail and her son, Samuel. They're going to stay with us."

Abigail held her arms out to the little girl. "Your daddy has told me much about thee. Can thee help me care for little Samuel?"

Melinda edged closer to her father. Then took a tentative step forward. "Hello, ma'am. I like your little boy."

* * * *

Rob built a blazing fire to ward off the evening chill. After finishing the cold supper sent by Thelma Faulkner, the small family sat around the table. Abigail laid her head on Rob's shoulder. He stroked her cheek, brushing back the fine tendrils of dark hair.

When Samuel started fussing Melinda jumped up and returned with her corncob doll. Kneeling down by the baby's blankets she held the doll out to him. "It's for you," she said, as she carefully placed the doll near him.

"I almost forgot," Abigail said. She also left the table and returned with a small box. "I met a man on the train who helped me when I dropped my case. He looked familiar, but I couldn't place him. As we talked, he asked if I knew thee. It was quite a coincidence. He asked me to give thee this for Melinda." She smiled as she handed him the box.

Opening it, Rob pulled out a gold locket. It was the same locket he had flung at Nate's feet on the day of Laura's funeral. He looked around at his new family, then into the depths of the fire. He had traveled a long way since 1861, but he felt the past reach out for him, even now on the happiest day of his life.

SOURCES

Ashby, Thomas A., M.D. *General Turner Ashby.* New York: Norton, 1943.

Branson, Ann. *Quaker Spiritual Writing: Journal of Ann Branson.* Pennsylvania: Wm. H. Pile & Sons, 1892.

Clark, Charles M, MD. *39th Illinois Volunteer Infantry.* Chicago: 1889.

Cohen, Stan. *Civil War in West Virginia.* 1982.

Farwell, Byron. *Stonewall.* New York: Norton Paperback, 1943.

Gilmore, Col. Harry. *Four Years in the Saddle.* New York: Harper & Rowe, 1866.

Johnson, Mary. *The Long Roll.* Boston & New York: the Houghton Mifflin Co., 1911.

Lesser, W. Hunter. *Rebels at the Gate: Opening of the War in Western Virginia:* Illinois Source Books, Inc., 2004.

Matinez, J. Michael. *Life and Death in Civil War Prisons.* Tennessee: Rutledge Hill, 2004.

McPherson, James M. *The Atlas of the Civil War.* Pennsylvania: Running Press, 2005.

Newbraugh, Frederick T. *Warm Springs Echoes, Vol. 2.* Maryland: Automated Systems Corp., 1975.

Pringle, Cyrus. *4th Vermont Infantry Recollections: Record of a Quaker Conscience.* Vermont Civil War.org Webmaster: Tom Ledoux, 2014.

Speer, Lonnie R. *War of Vengeance – Acts of Retaliation Against Civil War Prisoners.* Pennsylvania: Stackpole Books, 2002.

Tanner, Robert G. *Stonewall in the Valley.* Pennsylvania: Stackpole Books, 2002.

Webb, James. *Born Fighting.* New York: Broadway Books, 2004.

Wheeler, Richard. *We Knew Stonewall.* New York: Thomas Y. Cowell Co., 1977.

Wiley, Bell Irvin. *The Life of Johnny Reb. Missouri*: Bobbs Merrill Press, 1943.

www.ingramcontent.com/pod-product-compliance
Lightning Source LLC
Chambersburg PA
CBHW020757250626
47155CB00003B/1117